The Memoirs of WILD BILL HICKOK

AND

SHADOW ON THE SUN

★ RICHARD MATHESON ★

FORGE®

A TOM DOHERTY ASSOCIATES BOOK ‖ NEW YORK

THE MEMOIRS OF WILD BILL HICKOK AND SHADOW ON THE SUN

The Memoirs of Wild Bill Hickok copyright © 1996 by RXR, Inc.

Shadow on the Sun copyright © 1994 by RXR, Inc.

A Forge Book
Published by Tom Doherty Associates
175 Fifth Avenue
New York, NY 10010

www.tor-forge.com

Forge® is a registered trademark of Macmillan Publishing Group, LLC.

ISBN 978-0-7653-9347-0

Our books may be purchased in bulk for promotional, educational, or business use. Please contact your local bookseller or the Macmillan Corporate and Premium Sales Department at 1-800-221-7945, extension 5442, or by e-mail at MacmillanSpecialMarkets@macmillan.com.

First Mass Market Edition: September 2017

Printed in the United States of America

0 9 8 7 6 5 4 3 2 1

CONTENTS

The Memoirs of

WILD BILL
HICKOK

I dedicate this book
with much gratitude
to all those who helped me
in my writing career:

William Peden, Anthony Boucher, J. Francis
McComas, H. L. Gold, Harry Altshuler,
Ray Bradbury, Robert Bloch, Howard Browne,
Al Manuel, Albert Zugsmith, Alan Williams,
Malcolm Stuart, Rick Ray, Sam Adams,
Lee Rosenberg, Rod Serling, Buck Houghton,
Jules Schermer, Jim Nicholson, Sam Arkoff,
Roger Corman, Anthony Hinds, Dan Curtis,
Larry Turman, Steven Spielberg, Allen Epstein,
Jim Green, Stan Shpetner, Stephen Deutsch,
Jeannot Szwarc, Davidw Kirschner, Jeff Conner,
Davd Greenblatt, Gary Goldstein, Bob Gleason,
Greg Cox

and especially, Don Congdon

Introduction

Since I am best known as a writer of fantasy, it is appropriate, I feel, to state at the outset that this novel may well be a fantasy. While there is evidence supporting much of what I fictionally contend, at the same time I do not wish to offend historical purists who believe that Wild Bill Hickok was an authentic frontier hero. In any case, I did not write the book to demean Hickok in any way and, regardless of my take on his character, his reputation will continue to endure.

To the Reader

You may recall that, some years back, I was witness to the violent demise of famous gunfighter-lawman Clay Halser.

Following that tragic incident, I was requested by the management of the hotel at which Halser was staying to inspect what meager goods he possessed with the intent of returning them to his family in Indiana. This request was made of me because I had known Halser since we first met during the War Between the States.

In the course of examining his goods, I ran across a stack of record books in which Halser had kept a journal from the latter part of the war until the very morning of his death.

This journal was prepared and edited by me and published in May 1877 to some measure of success.

I mention this as introduction to the incident that occurred in September of that year in the town of Deadwood, the Dakota Territory.

As you may know, this was the town in which James Butler Hickok—known by the sobriquet of Wild Bill—was murdered by a drifter named Jack McCall, whose assassination of Hickok will doubtless be the single notable event of his life. McCall was hanged for the crime on March 1 of that year.

By coincidence, I happened to be present in Deadwood on assignment from *The Greenvale Review,* preparing an article on the aftermath of Hickok's murder: its effect upon the community, their reaction to McCall's hanging, their recollections of Hickok as a man and a celebrity.

I intended to incorporate, within these facts, some comment as to the perilous mortality of men like Hickok, who had not yet reached the age of forty when he was killed. Halser had, as a matter of fact, died even younger, at the startling age of thirty-one.

I was staying at the Grand Central Hotel, compiling the disparate elements of my article, when someone knocked on the door of my room.

I rose from my work and moved across the floor to see who it was.

A woman stood in the corridor; short, comely, with glowing red hair. She was wearing a dark brown dress with a white lace collar and a small brooch fastened to it. On her head was a brown bonnet with green ribbons. She wore dark gloves on her hands in which she carried a wooden box approximately twelve by ten inches in dimension, four inches thick.

"Mr. Leslie?" she asked.

"Yes." I nodded.

"My name is Agnes Lake Thatcher Hickok," she said.

I felt a tremor of astonishment at her words. How incredibly synchronous, I thought, that Hickok's widow should be knocking at my door at that very moment.

"I'm delighted to meet you," I told her. "Did you know that I am in Deadwood preparing an article about your late husband?"

Was that a flicker of uncertainty across her face? She seemed, for an instant, to be on the verge of drawing back.

"Nothing captious or lurid, I assure you." I told her hastily, "Only a generalized appraisal of the community's reaction to your husband's . . . death." I had almost said "murder," then withheld myself from the word, fearing that it might prove disturbing to her.

"I see," was all she responded.

I stepped back and gestured toward the room. "Will you come in?" I invited.

A natural hesitation on her part; she was a lady, after all, and not about to enter a strange man's room unquestioningly.

I was about to suggest that we retire to the dining room when she murmured, "Thank you," and came in. Later on, I arrived at the conclusion that she had not wanted to be seen in public saying what she had come to say lest it be overheard and misconstrued.

Quickly, I removed some books from the one chair in the room and set them on the room's one table. I gestured toward the chair and, with a "Thank you" spoken so indistinctly that I could barely hear it, she sat down, placing the box on her lap.

"Well," I said. I hesitated before sitting on the bed, thinking that it might make her uncomfortable, then decided that my standing would make her even more ill at ease and quickly settled on the mattress edge.

I forced a polite smile to my lips. "What can I do for you, Mrs. Hickok?" I asked.

She gazed at me with a restive appraisal for what must have been at least thirty seconds. Then she swallowed— the sound of it so dry that I considered asking her if she would like a drink of water—and clearly came, once more, to the decision that had brought her to my room in the first place.

"I have read your . . . presentation of the journal written by Mr. Halser," she began.

I nodded. "Yes?"

Another lengthy hesitation on her part. I heard her swallow dryly once again and, this time, did inquire as to whether she would care to have a drink of water.

She responded that she would, and I stood at once, moving to the table where I kept a carafe of water and two glasses. I poured some water into one of them and handed it to her. She thanked me with a bow of her head and took a sip from the glass.

She then placed the glass on top of the table and looked at me again.

"I have come to Deadwood to visit my husband's grave," she said. "I am traveling with Mr. and Mrs. Charles Dalton and Mr. George Carson."

I nodded, wondering why she told me this. I said nothing, however. Clearly, she was discomposed, so I sat in quiet, allowing her to proceed at whatever pace was necessary for her.

"We have all decided," she went on, "that the grave should remain undisturbed."

I nodded; still waiting.

"Accordingly," she said, "we have agreed that arrangements will be made to erect a fenced monument to my husband's memory."

"Of course," I said, nodding once more. "A splendid idea."

She drew in a long, somewhat tremulant breath and fell silent again. I had to wait further, sensing that, were I to press the situation, she might depart, her mission unstated. And I was beginning to sense—with a tingle of expectation—what that mission might be.

"I have, in this box," she said at last, "a journal written—*no,*" she broke off suddenly, "not a journal," she amended. "My husband *did* keep a journal, but that was burned."

Burned! The shock of hearing that obscured her continuing statement. *My God,* I thought; it was *true* then, the protracted rumor that Hickok had composed a journal. And it had been *burned*? I could not adjust to the revelation, it was so confounding to me.

"I'm sorry," I was forced to say. "I didn't hear that last remark."

She hesitated as though questioning my reliability.

Then she said—repeated, I assumed, "What my husband *did* leave behind was an account of his life based upon memory."

She patted the box. "I have it here," she said.

I tried not to reveal the eagerness I felt at what she'd told me. She had brought this manuscript to *me*? I was overwhelmed.

"I . . ." She swallowed again and required some moments to reach for the glass again and take another sip of water. I sat in restless silence, attempting with great difficulty to keep my fervor from showing. I doubt if I entirely succeeded.

"I presume—" she said, then drew in wavering breath, "that . . . the magazine you represent is willing to . . ."

She gestured feebly.

I don't know why I felt such a rush of terrible embarrassment for her. There was no reason whatsoever that such an astounding find should not be compensated. If she had mentioned this immediately, in a matter-of-fact manner, I would have merely nodded in agreement, thinking nothing of it.

Not that I felt any less that Hickok's reminiscences should be paid for. It was her awkward broaching of the subject that made me feel a sense of great discomfort for her.

She needed money; that was clearly the situation. She had every right to it and yet the obvious tribulation of her need for it was unsettling to me. *I* swallowed dryly now.

"Well, of course—" I began and had to clear my throat in order to continue, "I am certain that the magazine will be more than pleased to remunerate you for the manuscript."

I felt an inward groan assailing me. It was apparent that, no matter what I said or how discreetly I said it, it was going to come out wrong; which, of course, it had. Mrs. Hickok could not contain a blush of disconcertion and, from the warmth I felt on my cheeks, neither could I.

"You . . . feel they would be . . . interested then," she said.

"Oh, definitely. *Definitely,*" I replied, acutely aware that I spoke too loudly, too excessively.

Her smile was—I can use no more apt description— heart-wrenching.

"I never intended for the book to be seen by the public," she explained. "I thought of burning it as my husband had burned his journal. To keep it from the world, to . . . protect his reputation. However . . ."

I could only stare at her in mute distress. What could there be in the memoirs that she thought might harm her husband's reputation? For several moments, I felt an urge to tell her to leave immediately and take the manuscript along with her. I had a specific image of Hickok. Did I want to risk it?

What was there in the man's account that might conceivably undo that image?

Without telling them why I was asking, I approached a number of people who knew Hickok personally, seeking in their recollections some verification for the memoirs he wrote.

For a time, I convinced myself that the manuscript was fraudulent; that I had been the victim of a hoax.

That soon abated. The memory of Mrs. Hickok's unquestionable pain made it clear beyond a doubt that her words were sincerely motivated.

So, with due emphasis on this point, I present to you the memoirs of Wild Bill Hickok.

I have done a minimum of editing on them. Unlike Clay Halser's journal, this is not a day-by-day account, with the inevitable excesses of such a manuscript.

There is a minimum of repetition or irrelevant commentary in Hickok's memoirs. It is, instead, a remarkably clear-eyed appraisal of the events of his life, written with the intent of describing it exactly as it was.

The contents may surprise you.

Frank Leslie
July 19, 1878

My Intention,
Wise or Otherwise

I, James Butler Hickok, being of chafed mind and dilapidated body, hereby declare what I intend to accomplish by the writing of this account.

In brief, a presentation of the truth; the details of my life as they occurred, not as so many think they did.

For more than fifteen years, commencing after the war, I maintained a daily journal of my activities. It was, sad to relate, more than somewhat self-justifying if not self-aggrandizing. I reread it awhile back and found it to be a generous heap of cow chips. Sensibly, I put a match to it.

I am thirty-eight years old now, and it is time to set the record straight about my life. Despite my scarcely venerable age, I have a lingering impression that I am near the end of my trail. It is, accordingly, now or never.

If what I disclose offends or dismays those legions who have, over the years, shaped me in their minds as some manner of icon, a two-gun god set up on a pedestal—well, sorry; my regrets. But truth is truth and facts are facts and I cannot change that anymore, although I tried to do it once.

To begin with, then, step back in time to my childhood.

Growing Up
[as Much as Possible]

I was, as you may know, the youngest of four brothers. Oliver, born in 1830; Lorenzo in 1832 (another Lorenzo, born in 1831, died soon after birth); and Horace in 1834. In 1836, the family moved to Homer, Illinois, where I was born the following year. My two sisters, Celinda and Lydia, were born in 1839 and 1842.

Herewith, a brief quotation from a description—not mine, I rush to clarify—of my early life.

"The deadliest killer of men the West has ever known, James Butler Hickok was born in a tiny log cabin in Troy Grove, Illinois, on June 27, 1837."

It was a small house in Homer, Illinois, on May 27, 1837. The inaccuracies began immediately, you see.

"As a boy, Young Hickok [as a boy I could hardly be called Old Hickok] was enthralled by tales of the wild frontier, poring avidly over many a volume that recounted, in hair-raising detail, sagas of adventure in that barbarous land."

I see myself, about the age of twelve, a wispy, blond, extremely doe-eyed boy, sitting cross-legged by the fireplace, a book of true adventures on my lap.

Concealed inside it was a torn-out catalog page on which were illustrated ladies' corsets.

"In this, he was encouraged by his father, a kindly, tolerant man."

Visualize Young Hickok emitting squeals of utmost pain as his father hauled him to his feet by one ear.

Moments later, picture in your mind Young Hickok stretched across his father's lap, reddening buttocks being walloped with a belt. Young Hickok's blubbering has no effect on Elder Hickok, whose features, in moments of such stress, bore all the animation of a statue's.

"A Hickok is a gentleman," he told me, alternating blows with that reminder. "A Hickok is a gentleman." *Whop!* "A Hickok is a gentleman." *Whop!* "A Hickok—"

You get the idea, I think. All of this observed by my mother, watching in subservient distress, unable to prevent her favorite son from getting his bottom belabored.

Afterward (it was a regular occurrence, I assure you), my mother would apply—with tender, loving touch—goose grease to my fiery, stinging backside as I lay on my stomach on her bed, her tone of voice as loving as her soothing application.

"You must always be a gentleman, James," she would tell me gently. "Remember that. It is your birthright. You are descended from the Hiccock family of Stratford-Upon-Avon, Warwickshire, England. A noble line, James."

To which I snuffled pitifully, eyes bubbling tears, and murmured, "Yes, Mother."

Oliver and Horace and Lorenzo were tall, strong boys, my father was tall as well and constructed like a tree.

I, on the other hand, was a stripling, slender and graceful in appearance (if I do say so myself). Hardly a likely prospect to become "the deadliest killer of men the West has ever known"; but more on that anon.

I believe that my facial features were inherited from my father, a man of distinguished appearance, with dark hair, high cheekbones, and a Roman nose.

My disposition (I am glad to say) came from my mother, a warm-hearted, seraphic woman whom I loved intensely.

That my disposition came from her, I did not overly relish in my youth. The other boys in Homer treated me—what is the proper word?—*abominably?* Yes, that will do. They called me Girlboy, inviting (actually goading) me to wrath and fisticuffs.

Said invitation was rarely accepted by me unless their physical and verbal tormenting grew so extreme that I saw red and responded with sudden, mindless violence that, for a moment or two, sufficed to startle them into retreat. My fury vanished quickly, however—almost instantaneously— at which point they would, once more, charge and chase and cuff me to the point of tears.

I wept a good deal as a boy. My father hated that, so I attempted to conceal it from him as well as I was able— which, too often, proved impossible. My mother, bless her saintly heart, understood and sympathized with all that I was going through. Without that loving sympathy, I wonder now and then if I would have survived my childhood.

When I was twelve or thirteen, I cannot recall for certain, my father tried to teach me how to fire a revolver. I emphasize the word *tried,* for I was just about as far from being a candidate for "the deadliest killer of men," etc., as the Earth is from the stars.

See Young Hickok standing there, a look of calcified intent on his girlboy face as he aims a huge (to him) revolver at a distant target.

"At an age when other boys knew naught of such pursuits, Hickok was already mastering the art of pistol firing . . ."

Closing his eyes, a grimace of total apprehension on his

face, Young Hickok pulls the trigger, the violent recoil of the pistol flinging him into his (prevalently tenderized) backside, the revolver jumping from the grip of his delicate hand.

". . . aided always by the patient ministrations of his beloved sire."

Patient and beloved sire drags Young Hickok to his feet by his (also tenderized) ear and leads him to the fallen revolver. *"Again,"* he says through clenched teeth.

Young Hickok picks up the revolver gingerly. He aims, grimaces, shuts his eyes, and pulls the trigger once again. A repetition of the same, Young Hickok flung down forcefully onto his sensitized haunches, the revolver flying, the target as safe as a babe in church.

How many times did this go on? I believe the proper word is *interminably.* Until Young Hickok's face was smudged from the black powder smoke, his hand and arm and shoulder aching from the pistol's sharp recoil, and his behind on its way, once more, to peaks of throbbing pain.

Grimace, eyes shut, pulling of trigger, exploding percussion, Young Hickok thrown flat on his arse, beloved sire hauling him up by the ear, intoning, in the same sepulchral tone of voice, *"Again."* Until Young Hickok, injured and despairing, breaks into a fit of weeping, at which patient sire twists his son's ear and instructs him that "a gentleman does not cry."

If the blubbering did not cease forthwith, off came the belt, Young Hickok's trousers were lowered to half-mast, and another buttock drubbing ensued.

Followed, as the custom was, by my mother applying further layers of goose grease to my battered backside, comforting me, and reminding me in her loving way of my heritage.

I recall the day she opened up a family chest and drew

forth from its aromatic depths a copy of the Hickok family tree.

Our family can be traced back (she informed me) to one Edward Hiccox, Esquire, of Stratford, England. A relative named John Hiccocks was a Master of the High Court of Chancery from 1703 to 1709.

A William Hitchcock sailed to America in 1635, settling down in Connecticut.

A hero in the Revolutionary War was Aaron Hickok; he was, it is believed, present at the Battle of Bunker Hill.

"You see, son," said my mother on that occasion and many others, "you are descended from a fine and noble line."

I found that somewhat comforting and there were times aplenty when I needed that comfort to assuage the aching in my heart (and bottom).

I Become a Bibliolator

If you have read this far, perhaps you wonder at my command of language.

My mother constantly encouraged me to read in order that I might educate myself. This I did, keeping the habit as much a secret as possible from my P.A.B.S. (patient and beloved sire) since he felt that such a custom was a waste of time, a man's attention to be concentrated exclusively on the higher values of life such as commerce, farming, politics, and (I took it as a given) shooting pistols at targets so as to perfect the shooting of them at men. I find it beyond ironic that I ended up so deeply entrenched in this latter "manly" pursuit.

I have been, by necessity (I believed that it was necessary, anyway), obliged to conceal my reading and education from the general public, feeling that, in their eyes, it besmirched my image as the deadliest killer of blah ad infinitum. I have gone so far as to deliberately misspell words and misuse grammatical construction in order to maintain that image as a rough-and-ready pistoleer. Well, bah to that. The truth emerges now.

I have read—naturally—the novels of James Fenimore

Cooper such as *The Last of the Mohicans, The Leather-stocking Tales, The Pathfinder,* and *The Deerslayer.* I tried to read *Santanstoe* but found it less interesting than his other works and did not complete it.

I have also enjoyed a number of works by the well-known English author Charles Dickens, most notably *The Pickwick Papers* (which I found delightful), *Oliver Twist,* and *David Copperfield.* I tried to read *American Notes* but found a good deal of it quite offensive in its criticism of our way of life and broke off the reading.

I read (with many a shiver, I confess) Mary Shelley's novel *Frankenstein,* the idea for which (I read elsewhere) was derived from the witness of a certain alchemist who claimed to have created a tiny human being in a bottle; *homunculus,* I believe it was called. I also read much of Carlyle's *History of the French Revolution* and found it to be of much interest.

I have read some of Edgar Allan Poe's works but, in general, thought them oppressively dark in tone although his poetry is singularly powerful, particularly "The Bells" and "The Raven."

I have also read, throughout the years, *The Count of Monte Cristo* by Dumas, *Don Quixote* by Cervantes, *Gargantua and Pantagruel* by Rabelais, *Gulliver's Travels* by Swift, *The Memoirs of Casanova* (I sensed a kindred spirit there), *Pilgrim's Progress* by Bunyan, *Robinson Crusoe* by Defoe (I, too, have known that sense of utter isolation felt by Crusoe), *Tom Jones* by Fielding, *Ivanhoe* by Scott, and even *Uncle Tom's Cabin* by Stowe (of whom Lincoln, I recall reading, upon meeting her, said something like, "Well, here is the little lady who started the war").

All this in addition to a regular perusal of as many newspapers as I was able to lay my hands on.

Why do I mention this? As indicated, to square my

account. I intend to tell the truth regardless of its consequences. My Wild Bill image may be tarnished by the facts, but let that be. I wish it so.

I might add, since it is not a fact generally known, that my mother also introduced me to the subject of Spiritualism, telling me about it when I was a boy. Naturally, as in so many other areas of my life at that time, I did not (dared not) mention this to P.A.B.S. Nor did my mother tell any of my brothers about it; I was the only one she trusted with such information. I confess that, to this day, I am not certain how I feel about the subject. God knows I have been exposed to death in many ways, but as to its penultimate significance, I am not sure. Naturally, I would like to believe in a continuation of existence, although I do confess that the vision of men I have killed remaining about as lingering shades does nothing but chill my blood.

Birds, Bees, and Pistology

"Young Hickok spent many an hour in manly pursuits, his endless quest for bold, exciting enterprises leading him into more than one tight squeeze."

One of these manly pursuits was Hannah Robbins, who I lured into a haystack on a sunny afternoon, urged on by the mounting juices in my lower realm.

Unfortunately, P.A.B.S. happened to be passing by and found us there.

I recall his features—stonelike as always—as he hauled me upward, trouserless and jutting in a most unseemly way, and escorted me across the field (by ear, of course) while naked fourteen-year-old Hannah scrambled from the stack, snatched up her clothes, and ran for home.

Inside our barn, a typical posterior-hiding took place, my body (ungarbed below) stretched across my father's legs as he wore his belt down farther on my burning buttocks.

"A Hickok is a gentleman," he told me sternly. "Repeat."

"A Hi-Hi-Hi-Hi—" was all I could manage.

I cried out as another blow resounded leatherly across my bottom.

"Hickok isagen'l'man!" I blurted.

"Correct," my father said.

Another belt delivery to my hapless rump.

"Repeat," my father said.

"Oooh," I replied.

Another blow. *"Repeat,"* my father said.

"A Hickokisagen'l'man!" moaned I.

"Correct," he said. Another blow. *"Repeat."*

Another limping, weeping visit to my mother's consoling presence. Another gentle application of goose grease to my harrowed haunches. Another kind reminder of my legacy.

"You must always be a gentleman, James," she said. "It is expected of you."

"I *know,* I *know,*" I muttered dismally.

But it *did* sink in. I *am* a gentleman. Whatever else I have failed to be, I have always been a gentleman.

Has it served me well?

I wouldn't bet my stash on it.

Fourteen years of age: my father trying, once again, to teach me pistology.

"With constant practice, Young Hickok soon perfected that deadly eye, which was to serve him with such potency in days to come."

I aimed, I fired, keeping my eyes open at any rate and managing to stay on my feet, albeit staggering noticeably.

The target—a bottle standing on a boulder top—remained untouched, the ball whistling off into the distance.

"Again," my father said, features ossifying in their usual fashion.

I aimed and fired, tottering.

The bottle remained safe and sound.

"Again," my father said.

Not much point in putting down the further details. P.A.B.S. watching me with monolithic detachment, mute save for the one repeated word. Young Hickok contorting his greenhorn visage into a gargoyle mask of concentration as he aims, fires, teeters, misses.

With each new miss, my father took me by the ear and moved me closer to the target. I kept on aiming, firing, stumbling, missing. With each new miss, my father's incredulity at my ineptitude with the revolver mounted until his eyes were bulging so with his determination not to lose his temper that it would not have surprised me at all had they popped from their sockets. Soon, his "Again's" were delivered behind tightly clenched teeth.

On one occasion, at a distance of some fifteen feet, I managed to hit the boulder, the ricocheting ball knocking off my father's hat and causing him, from startlement, to topple, crashing to the ground.

Seeing that, a woebegone expression on his face, Young Hickok began to undo his trousers as his P.A.B.S. rose to his feet and began removing his belt.

I leaned against a tree as my father laid said belt (with special vigor) across my much harried fundaments.

"A gentleman is skilled in the use of weapons," he instructed me.

"A gentleman—" I began.

A wallop on my rump concluded my remark.

"You were not instructed to repeat," my father said.

I do not recall my exact response, but I feel confident that it was something in the neighborhood of "Oooh!"

Of course, in time, I actually learned to shoot, first with a Pennsylvania long flintlock, then a better rifle (a percussion-lock Remington). I did this minus my sire's patient and benign presence and learned much faster.

I have always preferred the rifle as a weapon. If I had been permitted to conduct all street confrontations with a rifle instead of a revolver, I would have faced these moments with far more equanimity than, in fact, I did. But I suppose it would be less dramatic for two opponents to face each other with rifles sticking out of their holsters.

During that period, Oliver traveled to California, where he found a profession (teamster) and lost an arm. Horace and Lorenzo worked on the farm, leaving me to spend the greater part of my time shooting squirrels, rabbits, deer, and prairie chickens to augment the family larder. I became quite good at that.

But then none of those critters were armed.

Egress and Egest

"Thus was Young Hickok admirably equipped to master any peril he might face—which soon proved necessary as he was exposed to the sound of hostile gunfire and the near proximity of death when he assisted his father in delivering runaway slaves from one station to the next of the so-called 'underground railroad.'"

I remember one occasion when I was fifteen, an evening on the road outside of Homer, my father driving a small hay-filled wagon, underneath said hay an assortment of fear-ridden slaves who had escaped from the South.

We had just turned a curve in the road when we caught sight of three mounted men ahead, waiting for us.

"Bounty hunters, I'll wager," my father said.

His words petrified my limbs. Bounty hunters made their living capturing runaway slaves and returning them to their owners—at gunpoint, needless to say.

I made, I fear, a feeble sound of apprehension.

"A gentleman does not show panic when in danger," said my father.

"Yes, but—" I began.

"Repeat," my father told me.

I answered through my teeth, which I was gritting to prevent their chattering. "A gentleman does not show panic when in danger," I repeated.

"Correct; repeat." Despite my dread, I knew, at that moment, what a brave man my father was.

The words had a tendency to vibrate in my throat as I repeated them.

"Correct; repeat," my father said. We were almost to the three men now.

"A gentleman does not—"

My voice choked off as my father shouted at the horses suddenly and cracked his whip above their heads. The bounty hunters began to draw their pistols, then were forced to yank aside their mounts to avoid getting run down as the team and wagon hurtled by them.

Behind, the bounty hunters opened fire and pistol balls began to buzz around us like infuriated bees. I sat on the seat, eyes wide and unblinking, utterly benumbed with fear, mumbling to myself, making an endless litany of my father's family maxim, "A gentleman does not show panic when in danger a gentleman does not show panic when in danger a gentleman does not—" And so on.

How long that chase continued is lost in congealed recollection. All I do remember is emerging from a blinding stupor of dread to discover that my father had steered the team and wagon behind a great clump of bushes, eluding the bounty hunters who were galloping by.

After they had disappeared, my father turned to me.

"You behaved well," he told me.

"Thank you, sir." Was that my voice I heard? It could have been that of a frightened girl.

P.A.B.S. patted me on the back. "You see. It *can* be done."

"Yes, sir," replied Young Hickok, hoping to God above

that P.A.B.S. did not notice the spreading puddle by his feet.

I plucked discreetly at my soggy trousers.

"Now you are a Hickok," said my father.

Somewhere Between Boyhood
and [Hoped for] Adulthood

A brief enumeration of the passing years and my varying occupations.

1853: Canal mule driver.

1854: Homesteader.

1855: Stable tender.

1856: Bull whacker.

1857: Freight wagon driver.

1858: Stagecoach driver.

This last employment, for three men named Russell, Majors, and Waddell, went on for several years and was, if you are not aware, a giant pain (literally) in the a————. Roads were little better than rutted tracks stocked with rocks and hidden stumps; only the open prairie and mesa country were accessible without danger of spinal havoc. The spring-steel brackets were of little assistance when the going was extreme, not to mention the clouds of dust that billowed around the coach as it rocked along, threatening to smother driver and passengers alike.

Toward the end of 1858, I fell in love with a young woman named Mary Owens and came close to marrying her and taking up a life of farming.

Lorenzo traveled to Kansas and convinced me that it was a mistake. I think of that often, not certain why I let him talk me out of it; could it possibly have been only because she was part Indian? I can scarcely believe that now, yet I did not marry her. I also think often that, had I married her, I might have lived a peaceful existence on that farm. It would, God knows, have been a simpler life.

As heretofore indicated, I did become as proficient with the pistol as the rifle.

Had I known what roads that skill would lead me along, I would have dropped the ability as quickly as I would have dropped a red-hot branding iron. But, of course, I didn't know. Accordingly, I disappeared into the woods at every opportunity to hone the edge of my revolver skill. Indeed, in time I derived undue pleasure in astonishing all and sundry with my mastery of the handgun.

But that is simple; don't you see. Time and practice, nothing more. Shooting an apple from a tree and putting a second ball in it before it hits the ground? No great achievement. An apple doesn't shoot back.

I had begun to read any periodicals that came my way by 1858 and was aware of myriad things occurring outside of my personal life.

For instance, Senate candidate Abraham Lincoln declaring that "the Union cannot permanently endure half slave and half free." Little did we know where those words would lead us.

That summer, the first Pony Express mail delivery traveled from St. Louis to the west coast in twenty-three days; an incredible feat.

The Seven-Year War with the Seminole Indians had concluded; cost: ten million dollars and the lives of fifteen hundred men. Does mankind ever come out in the black from a war?

On August 5, 1858, two steamers began to lay cable across the bottom of the Atlantic Ocean. Upon completion, England telegraphed our government: "Europe and America are united by telegraph. Glory to God on the highest; on Earth peace, good will toward men."

In September, the cable's insulation ruptured and the service discontinued.

By 1860, I was still a stage and wagon driver; not much progress there.

Homer's name was changed to Troy Grove since there was another Homer (larger) in Illinois.

Abraham Lincoln won his party's nomination for President of the United States (his progress had considerably outstripped mine). His vice presidential candidate was a man named Hannibal Hamlin. Where is he today?

In autumn of that year, none of the four presidential candidates obtained a majority vote, and Lincoln was elected with a plurality of half a million votes more than Stephen Douglas.

In December 1860, Congress debated and President Buchanan hesitated and the North stood by in hapless silence while the South made ready to redress their grievances with a plan to secede from the Union.

By January 1861, the South's secession was rolling along steadily; first Mississippi, then Florida, Alabama, Georgia, Louisiana, and, by February, Texas. The other states were soon to follow.

In Lincoln's inaugural address, he stated that he had no intention, directly or indirectly, to interfere with slavery wherever it might exist. I could not help but wonder— along with many others—what had happened to his conviction that the Union could not permanently endure half slave and half free. I presume that when politicians actually assume office, their convictions, of necessity, become more flexible.

In the spring of 1861, to my amazement (along with others), I read that the Confederacy actually hoped to establish its independence by means of peaceful negotiation. This was, to say the very least, substantially naive, considering that the United States government regarded supporters of Secession as traitors to the Union.

It is interesting to speculate, in retrospect, how different the war would have been if the man who was offered the command of the Union Army had accepted instead of resigning his commission and offering his services to his native state of Virginia, which, naturally, accepted this offer by Robert E. Lee.

Why do I go on about these things? Perhaps to avoid the beginning of it all: my appearance to the public eye, my notoriety and increasingly demanding residence in an outsize hornet's nest. But, heaven help me, it is time to tell the tawdry tale.

By July of 1861, I was about to secede from anonymity.

The Straight Goods

"Hickok's first manhood brush with violent death occurred on Friday, July 12, 1861, when he became involved in the horrendous incident that first revealed his lethal prowess as a slayer of men and brought to life the Hickok legend: *the Battle of Rock Creek Station.*"

Rock Creek Station was a stagecoach station six miles out from Fairbury, Nebraska.

I was there recuperating from some injuries I had incurred when a wagon I was driving ran over a bear, overturned, and pitched me to the ground. On the afternoon of July 12 (my imaginative biographer, Colonel George Ward Nichols, got the date right, anyway) I was in the sleeping quarters of the station, not, I must confess, sleeping but—well, let it be said—dallying with a most attractive young woman by the name of Sarah Shull. Both of us were on my cot, as the French would have it, au naturel.

I was lying on my back while Sarah spoke to me, alternating words and phrases with a rain of kisses on my face, my neck, my shoulders, chest, and—to be decorous—et al.

"Hickok was alone when it happened," Nichols wrote, fully on the mark, as usual.

"You ain't really going to leave your job here, are you, darling?" Sarah asked.

"Soon enough," I answered.

"Why?" she asked.

"A gentleman does not drive wagons and coaches for a living," I replied. If that sounds egregiously pretentious to you, you're correct. I had a manner of behavior then that, in recollection, makes me alternately smile and cringe. Some might say that I was full of myself. Actually, I was full of manure.

"What *does* a gentleman do?" asked Sarah.

"Something appropriate," responded I.

"Something *what?*" inquired Sarah.

I frowned at her in lordly disdain. "Ap*prop*riate," I pronounced the word again. "Something *fitting.*"

"Like what?" asked Sarah.

"I'm not quite certain yet," I let her know. "I'll find out, though."

"Marry me and take me with you," she pleaded.

After she allowed my lips their freedom once again, I looked at her, not so much in scorn but in surprise that she could even conceive of such an occurrence.

"You?" I said.

She stopped her kissing frenzy and looked sulky. "Why not?" she demanded.

I gazed into my (unpromising at the time) future and replied, "Because the woman I *marry* will have to be a *lady.*"

"Oh!" cried Sarah, angrily.

She glared at me for many moments, then once more pressed herself against me, snuggling close.

"If only you weren't so gorgeous," she said.

"No man is gorgeous, Sarah," I chided. But of course she was right. I *was* gorgeous then. What can I say? I looked in the mirror and there it was. No feather in my cap, of course; I know that now. Heredity; my father was a handsome man. My looks were not remarkable at all, but at the time I certainly made the most of them.

So when she countered, "You are," I did not contest the point. *Why argue with the unarguable?* I probably thought.

Idiot.

At that point, both of us looked toward the window as we heard the sound of approaching horses. Sarah gasped.

"I thought you said no one was coming here today," she said.

"I didn't think they were," I replied. I didn't either, or I wouldn't have arranged our assignation.

Sarah jumped up hastily and hurried to the window as I rose and pulled up my long johns over my (rapidly decreasing, let me tell you) equipment.

At the window looking out, Sarah caught her breath in such obvious shock that the sound made me twitch, lose balance, and topple to the floor from where I looked up at her with a combination of vexation and alarm.

"What's wrong?" I demanded.

"It's Dave," she said.

"Dave who?"

"McCanles."

"So?" I responded, struggling to my feet, rubbing my bruised elbow.

"He looks mad," Sarah replied uneasily.

I felt myself beginning to tense as I limped to the window and looked outside.

Some fifty yards away, dismounting by the corral, were three men, Dave McCanles, James Woods, and James Gordon (the identities of the last two of the trio I discovered later).

McCanles was looking toward the station with an expression that more than confirmed Sarah's observation. He looked, in point of fact, on the verge of spitting fire.

"What's he mad about?" I asked.

I looked at her inquiringly as she failed to respond.

"*Well?*" I asked.

Her smile was wan. "Us?" she said.

"*Us!*"

"Well . . . yes," she admitted. "I'm his . . . sort of . . . well, I'm sort of his mistress."

"You never told me that!" I cried, aghast.

Her face curled up. "You never asked," she offered feebly.

I looked back at McCanles, looked at Sarah, looked back at McCanles, and felt my breath cut off. I believed I leaned toward the window, my mouth as widely open as the window was.

McCanles was drawing a shotgun from its saddle sheath.

"That's not a shotgun," I actually heard myself say, my tone of voice incredulous and weak.

"Yes, it is," Sarah verified.

I saw McCanles say something to Woods and Gordon, the two men nodding grimly.

Then he started toward the station.

I gaped at Sarah, pointing toward McCanles. I attempted speech but failed to produce more than a succession of inchoate sounds, which fluttered in my throat.

Then I blew.

"Good Lord, girl!" I exploded.

She began to bawl. "I'm sorry!"

"*Sorry!*" I repeated at a higher, angrier pitch. "Don't you realize—?"

I pointed at McCanles with a trembling finger.

"—that man is going to get hurt?" I wheezed.

I grabbed her arm and pulled her to the bed, picked up her shift, and flung it at her.

"Put it on," I ordered, swallowed, pointed. "Then go out and tell him he's a dead man if he comes in here. You understand?"

She stared at me.

"You understand?" I repeated.

Sarah, whimpering and snuffling, nodded as she drew the shift over her head and down across her body. I shoved her toward the doorway.

"Go!" I cried.

She stumbled through the doorway.

"Tell him I'm a deadly shot!" I ordered. *"Tell* him!"

I felt the gases in my stomach taking flight, an involuntary belch escaping me. Turning toward the window, I assumed a stiff expression on my face.

"The man's a fool," I mumbled.

I belched again, eyes bulging as a wave of nausea plowed through my stomach. I looked outside.

McCanles was almost to the station. As he moved, he was loading his shotgun.

"Don't *do* that," I remember saying in a faint, offended tone.

I turned and strutted about the room in aimless patterns, lower lip thrust forward, a look of dignified affront on my face. It was an expression I had cultivated through the years—if not the knowledge of when it was appropriate.

With an abrupt descent, I plopped down on the cot and, with casual albeit palsied movement, pulled on my right boot. I looked toward the window, drawing in a deep, quavering breath, then looked toward the doorway.

Hastily, I stood and snatched my trousers off the chair back they were lying across. I tried to push my right foot through its proper leg but could not because I'd donned my boot first.

Nonetheless, I strained to shove the boot through. "D———n it, man," I muttered sternly.

With a stifled cry, I lost my balance and crashed down on my side.

"*D———n it, I say!*" I cried, pathetically, I fear. I tried to pull the boot free now, could not, and reaching down with quivering hands, yanked off boot and trousers both, almost pulling down my long johns.

I hurled away the boot and trousers, looking toward the doorway suddenly as Sarah's voice was heard outside.

"No, Dave!" she cried. That was not exactly reassuring.

I stumbled to my feet and lurched toward the bedside table, tripping over the right leg of my long johns, which I had partially removed with the boot. Flailing for balance, I banged against the table, knocking down the oval, gold-framed photograph of my mother. Setting it back up quickly, I pulled out the table drawer and jerked out my Colt Navy .36 revolver, whirling to face the doorway, gun extended.

"I warn you, sir!" I said. I'm sure McCanles never heard a word of it, so gargly was my voice.

With my left hand, I pulled up at my sagging long johns, listening to the voices of Sarah and McCanles outside as she tried—obviously in vain—to dissuade him from his purpose.

I received a sudden demented inspiration and tossed the Colt on the cot. I posed as nobly as I could, arms crossed, shoulders back, head high.

"Sir, I am unarmed, as you can see," I practiced. "Let us settle this like gentlemen, not—"

"*Hickok!*" roared McCanles.

I swallowed what felt like a large stone in my throat.

"A gentleman does not show panic when—" I started in a hurried whisper.

"Prepare to meet your maker!" cried McCanles.

So much for nobility. My stomach doing flip-flops, I lunged for my pistol, juggling it for several moments, then got a grip on it. I looked around for some location of advantage, seeing none. I heard the stomp of McCanles's boots as he entered the station, and I found it difficult to breathe. I mumbled to myself, "Have courage, Hickok." I did not convince myself.

Then, on impulse, I strode quickly to a pair of hanging blankets that served as a closet divider. Pushing in between the blankets, I turned and pressed my back against the wall, the Colt clasped to my chest. I forced my lips together, face a mask of willful and terror-stricken resolution. The approaching footsteps came closer and closer, entering the room. They stopped.

"Hickok!" shouted McCanles.

I was immobile save for my gaze, which dropped to a pair of boots set side by side against the blanket.

Carefully, I reached out one bare foot and nudged them forward.

McCanles obviously saw the boot tips sliding out beneath the blanket edge for he clumped across the room and, with a glare of triumph (I have no doubt), raised the shotgun, firing both barrels simultaneously at where he thought I stood.

I would like to say that my returned fire was deliberate, but the truth is otherwise. Jolting back in dazed shock as the double shotgun blast tore apart the blanket, I fired my pistol more by reflex than design. I heard McCanles cry out.

After a passage of moments, when nothing more occurred, I peeked around the tattered blanket edge, reacting to a vision in its pall of smoke.

McCanles stood motionless, a hole in his chest.

He inched his head around and stared at me.

I stared back, speechless.

Then he spoke, at best a wheezy, bubbly sound.

"You . . . dirty . . . cheating . . ." He gathered gurgling breath to complete his insult. ". . . luck-out son of a b————h, you."

I drew myself erect and answered, with distaste. "That is not a proper remark, sir. You insult my mother's good name."

I contemplated firing a second shot but found it needless as McCanles toppled backward like a fallen tree and stretched out on the floor, entirely motionless.

I had little time to savor my escape as I heard the sound of running boots outside and rushed back to the window.

Gordon and Woods were racing toward the station, pistols in hand, Gordon in the lead.

I stiffened with resentful dread. "But that's not *fair,*" I said, as if it mattered.

Another eructation puffed my cheeks and passed my lips as I looked from side to side, searching, once more, for advantage.

My harried gaze fixed on the fallen shotgun and I tossed the Colt onto the mattress of my cot. Lunging for the shotgun, I bent over, snatched it up, and posed dramatically, feet set apart, weapon pointed toward the doorway.

Several Argus-eyed moments ticked by before a disconcerting observation struck me.

"Hold on," I remember saying to myself.

Breaking open the shotgun, I winced at the sight of spent shells. With a sound of impending (if not already fully present) panic, I dropped to my knees beside McCanles's body, hissing at the pain it caused on my knees. With trembling fingers, I began to search the dead man's pockets, ransacking for additional shells. *Dear God!* The thought appalled me. *He had more, didn't he?*

He didn't, I discovered, stupefied by mounting dread, tossing coins, strings, keys, and a red bandanna in all directions, whines vibrating in my throat.

Boots pounded on the floorboards at the station entrance. Staggering to my feet, I bolted for the nearest window, trying hard to open it, in vain, of course. The whine increased in pitch and volume and I grabbed a chair to smash the window from its frame.

The thumping footsteps entered the room. I whirled, my cry of shock unheard beneath the shot's explosion. The ball chopped off a chair leg and, unthinkingly, I slung the chair at Gordon.

How I managed to hit him, I have no idea. Nonetheless, the chair slammed into him and drove him, staggering, back.

Diving for my cot, I grabbed the Colt and snapped off two shots, both of them missing Gordon as he dropped to the floor. Scrambling to his knees, he started firing back. I flung myself behind the cot, balls whizzing by me, powder smoke beginning to obscure the room.

From behind the cot, I had a view of Gordon's legs and, lunging underneath its frame, I fired upward twice, returning Gordon's rapid fire. One of the balls found its mark and Gordon made a grunting sound, began to stumble back and, clumsily, collided with Woods who was, just at that moment, running hard into the room. The two fell in a mutual heap, one alive, one, I discovered consequently, dead.

Rearing up behind the cot, a dread avenging angel, I aimed my Colt at Woods and pulled the trigger, greeted by the clicking of my pistol's hammer on an empty chamber. I palm-slapped back the hammer, pulled the trigger once again, then tried once more. Clicking, only clicking.

"Aw, no," I believe I mumbled.

Helpless and aghast, I watched Woods standing with a languid movement, a grin of vengeful satisfaction on his fat lips. Extending his arm, he pointed his revolver at me. I had read about ghouls but had never really seen one until that moment; Woods's leering visage qualified in spades.

Still on my knees, I think I said, "That isn't gentlemanly, Woods." Perhaps I only thought it; memory fails. I know the notion did occur to me however I expressed it, in my mind or with my mouth.

Woods's finger must have actually been squeezing at the trigger of his gun when Sarah rushed into the room, a grubbing hoe clutched in her hands, and smacked him potently across the back of his head. Woods staggered forward with a startled cry and dropped his pistol.

I watched with an open mouth as Sarah walloped Woods a second time. Reeling to his feet, bleeding profusely, he stumbled from the room, Sarah in pursuit.

Starting toward the doorway, overwhelmed by Sarah's unexpected action, I failed to notice the shotgun on the floor and stubbed my toe on its stock. Hissing with pain, I almost fell, cursing as I flailed about, then finally regained my balance and began to limp from the room, my hobble a conspicuous one.

At the station entrance I was forced by a wave of dizziness to lean against the door frame for support.

Far out on the station grounds, I witnessed Sarah, hoe brandished, chasing Woods away.

Reaction set in then; immediately, I was sick to my stomach and felt my cheeks puff out as I resisted losing the unstable contents in my stomach.

I went rigid as a pair of horses galloped hard around the station, reined in by their riders. They were, thank the Lord, two locals with no interest in McCanles's vengeful jealousy.

"What happened?" cried one. "We heard shots!"

I gestured with grandiloquence. That I was good at.

"Nothing in particular," I actually said.

I stepped aside and waved the two men by as they jumped from their mounts and rushed inside to investigate.

As soon as they were out of sight, I staggered from the doorway and moved away from the station, trying to effect a casual stride despite the loose-limbed state of my legs.

Reaching the well, I dipped both hands into a bucket of water and washed off my face. I cupped my right palm and took a drink, belched stentoriously, then hiccupped. Leaning on the rim of the well, I began to belch and hiccup alternately, trying—not with great success—to look assured despite the detonating, honking noises I kept making one by one.

Citizen Hickok
Makes a Gesture

"Self-Defense Verdict on Rock Creek Shootout!" howled the headline of the *Brownville Advertiser*. "Stage Driver J. B. Hickok Exonerated."

"Yay, J. B.!" exulted a patron of the Fairbury House saloon.

I stood at the counter, corraled by a horde of red-faced tipplers who pumped my aching hand, pounded my smarting back, and eyed me with respectful awe. It had begun, you see.

Jefferson once wrote, "He who permits himself to tell a lie once, finds it much easier to do it a second time." Not to mention a third and fourth and fifth time and beyond.

In other words, I did not refute their adulation but accepted it with regal deference. How easy it was.

"Here's to Jim Hickok!" cried one of them, his glass raised high in a toast.

Cheers. Applause. Further drinking. J. B. was near believing it had all occurred as they believed.

"Tell us how you did it, Jim!" a man's voice rose above the rest.

There was a sudden, eagerly respectful silence. Later, someone referred to it as a hush of awe.

I gestured modestly; I had perfected that display by then.

"There's really not that much to tell," said I.

Fervent protests ensued.

"Sure, there is!"

"Aw, *come* on, Jim!"

"Tell us, J. B., *tell* us!"

I conceded with that simple grandeur I had mastered. "Three men came to kill me. Three men died. That's all."

A rippling of veneration for my humble understatement.

Then a man said with a smirk, "By God, I just can't *wait* to see what happens when the rest of that McCanles clan shows up!"

The room was filled with sounds of happy expectation. "Yeah!" they bellowed. *"Yeah!"*

My stomach was filled with bubbles of curdling whiskey.

"They'll be gunning for you sure as hell!" some other follower elated, cackling loudly.

I maintained a frozen smile, although my eyes were glassy, I have no doubt.

"How many *are* there, Jeb?" another man inquired of the follower.

Jeb replied, exhilarated, "No more than *seven*! Mean as *sin* though." Another cackle. *"That'll* be a showdown! Yippee! I can hardly wait!"

Someone with a heavy hand slapped me hard across the back.

"What do *you* say, Jim?" he asked.

Everyone regarded me with eager anticipation. I managed an approximation of the modest gesture. Thankfully, my voice held steady as I spoke.

"If it comes, it comes," I told them.

Maddened cheering. I raised a glass of whiskey to my lips and downed its contents in a swallow. The liquor hit my stomach like a burst of sour flame. My cheeks inflated, and I barely managed to repress a belch. At that moment,

I decided it would be a grand idea to get blind drunk, so I poured myself another glassful, quickly swallowing it.

Some hours afterward, I had handily achieved my goal. The saloon floor tilted back and forth with gentle, rocking motions, my head and fingertips had lost all physical sensation, and my plight had satisfactorily been numbed away.

Near sundown, my comrades and I exited the Fairbury House, two of them supporting me like weaving bookends. Everyone was talking at the same time, laughing, snorting, singing, belching. I could not step back and view my face, but I believe it was a mask of absolute inebriation, eyes unblinking, staring, my expression one of hapless stupor. As the saying goes, I could not have hit the floor with my dropped hat.

Politely, I crimped the brim of said hat to a passing lady, discovering in the act that the hat was nowhere near my head, its location unknown. A belch escaped my lips involuntarily, and the lady frowned. I could not find it in my heart to blame her for that.

The two men now attempted to elevate me to the back of my horse. A flicker of awareness made passing contact with my brain and, offended, I armed my two assistants back away.

Assuming an expression of dignified aplomb on my torpid features, I raised my left boot toward the stirrup, missed it totally, and lost my footing, saved from falling only by my grip on the saddle horn.

"Hey, Jim, let me help you," said my first assistant, the words, you may be sure, not at all as clear as I have written them, something more like, "Heyjimle'mehel'ya."

I flung aside my right arm, barely hanging by my left. "Stand back!" I cried. "Stanba'!" I probably garbled.

Features set with stiffened resolution, I raised my left leg once again, located the stirrup, and stood on my right leg, swaying back and forth with the movement of my horse and of the ground itself.

I braced myself, clenching my teeth, and, inchingly, rose up to throw my right leg over the saddle. In doing so, I threw the weighted balance of my body too far to the horse's right and toppled to the ground with a hollow cry of disappointment. Fortunately, my left boot did not remain in the stirrup or my situation would have been inopportune.

My two assistants, mumbling words of consolation, pulled me to my feet again and helped me board the horse's saddle. There I wavered for a number of moments, on the verge of falling off again. I gripped the saddle horn with both hands. "D———n you, sir," I muttered, to whom I cannot say because I do not know.

"Yay, Jim!" my second assistant crowed. "You did it!"

They mounted their own two horses and we three started down the street.

"Jim can do anything," my first assistant claimed. "Jim is hell incarnate!" At the time I didn't have a clue what that connoted, but then I'm sure he didn't either.

"D———n right," I said, agreeing nonetheless.

"Those poor McCanles b———s," said my second assistant. "They won't know what hit them."

"Right," I mumbled.

"Jim'll get 'em, get 'em good." my first assistant added.

"Right," I mumbled.

"Jim'll blow their a———s off, that's what he'll do!"

"D———n right," I mumbled.

My friend cackled wildly. "I can't hardly wait!"

I attempted to maintain a look of unruffled determination but was close to spewing up my entire evening's consumption of both fluid and solid. Nausea swelled my stomach like the contents of a volcano about to erupt.

That is when I saw the sign—and my salvation—nailed to the wall of a building we were passing.

The Union Needs You! it huzzahed. Help to Fight the War Back East! Enlist and Leave Today!

The last two words struck fire in my soggy brain. Citizen Hickok, answering the crisis of his nation, decided to enlist.

Heroics: Pea Ridge
and Wilson's Creek

I joined the Eighth Missouri State Militia and was off to war.

Talk in Washington that first of July (1861) was of a ninety-day limit to hostilities. A somewhat imprecise estimation, shall I say?

I believed it, though, and went to join the fray, if not with overjoyed anticipation, at least with some degree of assurance that my tour of duty would be brief.

For a while, I was spared the ferocity of man-to-man combat by an assignment to be a sharpshooter. It was the first time I felt grateful to my P.A.B.S. for starting me on the path toward marksmanship. I confess I did not relish shooting down men from a distance but, at least, they *were* our enemies (or so we were told) and, at most, I didn't have to confront them face-to-face.

At the battle of Pea Ridge in Arkansas I even managed to acquire some reputation (as though I wanted it) without endangering myself when my commanding officer ordered me to find an advantageous spot overlooking Cross Timber Hollow, if I recall the name correctly, and pick off (lovely euphemism for *exterminate*) as many of the Rebels as I could.

I was there for several hours, virtually unseen, and what an irony it is that on that single afternoon, I killed more men than I ever did again. And from a distance, let me emphasize. Heroic? Doubtful. That was Pea Ridge.

I cringe to cite details of the afternoon near Wilson's Creek.

"Ever the loyal patriot, eager to serve his country in her hour of need, Young Hickok [getting older fast] joined the Union forces in the War Between the States during which his next audacious exploit took place: the ambuscade at Wilson's Creek!"

Our wagon train moved sluggishly along a dusty road, soldiers in the wagons, marching, or on horseback. Steep hills bordered both sides of the road.

I was driving one of the wagons (not too much advancement there) my uniform splattered with caked mud and layered with dust. We didn't know it, but a detachment of Rebel guerrillas was lying above us, crouching or standing behind boulders, bushes, logs, and trees.

We learned about it when an officer in charge of them leaped up and shouted, *"Fire!"*

Four cannons—two on each side—and a slew of rifles and pistols roared and crackled. Explosions started blasting all around us. Men cried out in shock as they were hit by balls and shrapnel.

I struggled to control my pitching, panicked team as with savage Rebel cries, the guerrillas started charging down the slopes, firing weapons, and converging on the wagon train. Union soldiers fired back and bodies toppled everywhere.

An explosion roared beside my wagon, the concussion throwing it aside. With a startled cry, I started over with its toppling, then leaped clear, landing at a dead run, the velocity of which I had to sustain in order not to fall.

This caused me to collide, head-on, with a hurtling Rebel, the violent impact knocking both of us backward, each emitting grunts of startlement. Dazedly, we gaped at one another. Then, hastily, I fumbled for my Colt.

The collison had caused it to slip below my waistband and I had to reach down clutchingly inside my trousers as the Rebel staggered to his feet and raised his rifle dizzily to fire at me. With teeth clenched, I jerked upward at my pistol, thumbed the hammer desperately, and blew a hole directly through the crotch of my trousers, yelping as the enclosed percussion burned my privates.

The Rebel crashed down, dying, as I lurched to my feet, whining with pain while I attempted, still in vain, to pull my pistol free despite its tangling in my long johns. Something hit and caused my hat to fly; making me hitch around so sharply that I lost my balance and went thudding down onto my left side.

The sound of galloping hooves nearby made me scramble around to gape at what I saw: a riderless horse bearing down on me at high speed.

I lunged up to avoid getting trampled and, leaping, managed to grab the horse around its neck. I was yanked precipitously from my feet and strained to pull myself aboard the horse's back, my boot heels alternately flying in the air and gouging at the earth.

My fourth attempt succeeded, carrying me across the horse's back and straight across its other side where I dangled anew, legs flapping uselessly, boots dragged or running along the ground.

I tried again and, finally, was successful, managing to throw my left leg over, not the horse's back, but its neck.

How long I would have stayed there is beyond my knowing. As it happened, the requirement was brief, as an explosion on the road ahead made the horse rear wildly, in so doing flinging me directly onto its back, unhappily straight down on the saddle horn, which stressed my privates even more.

With a heavy groan, I shifted backward quietly as the horse turned right and started charging up the slope. I hunched forward as a bullet skimmed through my hair, straightened up, then ducked abruptly once again as the horse charged underneath a low-hanging branch.

I glanced back in startled relief, then turned back, facing front again, and cried out in shock as the horse ran underneath another tree branch lower than the first.

I had no choice but to clutch at it and remain behind, legs dangling, as the horse raced on. A buzzing rifle ball ricocheted off the branch, making me gasp and twitch. Hastily, I pulled myself onto the branch, yelping as a fiery fragment of shrapnel creased the seat of my trousers. Further pistol balls whizzed by me as I looked up the slope.

A Rebel officer was riding down directly toward me, firing his revolver. I ducked and bobbed in desperation, trying to elude his aim. He jolted on the saddle suddenly as someone shot him; then he toppled off the horse.

I saw my opportunity and scrabbled around, not noticing that I'd caught my boot in a crook of the branch.

As the horse galloped by below, I made a dive for it, was caught, and wound up swinging upside down by one leg, hot lead flying all around me. It seemed as though my finish was inevitable until my pinned foot slipped free of its boot and I landed on my head below the tree.

Staggering up, I started hobbling up the slope, right foot shorter than the left by the height of one missing boot heel, causing me to lurch from side to side in clumsy rhythm. As I lumbered upward, I kept trying to remove the pistol from my trousers so as to use it without shooting off my groin. I kept tripping, sprawling, slipping, sliding, and flinching at the cannon's roar as I escaped the ambuscade below.

Reaching the top of the slope, I plunged into a clump of bushes and immediately began a headlong tumble toward the creek below.

I hit the water, rolling, swallowed more than some, broke surface, spluttering, then started thrashing toward the opposite bank, choking and gagging as I went, soaking wet and bruised from head to toe.

"Thus with an intrepid skill that bordered upon the uncanny did J. B. Hickok, two guns spitting fusillades of death, make good his escape from the Rebel entrapment!"

The Unsolicited Birth
of Wild Bill Hickok

Following my military triumph at the Wilson's Creek engagement, I found an unoccupied Confederate mule grazing in a field and commandeered it as a prize of war. Mounting same, my feet, one booted, one without, both close to dragging on the ground, uniform a filthy, rumpled miscellany of hanging threads, shreds, and tatters, I rode into the nearest town, the war on forced deferment for the moment, my need for a strong drink outweighing all martial interests.

I came upon a mob of grumbling men assembled in the street in front of the saloon. Dismounting, I began to shoulder through them, whiskey bound.

A man took firm hold of my arm and held me back. "I wouldn't go no farther, soldier," he informed me in a voice so deeply rumbling that it seemed to issue from his bowels.

I glared at him, in no mood to be hindered from the gratification of my thirst. "Why?" I demanded.

"Because a bad 'un's holed up in there," he said. "Had a shooting fracas with a couple of our local boys, killed one, near killed the other. We're just fixing now to lynch him."

I needed no additional information, my thirst restraining of its own accord. "Is there another saloon around here?" I inquired.

"Right down the street," he answered, pointing.

"That will do," I said with a nod. I turned away, moving past a couple in their sixties or seventies.

"You can't just lynch a man without a trial!" the old woman was protesting.

"You just watch us, Maude," the old man, who I assumed was her husband, replied.

"You're animals!" cried Maude. "Wild animals! Isn't there a man among you?"

Some of the men made angry noises at her as I pushed through their assembly and started down the street, eyeing the saloon some thirty yards away; a satisfactory distance from the unpleasantness, I estimated.

I started, gasping, as a man came staggering from the alley between the saloon and a dry goods store. Wounded in the shoulder, he could barely stand and flopped against me, causing me to grab him without thinking.

"For God's sake, mister!" he begged. "Get me to my horse!"

I didn't even have the time to think of a reply when someone in the mob caught sight of us and shouted, "There he is!"

I looked around in shock to see the mob surge in my direction, one of them brandishing a rope above his head.

I could only gape at them until the wounded man began to draw his pistol. Then I had to move.

"Wait a second," I muttered, wrestling him for possession of the revolver, at the same time trying to observe the approaching mob from the corners of my eyes. Let me say, they were an ominous vision as they stalked the wounded man and, for all I knew, me as well.

The man and I continued grappling for the pistol. "Wait, I said!" I told him frantically.

Suddenly, the man collapsed and, in abrupt possession of the pistol, my trigger finger jerked by accident and I fired.

The mob recoiled like a wounded beast as a man in its front rank was shot in the leg and flopped to the ground.

I stared at them and, in that moment, knew them for what they were: a company of craven cowards.

Smelling victory, I took the opportunity to vent my aggravation concerning every rotten thing that had occurred that day.

"All right, that's enough!" I yelled.

The mob—now a disorganized crowd—stared at me in silence.

With lordly mien, I instructed them to return to their homes.

No one stirred. I scowled at their slow-wittedness and fired over their heads, hearing a distant window shatter.

"I said return to your homes!" I shouted. *"Now!"*

The mob began dispersing hastily.

"And send your constable to hold this man for trial!" I added.

The old woman, Maude, raised her fisted right hand in a gesture of triumph.

"Good for you, Wild Bill!" she cried.

I was going to correct her, then decided that it wasn't worth the effort.

The story in the local newspaper the following week referred to me as Wild Bill Hiccock.

It was not the last time I would be misrepresented by the press.

Some Further History

In July 1862, President Lincoln called for three hundred thousand more volunteers. The ninety-day limit to hostilities had already been dead and buried nine months.

By the autumn of 1862, the national debt, enhanced by the war, reached the staggering amount of $500 million, an increase of $436 million in the past two years, a sum too vast to even imagine at that time.

As an interesting side note, in the summer of 1863, two French scientists discovered little rod-shaped bodies in the blood of animals infected with anthrax. They named them, logically enough, little rods, or bacteria. This could result in interesting health developments someday, I believe.

Back to the war: in October 1864, submersible boats were being utilized by the Confederates. The first of these, despite sinking five times in succession, was recovered each time and finally succeeded in exploding a torpedo underneath the Union ship *Housatonic,* which promptly sank. The submersible also sank again, this time permanently, drowning its entire crew.

At last, in April 1865, General Lee surrendered to General Grant at Appomattox Court House.

It turned out that the Union Army had lost three hundred

and eighty-five thousand men in the war, the Confederate Army ninety-four thousand men.

The cost of the war was—I still cannot fathom the amount—$8 billion!

It was, of course, stated that the Union had won the war but, in my opinion, no one won it and no one ever will win a war considering the cost and agony involved.

But enough of serious matters. Back to my life.

Until the end of the war, I served in various capacities: scout, wagon master, courier, sharpshooter, spy, and policeman. I was not, as claimed, a member of the Red Legs or the Buckskin Scouts.

After Appomattox, like most other veterans, I was without employment, which carries my chronicle to Springfield, Missouri, in July of 1865 and my next step up—or is it down?—toward nationwide acclaim.

Destiny and Springfield

At the risk of being repetitious, I must disclose that the incident began inside a hotel room with me in the company of an unclad young woman named Susannah Moore. I, too (need it be said?), was devoid of clothing.

The two of us were reclining on the bed while, with princely care, I trimmed my new mustache, scissors in right hand, mirror in left.

Susannah was pressed against me, playing with my hair, which I had now allowed to grow down almost to shoulder level.

"I just *love* your hair, Bill," she remarked. "It's so soft and shiny." It was that because, when I resided in a town or city, I washed it regularly.

You notice that she called me Bill. Mistake or not, I had gone along with the old lady's miscall and permitted the name to prevail.

Frowning at her careless touch, I put down the mirror and removed her hand from my hair. "Easy, girl," I told her, "you're snarling it."

Contrite, she began to stroke my hair more carefully as I returned to mustache snipping. "Sorry, Bill," she said. "I just lose all control when I'm around you."

"Try not to," I responded with a distracted tone. I really *was* that way. The memory makes me squirm.

I appraised the reflected trimming job and made a sound of satisfaction. "Not bad," I said.

Susannah flung an arm across my chest and pressed her cheek to my shoulder as I performed a few last snips of lip hair surgery. *"Watch it,"* I cautioned.

"Oh, Bill," she said, "why won't you marry me?"

I didn't even feel the need to answer that.

"I know you think I'm just not good enough for you because I'm not a lady," she went on, bearing out my lack of response. "But I could change, Bill. I could *make* myself a lady."

Did I really reply with such pretentious self-importance? I'm afraid I did.

"A lady is *born*, Susannah," I informed her. "The same as a gentleman is." My Lord in heaven above, how arrogant could a young man be? Susannah bristled, hurt. Who could blame her? "Well, I don't know what *you're* acting so high and mighty about!" she pouted. "You're just a no-count wagon driver!"

I gave her one of my self-engendered wintry looks, which caused instant repentance on her part.

"I'm sorry, Bill," she apologized. "I know you're only driving for a while. I know you're headed for bigger things. I'm sorry."

I nodded curtly. "Don't let it happen again," I said. Oh, if I could only step back through the corridor of time to give that fatuous idiot a hearty boot on the rump!

Susannah writhed against me, groaning. "Do me, Bill," she begged. "Don't make me wait no more." She reached down to hasten my readiness for same.

I was concentrating on the final stages of my mustache pruning. "Take it easy, girl," I said, "I'll get to it."

She rubbed against me more insistently. "Do me *now*,

Bill," she pleaded, the pitch of her voice rising at least an octave. "*Do* me." She worked at my utensil with increasing vigor. "Oh, *Bill*," she said.

"Oh, *h———l*," I responded.

Laying aside the scissors and mirror, I turned to face her on the bed and we began to kiss determinedly.

"Do me," Susannah muttered between osculations. "*Do* me, *do* me."

"All right, all right," I told her. "Just stop yanking at me, will you?" I yelped as she wrenched my appointment. "D———n it, girl!" I stormed.

"I love you, Bill!" she cried as we commenced. "I love you, love you! I could be a lady!"

"No chance," I gasped, at work now.

"You're the only man I'll ever love!" she moaned. "Ain't never going to see Dave Tutt no more!"

In the heat of the encounter, it took several moments for the words to register on my otherwise-occupied brain. But suddenly they did, and I grabbed her by the shoulders, jerking her devouring mouth from mine.

"What was that?" I demanded.

"What was what?" she inquired, breathless.

"You said Dave Tutt," I prompted her.

She tried to get at my lips again. "He don't matter none to me," she said. "You're the only one, Bill."

A cloud of gloom had drifted in above my head by then. "You're Dave Tutt's girl," I said.

She smiled at me adoringly. "Not anymore I'm not," she reassured me.

With that, she wriggled from my faltering grip and climbed all over me, kissing my face, my lips, my chest, my stomach, and prime points south.

"I'm *your* girl, Bill," she gasped between attentions, "*Wild Bill*. The strongest . . . toughest . . . *biggest* man in all the—!"

She broke off in dispirited perplexity. *"Bill,"* she said, "it's gone all *diddly.*"

The following selection is derived from an account of the Dave Tutt incident as described by a man who was self-named Captain Honest and notated by (who other?) Colonel Nichols, a double dose of bona fide accuracy.

The account, of course, had to do with Dave Tutt taking my pocket watch.

"This made Bill shooting mad, so he got up and looked Dave in the eyes and said to him: 'I don't want to make a row in this house. It's a decent house and I don't want ter injure the keeper. You'd better put that watch back on the table.'

"But Dave grinned at Bill and walked off with the watch. At which I saw that Bill was fixing ter get into a fight with Dave. 'It's not the first time I have been in a fight,' he said. 'You don't want me ter give up my honor, do yer?' He added that Dave Tutt wouldn't pack that watch across the square unless dead men could walk."

Well, first of all, if I'd ever spoken like that, I would have holed up in a cave with a book on English grammar until I learned how to speak correctly.

Second of all, it never happened that way.

Third of all, you know I'm going to tell you how it really took place.

Fourth of all, read on.

The incident occurred in a room in the old Southern Hotel on July 20, 1865.

I was playing poker with three gentlemen of my acquaintance, one of them the aforementioned Captain Honest. I remember wearing my one good article of clothing, a shabby Sunday-go-to-meeting coat. My watch, as was my custom, had been placed on the table so that I could keep track of the time as well as use it as an excuse to depart ("An early rising hour, I fear, gentlemen") in case I was losing too heavily.

I had already achieved some measure of social standing by virtue of the incident at Rock Creek and my reported heroics during the war, and one of the men, a Mr. Cosgrove as I recall, was using it to make conversation as we played.

"Mr. Hickok," he said.

"The same," I answered.

Chuckles from the trio.

"I have wondered," said Cosgrove, "in light of your increasing reputation as a man of cool nerve and action, whether you have ever given thought to the possibility of becoming an officer of the law—a constable perhaps, a U.S. marshal or a county sheriff."

"As a matter of fact, I have," I said offhandedly, although the thought had never crossed my mind for an instant.

"Splendid," said Cosgrove. "When may we anticipate your entry into this select endeavor?"

Now, I knew the English language passing well, but I confess to several moments of brain blankness before I got the gist of that inquiry.

"One of these days, for certain, Mr. Cosgrove," I declared then. "One of these days for certain," I repeated to emphasize my resolution on the matter.

"I sincerely hope so, Mr. Hickok," Cosgrove replied. "Since the war's conclusion, our frontier has become infected with scofflaw men of violence. We need your kind of stalwart to put them in their place."

"I observe that fact, sir," I began, completely in the mood of it by then. "And I assure you—"

I broke off speaking with a twitch of startlement as the door to the room was flung open so violently that it crashed against the wall. I jerked around so sharply that my chair was toppled.

Standing in the doorway was Dave Tutt, a man of frighteningly malignant countenance, an authentic nightmare of a man who contained his dread temper at the cost of straining breath and a voice that cracked at regular intervals.

"It was in the summer of 1867 [Nichols's flawless accuracy with facts again], in Springfield, Missouri, that Hickok's next man-to-man encounter took place: the justly celebrated gun duel between himself and gambler Dave Tutt. The cause: a card game difference of opinion."

As though nothing had occurred, I turned back to the table, set my chair back in place, and reseated myself.

"Shall we continue, gentlemen?" I said, hoping that my voice did not sound as hollow to them as it did to me.

The game resumed, albeit somewhat tentatively. I succeeded in maintaining visible composure (at least, I think I did) as Tutt clumped over measuredly and stood behind my chair, his voice as tight as the walls of my stomach as he muttered, "*Evenin'*, Mr. Hickok."

"Evening, Mr. Tutt," I replied.

I continued playing cards, teeth set on edge, the three men acting as though nothing out of the ordinary was taking place—not an award-caliber performance by any means.

They caught their breath as one man—fortunately obscuring my gasp—when Tutt raked out a spare chair from beneath the table and sat down heavily on it. I swallowed and began to add some money to the pot.

"Talking to Susannah Moore a while ago," Tutt said.

The money made a clinking noise as I dropped it prematurely on the table. "Who?" I asked, my voice not dissimilar to that of a jittery owl.

"Susannah Moore," he said, then added through clenched teeth, "My *woman*."

"Oh. Yes," I said, trying my utmost to keep my voice steady. "I believe I've met her."

"I *know* you've met her," Tutt responded.

I grunted, feigning full absorption in the game. Breathing hard, Tutt stared at me for several minutes before speaking again, at which time he said, "You owe me twenty-five dollars, *Mr. Hickok.*"

"What?" I asked. I heard but didn't know how to respond.

"You *do* recall our card game last week, don't you?" Tutt inquired.

"Oh. Yes," I said, reaching for my money.

"I believe the sum was twenty dollars, Mr. Hickok," said Cosgrove. I stared at him blankly. "I was in that game, if you recall," Cosgrove reminded me.

Idiot, I thought. But I was forced to agree. "Yes, I recall," I said. "It was twenty."

I picked up money from my pile and counted, "Ten . . . fifteen . . . twenty, Mr. Tutt. I believe that squares us." I held it out to him.

He made no move to accept it, so I laid it on the table in front of him. "There you are," I said.

"The sum was twenty-*five,* Mr. Hickok," he said.

I was painfully aware of the three men eyeing me with keyed-up expectation, and I sensed that I was trapped. I had conceded one point to the man. Another could be ruinous to my reputation. I lowered my head to conceal the movement of my bobbing gullet, then looked up at Tutt, praying to the skies that he noticed I was unarmed.

I guess he did, because he whined with repressed frustration as I continued playing cards. I suppose there is the possibility that my notoriety—as modest as it was—had some effect on him.

At least until, some moments later, he reached out suddenly and took my watch off the table, stood, and slipped the watch into his vest pocket. Then he spoke, again through clenched teeth (not too easy, try it sometime).

"This cheap, five dollar watch will make up the difference," he announced.

I didn't want to shudder, but I did. I hoped nobody noticed it or, if they did, mistook it for a shudder of rage.

"I'll be walking in the square tomorrow morning with this watch inside my pocket," Tutt informed me.

He glared at me in outright challenge, which I chose not to accept. Then he turned and left the room, slamming the door so hard that a picture fell from the wall, its glass front shattering, making all of us wince.

The three men stared at me. I cleared my throat, tried to speak, could not, cleared my throat again and managed, then, to speak. "Shall we continue, gentlemen?" I asked.

The game went on, but I could feel dissatisfaction hovering in the air. I know a statement was expected, so I made it.

"He will not be walking on the square with my watch in his pocket," I said, then added, with portentous melodrama, "unless dead men can walk."

A collective sigh escaped the lips of the three men; they were fulfilled.

As I continued playing cards, I felt my stomach moving and my cheeks puffed out in the repression of a belch.

I did not sleep that night.

How did I get into this insanity? I asked myself. *Because you haven't got the brains to keep your God d———ed trousers on!* I answered, furious with myself. First Sarah Shull, now Susannah Moore. Why was I so God d———ed handsome? (Yes, I really *thought* that, poor beleaguered fool that I was.) I actually felt sorry for myself for my appearance. Shake your head if you like. I am shaking mine as I write this.

What made me say what I did? *Unless dead men can walk*. It didn't even make sense; of course dead men couldn't walk! Stupid; idiotic. Pride goeth before a fall; no doubt of that. I had no inclination whatsoever to face Dave Tutt. He was a deadly shot and, unlike me, was accustomed to having men shoot back at him, one to one. He wasn't a falling apple, a fence post, or a bottle on a stump. The man intended to kill me, for God's sake!

For hours, I lay on my hotel bed, propped up by pillows and a bottle of rye whiskey. I felt ill and apprehensive. *Deadly killer of men?* The phrase would have been uproarious if it hadn't been unnerving.

Much of the time, I stared at the small framed photograph of my mother, which stood on the bedside table. In my mind, I heard her speak again those certain words, particularly unsettling at that moment.

"You must always be a gentleman, James. It is expected of you."

"Yes, Mother," I murmured, which finally brought about the notion.

At six o'clock the following morning, I packed my carpetbag and left my room. There was no one at the lobby desk. I'd send them the amount I owed them later on; I wasn't going to wake them up.

It pleased me to observe that the street was deeply misted and, as far as I could hear, unpopulated. I walked along the plank walk with unhurried strides, telling myself that I was not, in any manner, pressed for time.

Soon I stepped down from the walk and started across the square toward the livery stable, where the one sound in the world I didn't want to hear, I heard: Dave Tutt's voice.

"Morning, Mr. Hickok," he said. How could he have possibly known that I was getting up so early?

I opened my mouth, ostensibly to answer him, but nothing audible emerged.

"Up mighty early, aren't you?" he said. *D———n his bones, he'd been waiting for me!*

I stared at his form, barely visible in the mist.

"Going somewhere?" he asked. I knew that he was ready to explode by the cracking of his voice. I tried to estimate how far from me he was. I guessed it was fifty feet or so.

Clearing my throat as softly as I could, I told him, "Yes, as a matter of fact, I am."

"And where might that be, Mr. Hickok?" he inquired, his voice still breaking—not with fear, I was certain, but with blinding rage.

I answered gravely. "To visit my mother, if it's any of your business, Mr. Tutt."

He whined with held-in fury, voice continuing to crack as he responded. "My business, Mr. Hickok, is to meet you in the square this morning."

"I am aware of that," I replied, amazed by the unperturbed sound of my voice. "However, my mother's health takes precedence—"

"And what about *your* health, Mr. Hickok?" he interrupted.

I knew in that instant that I could not avoid this confrontation. Hastily, I tried to summon up (in his mind anyway) the exaggerated image that the newspapers and journals had created.

"Worry about your own, Mr. Tutt," I warned him.

Was it conceivable that he would back down from the act of facing Wild Bill Hickok? Lose courage and avoid the moment? For several, glorious moments, I actually thought that he might.

Then I saw that, indeed, he *had* reacted nervously to my image and was, now, incensed at himself for doing so. Intent on recapturing the frenzy of his rage toward me, he grabbed for his pistol.

His first shot knocked the carpetbag clear out of my

hand. Catching my breath, I clutched for my pistol, which was thrust beneath the waistband of my trousers.

Tutt's second shot knocked off my hat and sent it sailing. Stumbling backward in startlement, I opened fire blindly.

We blasted away at each other across the square. The dark, swirling powder smoke added to the mist and made visibility close to zero. I shot at him till my gun was empty and, in the sudden, heavy silence, squinted hard to see through the smoky mist.

When it had cleared enough, it revealed the sight of Dave Tutt, unharmed, grimacing fiercely as he reloaded his pistol.

"Sweet Jesus," I murmured.

I looked around abruptly for my carpetbag. Catching sight of it, I lunged to where it was and dropped to my knees beside it. Tearing it open, glancing constantly toward Tutt, I fumbled in the bag for my box of pistol balls.

I could not locate them right away and started yanking out shirts and socks and long johns, tossing them in all directions, muttering. *"Good God,"* through gritted teeth.

I gasped as Tutt began to fire again and flung myself onto my chest as lead balls whined and spattered around me. All shots missed, and I looked up again.

Tutt was, once more, invisible behind the black smoke and white mist.

Scrambling to my knees, I started searching in my carpetbag again, still unable to locate the box of pistol balls, and, with a scowl of demented fear, I upended the carpetbag and spilled its contents onto the ground. "Come *on*," I mumbled. "Come *on*."

Seeing the box, I opened it so hastily that balls spilled all across the ground. Shaking, dropping half of them in haste, I started to reload, glancing up and hissing with alarm.

Dave Tutt was advancing through the smoke and mist, pistol extended. As stunned as I was, I could not help noticing that, indeed, he did seem afraid of me, his graven features set in an expression of frightened determination.

That didn't help my nerves from threatening to shred as I continued struggling to reload.

Tutt opened fire again, and I grunted as a burning sensation tore a furrow through my right side. Pitching onto my chest again, I finished loading and began to fire back, holding my revolver with both hands, elbows braced on the ground. By the time I'd fired six times, Tutt was hidden in the smoky mist again.

Struggling to my knees once more, wincing at the pain in my side, I started to reload.

By then there were sounds around me: doors opening and closing, boots running, people shouting, "Hey, what's going on?" and "God above, what's happening?" and a woman's shrill voice, "Don't you dare go out there, Beauregard!"

As I reloaded, I kept glancing anxiously into the clearing mist and smoke.

Then, I stopped reloading and, pushing up shakily, moved across the square and stopped by Dave Tutt's sprawled and motionless body.

His eyes were open, his berserk grimace of fear and hatred still frozen hard on his features.

I stared at him; then, after several moments, reached down and tugged at the fob hanging from his vest pocket, pulling out the watch.

A ball had mangled it.

"Aw, s———t," I muttered.

I began to gather my belongings and stuff them into the carpetbag. Then I started back toward the hotel, limping as I walked. I could feel blood trickling on my right side and down my leg.

I do not recall the trip across the square and down the street to the hotel. I recall only moving through the lobby and starting up the stairs with slow, stiff movements, aware of the awed, admiring gazes of several guests.

As I moved woodenly along the upper corridor, a sock fell from my carpetbag and fluttered to the floor. A man, peering out from his room, stepped forward, picked it up, and held it out to me, mouth opening as though he meant to speak of it. My stonelike expression kept him still. I continued down the hallway like a trudging statue. A pair of long johns now dropped to the floor, but I did not essay to pick them up. Reaching my room, I unlocked the door (thank God I'd forgotten to leave the key on the lobby desk) and went inside. Closing the door, I relocked it, dropping the carpetbag as I did. Then, straightening up, I felt my eyeballs rolling back and toppled over in a dead faint.

Thus the "justly celebrated gun duel" between Dave Tutt and myself.

Enter the Lord of Liars

They indicted me for murder and I had to face a trial. The indictment was against one William Haycock for the death of David Tutt. I attempted to correct the spelling of my name and it was promptly amended to James Hickcock (one of many spellings of my name I have been saddled with). I gave up trying to achieve the proper spelling and the trial took place. The jury found me innocent, although public sentiment did not appreciate the judgment entirely, believing that it might not have been a case of self-defense but one of deliberately fomented murder or, at the very least, manslaughter.

In great discomfort from my wound, I purchased opium from a local druggist. In tandem with a jug of frontier corn whiskey, I remained in a state of semiconscious numbness.

I remained in that condition throughout the remainder of August and nearly half of September, at which time it was my lot (I will not say my good fortune) to meet that prince among prevaricators, that lord of liars, that emperor of exaggeration, Colonel George Ward Nichols.

I was lying on my bed reading the *Missouri Weekly Patriot* when there was a sudden pounding at the door. The

newspaper flew from my hands and I lunged for the bedside table, knocking it over. Diving off the bed, hissing at
the pain in my side, I snatched up my revolver and rolled
into a rigid crouch, teeth clenched, eyes slitted, expecting
members of the Tutt clan to come bursting in, guns firing.

When there was nothing, I asked (the epitome of manly
calm), "Yes?"

"Have I the honor of addressing Mr. James B. Hickok?"
asked a man's voice.

I rose, picking up the bedside table. "Who are you?" I
asked.

"Colonel George Ward Nichols, sir!" the man responded.

"Who?" I asked, suspiciously.

"Colonel George Ward Nichols, Mr. Hickok!" he replied.
"Assigned by *Harper's Magazine* to interview you!"

"Interview me?" I mumbled in confusion.

"May I come in, sir?" inquired the voice.

"Are you alone?" I asked.

"Alone, yes!" cried the voice, so loudly that it made me
twitch. "Empty-handed, no! For I carry with me, sir, an
all-consuming admiration for your bravery and courage!"

"Huh?" I muttered.

"The world awaits your story, Mr. Hickok!" cried the
voice. "May I enter to seek it out?"

I hesitated before moving to the door. There, to be on
the safe side—I was still gun-shy from my battle with
Tutt—I unlocked it, then stood with my back to the wall,
pistol at the ready.

"Come in," I said.

Colonel George Ward Nichols burst in eagerly, a heavyset, florid-faced, overdressed man in his fifties. On his seeing no one, his mouth fell open in astonishment. Then he
whirled. "Ah-ha!" he cried delightedly. I flinched a little
at the volume of his voice. "Always on the qui vive, sir!
Argus-eyed! Prepared for bloody confrontation at a mo-

ment's notice! *Wild Bill!* Alert and vigilant! *Semper paratus!* My *dear* Mr. Hickok!"

I must have gaped at him. Right from the start, he seemed unhinged to me.

He snatched his card from a vest pocket and proffered it grandly.

"Colonel George Ward Nichols, sir!" he proclaimed himself. "Former aide-de-camp to General Sherman on his heroic March to the Sea! [I swear I heard capital letters in his voice.] Your obedient servant, sir! As one gentleman to another—"

He caught me in that moment; that was my Achilles' heel, all right.

"—may I express to you my heartfelt approbation and respect! You are a giant, sir! A *giant!*"

What is it that narrators always comment in those Gothic novels?

Had I but known . . .

How apropos to the occasion. Had I but known the perilous byways Nichols's articles would route me through, I would have flung him through the doorway of my room—perhaps even the window. He is the author of the role I have been cast in, the legend I have been imprisoned by. D——n his bloodshot, twinkly eyes for doing that!

Still, he was just a reaper, not a sower. I can see that now, although I certainly didn't at that time. I thought myself a victim then. That I had given full cooperation to the deed was not a part of my awareness. My conceit and deluded arrogance would not allow me to admit the truth. So who am I to blame this blustering equivocator, this frontier Munchausen? I gave him the raw materials; he only manufactured them to sell his articles. Did it ever occur to him for an instant that his grandiose depiction of me was not only blown completely out of proportion but that, in fact, it would, in addition to aggrandizing me, put my life at considerable and mounting risk? I'm sure he didn't. How could he? *I* didn't even consider it.

For instance, how could I allow myself to swallow, much less digest, the following?

"This verbatim dialogue took place between us. 'I say, Bill, or Mr. Hickok, how many white men have you killed to your certain knowledge?' After a little deliberation, he replied, 'I would be willing to take my oath on the Bible that I have killed over a hundred.' 'What made you kill all those men? Did you kill them without cause or provocation?' 'No, by heaven! I never killed one man without good cause!' "

And the following, me as "quoted" by Nichols:

"Just then McKandlas [McCanles] poked his head inside the doorway, but jumped back when he saw me with a rifle in my hand.

" 'Come in here, you cowardly dog!' I shouted. 'Come in here and fight me!'

"McKandlas was no coward, even if he was a bully. He jumped inside the room with his gun leveled to shoot; but he was not quick enough. My rifle ball went through his heart. He fell back outside the house, where he was found afterward holding tight to his rifle, which had fallen over his head.

"His disappearance was followed by a yell from his gang and then there was a dead silence. I put down the rifle and took the revolver and said to myself, *Only six* shots and nine men to kill. Save your powder, Bill, for *the death-hug's a-comin'*."

And this:

" 'I hardly know where to begin. Pretty near all these stories are true; I was at it all during the war.' "

And, of course, the following, straight from the mouth of Captain Honest to Colonel Nichols's ear and pen:

"The instant Bill fired, without waiting ter see if he had

hit Tutt, he wheeled on his heels and pointed his pistol at
Tutt's friends, who had already drawn their weapons.

" 'Aren't you satisfied, gentlemen?' cried Bill, as cool as
an alligator. 'Put up your shootin' irons or there'll be more
dead men here.' And they put 'em up and said it was a fair
fight."

When Nichols first began to question me, I made no
attempt to conceal my knowledge of the English language.
As I spoke, however, it became apparent that he expected,
even probably yearned for, a more rough-hewn manner of
speech, so I began to drop the bandbox image and feed
him more the lingo he was looking for; thus my use of the
vernacular in describing the Rock Creek incident (the fan-
ciful building of the facts was Nichols's).

Does it go without saying that I have mulled interminably over my decision to wear the blinds where it came to
factuality about the more sensational events of my life? I
do not know whether it does, so I will state clearly that yes,
I have gone over it as many times as you could possibly
imagine.

Not that I was capable of facing pure and simple truth
when Nichols, Henry M. Stanley (of Africa fame in finding Dr. Livingston), and the others wrote and published
their inflated accounts of my stout-hearted feats of valor.
No—*Tell the truth now; Hickok*—I could not resist the
journalistic blandishments enough to say them nay. Consider: I was twenty-eight years old. I should have known
better, there is no denying, but I simply didn't. I *enjoyed*
it, basking in the sunlight of the public's reverence for
my accomplishments. I was just a farm boy after all, no
city-bred sophisticate. How could I resist? I ask you.
How?

Anyway, I didn't. Oh, I knew that they were stretching
the blanket out of shape but, when I considered it, I told
myself that those distorted articles were nothing but a lark,

something to chuckle over in private but not be overly concerned about.

My mistake.

In time, while never noticing the day-by-day construction, I built a wall in my mind that separated facts from fancies, truth from lies.

Guess which side of the wall I chose to live on?

Into the Law
and Out of It

Very few know of this, but I was briefly—oh, so briefly—a constable in Morgan City, Kansas, in July and August 1866. I was not, as some have stated, a marshal. I was an underpaid and overwrought constable. Because of my "triumphs" at Rock Creek and during the war and in Springfield, I allowed myself to be coerced (my own failure to differentiate fact from fable) into taking the job where, for several months, I was an agitated misfit of a man, snapping pettishly at everyone, despite the fact that it was a relatively well-behaved community, and in short order, getting the blazes out and returning to safer employment.

Fort Riley

Despite my mounting glory as a man of action, I continued to be a wagon driver to support myself.

Picture me, inside a wagon in a wagon camp, sprawled against the tailgate, wearing filthy work clothes, a week's growth of beard on my cheeks, a layer of grime on my skin, hair a greasy mat across my shoulders, as I read by candlelight the premiere article by Colonel Nichols in *Harper's Magazine*. I could not, of course, have seen my face, but I would wager its expression was akin to that of my twelve-year-old self, open-mouthed and vacantly enthralled, as I pored over the torn-out catalog page on which were illustrated women's corsets.

"His is a quiet, manly face," the article read, "so gentle in its expression as to utterly belie the history of its owner. Yet it is not a face to be trifled with—[I narrowed my eyes] the lips thin and sensitive [I pursed my lips], the jaw not too square [I shifted my jaw], the cheekbones slightly prominent [I attempted in vain to move my cheekbones], a mass of fine, dark hair [I frowned at that. "Dark?" I muttered] falling to well below his shoulders ["Below my shoulders?" I said], the eyes as gentle as a woman's. [*"What?"* I snapped.] In truth, the woman nature seems prominent throughout."

"God————n!" I slapped down the magazine and glared at it. But I could not ignore it very long and picked it up again.

"You would not believe that you were looking into eyes that have pointed the way to death ["All right," I grumbled] to hundreds of men."

My mouth fell open; it was the first I'd heard of that.

"Yes, Wild Bill, with his own hands, has killed hundreds of men; of that I have no doubt. As they say on the border, 'He shoots to kill.' "

I stared at the article with undecided detachment. At least I had the moral decency to feel dubious about it in the beginning.

Footsteps sounded outside, and I quietly hid the magazine behind a wooden crate.

It was the wagon train leader. "Bill?" he said.

I cleared my throat (thickened by emotion because of what I'd read? Who knows?). "Yes?" I answered.

"You signing on for the drive back to Fort Riley?" he asked.

"What's the pay?" I countered.

"Still fifty a month. You in?"

I replied without enthusiasm. "I suppose."

"I'll put you on the list then," he responded.

After he'd walked away, I thought, *He obviously hasn't seen the article*. Was fifty a month for wagon driving the best I could do?

A man of my stature?

Fort Riley was aswirl with dust and din as I steered my wagon into the quadrangle. Braking it to a halt, I stepped down, slapping dust from my clothes as I crossed to the nearest water barrel. I detested being dirty!

Removing the barrel top, I lifted up a dipperful of water and flung it into my face. Blowing out spray, I removed my hat and dumped another scoop of water over my head, then another. I poured some water into my mouth, worked it around, and spat it to the ground. Then I stood immobile, hair plastered down, face dripping wet, feeling thoroughly disgruntled. "Son of a b————h," I remember muttering. "I have got to find a better way." *You deserve more than this,* I told myself, slapping a cloud of dust from my shirt.

Did the cosmos answer me? You be the judge.

I turned as the wagon leader ambled up to me, speaking my name. Well, not my real name of course, the one that old lady had christened me with.

"What?" I asked.

"Captain Owens asked to see you."

"Who?" I asked.

"Captain Owens, Post Quartermaster."

"Why?" I asked.

"No idea. He just wants to see you."

"Where?" I asked.

"His office." The wagon leader pointed. "Over there."

"When?" I asked, covering the journalist's Five W's in record time.

"Now," the wagon leader said with not a little aggravation.

I walked over to the building pointed out to me and knocked on the door.

"Come in," said a voice. It might have been that of a prepubescent boy.

I went inside to face a pudgy, pink-faced balding man in his early forties. He looked like a prepubescent boy as well, playing soldier in somebody else's cut-down uniform.

I walked up to his desk, exuding dust, and stopped in front of him. "You asked to see me." I told him not too genially, I fear. I was truly disgusted with my lot.

Captain Owens pointed at me, clearly thrilled. "You awe *Wiwd Biw Hickok*?" he inquired.

I blinked. The man lisped terribly in a voice pitched as high as that of a choirboy. This was not to be an easy interview, I saw.

"Yes?" I said.

He sprang to his feet, pink, pudgy hand extended. "My honow, siw! We have heawd much good about you! *Much* good!"

He pumped my hand relentlessly. I was speechless, which was just as well, as he plunged on, his tone abruptly grim. That I kept a straight face is a tribute to my acting skill.

"May I discuss with you a cewtain vexing pwobwem which contwonts us hewe in Fowt Wiwey?" he inquired.

"Uh . . . *sure*," I managed. *God, don't laugh,* I thought; *he is a captain.*

He replied with reverent appreciation. Obviously he'd read the article in *Harper's*.

"*Thank* you, Mr. Hickok" (I cannot convey what he did with the word *Mister*). "Thank you vewy much." His expression altered to one of deep gravity. "As you may ow may not be awawe, Fowt Wiwey is the home station fow the undewpaid, undewfed, dissatisfied, and bwawwing subdivision of the United States Awmy. Mowawe is at wock bottom." (That almost got me, I confess.) "We awe suwwounded by undesiwabwe wecwuits who have enwisted onwy fow the puwpose of being twanspowted west at ouw expense, Mr. Hickok, at *ouw expense*!"

I hung on his every word now, hoping that by concentrating intensely on the meaning of his words, I would not be toppled by the sound of them.

"Many of these wecwuits" (that word again; it pummeled at my will to keep from collapsing into laughter) "desewt soon aftew awwiving at the fowt," he continued, unaware of my intense struggle to remain of serious mien. "Consequentwy, thew is uttew *chaos,* don't you see. Open hostiwity between scouts and twoopers." (Twoopers! God in heaven!) "On the scouts' side awe the teamstews and the wabowews" (that one I almost didn't get at all until I realized that what he was trying to say was *laborers*), "on the othew side are what the teamstews cwudewy wefew to as *bwue bewwies.*"

"I beg your pardon?" I said; I missed that entirely.

"Bwue bewwies, bwue bewwies," he repeated testily. *Why should the teamsters refer crudely to blueberries?* I wondered, then realized, as he went on, that he meant to say *blue bellies.*

"Thewe awe not, you see, enough twoops to fowm a weguwar peace patwol."

Oh, Jesus, wind it up before I crack, I thought, face straining to remain composed.

"That is why we need you, Mr. Hickok."

Fortunately, curiosity replaced my resisted urge to guffaw in the man's pink, pudgy face. "Me?" I said.

Again, he pointed at me as though identifying me to a crowd that wasn't there.

"*You,* siw, and no othew. Thewe is a big job to be done hewe at Fowt Wiwey. It calls fow a big man. You awe that man, Mr. Hickok. Bwave. Intwepid. A dauntwess, pistow mastew." Despite my curiosity, I almost snapped at that.

"Wiw you," challenged Captain Owens, "accept the position of United States marshaw, siw?"

I was stunned. "United States—" I began, then couldn't finish.

"Youw sawawy" (salary, I gathered) "wouwd be one hundwed dowwaus a month."

"A *hundred,*" I murmured, forgetting how he spoke in the shock of the moment.

"Can we count on you, Mr. Hickok?" Owens pleaded. "Wiw you wend us youw gweatness in this houw of need?"

He gazed at me dramatically. *Just don't say anything to destroy this moment,* I thought.

"No one else can fiw the biw, sir. Onwy you awe big enough to meet this chawwenge; onwy you awe wedoubt-abwe enough to cast this gauntwet with wespwendent twiumph!"

I had to settle for a fit of coughing, which I told him was caused by dust in my lungs.

Duding Up for Doom

Obviously, I did not consider the matter too deeply, thinking only that I'd double my income and be able to bathe regularly; not exactly an exhaustive appraisal of the job of U.S. marshal. I was in the way of being desperate, though. I hated wagon driving, hated being dirty, felt underpaid and, more to the point I'm afraid, underappreciated for my burgeoning prestige. I was already pushing aside any memories of Morgan City.

So I accepted Owens's offer, although I vowed to converse with him as little as possible. After bathing to a fare-thee-well (the ablutions extending to more than an hour) and burning all my clothes except for those I had to wear to the post store, I went there to prepare for my new position of importance with an outfit of appropriate distinction.

First of all, I purchased new undergarments, new buckskin trousers, boots, and a fine white shirt with a ruffled front.

Then I got down to serious dressing.

The clerk began it all by carrying an ornate buckskin jacket to where I was standing in front of a full-length mirror, putting the trouser legs over the boots for appearance's sake.

"Try this one on, marshal," said the clerk. Smart man, he, to address me as such even though I didn't have my badge yet.

"Right," I said.

I put the jacket on and started to button it but stopped, not caring for the effect. I removed the jacket and handed it back to the clerk. "Have you nothing larger?" I asked.

"Yes, we do," the clerk said, beaming.

"Fetch it then," I told him.

"Yes, *sir*," he said, moving off from me on dancing legs.

While he was gone, I eyed myself in the mirror, leaning in to fiddle with my mustache; I was not quite satisfied with it even then. I nodded, approving of my general handsomeness. I squirm to say it, but a picture of that younger me is necessary to explain the pitfalls I so persistently allowed myself to fall into.

The clerk returned on the run, carrying a longer, far more elaborately decorated buckskin jacket, so pale it was almost white.

"I think you'll like this better, Mr. Hickok," he said.

He was right. I liked it on sight. I slipped it on and regarded my reflection, an expression of carefully calculating assessment printed on my face.

"It's a beauty," said the clerk.

It was. Nonetheless, I sustained the questioning look. "I don't know," I said. "I just don't know."

At which point, I did *not* know. This was a significant moment in my life; I sensed that strongly. I did not want to make a mistake. I liked the jacket and knew that I'd be happy with it. Still . . .

"Have you nothing . . . larger?" I inquired.

"Well . . . *yes,* sir," said the clerk as I removed the jacket. "There *is one* but . . ." He hesitated.

"What?" I asked.

"Well . . ." he said. He took back the jacket I'd removed. ". . . it's . . . awful expensive, marshal."

Did he know that he would twang a nerve in my self-regard when he said that? Probably; he was a *sales* clerk after all, not a philosopher.

Whatever the case, the nerve was twanged, and I responded grandly, "Fetch it, my good fellow!"

"Yes—sir, Mr. Hickok!" he responded, fairly leaping off to do so.

I turned to examine myself in profile, drew in my stomach tightly, crossed my arms, and raised my chin, a positively noble expression on my face. What an ass I was! But then, I must look back with greater charity on that deluded young fool. He knew no better.

The clerk came running back, a little breathless now. In his arms was the most ludicrous jacket ever styled by man. It had a fur collar, double fur ringlets at the wrists, a double fur trim with heavy buckskin fringing at its bottom, and buckskin fringe on each arm.

It was perfect.

Slipping it on, I gazed at myself in the mirror, trying hard to look uncertain and wary again but hard put not to reveal that it was love at first sight. I plucked at the jacket, stirring it around my knees; that's how long it hung. "Hmm," I said. Then, finally, unable to restrain my feelings anymore, "This is more like it."

"It looks *wonderful,* Mr. Hickok," said the clerk, all choked up, no doubt from calculating the total sale receipts.

"Yes," I agreed, regarding my reflection with intense satisfaction. Then I nodded. "Now a sash," I said.

The sales clerk's face went suddenly devoid of all expression. "A—?" he started.

"Scarlet," I instructed.

"You—?" he started.

"Want a sash," I said. "A *scarlet* one."

"I see," he replied.

My gaze shifted to his reflection in the mirror. "You *have* one, don't you?" I asked, a trifle testily. Who was he to question my fashion acuity?

"Oh . . . *yes,* sir, Mr. Hickok!" he replied, scuttling backward like a threatened crab.

As he turned away, I buttoned up the coat, trying to repress a smile but too pleased to manage it.

I forced the smile away as the clerk dashed back with a broad, scarlet sash in his hands. "It's a little wide, Mr. Hickok," he apologized.

That didn't bother me. "Is it your *best?*" I demanded; that was more important.

"Oh, *yes,* sir, Mr. Hickok," vowed the clerk. "Absolutely. Made in Boston."

I grunted and began to tie the sash around my waist.

The clerk and I appraised my reflection.

"What do you think?" I asked. I'd already made up my mind but wanted verification.

"It looks," he said, straining for the proper word. "—*lovely.*"

"What?" I growled.

"I mean—tremendous, marshal! *Tremendous!*" cried the clerk.

I looked at his nerve-wracked reflection for several moments, then, clearing my throat, reached out and took my Navy Colt from a nearby table and slipped it under the sash.

It looked drab against the sash and jacket.

I said so.

"Mr. Hickok?" inquired the clerk.

"*Drab,* I said."

"Oh," he responded. "Yes." He had no idea of what I was saying.

"I saw some over there with ivory handles," I said.

"*Yes,* sir!" he cried in total delight, bouncing off.

"The .36 caliber Colt Navy, mind!" I called after him. It was, of course, my favorite weapon. The 1851 model with the seven and a half inch barrel; very accurate and hard-hitting, always the most popular of Colt's percussion revolvers.

In the clerk's absence, I returned to mirror-gazing, tossing back my hair, which I'd decided to grow longer yet in keeping with my new image.

The panting clerk rushed back to me, carrying one of the revolvers. Taking it from him, I slipped it underneath the sash on my right side, butt to the rear as was my custom.

I stared at my reflection, pleased. The ivory handle looked very smart indeed.

"I thought—" the clerk began.

"Yes?" I asked.

"Well," he said, "I thought you carried *two* revolvers, sir."

"What?" I looked at him, confused.

"That's what Colonel Nichols wrote in his article," the clerk explained. " 'Mr. Hickok always wears a brace of pistols at his waist.' " *My God,* I thought, *the man can quote from the blasted article!*

I cleared my throat again. "Well . . . yes, usually I do," I lied. "Sometimes one needs a deuce of weapons in a pinch." I gestured regally. "So bring me another," I told him.

"*Yes, sir!*" he exploded, disappearing in a flash of movement, returning quickly with the second ivory-handled Colt. I took it from his hand and thrust it underneath the sash on my left side.

"Do you think that, perhaps—" the clerk began to say.

He broke off, both of us wincing as the sash was pulled

loose by the weight of the two pistols. I tried to grab at them but missed, and both clattered to the floor. The sash I managed to catch.

The clerk and I regarded each other. I attempted to cover my embarrassment with a look of aggravation. "*That* is why I only use one pistol with a sash," I said.

"Yes, sir," said the clerk, picking up the pistols and handing them back to me. "I—I wonder," he faltered, "if a—a—a *belt* might be more . . . you know, Mr. Hickok, more . . . *practical*?"

"For *two* guns, *yes,* of *course,*" I scoffed. "Very well—" I gestured with impatience. "A *belt* then."

"*Yes,* sir," said the clerk and ran off.

I hefted the two revolvers. Awfully heavy, I thought. I tried to twirl them both and about dropped them, glancing quickly toward the clerk to make certain he hadn't seen.

He was occupied in searching for a belt.

I turned back to the mirror and posed abruptly, both revolvers pointed at the mirror, my eyes narrowed, an ominous expression on my face.

"As they say on the border, 'He shoots to kill,'" I mumbled. *Oh, Hickok, Hickok.*

I lowered the pistols as the clerk returned on the run, carrying a belt, gasping for breath as he handed it to me, "Here you are, marshal," he wheezed.

I looked for a place to set down the pistols while I put on the belt. Finally, I handed them to the clerk and fastened the belt around my waist; it was a little snug. I had to suck in my gut to fasten the buckle. "The revolv—" I stopped; my voice was wheezy now. I drew in a deep breath. "The revolvers, if you please," I requested.

The clerk handed them to me and I managed with some effort to force them under the belt on each side. Unfortunately, my arms would not hang normally now. I frowned, not knowing what to do, then sighed and reversed the pistol butts.

"Prefer the cavalry draw," I told the clerk.

"Yes, sir. That's what Colonel Nichols wrote," he said.

"Oh, yes," I responded.

"You'll also need a knife though, won't you?" he inquired.

I stared at him.

"Colonel Nichols said that in the battle of Rock Creek Station you used a knife against those ten men."

"Oh. *Yes*." I nodded. "A *knife*."

"I'll get it right away, sir," said the clerk, running off, shoes thumping on the floor.

I made a face, uncomfortable because the belt was so tight. I tried to loosen it but couldn't without removing it entirely. I belched as softly as I could, then forced back a look of majestic composure as the clerk rushed over, carrying a knife so huge it would have made Jim Bowie pale. "I brought the biggest one we have!" he said unnecessarily.

"Good," I said. I nodded. *"Good."* Idiots, both of us.

I took the knife away from him and slid it gingerly beneath the belt, hissing as it slid across my stomach. I shifted it to the left.

"Oh, *Marshal Hickok*," said the clerk in awe.

"You don't think it's . . . a bit much?" I tested; I already knew it was.

"Oh, *no,* sir, marshal, *no,* sir! You look *wonderful*!"

I nodded again. *I don't look bad,* I thought.

"You should get a photograph taken!" enthused the clerk.

Good idea, I told myself. "Well," I responded gravely. "Perhaps, for my mother."

"Yes, sir!" cried the clerk.

Some of you may have seen that photograph. It has been reprinted many times.

If you do happen to see it, remember how it came about.

And remember the young man who had no conception of the billy hell he was about to raise.

If My Brains Were Dynamite

The saying goes: If his brains were dynamite, there wouldn't be enough to blow his nose. Another states: He was so ignorant that he couldn't drive nails in the snow. Either applied to me in those days.

Within a day of my assumption of office and formal pinning on of my badge by Captain Owens ("It is my gweat pweasuwe, Mawshew Hickok, to pwace this on youw manwy bweast"), my first emergency broke out: a full-scale brawl between the teamsters and the soldiers.

I watched it from around the corner of a building, dressed in all my finery, my stomach gurgling.

Across the quadrangle, I saw Owens waddling from his office, looking agitated; heard him dispatching soldiers in all directions to "find Mawshew Hickok!"

I looked back at the brawl, my nausea increasing. I then looked back at Owens and felt my body stiffening as though with instant rigor mortis.

He'd caught sight of me by the building and was staring, half expectant, half dismayed.

I had no choice. More loathe to face a sudden loss of image than to face this challenge to my office, I lurched forward as though I was just arriving to notice the brawl, forcing a look of stern disapproval to my face as I strode toward the battle like an offended king. I was considering, as a matter of fact, that if it came to it, I'd rather be involved in a fistfight than a gunfight. It wasn't likely that one could die from a fistfight.

Reaching the fringes of the brawl, I stood there royally and haplessly unnoticed for several moments before raising my voice.

"All right, uh . . . *here*," I said. "That's quite enough of this."

The battle raged on as though I had achieved not only inaudibility but invisibility as well. I was, to say the least, nonplussed. I glanced at Owens, who was watching me with uneasy curiosity. I had to do something and do it fast.

Without thought, I drew both Colts from beneath my belt and fired them into the air.

The explosions made everyone stop fighting simultaneously and look at me. I swallowed hard.

"The name—!" I stopped, forced to clear my clogged throat as hastily and quietly as I could.

"The name is Hickok!" I said then, my voice, thank the Lord, now booming over the quadrangle. Not wishing to take any chances, I added, very loudly, *"Wild—Bill— Hickok!"*

To my relief and utmost gratification an immediate buzzing of impressed, excited conversation began. I let it spread a bit, then fired two more shots into the air. Instant silence ensued.

"I have been appointed as the U.S. marshal at this fort!" I said. *"As* such—" I had to clear my throat again. *"As* such," I repeated, "I intend to see that brawls like this do not take place!"

I drew in a deep (and shuddering, that part fortunately unnoticed) breath and completed my declaration.

"Now, return to your work!"

Crucial moments passed as all the gathered men observed me standing there, the picture of unruffled vigilance. *For God's sake, go, I was thinking.*

Then (bless the man) one of them said, loud enough for most to hear, "Hell, let's not screw around with *him*."

I did my all to repress a smile of relief, managing to do so by elevating my chin and willing back the look of watchful self-possession; slightly undone, I'm afraid, by a puffing of my cheeks as I stifled escaping stomach gas.

"In the weeks that followed [more drivel from Nichols], Hickok proved beyond a shadow of a doubt that his reputation was no journalistic fancy but a hard, cold fact of life."

I kept the door to my office locked as often as I could.

"The office where he quartered soon became the center of control and retribution at the fort."

Even if anyone had managed to enter the office, they would most likely have found it empty.

"All problems of misdeed and discipline forthwith ceased to exist."

My real center of control was out behind the office.

"Each day, Hickok gained in stature and authority, his will unquestioned, his dominion firm."

If such is possible with trousers down, head slumped against the door, bent over, groaning, in the outhouse.

I kept a bottle of whiskey there with me from which I would take periodic belts, grimace, cough, hiss, and belch.

More than once, a nearby horse's neigh or someone shouting or (God forbid) calling my name as I drank would cause my hand to twitch so sharply that I threw whiskey on my clothes or in my face, and I was forced to dry myself with a torn page from the current mail-order catalog.

I pondered, more than once, over what President Lincoln

had said (when he was still alive). "What kills a skunk," he'd said, "is the publicity it gives itself." Not that I believed I was a skunk, but I feared the publicity I was getting just might end up killing me.

Once (I forget the year) I made the mistake of revealing the truth to a journalist. "I'm not ashamed to say," I told him, "that I have been so frightened that it appeared as if all the strength had gone out of my body and my face was as white as chalk."

I regretted saying that to him, as I regretted far more deeply making a similar confession years later; but I will speak of that presently.

Not, in the long run, that it mattered in the least what I said to that journalist or any other journalist for that matter. As time went by, they all ignored me as a human being anyway, so intent were they in making me a legend.

There were moments when, despite the puffing pride I felt at what they wrote about me, I yearned to run across a skeptic. When the tales became too tall for even me to overlook, I, of course, continued my attempt to feel amusement at the exaggerations and downright lies; but it grew increasingly difficult, especially as each new grandiose account put my life a little more in jeopardy.

Not that everyone adulated me. There were a number of my contemporaries who regarded me (and said so) as a bully, a braggart, a cheat, and a rogue.

There was even such an article written about me in *The Kansas Daily Commonwealth* in 1873. I carry it in my wallet.

"It is disgusting to see the eastern papers crowding in everything they can get hold of about 'Wild Bill.' If they only knew the real character of the man they so want to worship, we doubt if his name would ever appear again. 'Wild Bill' is nothing more than a drunken, reckless, murderous coward who is treated with contempt by true border men and who should have been hung years ago for the murder of innocent men."

A little overstated surely, but at least it was counterbalance for the exasperating mountains of horse turds piled up by the fabricating worshipers.

One day, while sitting in my second office, I heard someone call my name.

I was going to remain silent, then decided that there was no point to that; they'd locate me sooner or later, anyway.

"What?" I called back, wincing as my stomach juices bubbled.

"Captain Owens would like to see you, sir!" the man replied; a soldier, I discovered consequently.

"All right!" I said. "I'll be there in a while!"

What now? I wondered. Had I deluded myself into believing that Owens—albeit a fool—had failed to notice my complete ineptitude at marshaling?

My stomach growled and bubbled. I drained the bottle of whiskey, dropped it into the pit, and bent over once again, groaning, leaning my head against the door.

Twenty minutes later, calm and dignified as always (my public self), I entered Captain Owens's office.

"You wished to see me?" I inquired.

"It is my pwiviwege, Mawshew Hickok," he declared, "to intwoduce you to Genewaw Wiwwwiam Tecumseh Shewman."

I started, looking around. I hadn't noticed the man standing by the window who turned to regard me. He was tall and strong faced, barely bearded, with receding hair and probing eyes.

"I'm honored, general," I said.

"Marshal," Sherman replied in a noncommittal voice.

"Genewaw Shewman has just awwived at Fowt Wiwey,"

Owens said, "showtwy to commence an inspection touw of the awea. Accowdingwy, despite awe need fow youw sewvices, I am appointing you majowdomo fow him."

I thought I'd gotten it, but I wasn't quite certain. "Major—?"

"Domo, domo," Owens repeated. "I want you to wun his wagon twain."

"Oh," I said. Now his lisping was a wonderful sound to my ears. He *hadn't* found me out. I felt like laughing aloud.

I masked my face with dignity, however.

"It will be my honor, General Sherman," I told him.

I was thinking: *Hallelujah! I'm reprieved!*

Buttons and Bows

As we moved from the fort, Sherman and I at the head of a column of men and wagons, I looked back to throw a farewell glance at my problems.

I saw a soldier and teamster circling one another with drawn knives, a group of men observing.

Hastily, I turned back to the front lest anyone think I'd seen what I had. I cleared my throat portentously.

"I understand we have a mutual acquaintance, general," I said.

He glowered at me. *"What?"* he snapped.

"I understand that we know the same man." I revised my words.

"I doubt it. *Who*?" he replied.

"Your former aide-de-camp, Colonel George Ward Nichols."

Sherman made a snorting noise. "Aide-de-camp, my a———!" he snarled. "He ran some wagons for me, just like you're doing. And he was no more a colonel than my horse!"

I must confess to being blanked out by his harsh response. I stared at him, speechless. Then, at length, I cleared my throat again, this time not portentously in any way.

"Well," I said, "time to go check the wagons."

"Do that," Sherman told me.

I pulled my mount around and rode along the train, feeling properly chastened. I'd known that Colonel (hell, I wouldn't call him *that* anymore!) Nichols was a man fully skilled in stretching the truth like taffy, but I hadn't known that the stretch included his title as well.

After riding back three wagons or so, I turned my horse and rode along beside one of them. I'd leave Sherman to himself, I decided, do my work, and expect no more. Curse Nichols's dissembling bones anyway!

Lost in depressed thought, I had not noticed the small girl of eight or so sitting on the front seat of the wagon by her father. It took a while before I grew cognizant of her coquettish glances. I looked over at her, and immediately she averted her eyes. I had to smile. She was an absolute darling of a girl.

When I looked away, she looked back at me again. I looked back at her; she looked away. I had to chuckle now as we commenced a duel of sidelong glances and eye evasions. Finally, after some time, I contrived to catch her eye and winked at her. Instantly she was reduced to hand-stifled giggles.

"What are you doing?" her father asked.

"Being a delightful young lady, sir," I told him and nudged my horse forward.

As I rode beside the next wagon up, I smiled to myself, considerably cheered.

"All right, stay together now!" I ordered. "Don't start lagging! We've got a long way to go!"

I felt good now; away from that hateful fort and out on the plains again. And all because of the innocent flirting of a little girl. *How marvelous,* I thought.

I may forget or simply not get around to revealing my admiration for the charm of children.

I have always found myself at ease with them, able to enter, as it were, their world in place of my own, become a child along with them, and enjoy their pleasures as my own. Few know this of me. Accordingly, I feel it not amiss to comment on it now.

I must add that children have always warmed to me and liked my company, whether it was to play their childlike games along with them, spend a carefree afternoon fishing with them, or take part in serious discussions with them about their dogs or cats or dreams. To sit with a child or with children and chomp on an apple or candy while conversing on any subject that appealed to them was more than just a pleasure to me, it allowed me to forget whatever cares were besetting me and escape to a relaxing, peaceful period of time.

I remember, in particular, when the wagon train stopped at Marysville, Kansas, how I spent an enchanting afternoon with the young daughter of a certain Dr. Finlaw, scrambling along a riverbank and consequently getting horrendously muddy, me laughing until tears ran down my cheeks, the small girl bursting with peals of hysterical amusement while we tried to catch bullfrogs, totally in vain I must add.

Custered

A particularly ironic quote from Nichols's account of my activities at that time: "Some months later, General Sherman's tour of inspection having been concluded, Hickok happily returned to his duties at Fort Riley."

Ironic, did I say? I should have termed it crackbrained; farcical. I felt devoured by gloom as the wagon train moved toward the distant fort, my future there a dismal prospect as I saw it.

But then, as I rode in apprehensively, I reacted in great surprise to what I saw.

Everything was spit and polish, total order, total discipline. *What had happened while I was gone?* I wondered. *Had Owens gone insane and turned from a hapless lisper to a hard-edged disciplinarian?* I found that difficult to believe. Yet something had to explain this wondrous transformation: soldiers drilling smartly; teamsters working hard, with much efficiency; everything in view running like a well-oiled clock.

I had, I confess, been keeping my marshal's badge in my pocket, planning to avoid the pinning of it to my shirt as long as possible. Seeing this miracle taking place before me, I removed the badge from my pocket and pinned it back in place, thinking, *How?*

The answer was not long in coming: Custer.

I was taken to Custer's office, and instantly I took notice of his appearance. As a handsome man myself (remember, I speak now as I thought then) I appreciated his flamboyant grace; thick, blond hair hanging as long as mine, full, drooping mustache and goatee, flashing eyes and teeth, dressed in an immaculately tailored uniform. Is it retrospective imagination that causes me to remember an atmosphere of threatening, even impending mania about him? Perhaps memory errs. Still, why do I recall this if it wasn't so?

Seeing me, he thrust his hand out with the swiftness of a sword thrust. "Colonel George Armstrong Custer—*at* your service, Mr. Hickok," he said.

I shook his hand, trying not to wince at the strength of his grip. "Honored to meet you, sir," I responded.

There was another man in the room, a cruel-faced, glowering man. I will always think of him as such.

"This is my brother, Captain Thomas Custer," the colonel told me.

I extended my hand. "My pleasure, captain," I said.

He did not take hold of my hand immediately but made me wait for the gesture, running his gaze over my face and outfit with an attitude of contemptuous amusement.

Then he took my hand and squeezed it even harder than his brother had. *"Marshal,"* he said. Somehow, he made it sound like an obscene word. I didn't know what to make of the man. Clearly, he looked down on me; why, I had no conception. Still, in those opening moments, I seemed to understand that Captain Thomas Custer was going to be a large burr underneath my saddle.

I turned back to the colonel as he spoke.

"As you have doubtless observed, Marshal Hickok," he

said, "the discipline problem at Fort Riley has been duly solved."

"Uh . . . no," I said; unconvincingly, I think. "I hadn't noticed, having just come in."

Custer had continued speaking over me, as though he had no time for either listening or reacting. "Accordingly," he said, "I must request that you relinquish your assignment as United States marshal, the necessity for your services no longer existing."

God's in his heaven, it occurred to me; *all's bright in the world*. I pressed down any facial expression that might reveal my thoughts and said, "Of course. I would have suggested it myself as soon as I'd noticed . . ."

My voice trailed off and, as the Custers watched, Tom with a scornful smile (How could he dislike me so soon? It usually took awhile.), I unpinned the badge, tossed it on the desk edge where it fell to the floor, bent over, picked it up, and set it back on the desk.

"Thank you, Mr. Hickok," Custer said.

I smiled and nodded and began to turn away.

"And now, perhaps, you'll sign on as a scout with us," said Custer.

I turned back, unable, I'm afraid, to conceal my surprise. I saw Tom Custer's look of scorn return and deepen. "Uh . . . well, I—" I began.

"We need you, sir," said Custer, overriding me again. "Need you badly." He smiled that toothy smile for which he was so well known. "I've been counting on your help."

Once more, as on so many other dark occasions, I was cornered. "Oh," I said, "well, naturally I—"

I flinched as Custer clapped me on the shoulder; heartily, I suppose it would be called; painfully, is how it should be described.

"Splendid, Mr. Hickok!" he said, enthused. "As our British cousins say: *Good show!*"

He smiled and pointed at me, looking every inch the potential lunatic he was. No, memory does not err. It was all there in his face: a madman's glee.

"I understand your hesitation, however, I assure you," he said.

I felt myself tensing. *He did?*

"Fear not, however," he assured me, "I can promise you that life with us will not be dull."

"I—" was all I managed to utter before he rolled on across me, a grinning juggernaut, his eyes gone glittery.

"Orders have come through from Washington," he said. "To wit: 'Settle with the Red Man at any cost.'"

I felt my smile—polite as always—ossifying.

"I am therefore," Custer went on (I am tempted to write "raved on" but his voice was not that rabid even if his brain was), "launching an immediate and mass campaign against the Sioux, the Cheyenne, and the Kiowa Nations."

He smote the air elatedly. "Much excitement lies ahead, Mr. Hickok!" he cried. "I'm *delighted* you'll be with us all the way!"

Snatching up a piece of paper from his desk, he slammed it down in front of me, grabbed a pen, and jabbed it into his inkwell with the stab of a deranged picador, then held it out to me, white teeth flashing in a dazzling smile.

"Your contract, sir!" he cried.

I stared at him, the polite smile still frozen on my lips.

I then took hold of the pen and leaned over to sign. As I did, I saw, from the corners of my eyes, the Custer brothers exchange a look, Custer's one of satisfaction, his brother's one of continuing scorn. To his credit, Custer, at least, frowned at his brother.

I wish he could have done more to control him.

Scouting Days

Henry M. Stanley was, for a time, a special correspondent for the *Weekly Missouri Democrat*. It was for that publication that he penned the following. "Riding about in the late field of operations, he was seen by a group of red men who immediately gave chase. Too soon they found whom they were pursuing and then commenced to retrace their steps but not before two of them fell dead before the weapons of Wild Bill. A horse was also killed and one wounded, after which Wild Bill rode unconcernedly on his way to camp."

I interpolate in Stanley's account of the same event to show you how it really happened.

Visualize me, if you will, galloping at high speed across the prairie.

"Among the white scouts in Custer's Seventh Cavalry were numbered some of the most noted in their class. Nonetheless, the most prominent of these was 'Wild Bill' Hickok."

The reason I was galloping at high speed was that three Indians were chasing me, shooting arrows at my back.

After a while, I steered my horse into a canyon, looking back across my shoulder, relieved to see that the trio of Indians was not in sight at the moment.

"He was a plainsman in every sense of the word, ever watchful and alert."

The three Indians came charging from a side canyon ahead, catching me completely by surprise. I had to yank my horse around and gallop in the opposite direction.

Soon I faced a slope and drove my mount up the boulder-filled incline. The Indians were out of sight again. Lifting myself in the stirrups to twist around and get a better view, I lost balance and toppled from the saddle, tumbling to the ground.

"Whether on horseback or on foot . . ."

I staggered to my feet and hobbled dizzily after my horse.

". . . he was one of the most perfect examples of physical manhood the West has ever known."

I dived for my horse's tail and managed to grab hold of its tip. I tried to run but tripped over a rock and was dragged by the horse for several yards before letting go. I somersaulted over, then sat up on the hot ground, panicky and furious at the same time. "S———t!" I cried.

"Of his courage, there can be no question."

Moments later, face bloodless, eyes slitted, teeth clenched, features tight with apprehension, I crouched in the center of a boulder formation. At the bottom of the slope, the three Indians were riding past, searching for me.

As they rode out of sight, I stood and backed off slowly, a pistol in each hand.

I cried out, startled, as I backed into a cactus, flinging up my arms, and dropping my revolvers, one of them bouncing off my head. Dazed, I glanced back groggily, saw the cactus, and scowled.

Abruptly, I looked up the slope. The Indians had doubled back and were now above me. Grabbing my pistols, I began to run and leap down the slope, glancing across my shoulder. The Indians came riding quickly down the slope, shooting arrows again (thank God they had no rifles). I opened fire as I fled.

"His skill in the use of the revolver was unerring."

My pistol balls knocked dust into the air everywhere but near the Indians.

Racing down the slope, I skidded, slipped, and rode the seat of my pants down the rock-strewn incline, teeth set against the fierce abrading of my bottom. I hit a boulder, feetfirst, reared up, and flew across it, headfirst.

Landing hard, I struggled to my knees, very dizzy now, and looked across the boulder. (Unless I imagined it, the seat of my pants was smoking.)

The three Indians still charged down the slope on their ponies, shooting arrows.

Raising my pistols, I pulled the triggers, looking at the guns in shock; they were empty.

Suddenly, I cried out as an arrow flew into my right hip, causing me to topple over. Laboring up, convinced that I was finished, I looked up at the Indians to see, with astonishment, that they had dragged their mounts around and were charging up the slope in flight.

I watched them dumbly, totally perplexed.

Then I heard the thundering of hooves and looked around. A cavalry patrol was galloping toward me with —of all people—Tom Custer in command.

I stood slowly, grimacing with pain, looking rather awkward with an arrow jutting from my hip. The cavalrymen galloped by on each side of the boulder, pursuing the Indians; Tom Custer reined up to talk to me. Despite the agonizing pain, I tried to look blasé; I gestured casually.

"His deportment was entirely free of bluster and bravado; always well controlled."

I collapsed and fainted dead away.

When I came to some minutes later, still lying on the ground, it was to see a sadistically smiling Tom Custer heating a knife blade in a fire, troopers watching.

"Even when severely wounded, as he often was, Hickok bore his pain with Spartan resolution . . ."

Custer kneeled beside me and, before I could speak, began to gouge the red-hot knife tip into my hip, digging for the arrowhead.

". . . never uttering, at any time, so much as a murmur of complaint."

If there truly is a God in heaven, I believe he had no difficulty whatsoever hearing my squall that afternoon echoing and reechoing across the terrain.

Elizabeth

Since I do not anticipate that this manuscript will ever be published—or, if it is, that it will not be published for many years—I feel it is appropriate—well, no, that is not the word for it; say, rather, it is in the name of truth—that I add the following. Not that I intend to spell it out in lurid detail; far from it. I have too much deep respect for the person involved. Well, call it ego then; perhaps I have not matured quite as much as I would like to believe and it makes me feel a sense of personal pride to say this.

I believe that Elizabeth Custer was in love with me.

I hasten to add that, beyond a host of exchanged looks (some of them definitely fervent) and a single, passionate kiss, there was never anything untoward in our relationship. I respected her marriage as well as the lady herself and would never have compromised or sullied her name in any way. If this sounds hypocritical in light of what I have already indicated about Sarah Shull and Susannah Moore (and others I have not mentioned) remember that Elizabeth Custer was a genuine lady and I respected that.

I met her, of course, while I was a scout for Colonel Custer at Fort Riley, and during the period of my recuperation from the arrow wound, I got to know her well.

We discovered that we had a mutual interest in the subject of Spiritualism. She let me read several books she owned on the subject and we discussed their contents at length. Her husband—and brother, thank the Lord—were in the field most of the time, so we had uninterrupted hours together. I wondered more than once whether anyone who saw me entering her quarters suspected the worst. If they did, they were in error and, at least, nobody chose to speak of it to either Custer or his brother.

Elizabeth was a truly lovely person. I thought on occasion that she was too good for her posturing spouse, but she maintained a steadfast loyalty to him that I am certain will endure long after Custer's unfortunate death.

What drew us to one another may have been as simple as a physical attraction between two handsome people. (I *was* good-looking; then at least.) But I feel it was more, in fact. She seemed impressed by my family background, as I was with hers. We were both fundamentally genteel (I know this sounds bizarre considering my reputation, but it's true) and soft-spoken. And, as I have already indicated, we shared an interest in Spiritualism and enjoyed long conversations on the topic.

The looks we exchanged, the sudden drawing in of breath by her at times, and, of course, the one kiss during which we clung to one another tightly—all these verify, in recollection, my belief that she cared for me.

One more piece of evidence does the same.

I carry, in my billfold, a page she wrote. She said that she had planned to use it in a book about her life with Custer but decided against it as it might disturb her husband. I was truly honored that she trusted me to keep it in my possession.

Herewith: "Physically, Wild Bill [I have always been sorry I did not ask her to call me James] is a delight to look upon. He walks as if every muscle is perfection and the careless swing of his body as he moves seems perfectly in keeping with the man. I do not know of anything finer in the way of physical perfection than Wild Bill when he swings himself lightly from his saddle and, with graceful, swaying step, squarely set shoulders, and well-poised head, approaches. I will not discuss his features, but the frank, manly expression of his fearless eyes and his courteous manner give one a feeling of confidence in his word and in his undaunted courage."

Not the words, I submit, of a disinterested woman.

Home

Two things made me leave the fort when the condition of my wound had improved. One was, as indicated, to leave behind any temptation that might exist between Elizabeth Custer and me. The other was more in keeping with my general desire to avoid danger.

My wound was getting close enough to healing to present me with the likelihood of Custer asking me to scout for him again, so I decided that it was a most propitious time to visit my mother.

Accordingly, I purchased a dress from the fort post, announced my plan, and packed my carpetbag.

The day I left, I limped to my horse with the aid of a cane and tied the bag and cane behind the saddle.

As I did, I saw Tom Custer walking across the quadrangle, heading in my direction.

"B———d," I muttered under my breath. "Don't know which of them is crazier."

I lifted myself onto the horse, wincing at the pain in my hip.

"*Leaving,* Hickok?" Tom Custer asked.

"Yes, sir," I replied, sounding as genial as I could. "Going home to Illinois to visit my aging mother."

"So I heard," said Custer, almost interrupting me. "You *will* return though."

"Oh, yes. Definitely," I replied.

Touching the brim of my hat, I turned my horse away, murmuring to myself, "The day hell freezes over."

My mother was overjoyed to see me, though my family made it clear that bringing a dress and a few other trinkets was scarcely adequate when she really needed contributions toward her welfare; that I had never made such contributions annoyed them mightily. Since I was now, in their eyes, a celebrated personage, they assumed that I was rolling in money. Why they would think that I have no idea, but I was too proud or angry to let them know that my income for the past few years could be described with one word: *sparse*.

While I was home, my wound began to suppurate and a doctor had to come to lance the wound and scrape the bone.

Nichols's version:

"The doctor made four cuts outward from the wound, making a perfect cross. Then he drew the flesh back and began to scrape the bone. I [my sister Lydia] was holding the lamp and felt myself getting faint. 'Here, give it to me,' said Bill. He took the lamp and held it while the doctor scraped away, never flinching once."

The truth:

As soon as the doctor made the first cut, I fainted dead away and was out cold through the entire operation.

The year 1868 was rather strange.

Mount Vesuvius erupted in Italy.

Mount Etna did the same.

Earthquakes troubled England.

A cyclone hit the island of Mauritius, making fifty thousand people homeless.

The Hawaiian Islands were swamped by a tidal wave sixty feet high, and Mauna Loa erupted.

Gibraltar was struck by an earthquake.

Peru and Ecuador suffered enormous earthquakes. Mountains collapsed and immense tidal waves swept towns away and carried huge ships far inland.

Gigantic waves hit California, Japan, and New Zealand.

An earthquake hit San Francisco.

With such things taking place, even Nichols was hard put to find anything exciting to write about me.

After conducting a short-lived freighting business with a man named Colorado Charlie, I traveled from town to town, looking for a place to settle down, a place where everything was peaceful.

The pattern of my stops at any given community was similar.

I would seek out some old-timer sitting in front of the general store, usually with his chair tipped back. Approaching him, I would crimp the brim of my hat and say good afternoon. He usually responded, "Howdy."

"Nice community you have here," I would comment, testing the waters.

In one place, the old man spat and said, "Like h————l it is."

I gazed at him reflectively, recrimped the brim of my hat, and wished him a good day. Then, remounting my horse, I rode back out of town.

In another town, I reined my horse up near another old man sitting in another chair in front of another general store. I touched the brim of my hat, said good afternoon, and commented on what a nice community he had.

"That's what you think, bub," said the geezer, spitting.

Without another word, I tapped the brim of my hat, steered my horse away, and started out of town.

I have lost count of the number of communities I briefly visited this way.

"Ever on the search for new adventure," Nichols wrote, "Hickok rode into Hays City, Kansas, in the summer of 1868."

I reined my horse up by yet another general store porch on which yet another old-timer leaned back in his chair and, yet another time, crimped the brim of my hat; it was thinning from the surplus of crimping it had experienced.

"Nice community you've got here," I said.

The old man spat. "We like it," he said.

I leaned in toward him.

"Good marshal?" I said.

"Nope," he answered.

I straightened up with a frown. "You don't have one?" I asked.

"No, sir," said the old man. He gathered spit. "Sheriff," he explained, then spat. "Tom Gannon."

"*Ah,*" I said, leaning forward again. "Good man, eh?"

The old man looked around and gestured with his aged head. "Judge for yourself," he told me.

I looked around to see Tom Gannon lumbering along the plank walk, an enormous, ominous-looking man with a handlebar mustache and a derby hat, a shotgun tucked beneath his right arm.

The sight of him warmed the cockles of my heart.

"Yes, sir," I observed. "A nice community."

Hays was, of course, far more than a community. It was the terminus of the railroad, so the roundhouse, the turntable, and all the other buildings that go to make a railroad town were located there.

North and South Main Streets were built on either side of the railroad tracks.

On them were such establishments as the Capless and

Ryan Outfitting store, the Leavenworth Restaurant, the Hound Saloon and Faro House, Howard Kelly's Saloon, Ed Goddard's Saloon and Dance Hall, Tommy Drums Saloon, Kate Coffee's Saloon, Mose Water's Saloon, Paddy Welsh's Saloon, and so on. You may observe that drinking was a major feature of the social life in Hays.

The others were gambling and prostitution.

Someone wrote the following about this final occupation. I have carried it with me all these years, thinking that I might make use of it.

"Streets blazed with the reflection from saloons and a glance within showed floors crowded with dancers, the gaily dressed women striving to hide, with ribbons and paint, the terrible lines that the grim artist Dissipation loves to draw upon such faces. With a heartless humor, he daubs the noses of the sterner sex a cherry red but paints under the once bright eyes of women a shade as dark as the night in the cave of despair."

Where did all these women come from? Every European nationality was represented and, occasionally, the Far East. They came in every shape and size. Some were pretty, many were not. Some were mean and vicious, carrying knives or pistols. Age was no barrier, but those older than thirty were the exception. Most of the girls were in their teens, and once I met a fourteen-year-old.

Many entered the profession unwittingly, answering advertisements for domestic servants only to discover on arrival their dreadful mistake.

A few escaped their fate but, for the rest, there was only constant degradation and the threat of disease. Some died naturally, but more took their own lives, laudanum the preferred method.

I had not intended to convert this tale into a tract. Perhaps I do it from guilt, for I was no abstainer from these women who were "horizontally employed" as it is said.

Leave it to us men to denigrate these poor soiled doves with such mocking sobriquets as *ceiling expert, nymph du prairie, frail denizen,* and *crib girl.*

Excuse me for this bleak diversion but it is my story and I'll tell it as I choose, especially since no one is likely to read it, anyway.

I have wondered, now and then, if my descent into drunken and libidinous pursuits in 1868 could have been the result of my bitter disappointment that I could never possess Elizabeth Custer.

But then, perhaps that is no better than a foolishly romantic excuse for what I did. God knows I was no stranger to the artist Dissipation at that time, a more than willing companion to his every carnal blandishment.

Because a book was published at that time *(Wild Bill Hickok—King of Pistoleers* or was it *Hero of the Plains*? I forget) purporting to be a true account of my adventures, the descriptions of my character were so adulatory that they made me feel guilt about the unseemly life I was leading. Accordingly, I tapered off my profligacy and attempted to resemble more closely those glorifying words; probably the only time that lies improved the truth. Certainly, it was the only time one of those toadying accounts served to help me rather than hinder.

At any rate, I no longer cut the wolf loose. I caroused less with the ladies of the night and played my cards closer to the vest. Accordingly, my health, my energy, and my income were all enhanced and I began enjoying life again.

Until that afternoon.

Served Up Brown, Twice

I was playing poker in Tommy Drums Saloon, my fellow gamblers a trio of local men, all well respected, as I certainly was by then. A gathering of male and female admirers watched the game, drinking in my every word and gesture.

I tossed down my hand. "Well," I said, "the cards are certainly not cooperating with me today." Not a particularly witty observation, even by the most lenient of standards. If anyone else had said it—or if I had said it in a world (blessedly) free of Nichols and his hyperbolizing ilk—not a glimmer of appreciation would have ensued.

As it was, a wave of intense amusement ran through the assemblage. I picked up my dwindling pile of chips and made a face at its diminutive size. More laudatory chuckles from the Wild Bill Congregation. I tossed down the chips in disgust. Crinkled eyes and delighted laughter. "Perhaps I should have stayed in bed," I said.

An old man slapped his thigh and cackled as though my remark was the funniest thing he'd ever heard in his life. The others joined him in merry mirth; by God, this Hickok fellow belonged on the stage.

The next hand was dealt.

One of the players inquired of me, "Do you think you'd become our sheriff, Mr. Hickok, if Tom Gannon wasn't here in Hays?"

"Oh . . . I suppose I might," I responded offhandedly.

"Wouldn't *that* be something," said another of the players.

A thrilled murmur flowed through the room. "Yeah!" "Wouldn't it though!" "I sure would like to see *that* day arrive!" et cetera, ad nauseam.

I examined my cards, continuing grandly. "However," I declared, "Ellis County *does* have a sheriff. And a d———ned fine one, we must admit," I added generously.

"Oh, well, sure, of course," another man begrudged.

"You'd be better, Wild Bill," player number three observed.

"Ay-men!" a woman cried.

I nodded, smiling graciously. (These moments I could not resist. Could you?) "Well," I drawled, "I guess I'd get the job done somehow."

"Somehow?" "S———t, man!" "Huh!" Incredulous sounds from all and sundry.

"We'd *never* have a problem if *you* were sheriff!" Player number two was positively effervescing.

I gestured with princely restraint. I was really good at it by then; my gestures could not have been improved upon. "I appreciate your confidence, gentlemen," I told them self-effacingly, "and truly hope that, one of these days, I can repay it with deeds instead of words."

I looked askance at my cards.

"I also hope that, one of these days, I'll be dealt a decent hand."

Much gladsome risibility. I was a hit. Basking in their wide-eyed admiration, I began to speak again, saying, "Well, now—" when I had to break off as the batwing doors were flung ajar and a young man pounded over to us. His name (Do I remember that because he was the bearer of ill tidings?) was Bob Cooney and he was panting, wheezing, sweating. "Bad news, boys!" he cried.

"What?" "What is it, Bob?" "What happened?" All queries, virtually simultaneous.

"Sheriff Gannon's been shot from ambush!" he told us.

I recall a nerve twitching in my cheek.

"Is he *dead*?" someone demanded.

"Deader than a mackerel!" cried Bob Cooney.

An awed sound rippled through the group. Then, almost as one person, everyone turned their eyes toward me, trying not too successfully to restrain their enthusiasm so soon after learning of Gannon's murder. I felt my cheeks puff as my stomach made its presence known.

"Well, now," I said, hoping that my voice was not quite as faint as it sounded to me.

Walking back to my hotel, still limping slightly, I tried to pretend that I didn't notice everyone's anticipating looks.

"Hey, Jeb, you heard about Gannon?" someone shouted from across the street, making me start.

"Yeah!" said Jeb; he was walking behind me. *"Wonder who they're going to get to take his place!"*

"Yeah! I *wonder*!" shouted back the man across the street.

I tried to freeze my face as though absorbed in momentous thought. Two women (ladies, I presume) passed me on the walk, casting sidelong glances; I was so distracted I forgot to touch my hat brim, much less respond to their glances.

I passed an older man who smiled at me broadly. "Afternoon, Mr. Hickok," he said.

My returned smile was closer to a momentary wince, I think.

"Heard about Sheriff Gannon?" the older man inquired.

I pretended not to have heard the question, increasing the length and speed of my stride. Gaze fixed straight ahead, I limped by a group of men who murmured eagerly among themselves, looking toward me with equal eagerness.

"*Now* we'll see some action," I heard one of them say as I left them behind.

"Boy, *will* we!" vociferated another.

I clenched my teeth and walked faster yet, even though it made my hip ache.

I entered the lobby of my hotel and, crossing to the stairs, ascended them. Happily, no one present there had heard the news, and all I had to deal with was the usual goggle-eyed veneration.

Reaching my room, I unlocked the door and went inside, closing and relocking the door, then taking off my hat and slinging it onto the bed. Moving to the bureau, I picked up the bottle of whiskey there and poured myself a glassful; the neck of the bottle rattled on the rim of the glass. Putting down the bottle, I emptied the glass's contents in a single swallow and stared morosely at my reflection in the mirror.

My stomach let go and I exploded with a deafening belch.

"Good . . . *God,* sir!" I addressed the white-faced craven in the mirror. "You *offend* me!"

It was almost dark now; night was coming as it always did despite man's fear of it. Correction: despite *my* fear of it.

Boots off, I was sitting on the bed, staring glumly toward the window, more than just a little drunk.

Reaching out, I picked the bottle off the bedside table and poured the last of its contents into my glass. I held the bottle upside down for near a minute so the final drops would not be lost.

I then drank the glass empty, sighed, and hiccupped. I was waiting for what I knew was coming. I asked myself why I was doing so, why I wasn't getting out before it came. I had no answer; I sat waiting helplessly. The edges were numbed by liquor, but the core still pulsed with that apprehension I'd experienced so often in the past.

I looked now toward the door as footsteps approached my room. I felt paralyzed. Would I be able to react at all to what was now about to happen? I had no idea whatever.

The footsteps stopped. I felt myself begin to tighten with involuntary prescience.

Then I flinched, legs jerking, as someone knocked on the door.

For an instant, I visualized Death in his black, cowled robe standing outside, skeletal hand poised to knock again.

He did, and I flinched again. I stared mutely at the door.

"Mr. Hickok?" said the voice.

Absurdly, I thought, *It couldn't be Death, he wouldn't call me mister.* I drew in a trembling breath.

"Mr. Hickok?" the voice repeated.

I was tempted not to answer; I wasn't there, I'd gone out for the evening, I was riding, I was sleeping, I was dead.

The temptation affronted me. I raised my chin, assuming, even in the semidarkness, my most imperious expression. "Yes?" I asked.

"This is Mayor Motz," he told me. "May I enter?"

I swallowed with effort. That I couldn't handle. "I'm not dressed," I told him.

"Ah, well . . . in that case." I heard him clear his throat. "As you have no doubt heard by now," he continued, "Sheriff Gannon has been killed in the performance of his duty, and as mayor of Hays, it is, therefore, incumbent upon me to appoint a temporary sheriff until a new election can be held."

Stop babbling and get on with it, I thought.

He did. "I would be pleased and highly reassured if you would be that man, Mr. Hickok," he said.

I gazed at the door with lifeless eyes.

"Your salary," he babbled on, "would be one hundred and twenty-five dollars per month plus fifty cents for each unlicensed dog you shoot. However, after the election— which I *know* you'd win hands down—those figures can, I guarantee you, be improved upon."

I opened my mouth to speak, then closed it without making a sound.

"What do you say, Mr. Hickok?" asked the mayor. "Does that sound agreeable? Can we count on you?"

I drew in a very long, very shaky breath and braced myself.

"I'll think about it," I told him.

The silence in the hall was like a knife blade sinking slowly into my heart.

"I'm *supposed* to be reporting back to Fort Riley after my hip is better," I explained unconvincingly.

It was a lie I could not maintain. I tensed with aggravation, resenting Motz for putting me in this position.

"I'll let you know in the morning," I told him stiffly.

"Fair enough, sir!" Motz responded cheerily. "In the morning then. But please— don't let the salary affect your decision, for, as I say, it can definitely be improved upon."

He paused, then said, "Until tomorrow then," and left.

I slumped back weakly on my pillow. "Sure," I muttered, "it's the salary that will affect my decision."

Approximately twenty minutes later, I retrieved my carpetbag from the closet and began to pack it with my few belongings. *Time to move on once again,* I thought.

I looked at my mother's framed portrait for a while before putting it into the bag, trying not to think of what her reaction would be to this, much less—I shuddered at the image—my father's.

It is hard to believe that an illustration from a magazine altered the direction of my life.

Still, as I began to put it in my bag, I stopped and found myself staring at the well-worn copy of *Harper's Magazine,* the article about me and illustration of me prominent.

It was how I looked in that illustration that struck me so hard. Grand and noble. A gentleman par excellence.

It reminded me of how I looked when I first read that article; dirty, lying in filthy attire in the back of a wagon, a drifter and a derelict par excellence.

Was I to take the risk of sliding back to that?

I could not. Whatever the risks (and, of course, I downplayed them in my mind, believing that my reputation would enable me to once more triumph over any situation), I would not permit myself to retreat. I was here, I was wanted and admired, and Hays had not, in recollection, been all that woolly a place since I'd arrived.

Revealingly, the first thing I removed from my bag was the framed portrait of my mother, which I set back up on the bedside table. Sitting down, I gazed at it, remembering how she told me that I had descended from a long and noble line.

"I will not dishonor it," I promised her.

At the Hays City Tailor Shop I did my best to bring that illustration to reality. Once more my personal self was imitating my created one; very strange behavior, I can see now more than I did then.

When I finally stepped forth onto the street, sheriff's badge displayed for all to see, I was the very model of sartorial splendor in my pleated shirt of finest white linen, my flowered waistcoat cut low to reveal my silk cravat, my Prince Albert frock coat with silk collar, my black salt-and-pepper trousers tucked into custom-stitched boots with two-inch heels, a scarlet silk sash fastened snugly at my

waist, my two new pearl-handled revolvers under it
(Colt Navy .36, of course), and my low-brimmed black
hat. I was a true-life version of the *Harper's* illustration
except, I feel compelled to add, even grander. I had achieved,
at least as far as my clothing was concerned, my greatest
dream. I was a living fashion plate.

Strutting along the plank walk, I paused by the window
of a store to admire my reflection, and it seemed as though
I saw in the glass my mother's smiling face as she reminded me to always be a gentleman.

"I *am*, mother," I assured her.

I stepped down from the walk to cross the street, im-
pressing everyone who saw me, then stepped aside with
fearful reverence to let me pass. Horses, mules, and wagons stopped. Dogs paused to wonder and adore. (All right,
that's a Nichols worth of bologna.)

"Thus," he really did write of that afternoon, "did this
Beau Brummel of the frontier bring his glory and magnifi-
cence to the job of sheriff of Ellis County, Kansas, in the
United States of our America!"

A slight exaggeration granted but, on that occasion, I believed it to be the only time the foolish man had put down
God's unvarnished truth.

The Peace Pipe
Goes Out

Six weeks passed by in blessed and unexpected tranquillity, convincing me that I had made the right decision.

I practiced regularly with my pistols and must say that my increasing skill with same was virtually akin to awesome. I could center hit a two-foot circle at a hundred yards, hit two telegraph poles seventy feet apart by firing from a point midway between, and drive a cork through the neck of a whiskey bottle without breaking the neck. I even developed a dazzling quick draw, my speed "as quick as thought." Guess who wrote that?

Still (as I have indicated) to draw with speed and fire accurately, hitting dimes and a top fence rail is meaningless, because the dimes do not lug sidearms and they never wished me malice.

That was not the case with Bill Mulvey on that August afternoon in 1869.

I was in Kate Coffee's establishment, standing at the counter, having a drink, my right boot propped on the brass rail. Ralph, the barkeep, and I were alone in the saloon. I raised my glass in a toast to him, my comportment that of a man imbued with confidence, which, at the moment, I was.

"Your health, sir," I wished him loftily.

"Thank you, sheriff," Ralph replied.

I drank down half the glassful and sighed with satisfaction. Ralph and I exchanged a smile, mine eminent, his reverent.

"Things have sure been mighty quiet since you took over, Mr. Hickok," Ralph observed.

"Which is the way we like it, Ralph. That is the way we like it," I responded, my tone of voice indicating that it was, of course, a joke. I winked at him and downed the remainder of the glass's contents, Ralph chuckling with appreciation at my subtle jollity.

"Seriously, though," he said then, "you must be bored stiff after a month and a half of absolutely *nothing* going on."

"Well," I said, admitting it, "a *little* action might not be too disagreeable." I held up the thumb and index finger of my right hand to indicate how much.

I chuckled amiably as Ralph poured me another drink, chuckling in response. Then he glanced toward the front entrance.

"After marshaling and scouting at Fort Riley," I began, "this *is* a bit—"

Ralph interrupted, muttering, "Uh-oh."

My hand twitched just enough to spill some whiskey on the bar. Ralph didn't notice, leaning toward me to murmur, "Looks like you might be getting that action right now, sheriff."

With his head, he gestured slightly toward the entrance. I looked in that direction, tensing at what I saw: a nasty-looking young man glaring over the batwing doors, eyeing me with hostility.

"I haven't seen *him* before," I said, turning back to Ralph.

Ralph was gone. I turned my head to see him heading

quickly for the back room. I began to speak to him, then realized that there was nothing to say, and gave it up. I saw him shut the back room door. "Son of a b————h," I murmured. He'd certainly retreated fast.

I turned my head so quickly that my neck bones crackled as I heard the swinging doors creak open. The young man started toward me, boots clumping on the wood floor. I took my right foot off the brass rail and replaced it with my left so I could face him.

He stopped before me. "Hickok?" he said. Not mister nor sheriff; I was in for it, I saw. His eyes were wild, his expression bordered on mania; a veritable Dave Tutt, Jr.

"The name is Mulvey," he informed me.

"Well, I'm—" I began.

"*Bill* Mulvey," he cut me off.

"Well, I'm—" I tried again.

"*Wild* Bill Mulvey," he interrupted me again. "What do you think of *that*?"

The breaking of his voice told me what to think; he was afraid of me.

"Pleased to meet you, Mr. Mulvey," I greeted him coolly.

The tremulous snicker in his throat reinforced my conclusion as did his lamentable attempt to sound mocking as he repeated, "Please t'*meet*cha Mistuh Mulvey."

He tried to laugh, did not succeed, and stopped, face stiffening with anger.

"Well, *I* ain't glad to meet *you*, Hickok," he declared, his voice breaking again. My confidence increased.

"Mr. Mulvey, I suggest—" I started.

He broke in, features twitching, obviously terrified. "And I suggest your father was a chicken and your mother was a pig!" he ranted.

I smiled at him, amused.

"I believe that you're confusing your parentage with mine," I said.

His eyes bulged. He sensed that he was being defamed but couldn't quite comprehend how. He leaned forward, lower jaw jutting out. *"Say that again,"* he ordered.

I had only to threaten him with death now; that was obvious.

"Go home, Mr. Mulvey," I told him. "This is more than you can—"

I stopped, went rigid, as he stepped back quickly, right hand poised to draw.

"I told you to say it again," he said, "You yellow, long-haired, leaky-mouthed, no-souled, egg-sucking dandy!"

I might have taken pleasure in his vivid, creative epithet had I not, at that instant, come to the stunned realization that, despite his terror-stricken state, he was determined to go through with this. It was a new variety of plight for me. My mind went blank.

Then, inspired, I looked abruptly toward the entrance.

"Don't shoot, boys!" I ordered.

Mulvey jerked around, deceived. I grabbed for one of my pistols, moving so precipitately that my boot slipped off the brass rail and I crashed down to the floor as Mulvey whirled back, drew, and fired at the spot where I had been.

Sprawled, I fired upward, hitting him square in the gut; not a fatal shot but one that gave him such a shock, his brain was paralyzed. He stumbled backward, trying to raise his arm to fire a second time. My second pistol ball, more accurately aimed, entered his heart and killed him, causing him to topple over clumsily.

I stared at him, heart pounding, then glanced around as Ralph's muffled voice emitted from behind the back room door. "Is it over, Mr. Hickok?" he inquired.

I scrambled to my feet, replaced the Colt beneath my sash, and brushed my clothes off hastily. Straightening up, I swallowed hard.

"Yes, it's over," I responded sonorously.

The back door opened and Ralph peered out uneasily.

Seeing me on my feet, stately and composed, he emerged and looked across the counter, eyes widening as he caught sight of Mulvey's body lying motionless nearby.

"Holy . . . jumping . . ." he mumbled.

"Best fetch the undertaker, Ralph," I instructed calmly. "I'm afraid our friend here just cashed in his chips."

Turning, I strode toward the doorway, wincing as I felt my legs begin to quiver. I fought it off as two men rushed in, causing me to twitch in startlement.

"What happened, sheriff?" one of them asked in an excited voice.

I gestured airily. "Ralph will explain," I told him.

They watched me, open-mouthed, as I departed.

A good thing for me they weren't watching minutes later when I lost my lunch and part of my breakfast.

Several points that no one seems to know about.

In all the elaborations on my skill in the use of my pistols, never once have I read a single word about my constant efforts in maintaining them; as though the blasted things functioned perfectly with no attention paid to them whatever.

Far from it, let me tell you.

Almost every day, I took the trouble of refurbishing my Colts.

With me living in this h———lish climate filled with ever-present sand and dust, using salt-laden black powder, which attracted moisture like a drunken man, my revolvers would have, very early on, ceased to perform as needed if not constantly kept intact.

First I would empty them and meticulously clean out the chambers, pushing a pin or needle through the nipples until, by holding the cylinder at eye level, I could see daylight through the rear of each chamber.

I would then carefully load each chamber with powder, ram home the lead balls (five, of course, the hammer left on the empty chamber; "five peas in the wheel," as they say). Finally, I would inspect each copper cap—filled with fulminate of mercury—before placing it on the nipple.

In that wise, I made certain that my guns were never damp in any way.

I already had enough problems using my pistols in defense of my life.

My second point has to do with my use of the English language.

It began to be more and more apparent to me that to present myself as an educated gentleman might have a tendency to vitiate the image I'd acquired in the past eight years as a tough and rugged man of action, someone to be feared and respected.

Accordingly, I began consciously to write with more deliberate care, taking the time to misspell; words and twist the rules of grammar out of shape, for example, "you would laugh to see me now Just got in Will go a way again to morrow Will write in the morning but god nowse when It will start," and so on.

Easy enough to do. *Wright* instead of *write*. *Noncence* instead of *nonsense*. *Marryed* instead of *married*. *Agoing onn* in place of *going on*. *Achres* in place of *acres*. *Pririe* instead of *prairie*. You get the idea.

Actually, I think I overdid it and hope, with this account, to correct the misapprehension that I have been and am an uneducated clod with little to recommend me in the intellect department. Of course, would it have really mattered if I had let it be known that I had full use of the English language? Who can tell?

Smitten to the Core

It was a peaceful, sunny afternoon in the spring of 1870. Life in Hays had been remarkably placid, except for a brief incident the previous September when I was forced to shoot a man named Sam Strawhun, who was behaving in a threatening manner in John Bitter's saloon. To maintain my verity, I feel compelled to mention that the threatening gesture he was making toward me was with a beer stein, not a pistol, when I shot him through the head. The jury found the homicide justifiable, "being in self-defense."

Oh, there had been a brief confusion in October when the governor of Kansas—one James M. Harvey—had approved the refusal made by a certain Colonel Gibson to honor a warrant for arrest I had tendered him, claiming that he didn't recognize me as the sheriff of the county. But that was of little consequence in my life since no exchanged pistol fire was involved.

Indeed, the *Daily Commonwealth,* in December of that year, remarked that "Hays City, under the guardian care of 'Wild Bill,' is quiet and doing well."

That afternoon I ambled slowly along the plank walk, a monarch strolling through his kingdom, touching the brim of his hat as he passed various women, nodding (once) with

regal recognition as he passed various men, patting
(benignly) the heads of children as he passed them. All
regarded me with the mien of worshipers, murmuring,
"Afternoon, sheriff," or "Good afternoon, Mr. Hickok," or
"Good afternoon, sir." Oh, let me tell you, I was truly into
it by then, playing the role to the very hilt, not allowing to
myself for a second the faintest glimmer of recognition
that it was a role and nothing more.

I remember stopping on the walk and standing there,
stroking the index finger of my right hand underneath my
mustache as I gazed across my domain.

Then I heard a distant sound I did not recognize at first.
Only after a number of perplexed moments did I recognize the sound as being that of a calliope. I stepped out
into the street to get a better look. The calliope music grew
louder, coming closer. The monarch smiled.

Approaching down Main Street was a traveling circus:
animals in cages, elephants, costumed midgets, clowns and
performers walking and on horseback or in wagons, acro-
bats performing cartwheels along the dusty thoroughfare;
all to the shrill accompaniment of the calliope. Printed on
the wagon's sides I saw the name: Lake's Hippo-Olympiad
and Mammoth Circus.

I watched with a kindly smile. The king was pleased.

As the circus continued moving along the street, more
and more citizens emerged from their stores and offices
to watch in grinning delight. It was not often that the torpid
tempo of the community (which I, of course, found very
much to my taste) was broken in such a captivating way.

Along with the citizens, I watched with high good spirits.

Then I caught sight of something—some*one* I should
say—who abruptly galvanized me to the bone.

It was a mounted woman wearing red tights. A silk cloth
on her horse's back bore the stitched name Madame Agnes
Lake.

I ran an awed, admiring gaze along her shapely legs, up to her voluptuous, tightly bound figure, then farther up to her lush, red-haired beauty. Since this entry will, as likely as not, never be seen by the prurient eyes of man, I can reveal these things that ordinarily, as a gentleman, I would not deign to mention. I can add as well (I know it now, I didn't then) that Agnes Lake's appearance was greatly similar to that of my beloved mother.

At any rate, she smiled at the people as she rode by, nodding and gesturing gracefully. I find it amazing now to realize that she was forty-three years old at the time; I would have bet my stack that she was in the lower portion of her thirties, that at most.

I think I gaped at her, eyes unblinking, mouth (I hope not, but I fear) hanging partly open.

In fantasy, I saw her floating by me in a glowing, pink cloud, the shrillness of the calliope music somehow muted to my ears, even sweetened now.

I was, in brief, struck dumb by amour, let there be no doubt about that.

I was positively stupefied by Madame Agnes Lake.

And when, as she passed me by and saw me standing there, she extended me not only a dazzling smile but a gestured flirtatious greeting, I was an instant victim of calico fever. I had always believed that I would eschew all thoughts of matrimony until cows climbed trees, yet here I was, seconds after viewing her for the first time, already contemplating a quick jump over the broomstick.

Shortly thereafter, I strode across the circus grounds on a search for her.

I found her giving orders to some tent hands. "Now remember, boys, we have to set up quickly, here," she said, her voice (as I'd hoped and was enraptured to hear) was as melodious as her looks were ravishing.

"Madame Lake?" I said in as deep a baritone as I could summon.

"Yes, what is it?" she asked, turning to face me.

The word "it" popped like a soap bubble in her mouth when she saw me and I knew with instant felicity that she found me as attractive as I did her. Actually, with the ego that nurtured me so resolutely in those days, I most likely would have been stunned if she hadn't been attracted to me.

However, I could tell by her smile and the sudden way in which she started fussing with her thick red hair that she did find me attractive.

"I am Sheriff Hickok," I told her. "If there is anything at all that I can do to assist you . . ."

Her eyes had widened at my words. "Wild Bill Hickok?" she asked in awe.

I was hard put to restrain my heart's delirium.

"I have been called that on occasion, yes," I responded.

She pressed the fingers of her left hand to her (copious, shall I describe it?) bosom, gasping prettily.

"Oh, my," she murmured.

Thus did we stand there, dumbstruck by each other's beauty and position.

That evening, I attended the premiere performance of Lake's Hippo-Olympiad and Mammoth Circus.

Not that I paid much heed to the bulk of it. I was too intrigued by Agnes Lake. I stared, spellbound, as, costumed in her blue figure-hugging tights, she rode around the ring, upright on her cantering horse. I know that there was music being played by a band as she performed, but I don't remember hearing it, bewitched as I was by her appearance and her supple movements.

Each time she passed the stand in which I sat and turned her head to look at me, a delicately sensuous smile on her lips . . . well, I was a resident of Paradise, a feeble sound of ardor quivering in my throat.

My ecstasy soared completely when, later, she performed a high-wire act, a yellow, even more close-fitting outfit on her eye-filling form. High above, she smiled down at me more than once, and I was certain (perhaps it was no more than self-delusion at that particular moment) that I saw invitation in her eyes. Looking up at her, I felt my Adam's apple bob with laborious effort.

Later still—it was nearly too much for my stricken heart—adorned by yet another skintight costume, this one green, she entered a cage with two lions and a tiger and made them sit on boxes, cracking her whip above their heads, then raising both her ivory arms in triumph. I was overwhelmed. My hands grew red from pounding them together. Fortunately for me, I didn't have to draw a pistol that night; I could never have done it successfully.

Even from the cage, she looked at me and I could not help but dream that she, like I, had romance in mind; I returned her looks with total fervor.

After the performance, following a chat with several citizens (me pretending to be casual about the circus and its owner), I strolled (instead of running, which I yearned to do) to the wagon in which Agnes Lake resided while her show was traveling, and knocked on its door.

"Who's there?" I heard the voice that thrilled my body to its marrow.

"Sheriff Hickok," I replied.

A rustling sound. "One moment, sheriff," she responded musically. Breath faltered in me as I visualized her drawing a robe over her provocative figure. I stood on the doorstep, feeling as though time had stopped completely and would not resume its movement until I had her in my gaze again.

She opened the door and I saw that my imagination had been on the mark, the silk robe clinging to her obviously unclad curves and valleys. I could not recall the way in which I breathed, all movement ceasing in my chest.

It did not cease in hers. A deep breath swelled it out with maddening inflation. "Yes?" she inquired.

I want to get in bed with you and let my bodily derangement satiate itself.

Of course, I didn't say that; couldn't. "May I offer you a late supper at the Leavenworth?" I invited.

"The Leavenworth?" she asked.

"Our finest restaurant," I told her.

"Ah," she responded, hesitating momentarily. Was it possible that she would not go? It was, after all, late in the evening and she could—understandably—be weary from the performance.

But no—my heart danced at the sight—she smiled and said, "That would be lovely, Mr. Hickok. If you'll wait, I'll put some clothes on."

Don't; just take the robe off and we'll dive into a pool of heavenly passion!

"Of course," I said, "I'll wait outside."

We sat in the restaurant long after every other patron had departed, our only company a lone waiter who stood yawning by the kitchen door. It was an occasion (one of many, actually) where my status in the city kept the owner from requesting that we leave, that it was late, he had to lock the doors and go to bed. Instead, he waited patiently by the front door, sitting and reading a newspaper, smoking a cigar as he did.

I will not put down our conversation, even if I could remember every word of it, because it went on for hours. I will only say that we spoke of many things as we drank champagne and ate, our eyes gazing intently at one another.

You already know about me so it is not necessary that I repeat my side of the exchange. It is enough to encapsulate her recital, which I drew from her with rapt attention.

Her birthday is August 24, the year unrevealed, nor did I intimate that I wanted it revealed; it is, of course, a lady's prerogative to keep that information to herself, a gentleman's duty to make no effort to uncover the information.

She did reveal to me—an honor, I felt that she trusted me so—that although she tells everyone that she was born in Cincinnati, she was, in fact, born in Alsace, Germany, and her last name was Mersmann. Her parents had immigrated to this country when she was three, settling in Cincinnati, where she grew up.

At the age of sixteen, she met a circus clown named William Lake Thatcher and ran away with him to join the circus. After her husband spent a winter in Mexico with the Rich Circus, leaving her in New Orleans, he barely escaped with his life as *americanos* were not popular at the time. The war between Mexico and the United States was shortly to break out. Completely devoid of funds, the couple returned to Cincinnati, where her parents were not exactly overjoyed to see them.

For a while, the couple struggled with their careers, working in various theatrical companies, then joining the reorganized Rich Circus, where they remained for two years before joining the Spaulding and Rogers Floating Palace. They stayed with this show for eleven seasons, during which period Agnes bore a daughter, Emma, who I would later meet, a charming and highly versatile fourteen-year-old.

The couple and their child rejoined the show Lake had been attached to when Agnes had first met him. When this show did poorly, the Lakes, by now very experienced in the circus business, formed their own show, which succeeded in great part because of Agnes's skill as an equestrienne, lion-tamer, and queen of the high wire.

Their success was marred by tragedy when a patron ejected from the show by Lake returned later and shot him dead.

Her husband's murder was an enormous shock to Agnes, which she was compelled to bear since she was now the sole owner and operator of the circus.

Under her management, the circus prospered, its current tour bringing her to Hays, where she entered my life.

Even though I truly do expect that this account will merely languish on a dusty shelf or, at the very most, receive a limited publication many years after I have taken up residence in the bone orchard, I find most difficult the prospect of revealing the more intimate details of those days with Agnes.

We took drives in the daytime, Agnes with her parasol protecting her face from the blazing rays of the sun.

Sometimes, we would only go for a ride. At other times, we would find a peaceful glade on a stream where we would share a picnic lunch, which either she had packed in a basket hamper or I would have the Leavenworth prepare for us.

There, in the glade, we would converse, hold hands, then, later, share a gentle kiss, a clement embrace.

I went to each and every performance of the circus, naturally, pleased yet somewhat embarrassed when Agnes blew me a kiss as she galloped by, standing on her horse.

More and more, I would come to her wagon at the conclusion of the performance, there to hold her hands, then, later, embrace and kiss her with increasing passion.

We shared candlelight dinners in her wagon, gazing at one another with undisguised infatuation.

Finally, with candles extinguished, we consummated our relationship; I find myself able to say no more; she is, after all, a lady.

All was progressing splendidly, or so I thought. But, then, I have always had a flawless gift for counting my eggs before I even had a chicken.

My Horns Sawed Off Again

I was sitting in my office, whistling cheerily as I opened official mail, when the front door opened.

Looking up, I saw a small, timid-looking man standing in the doorway.

"Mr. Hickok?" he said inquiringly.

"Yes?" I answered.

I saw his Adam's apple bob as he swallowed. "Don't you remember me?" he asked.

I regarded him for a moment or two, then replied, "Can't say I do."

"Charlie Gross, Mr. Hickok," he said. "We knew each other in Homer years ago."

"Ah, of course," I rejoined with not a scintilla of recollection. "How are you, Mr. Gross?"

"I'm fine, Mr. Hickok. Fine," he said. I think he knew that I didn't remember him.

We stared at each other in silence.

"Well," I said.

"I'm a bookkeeper now," he told me. "In Abilene."

"Are you?" I said, politely.

"Yes, sir. I work for Mayor McCoy."

"Ah-ha," I said.

"When I told him that I knew you, he sent me here directly to ask if you'd be our city marshal."

Sure, I thought. *When pigs can fly and robins oink.*

"Your salary would be one hundred and fifty dollars per month plus one quarter of all collected fines; if that would be agreeable."

I smiled, amused.

"That would be entirely agreeable," I began to reply.

"Then may I—?" Charlie Gross broke eagerly into my answer.

"—if I were looking for a new position," I interrupted his interruption.

He opened his mouth to interject, but I continued.

"I am not, however," I informed him. "I am quite content in Hays and fully expect to remain here for the remainder of my life." (Complacency, thy name was Hickok.)

I should have known that my state of affairs was about as lasting as corral dust.

We were lying in my hotel bed, unclad, cuddled close together. That much I'll reveal.

I was feeling petulant.

"I surely wish that you could cancel at least *some* of your engagements, Agnes," I said.

She stroked my hair soothingly, but I wasn't soothed. "I do, too, love," she replied. "You *know* I do. But there are contracts. I'm required to appear with my circus, just as you are under contract to be the brave, wonderful sheriff that you are."

"Oh, I suppose," I answered, grudgingly. As you can see, I still held myself in very high esteem.

"It won't be long, Bill," she assured me. "I'll be back in less than two months, put the circus up for sale, and settle down with you and Emma."

She kissed me tenderly. "And I *will* be Mrs. Wild Bill Hickok before I leave Hays," she said.

I nodded, sighing. "Two months, though," I said.

"I'll write you every day, Bill," she promised. "Every single day in the week. And maybe you can take some time off from your important duties to come and visit me. Or maybe I can take some time off and see you here—or, meet you someplace."

I sighed again. She kissed me again.

"It won't be bad, my love, my precious Bill," she said. "In two short months, we'll be together permanently—Mr. and Mrs. Wild Bill Hickok. We'll buy some property, build a home, settle in for good, maybe even have another child."

She hugged me enthusiastically, face radiant with anticipation.

"Oh, it's going to work out, Bill!" she almost cried aloud. "You'll see! I'll make it work! For my Bill, my Wild Bill."

I remember clearing my throat, wondering whether to say it, then deciding that I must. "You, uh, *know* . . . that my real name is James," I told her, wanting her to see me more as myself than as the dime novel hero.

"*Is* it, love?" said Agnes languidly.

"Yes," I continued. "James Butler Hickok. Of the Warwickshire Hiccocks in England." I cleared my throat again. "A noble line," I said.

"Oh, I'm sure it is, Bill," she replied. She laughed, amused by her unwitting mistake. "I'm afraid you'll always be Bill to me," she said. She sighed with happiness. "My Wild Bill Hickok."

I felt myself withdraw inside. *Not the right time yet,* I thought.

"I've read that you've killed hundreds of men," Agnes said, startling me. She shuddered with excitement, I could tell. "That isn't true, is it?" she asked in a tone that told me she hoped I would say it was true.

"Well," I answered, awkwardly, not really knowing what to say. "That may be cutting it a little fat."

"How many were there?" she inquired timorously.

What to say? I wondered. *Lie? Tell the truth?*

"Let's just say I've lost count," I told her. Even as I spoke, I winced within.

"My God, what a man you are," said Agnes. "What a *man*."

Stimulated, flushed, she turned to face me, kissing me passionately.

"Oh, Bill," she said, breathing with effort. "Bill. *Lover*."

"Yes," was all I could manage.

"I *love* you, Bill!" she said. "I worship you! I'll make you so happy! I will, I *will*!"

"Agnes," I responded, barely able to speak. I did love her something powerful. I hated having to spread the mustard with her, but I didn't want to disillusion her, either.

We pressed together in passionate liaison.

Abruptly, then, we twitched and looked around in startlement as gunfire erupted somewhere down in the street; the drunken hoot and raucous laughter of a man, the shattering of glass.

"My God, what's *that*?" gasped Agnes.

I didn't reply, staring uncomfortably toward the window.

Agnes rose and moved in that direction. "Be careful," I told her. "Best not . . ." my voice trailed into silence as she continued to the window.

Outside, the shooting, hoots, shouts of laughter, and shattering of glass continued.

"There's a man on Main Street," Agnes told me.

I heard another shot and the crash of breaking glass.

"He's shooting out store windows," she told me.

"Oh?" I said.

Another shot, another crash of glass.

"And a lamppost," Agnes described.

A shot. A yelp.

"And a dog," she said.

She turned back and moved to the bedside, looking down expectantly.

"Well," I said, feigning a tone of mild exasperation, "I guess I'd better take a look."

She smiled at me with adoration.

"They're so lucky to have you for the sheriff here," she said. "Someone could get hurt."

I felt certain that my smile was somber. "I know," I agreed.

As slowly as I could without being transparent in my reluctance, I dressed and left the room with Agnes's plea to "Be careful, Bill" in my ear as I descended the stairs to the lobby. By then, silence had fallen.

Three guests plus the desk clerk were down there, peering outside. As they turned to face me, I yawned extravagantly. "Did I hear gunfire?" I asked.

They stared at me as though to say, in mutual incredulity, "You did unless you're stone deaf."

"What's been going on?" I inquired casually.

The desk clerk answered me, "A soldier's been burning powder," he said. "Shot out nine store windows, broke six streetlights, wounded two dogs, one cat, and a midget."

That made me blink. "A *midget*?" I said.

"From the circus," the desk clerk explained. "Took a slug right in his tiny butt."

"Interesting," I said. "Curious I slept through all that."

The repressed grin of the desk clerk suggested to me that he didn't find my physical exhaustion curious at all; I had tried to get Agnes to my room in such a manner as to preserve her reputation but did not always succeed. I pretended not to notice his smirk but moved to the doorway and peered outside. "Soldier gone now, is he?" I asked, trying to disguise my hopefulness.

"No, sir," said the clerk. "He's in Kate Coffee's place. Claims he's going to shoot the whole damn town up, make a fool of you."

"Oh?" I said; I felt my stomach walls begin to close in on my dinner. I cleared my throat to hide my swallow. "Well, we'd better see about that."

I felt a tremor of excited expectation from the desk clerk and the three hotel guests.

I stepped outside and started along the plank walk, moving against my will toward Kate Coffee's Saloon. I drew in a deep breath, pulled back my shoulders, and strode as erectly as I could, looking straight ahead. *He's just a soldier,* I consoled myself. *When he sees who he's up against, he'll quail and back off fast.*

Notwithstanding, I paused outside Kate Coffee's batwing doors to peer inside.

A number of men were clustered at the counter, talking in excited murmurs. Ralph caught sight of me and smiled with great relief, gesturing hurriedly for me to enter.

Bracing myself, I pushed open the swinging doors and went inside. The men at the bar descended on me like a pack of vultures sighting dead meat.

"Thank God you're here, sheriff!" said one of them, as quietly as he could, considering his mad exhilaration.

"We been looking for you everywhere!" another said, equally deranged by eagerness.

"Well, I was—" I began.

"He's in the back room, Mr. Hickok," said Ralph, flapping in to join his fellow vultures. "Dead drunk. Mean as hell. Says he's going to—"

"Yes, I heard, I heard," I said, cutting off his melodrama.

I looked toward the back room. Everyone looked at me, contemplating gunfire. I planned to disappoint them on that score, boogering the soldier into frightened submission. I started away from them.

"Better not kill him, sheriff!" said one of the men. "He's a captain in the cavalry!"

"I'll try not to," I responded, hoping that they didn't hear the disparagement in my voice. I started forward again.

Ralph whispered after me, "Says he's Custer's brother!"

I froze in midstep; stood there like a statue on a town square: Sheriff Hickok Above His Head.

"Sheriff?" said Ralph.

No answer from yours truly.

"Mr. Hickok?"

When I didn't stir—paralyzed by indecision—Ralph moved up behind me and tapped me on the shoulder. I had never in my life before taken leave of my skin, but I very nearly did at that instant, jerking out both pistols in the fastest draw of my life, and whirling in the quickest spin.

Ralph recoiled with a stricken gasp, and the men scuttled backward like a startled multiform crab.

"Don't . . . *do* that!" I whispered fiercely to Ralph.

"Sorry, Mr. Hickok," he apologized, backing off to join the men. I glared at all of them; for the moment, they represented, to me, the major source of my troubles.

"Stand back!" I ordered them in a hoarse whisper. "Just . . . *stand back*."

"Yes, sir," they said as one man, retreating, again, as one crab.

I made an angry, hissing sound and turned back toward The Room of Peril, staring at it gloomily.

I forced myself to edge forward then, pistols extended. I could almost feel the beady-eyed stares of the men on my back as they hoped for the best (for them), an eruption of exchanged gunshots, a body (preferably dead) sprawled on the floor, an eyewitness thrill of watching Wild Bill in bloody action.

I hesitated, looking down now at my Colts. I could not allow it to appear that I was taking unfair advantage over

Tom Custer; that was alien to my prestige. Reluctantly, I pushed them loosely back beneath the waistband of my trousers; I'd had no time to don my sash. My face twitched as I struggled to repress a stomach eructation.

Reaching the bead curtains that separated the main saloon from its back room, I peered inside, reacting to what I saw—and instantly suppressing that reaction.

Tom Custer had passed out cold on a chair, his upper body sprawled across a table.

I shut my eyes, releasing a cheek-puffing exhalation of relief.

I was about to turn and tell the men when, suddenly, a thought occurred to me. I didn't like it but could not dissuade myself from it. I turned, face adamantine, and flicked the wrist of my right hand in a signal for the men to step back. They did so, eyes widening, breath bated. Life and death was on the line; they knew it, they loved it.

After they had completed their backward movement, I turned and, standing tall, pushed through the bead curtains, wincing at the slight rattling noise they made, bracing myself in the event that the noise awakened Custer.

It didn't. Bracing myself further, I said, in a loud, ringing voice, "I'll have that pistol, captain!"

I mimicked a drunkenly rumbling reply, "Like h———l you will."

"I'd just as soon not pull down on you, captain!" I emoted as myself again. "I respect the uniform you're wearing but I don't—"

I broke off, stunned, as Custer stirred and began to sit up.

Jerking out one of my pistols, I laid its barrel across his skull and he collapsed back onto the table.

"Sorry—!" I gurgled. I cleared my throat as quickly and softly as I could. "Sorry I had to do that, captain!" I cried out, nobly.

Then I swallowed hard and had to gulp down several times in order to regain my breath. I belched softly and hiccupped seven times before controlling my system at last and turning back toward the main room of the saloon.

I came out, an expression of sovereign command on my face; I could still do that to a fare-thee-well.

"Will two of you boys carry the captain down to the jail for me?" I asked.

I moved toward the exit as the men came galloping to see what had occurred to Captain Custer.

I knew they would be disappointed at the lack of blood.

Tom Custer's fingers gripped the cell bars so tightly that they were white, drained of blood. There was a purplish lump on his forehead where I had clouted him. His face was a living testament to homicidal rage.

"I'm telling you, Hickok," he muttered, "you better clear out of Hays right now, because when my brother gets me out today, I'm going to curl you up, you hear me? I'm going to *kill you dead.*"

I stood before the cell, regarding him in silence.

"You *hear* me?" Custer shouted.

I turned away, then stopped as he continued ranting.

"You may have everybody else bamboozled, but you don't have me!" he said. "Because I know what you really are! A *coward*, Hickok!"

His voice became a slow, grinding, knife-twisting sneer as he continued, "A yellow-bellied, white-livered, spineless, two-bit, no-good, big-talking s———t of a coward!"

My heart was pounding as I looked down at my right hand.

It was clutched around the stock of a half-drawn pistol.

Appalled to find myself in this revealing state, I shoved the pistol back beneath my sash and moved abruptly toward the doorway to my office, ignoring Custer's further words.

I shut the door to the cellblock, locked it, and pulled the key loose, trembling, shaken to the core by what I had been—without thinking—on the verge of doing.

A gentleman about to commit murder?

Moving to my desk, I sat down heavily behind it and opened a lower cabinet, removing from it a glass and a bottle of whiskey. Pouring myself a large drink, I downed it hurriedly, then sat there gazing into troubled thoughts.

Approximately twenty minutes later, I exited the office and locked the front door, dropping the key ring into my coat pocket as I started down the street.

When I arrived at the circus grounds, Agnes was rehearsing Emma for her specialty horseback act.

Seeing me, she ran over and we came together in a fiery embrace and kiss. I did not usually care to display my passion in front of others, but there was no time for niceties at that moment.

"I heard what you did last night," she said.

"It was nothing," I replied, distractedly.

"Nothing!" she cried. "My *God,* what a man!"

I held her tightly, dreading that it was the last time I would ever see her.

Then I said, "Agnes?"

"Yes, love?" she responded, drawing away to smile at me.

I hesitated, then got it out. "I'm leaving Hays today," I told her.

She caught her breath. *"Today?"* she said. Then, "Why, Bill? Why?"

I tried not to swallow but couldn't help it.

"Well, you see," I explained, "I've been offered the position of city marshal in Abilene—at a considerable raise in salary."

"Well . . . yes, I understand," she said, obviously trying to do so. "But . . . why do you have to leave today? So suddenly?"

"Well, you see," I responded, "they have no marshal at the moment, and they're in dreadful need of one."

"I see," she murmured. Was she convinced? I doubt it, because she quickly added, "But what about our marriage? Can't you delay your departure a day or so for *that*?"

"Well—" Lord, I sounded unconvincing! "I rather promised them, you see. Signed a contract."

"I see," she murmured. "I just wonder . . . why you didn't tell me before."

"I had no chance," I lied. "Their message just arrived today."

"Mm-hmm," she said.

Heavy silence weighed us down. I was terribly uncomfortable at her expression: one of disappointment mingled with a palpable suspicion that I was running out on her.

She tensed as I put my arms around her.

"We'll write each other every day," I said. "And your circus *is* scheduled for Abilene, isn't it?"

"Not for quite a while," she answered.

"Well, I'll be waiting for you there," I said as reassuringly as possible. "All right?"

She did not respond.

"All right, Agnes?" I asked.

She tried to smile; it was extremely forced. "All right," she said, "if you have to go."

"I really do," I said in my expansive tone. "They're rather in a muddle there, it seems. Need a firm grip on the city reins," I finished with my famous crooked smile.

She nodded again, her smile even more strained. I kissed her, held her close.

"Don't fret now, Agnes," I told her. "Everything is going to be all right."

It was not a hand I would have bet on.

Fording a stream a few miles out of town, I reined in,

took the ring of keys from my pocket, and tossed it into the water, then rode on.

"And so, his work well done," Nichols later wrote, "Hays City now a peaceful, law-abiding township, Hickok rode on to his next appointment with historic destiny: Abilene."

Out of the Frying Pan

Of Abilene it was written: "There is no law and no restraint in this seething caldron of vice and depravity."

A perfect place for me to be the city marshal. Fortunately—or unfortunately depending on one's point of view—I didn't know how bad the place was when I went there. If I had, I doubt if I would have gone. Where I would have traveled is anyone's guess. Back into the wilderness, perhaps. At least it would have been safer than in what we naively label civilization.

Now that it is all concluded, I can quote extensively without my hair turning white as it well might have done had I been aware of these quotations prior to my journey to Abilene.

"It is a place where men shoot off their mouths and guns both day and night."

"Money and whiskey flow like water downhill."

"Youth and beauty and womanhood and manhood are wrecked and d———ed in that valley of perdition."

"Plenty of rotten whiskey and everything to excite the passions are freely indulged in."

"Here you may see young girls not over sixteen drinking whiskey, smoking cigars, cursing and swearing, until one almost loses respect for the weaker sex."

Pure heaven on earth for a gentleman descended from the noble line of Hiccocks of Warwickshire, England.

Thank God I had no idea what was in store for me. Or, were I inclined to profaning: d———m God for keeping it a secret from me.

The darkest irony of said secret being that the year I was there was the concluding year of Abilene's supremacy as a cow town.

Named after the biblical city, the Tetrards of Abilene, the city was, a mere four years before my arrival, no more than a frontier village. If only, for my sake, it had remained one—although, of course, in that event, they would not have needed a city marshal in the first place.

Then Joseph McCoy, searching for a location that would serve as a shipping point for cattle, found Abilene, which, as he described it, was "a very small, dead place consisting of about one dozen log huts." It was, however, situated in the middle of grassland and water. Therefore, it was but a matter of time before he had seen to the construction of a barn, a livery stable, an office, a hotel, a bank and, most important, a thousand-head-capacity shipping yard. Negotiations with the Union Pacific Railway Company followed.

Within a year, the log hut settlement had become a city to which cattle herds were driven in constantly increasing numbers.

By the time I arrived, hundreds of drovers (some called them cowboys or cowpokes or cowprodders or cowpunchers, etcetera) were nursing tens of thousands of cattle to Abilene in preparation for their long train ride to Chicago stockyards. These drovers, after spending months on the trail, wished only to "let her rip."

Riding into Abilene in April 1871, I took a look around what was to be my new domain. I was not, in any way, expecting the peaceful time I had in Hays.

Running east and west and parallel to the railroad tracks was Texas Street. Its main intersecting thoroughfare was Cedar Street, off that street the smaller one named A Street, at the end of which was Drovers Cottage (no cottage but a three-story hotel) and the Shane and Henry Real Estate office.

North of the railroad were the dance halls and the brothels. These, too, would be of concern to me since drovers were, as always, a natural prey for gamblers, pimps, and prostitutes as well as rotgut whiskey and, on occasion, lead poisoning.

In Mayor McCoy's office, the worthy gentleman pinned the city marshal's badge on my vest and declared, "With the authority vested in me as mayor of Abilene, I now appoint you city marshal."

I shook hands with him and with my deputy, Mike Williams.

"Congratulations, Mr. Hickok!" the mayor said. "Or should I say Marshal Hickok!" He laughed. "We're delighted that you changed your mind!"

He leaned in close to confide in me: "As for myself," he told me, "I feel that I can finally draw an easy breath now that you are in charge. Hays City's misfortune in losing you is Abilene's good luck."

"Thank you, mayor," I responded in my accredited florid wont. "I shall certainly do everything in my power to earn your praise."

"I'm sure you will, marshal," the mayor replied elatedly.

"Congratulations, marshal!" Williams said.

"Thank you," I responded. "And now, if I could see my office."

"Yes, sir, marshal!" Williams cried; he had a minimum of teeth, I noticed. "Right away!"

Leaving the mayor's office, we walked down Texas Street to the jailhouse, a fortlike structure built of stone.

"First building in the whole d———n town made entirely of stone!" Williams informed me; I noticed, as well, that he invariably shouted rather than spoke. I suspect that he was on his way to deafness, though he never mentioned such a failing.

"Why stone?" I asked him as we went inside.

"Used to have a wooden one!" he answered. "Drovers used to pull it down with ropes!"

He chortled merrily. "Those Texans, they're like wild gorillas when they come in off the trail!"

I glanced around the interior with its beat-up, rolltop desk, an oil lamp on its top along with some obviously never-used law volumes. A chair sat in front of the desk, a spittoon on the floor, an old rifle and a plethora of wanted posters hanging on the walls. Versailles it was not.

"Yes, sir!" Williams continued. "Them Texans are a bunch of maddened creatures, they are! In April, the city population is five hundred! By June, it's up to seven thousand with the drovers! Sleep everywhere, they do! In houses, hotels, tents, or in blankets on the ground! D———n, they're loco! Yelling like Comanches! They'll do anything! *Anything!* So tough they'd fight a rattlesnake and give it two bites to start! Just wait! You'll see!"

"How interesting," I told him, the old stomach walls contracting once again.

"Old Tom Smith kept them all in line, though!" Williams said.

"My predecessor?" I observed.

"Your *what*?" asked Williams.

"The man who was marshal before me," I said.

"Yes, sir! *Yes,* sir!" Williams said. "That was him! Old Tom Smith! Never even used his pistols either! Did it with his *bare hands,* with his *fists*!"

Smart man, I thought.

"Sure glad they got *you* to replace him, Mr. Hickok, *Marshal* Hickok! Ain't no one else I know of who could handle Abilene! No, sir! This place is like a crazy house come shipping season!" He cackled wildly. "It'll take a man like you to fill old Tom Smith's shoes and that's a fact!"

"What made him leave?" I asked.

"Didn't leave! Never left!" said Williams. "Got hisself all chopped up by an ax, he did!" He grunted grimly at the memory. "Almost took the head right off his shoulders!"

I stared at him in silence. *Thanks for telling me,* I thought.

Several minutes later, I was walking numbly down the plank walk, staring straight ahead. I didn't see the woman's face as I was passing her.

"Bill!" she cried.

My twitch was so violent as I jerked around with a gasp, clutching for one of my pistols, that the woman flinched and backed off sharply, gaping at me; at which point I recognized her.

"Susannah," I said.

"Bill Hickok. Of all people." She was smiling now. "What are you doing in Abilene?"

I shuddered.

"I'm the city marshal," I told her.

"Well, isn't that exciting!" she said. She stroked my arm. "I've missed you since Springfield," she murmured. "I hope I see you again."

I swallowed, my throat as dry as desert dust.

"I'm sure you will," I lied.

I sat in my hotel room, writing a letter to Agnes.

"Well, I have arrived in Abilene and everything looks fine."

I'd like to tell her the truth, I thought, but, of course, that was impossible.

"Although my task as city marshal promises to be a stiff one, I foresee no problems." All I *did* foresee were problems.

"I have handled worser situations in my day and I expect—"

I stopped writing. *Worser situations?* I thought. *What brought that on?* Was I trying to coarsen my image to her as well? If so, it was a stupid effort.

I stood up from the table and walked to the window. My room was on the third floor of the Cottage and from its vantage point, I could see across Abilene, out to the plains. I gazed toward the south, visualizing the cloud of dust that would give evidence of the first cattle drive approaching from Texas. The vision chilled me. In my mind, I heard Mike Williams chirruping, *"Just wait! You'll see!"*

I shivered convulsively. *"This place is like a crazy house come shipping season!"* I heard, in memory, Mike Williams's crazed remark. *"A crazy house!"* My stomach made a noise. It was preparing for the onslaught.

It is truly indescribable, the Entry of the Drovers. (I think of it as some insanely operatic scene.)

First, as noted, comes the cloud of dust. Then the drum and rumble of hoofbeats, which come closer and closer.

Then, at last, the horde of wild-eyed drovers gallop into town, screaming and whooping, hurling their hats, and shooting their pistols into the air, as they charge down

Texas Street, rein up death defyingly, leap down, and charge into saloons, dance halls, and brothels, intent on abandon of every sort and vice of all varieties.

This was now my world.

It was my first night on the job. All establishments devoted to depravity were filled to capacity and beyond. The air was alive with shouts and laughter, singing and tinkling pianos, shots and sounds of breaking glass.

I was sitting in the jailhouse with all lights extinguished. Coat off, unarmed, drinking steadily, shaking so much that the bottle neck rattled on the lip of my glass as I poured, whiskey spilling on the desk. I felt a face tic jumping on my right cheek at particularly alarming noises on the street.

I tensed as someone came running along the walk and tried to open the door, which I had locked some hours earlier.

"Marshal!" I heard Mike Williams call.

I flinched as he knocked on the door. "Marshal Hickok?" he asked. "You in there?" He was silent, then said, "J———s C———t, where *is* he?"

I started as he shouted to someone, "Hey, Sam, you seen the marshal?"

"Ain't he in his office?" Sam shouted back.

"No, he ain't!" cried Mike.

"What about the Cottage?"

"Ain't there, either!" Mike responded. "Nor any other place I looked! God d———n it! He's supposed to do the night patrols, not me! Oh . . . *hell*!"

I heard his running footsteps move away. *Thank God he doesn't have a duplicate key for the door,* was all I could think.

I poured myself another drink and downed it in a swallow, coughing at the fiery flare in my throat.

Then I froze as two men started talking just outside the door. *Oh, God,* I wondered, *had they heard me cough?*

"Hey, Bob, you seen the marshal?" one of them asked; it sounded like Sam.

"No. Why?" Bob asked. "What's up?"

"He's supposed to be patrolling," Sam responded. "Just talking now with Mike Williams. Says he can't find Hickok anywhere."

"That's odd," said Bob. "Don't sound like Hickok. 'Less he's with a girl or something."

"Or he's *scared,*" replied Sam.

"Hickok *scared*?" said Bob. "You crazy? Man, he's not afraid of *anything*! You know that, Sam!"

"Well . . ." Sam faltered. "Where is he then?"

Nothing more was said and their footsteps moved away. Standing, I began to pace, then after a while, caught sight of myself in a wall mirror and, stopping, gazed at my shadowy reflection. I felt something rising in me, something dark and filled with corrosive bile.

"A gentleman does not show panic when in danger," I muttered to myself, my tone a caustic one.

My breath shook suddenly and I began to punch the wall at every repetition of the word *gentleman*.

"A *gentleman* does not show panic when in danger. A *gentleman* does not show panic when in danger." My voice was now savage. "A *gentleman* does not—!"

I broke off with a sob of pain and clutched at my right hand, trembling strengthlessly, staring at my dark reflection in the mirror.

"Coward," I snarled.

The word impacted on me violently, acting as a purgative, and, whirling, I staggered to the trash basket where I lost the contents of my stomach in gagging spasms, doubled over like a man just gut shot.

At last, I straightened up and lit the oil lamp. Moving to the table by the wall, I poured some water into the pan and washed off my face, rinsing out my mouth.

I dried myself, then walked to the wall rack, took down my coat and donned it, putting on my hat then, watching myself in the mirror as I adjusted my tie, my features ashen, like the face of an unfamiliar statue.

I moved to the desk and picked up my brace of Colts, thrusting them beneath my sash. I poured myself an inch of whiskey, took a swallow of it, then put down the glass and turned for the door.

Unlocking it, I came out and shut the door again, relocking it. I turned my gaze toward Texas Street, that suburb of Dante's Inferno.

Drawing in a long and cheek-expanding breath of air, I started to walk along the plank walk, only semiconscious of where or who I was, knowing only one thing: that I had to make that walk or die.

Reaching the first saloon, I moved aside and stopped, gazing with apparent apathy at the festivities before me. The din decreased and I became aware of murmuring voices, of reactions. "It's *Hickok*!" "It's *Wild Bill*!" "It's the *marshal*!"

The saloon did not grow deathly still, but the contrast between its babel as I'd entered and its present sound was extreme; so much so that I thought I heard my stomach gurgling. Turning, I left.

Outside, I continued down the walk, moving with a passing semblance of calm, and went into the next saloon, stopping, once more, just inside the entrance, evincing the same reaction, the ratio of noise to silence altering noticeably. Once again, the voices, murmuring, "It's Marshal Hickok!" "Wild Bill!" "It's *Hickok*!" Once again I stood in silence, moving an arctic gaze across the room, focusing on no one. Then I left.

My first patrol was—albeit only partially aware—an unqualified success.

My reputation had preceded me well. That plus my

stiffly ominous appearance, caused to a large extent by petrifyingly suppressed terror, brought me deference wherever I went.

As my patrol progressed, I walked more and more erectly and with mounting poise, my stride that of a king en route to his coronation, its pace no doubt in rhythm with some regal pomp.

Later, I returned to my room at the Cottage, locked the door and, in silence, removed my hat, coat, pistols, sash, and vest, my face still set in the imperious expression I effected on my patrol.

I unbuttoned my shirt and removed it. Face unchanging, I began to wring it out; it was so soaked with sweat, it might have just been washed. I listened to the dripping perspiration on the floor, trying to avoid considering what I would have done had anyone challenged me.

"Thus," wrote Nichols consequently, "did Hickok—quickly and irrevocably—establish his omnipotence in Abilene."

"Never did a man confronted by such overwhelming odds behave with such composure and authority."

I kept two bottles of whiskey in my desk in case one of them ran out unexpectedly. Before going out on patrol, I drank enough to ossify my nerves. What the townspeople took for granite sovereignty was, in fact, paralysis by liquor.

"Each night, he patrolled on Texas Street, his dominion absolute."

Stiff-faced with inebriation, I strode the walks, unchallenged. (Well, almost.) I suppose it was my pistols and my assumed willingness to utilize them should the need arise that kept Abilene more or less under control that summer, which was its greatest and its last season as the cattle shipping center of the nation.

I had, some time before, come to the realization that my

long, drooping mustaches and shoulder-length hair looked absurdly affected but, by then, I also realized that they were part of my imposing persona and I was stuck with them, not wanting to take any risk of weakening that image in any way. Too bad. I would have enjoyed an extended visit to the nearest barber shop.

So, long-haired and fully mustached, fortified with stomach pills and whiskey, I walked abroad on Abilene's h ———lish streets, maintaining as menacing a posture as I could with my stomach rumbling like Vesuvius.

I said *almost* unchallenged for, on a number of occasions, attempts were made to bushwhack me. Fortunately, the aim of your average drover leaves a lot to be desired, and the pistol balls aimed at putting a window in my skull usually whistled by my head or slammed into a nearby wall, causing me to take a startled header and hide behind whatever might be handy, whether it was a hay bale, a water barrel, or horse trough.

"Never did a man endure such daily peril with such utter equanimity."

I shaved in my room, not trusting a barber shop with its chair backs to the entrance, nor my reaction time, should I note an attack reflected in the mirror. Even in my room, I angled my mirror to reflect the locked door, my pistols close at hand, my hand at times so palsied that I nicked my skin more than once.

"Never flustered, never disconcerted, Hickok faced his day-by-day duties with that calm sobriety of purpose for which he is so justly famous."

I had begun to supplement my artillery with a pair of Remington derringers, which I kept in my vest pockets, one on each side, concealed beneath my frock coat. The two Colts I maintained as always underneath my sash and, as always, I maintained in my system two glasses of whiskey before essaying out each evening.

"Night after night did this man of steel discharge his obligations with unswerving zeal."

My face congealed by alcoholism, I paced the plank walks of Texas Street, no longer entering alleys, having come close to being shot in those dark passages.

Even when I stayed on the *main drag,* as the drovers called it, a badly aimed shot might shatter a nearby window, causing me to fling myself plankward, panicked eyes searching for the source of the shot and never finding it.

"Week after week did Hickok display his courage and unyielding stamina."

By August, when I shaved, my cheeks and throat were festooned with fragments of blood-soaked paper. More often than not, I would sling aside my razor in a fury of frustration, yearning to lean back in a barber chair and have a barber's steady hand slice off my whiskers, not—as I was doing—shards of my epidermis.

I was, by then, so far into foreboding that I wore my sash on my long johns, one of my Colts beneath it for immediate use, if needed.

I had, in addition, purchased a shotgun and hacksaw, cutting the double barrel short. This I carried slung across my left shoulder, still packing the pair of derringers in my vest pockets and my two Colt revolvers under my sash.

I could feel my body sag with each new arsenal addition. One afternoon, draining an oversize glass of whiskey, I tilted back so far that I lost balance and crashed to the floor, spilling whiskey on myself.

"Texas Street became the unchallenged kingdom of this Prince of Pistoleers, the all-encompassing domain of this gun master of the border, whose name shall always be emblazoned in the annals of the West: Wild Bill Hickok!"

Thus I trod the boards of my domain, if the overweighted, drunken hobble I managed to achieve can be considered walking. I skulked from shadow to shadow, moving hastily past doors, windows, and alley entrances.

It was an evening in early September that, stepping off the walk to cross the street, I lost my balance and tumbled to the ground. Pushing to my feet, infuriated and, of course, embarrassed, I muttered to myself as follows:

"To h————l with this patrolling s————t! Let toothless do it! From now on, I stay inside!"

I groaned and whispered fiercely, "J————s C————t and twelve disciples, I must weigh a *ton* with all this s————t on!"

I hobbled on, stumbled on a street rut, almost fell again. "J————s C————t!" I snarled, not even caring anymore who saw or heard me.

Nichols, you're an idiot!

The End of the World

From that day forth, the location of my office changed to the Alamo Saloon, which was more in keeping with my taste and disposition; they even had an orchestra, by God, playing forenoons, afternoons, and evenings. Just the place for yours truly, J. B. Hickok of the Warwickshire Hiccocks.

There I spent the bulk of my time playing poker, my back to the wall (a habit I had taken up out of self-preservation), a bottle of whiskey and a pistol at close hand on the table.

I even had the time to read an interesting book about one of my favorite subjects: cards.

I learned that, from a fifty-two card deck, it is possible to deal 2,598,960 different five-card hands. Of those hands, 1,088,240 will contain a pair, 123,000 will contain two pairs, 54,912 will contain three of a kind, 10,200 will contain straights, 5,108 will contain flushes, 3,744 will contain full houses, 624 will contain four of a kind, 36 will contain straight flushes, and (no wonder I've never drawn one) 4 will contain royal flushes.

I was interested to learn that playing cards were derived from the tarot fortune-telling deck, cups, wands, coins, and swords becoming hearts, clubs, diamonds, and spades, kings and queens remaining, but knights becoming jacks.

During the French Revolution, kings, queens, and jacks were removed from the card deck (too Royalist) and replaced by nature, liberty, and virtue; hearts, clubs, spades, and diamonds becoming peace, war, art, and commerce. I suspect it made betting somewhat complicated.

I also suspect that I am taking up space to avoid continuing with my story—and the worst experience of my life.

"The first major challenge to the iron rule of Abilene's marshal occurred one day in the fall of 1871. Hickok was, as customary, working in his office when it began."

I pushed several chips across the table. "See you twenty and raise you ten," I said, deeply involved in marshaling duties.

I glanced toward one of the doorways as Mike Williams came in. The deputy's attitude toward me had changed somewhat since I had converted my patrols to poker games; not exactly disrespectful, but not as impressed anymore. I had decided I could live with that, the key word being *live*.

He came up to the table. "Marshal?" he said.

"I'm here," I answered, peering closely at my cards; I was seeing them a tad more blurrily those days.

"Could I talk to you?" he asked.

"I'm right here; talk," I told him curtly.

"In private?" he asked.

I started to flare, then held it back. Standing, I picked up my Colt and slid it underneath my sash as we moved into an empty corner.

"Well?" I asked.

"Town council has laid down the law. Faro tables in the Bull's Head Tavern can't stay in the back room anymore; too many complaints about cheating."

I stared at him, considering whether to object to the order. Then, seeing that I couldn't, I scowled and turned toward the street.

As we walked along the plank walk, Williams said, "Mayor also said the 'no guns while in town' rule isn't being strictly enforced."

I shook my head, affecting irritation. "That's ridiculous," I said. "Any man who wears a gun might have to face me in a showdown. In light of that, how many men are wearing guns in town?"

"A lot," said Mike.

He winced as I glared at him.

"It's what the mayor says, not me," he told me.

"Well . . ." I grumped, "the mayor's wrong."

Mike sighed. "If you say so," he responded. I tried to ignore the obvious disappointment in his voice and manner.

We turned in at the Bull's Head Tavern. One of the owners, Ben Thompson, gave me pause; I'd heard about him, nothing good.

But we were there, and I couldn't very well back down. *Time to play the role again,* the thought occurred; *the Prince of Pistoleers in action once more.*

The other owner of the Bull's Head, Phil Coe, was taller than me, better-looking than me, stronger-looking than me; I hadn't counted on any of this. When I informed him of the mayor's wish, he only glared at me.

I didn't really want to, but I turned to his partner, Ben Thompson, a square-jawed, burly, black-haired, blue-eyed, inky walrus-mustached Englishman.

"I beg your pardon?" he inquired coldly.

I was, of course, aware of their hostility but, at the same time, I was now possessed of the numbing self-delusion that, whatever the situation, no one would stand up, face-to-face, with Wild Bill Hickok, since no one ever had since I arrived in Abilene. At that moment, I'm afraid the legend was propelling the man.

"The faro tables have to come out from the back room," I repeated, knowing that he'd heard me perfectly well.

"Do they, now?" he said in the iciest voice I'd ever heard.

"They do," I said, starting for the back room.

I knew the sound behind me and froze; it was that of a pistol pulled from its holster. Clearly, I could not defend myself and could only hope that whoever had drawn the pistol wasn't the sort to shoot a man in the back.

Very slowly, I turned back. It was Thompson, his revolver pointed at my chest.

"What are you doing?" I asked as though I didn't know.

"What does it look like I'm doing?" Thompson answered with a question.

The oddest thing about the moment was that I really couldn't believe he was opposing me.

"Put the gun away," I said, fully expecting compliance.

I twitched as Thompson stepped forward and jabbed the end of his pistol barrel into my stomach.

"You don't seem to catch my meaning, *marshal*," he said and —oddly again—I was very much aware of the refinement of his English accent. The thought flitted across my mind of telling him that my family line went back to Warwickshire.

"The faro tables stay in back," he informed me.

He jabbed the barrel end into my stomach even harder.

"What's more," he said, "if I see you on the streets at any time from this day forth, I shall take the extreme pleasure of blowing out your guts."

Another jab; it hurt. "You *understand*?" he demanded.

I was riven to the spot, my expression—I'm sure—as indecipherable as my thoughts. For a while, I couldn't seem to determine whether to stand or retreat.

Then the soft but audible gurgle of impending nausea

in me revealed to them—and worse, much worse, to me—
that the self-delusion had been shattered.

I saw Coe smiling with contempt. I noted my deputy
staring at me unbelievingly, the remainder of his respect
fading fast. I stood immobile for several moments longer,
returning Thompson's ominous gaze.

Then I said, in a hoarse and unconvincing murmur,
"This isn't over," and, trying to summon (and failing) a
look of dignified aplomb, I turned and headed for the front
door.

The sound of Coe beginning to chuckle came close to
making me whirl and draw, the agony it gave me so severe as to wipe away all sense of fear. The moment ended
quickly, evidenced by little more than a tensing of my body
as I continued across the room. I did not fully realize it at
that moment, but my world had just collapsed.

Tarantula Juice Interval

In the event the reader of this chronicle (if, in fact, there are any) fails to comprehend the title of this section, let me pass along the following piece of information.

Booze has a multiplicity of names.

It seems to be a characteristic of man that, where it comes to his most profound weaknesses, he cannot help but create endless words for same. Why this is so, I cannot say. Perhaps men's fascinations need many means of depiction because men speak of them so often that they must have varied ways of accomplishing it lest boredom set in. Perhaps they are compelled to derive an infinite number of ways to describe them because they are obsessed with them. Or perhaps, fearing their compulsions, they devise endless ways of portraying them in order to dilute inner fear with outer words.

Whatever the reason, man certainly does have multiple descriptions for killing, sex, and liquor. Being a gentleman, I will not essay to enumerate the many sobriquets for sexual parts and congress; the reader can supply these from immediate memory.

Killing people (men primarily) has, of course, its ready lexicon of terms such as: bed him down, curl him up, down him, kick him into a funeral procession, make wolf meat of him, serve him up brown, wipe him out, put him in the wooden overcoat, and such.

For liquor: brave maker, bug juice, coffin varnish, dynamite, gut warmer, leopard sweat, pop skull, prairie dew, snake poison, sudden death, tonsil paint, and, as already noted, tarantula juice.

I had no use whatever for all the words comprising death descriptions. I confined myself to the two remaining areas of man's ruling passions. In brief, in the following weeks, I drank without cease and remained in bed the better part of each day and night in the company of any soiled dove I could purchase or lure to my room.

The shade was drawn, the room in shadows. I had come to eschew the sunlight in any way I could.

I was abed with Susannah Moore, who I had not seen in my early days in Abilene, wishing to remain as faithful as I could to Agnes.

Now she was back in my life, one of many I craved to provide physical and mental surcease from unending depression.

I must have looked a tragic sight: red-eyed, unshaven, unbathed, uncombed, and generally disreputable in appearance. Even Susannah, not exactly a paragon of judgment, seemed to recognize my wanting state.

"Bill, you can't stay up here *all* the time," she told me, "Everybody's talking, saying you're afraid of Thompson. Phil Coe's telling everybody you're a coward."

"Shut up," was all I said; slurred and barely understandable.

"You're not afraid of Thompson, are you?" asked Susannah. "Are you? After all the men you've killed?"

"Shut *up*," I repeated.

"You've killed hundreds of men," she told me. "How can one man—"

I stopped her lips with mine, kissing her with brutal force. She struggled in my grip and finally managed to wrest herself free. "You're hurting me!" she complained.

I grabbed her again; she twisted loose.

"You're *hurting* me, God d———n it!" she cried.

I shoved her away as hard as I could. "Then leave!" I ordered as she went flying off the mattress, landing on the floor with a loud thump.

She bounded to her feet, infuriated.

"D———n it, who the h———l do you think you are?" she raged.

"*Get out!*" I yelled.

"You no-good b——— d!" she cried. "You *are* afraid of Thompson!"

I started to lurch up after her, making her retreat so quickly that she slipped and fell again, banging her left elbow on the floor.

She began to cry and gather up her clothes. "You dirty skunk," she ranted. "You lousy, no-good son of a b———h."

I sat up on the edge of the bed, my upper body weaving, my lower body aching from residual pain in my hip. Reaching out to the table, I picked up the bottle of whiskey and poured myself a glassful.

"Drinking whiskey won't change anything," Susannah said. "You're still a yellow b———d."

My voice was soft and trembling as I told her to get out.

"I'll get out," she said, "and *stay* out. B———d! You'll be sorry! You can't rough me up and get away with it!"

She sobbed in fury. "That's how God d———n brave *you* are!" she said. "Have to beat up *women*!"

"You're no woman," I muttered.

"What?" she snapped. "I can't hear you! Can't you even talk now?"

"You're no woman, you're a whore!" I said.

"And you're a coward!" she responded almost apoplectically. "A lousy, stinking *coward*!"

I hurled the bottle at her, missing her by inches, the bottle exploding into fragments on the wall. Susannah's fury vanished and, with a look of dread, she sidled toward the door, her gaze fixed on my face.

"You're crazy," she said, shakily. "You've gone crazy."

I watched her, dull-eyed, as she started to unlock the door.

"Sorry," I murmured. "Not a thing a gentleman should do."

"A *gentleman*," she said contemptuously.

She opened the door and a pair of startled gasps made me tense and squint to see what was there, my sight somewhat blurred by whiskey and the other problem I had not addressed yet.

When I saw who was standing there, I felt the inside of my stomach drop as though I'd just then swallowed an anvil.

It was Agnes, her expression a mirror image of mine: total shock and disbelief.

Susannah stared at her, open-mouthed. I stared at Agnes, open-mouthed. Agnes was the only one who gave the tableau movement by turning her head from side to side, looking at Susannah, then at me; at Susannah, at me.

I pushed to my feet and Agnes wrenched herself away from the doorway, a sound of revulsion in her throat.

"Don't go!" I cried.

Lurching to the doorway, I started out exactly at the moment Susannah tried to leave. Like some team of amateur clowns, we were wedged together between the two sides of the doorway. "Look out!" I gasped. "Look out yourself!" she gasped back.

I shouldered her so fiercely that she reeled across the room, collided with the bed, and toppled to the floor with a cry of pain and outrage. By then, I was gone, pursuing Agnes, staggering from side to side, calling out her name in drunken desperation. My gait a wildly reeling one, I neared the staircase down which Agnes was beginning to retreat.

"Agnes, wait!" I begged.

I started down the staircase after her, so stunned by dismay that I didn't even turn back as I saw a couple turning on the second floor landing to ascend.

Seeing me, the woman made a sound not dissimilar to the squeak of a mouse, her eyes rolled back discreetly from the dreadful sight, and she slumped, unconscious in her companion's grasp. I lunged by them, uncaring for their plight, and raced around the landing, calling Agnes's name again.

As I reached the head of the next flight, my hip gave way, causing my left leg to crumple and, with a startled cry, I began to fall.

I saw Agnes stop abruptly to look back at me as I tumbled down the stairs at high speed. She had to press herself against the stairwell wall so I wouldn't carry her along on my juggernaut descent.

I couldn't stop myself, the inertia of my flailing fall continuing until the external force of a wall concluded it, my head and body slamming hard against it. "Bill!" I heard Agnes cry out, horrified.

I heard her rapid footsteps coming down the stairs and looked up at her groggily as she kneeled beside me, her expression one of apprehension.

"Means nothing to me, Agnes," I remember murmuring.

Her face began to fade away in darkness then. "Agnes?" I said frightenedly.

Then I fell unconscious.

My eyes fluttered open and, to my surprise, I saw that I was back in my room. *Had I dreamed it all?* I thought, staring at the ceiling.

Then I sat up, gasping at the pain in my head, clutching, at once, at my skull.

"Bill!" I heard her say.

Turning, gasping further at the pain it caused, I saw Agnes hurrying across the room.

She sat on the bed beside me.

"Agnes," I murmured. I had never been so happy to see another human being in my life.

Ignoring the pain, I clung to her as she stroked my hair. "Shh, it's all right, Bill," she comforted. "It's all right."

"Agnes. Agnes," I whispered, knowing I was close to tears.

She held me for some time, until my bodily and brain pain eased somewhat. Then she drew back from me, smiling; was it teasingly?

It was. "You were a naughty boy," she said.

"She's nothing to me, Agnes, nothing." That was true enough. "Things have been bad here; I was only—"

She stopped my apology by laying a gentle finger across my lips. "You don't have to explain," she told me.

I took hold of her hand and kissed the back of it repeatedly before pressing it to my cheek.

"It's the only time since we were separated, Agnes," I said. "The only time; I swear." I felt I had to stretch the blanket there lest I lose her.

She stood and smiled at me.

"You don't have to explain, Bill," she said, starting to disrobe. "I understand. I understand my Wild Bill."

I watched her, comforted by her presence and desire for intimacy with me, but distracted by the uncomfortable realization that she didn't really understand at all.

"I'm not sure I can—" I began, awkwardly.

"I don't expect it, Bill," she said with a soft laugh. "I just want to lie next to you."

"Please," I said, overwhelmed by gratitude for her acceptance of me, however ill-informed.

She got into bed with me and we embraced. To my astonishment, my manhood made an instant assertion of itself, springing to life. "Bill," she said, "don't hurt your head now."

"I won't," I said, not caring if I did.

Ten minutes later, I was sleeping soundly in her arms, at peace for the first time since I'd retreated from the Bull's Head Tavern.

I sat on a chair, face lathered, Agnes shaving me. I could not have trusted my own hand with the razor.

"I'm surprised at you," she chided. "Letting your appearance go like this. That's not the Wild Bill Hickok I know."

"Well . . . Agnes." I hesitated. "It's been very demanding here. Hays was like a holiday compared to Abilene. The strains, the tensions. You wouldn't believe what goes on here."

"I'm sure it's terrible, Bill," she said. She scraped off whiskers. *"Lord,"* she said, "if *you* have trouble, it *must* be terrible."

"It is," I said, "it *is*. I have to be alert to danger night and day."

"Don't nod, dear," Agnes cautioned me.

"Oh, sorry," I replied.

I closed my eyes with a contented sigh as she continued shaving me. It was quiet for a short while. Then she spoke again.

"Well, at least you won't be alone anymore," she said.

My eyes popped open. What was this?

"I'm going to stay with you," she explained. "The circus can get by without me for a while."

"No," I said, impulsively.

She looked at me, surprised. *"No?"* she asked.

I stared at her in hapless silence, then cleared my throat and braced myself.

"Absolutely not," I told her, trying to sound stern.

"But *why,* Bill?" she asked.

I gazed at her gravely, trying hard to think of a convincing answer.

"Because it's dangerous here," I finally said.

"But that's exactly why I want to stay," she told me. "So I—"

"No," I interrupted. She could not stay, that was certain; I could not allow it. "It isn't safe, Agnes."

She was still for disconcerting moments.

"It isn't," I insisted.

"Bill, are you trying to get rid of me?" she asked.

"Yes," I said. I saw her look. "I mean *no,*" I amended. "I mean *yes!*" I said, exasperated. "From Abilene! Not from my life."

She gazed at me in silence, obviously wanting to believe my words but having difficulty doing so. Making matters worse, it was the first moment since we'd met that I grew conscious of the fact that she was a number of years older than me.

I stood up. "Agnes," I said. I took her in my arms and pressed a lathery cheek to hers.

"Don't you understand?" I explained, "Abilene's a powder keg. I have so many things to settle. They're bad enough by themselves. If I had to worry about you, I just couldn't handle them."

Still, she was suspicious.

"I won't be here much longer, Agnes," I went on. "I've had the offer of a better job. In Newton. You can meet me there and stay with me. It won't be long. A few weeks maybe." *How will I get out of this?* I wondered.

"I just don't like it here in Abilene," I lied on. "Oh, I can handle it all right, but why should I go on living like this?" I drew back to smile at her, then had to chuckle as I saw the foamy lather on her face.

Removing the towel from around my neck, I wiped off her cheek. Still that uncertain look remained on her face.

"Agnes," I said.

I kissed her as passionately as I could. She remained unpliant for a few more moments, then abruptly, clung to me with desperation equal to my own. My heart leaped, overjoyed.

"You *do* love me, Bill, don't you?" she asked.

I gazed into her eyes.

"I love you with all my heart and soul," I told her, and I did—and do.

"Oh, Bill," she said.

We kissed tempestuously; and there were tears of happiness in both our eyes: hers I saw and mine I felt.

Dust and Double Death

I opened the front door of the hotel a crack and peered outside.

Seeing no one there, I opened the door for Agnes.

"Are things *that* bad, Bill?" she asked me, sotto voce. "You can't even walk out a door without checking first?"

"You have no idea," I replied, quite truthfully.

We started along the plank walk, my eyes darting in all directions for any possible sign of Thompson.

"Oh, Bill," Agnes said, "you should—"

She broke off as I pulled her underneath the shadow of an overhanging roof. "Stay out of the light," I told her.

"Oh, my," she said.

I repressed my sense of guilt toward her as we continued on.

"You *should* leave, Bill," she said. "It makes no sense to live like this. A little danger, yes; that's your profession. But *this*? You should take that job in Newton as soon as ever you can."

"Yes," I mumbled, distracted, still on the lookout for Thompson.

"Bill, Bill," she murmured, clinging to my arm. She looked at my leg. "That limp is bad," she said.

"Yes," I said, "my old arrow wound. That's what made my leg give way yesterday."

"Oh, my poor Bill," she said. "I had no notion it was so distressing here. I just wish I could stay with you."

"I know, I know," she added hurriedly as I gave her a look. "I just hate to see you have to be like this. It isn't fair."

I managed a twisted smile.

"It goes with the job, love," I replied.

A few minutes later, we were at the stage station. Agnes pressed her cheek to mine as I edged her toward the coach, my eyes shifting constantly, nervously.

"I'm going to miss you, darling," Agnes said.

"I'm going to miss you, too," I told her. "It won't be long, though. I'll write as soon as I know my plans."

"We'll be in Kansas City for another month," she said.

"I won't forget," I promised. "Good-bye, love."

I pressed her into the coach and tried to draw back, losing balance and toppling forward as she pulled me to her for another kiss. I disengaged myself, eyes still darting. "Good-bye," I said with a straining smile. "Good-bye."

"Good-bye, Bill," she said. As she saw me back into the shade again, she added, worriedly, "Oh, *Bill*."

"Don't worry now," I reassured her. "Everything is going to be all right."

As the coach pulled off, Agnes leaning out the window, waving, I exhaled heavily, my shoulders slumping with relief. *Thank God she's gone,* I thought.

When the hand tapped me smartly on the shoulder, I whirled with an astonished cry, clutching for one of my pistols, which I drew so fast I lost hold of it so that it flew away and splashed into a nearby horse trough.

Mike Williams lurched back, almost falling. "Hold it!" he cried.

I staggered, then regained my balance, wincing at the

pain in my hip, pressing a hand against it. "What the h————l are you doing?" I demanded.

Williams straightened up, a look of aggravation on his face.

"Just thought you'd like to know," he said, "Ben Thompson sold his half of the Bull's Head Tavern. Left Abilene this afternoon."

Albeit bathed in cool deliverance, I drew myself erect and looked at Williams with disdain. "Why should that mean anything to me?" I said.

"Oh, C————t," said Williams, turning to walk away. Despite his obvious scorn, I felt a sense of unutterable peace. Drawing in a long, deep breath, I started toward the Alamo Saloon, then, remembering, turned back and, pulling a coat and shirtsleeve as far up as it would go, I felt around distastefully in the murky water of the trough.

After a quick drying and cleaning of the submerged Colt, I left my room and sauntered to the Alamo, ready for a celebratory drink.

Entering the saloon, I strode to the counter and ordered a drink.

It tasted like ambrosia.

"Haven't seen you in a spell, marshal," said the bartender, a goading tone in his voice.

I didn't let it bother me. "I have been indisposed," I informed him.

"That so?" he said.

"Indeed," I replied. "An old scouting wound in my hip."

"Uh-huh," he said.

I poured myself another drink.

"It happened near Fort Riley, several years ago," I recounted. "I was out one day when seven hostiles started to pursue me." I looked down at my right hip. "One of them managed to imbed an arrow in my hip," I said. "I lost considerable blood but—"

I looked up quickly as the bartender started edging off, an uneasy expression on his face.

"What's wrong?" I asked.

I had only a moment to jerk my head around and see Phil Coe's twisted countenance in the mirror before I was flung around and his right fist hurtled into my jaw. I stumbled backward, skidded across a table, breaking up a six-hand game of poker, and landed on the floor, my hat flying off.

I sat up dizzily and shook my head, just in time to see Coe charging me again. Hauling me to my feet, he snarled, "Beat my girl up, will you?"

"What?" I asked.

He walloped me a second time and sent me flying backward, where I broke up a second poker game as I sprawled across the table, scattering chips, cards, drinks, cigars, and players in all directions.

I staggered up, attempting to remove my coat as Coe ran at me once again, face twisted with rage. He drove his left fist deep into my belly, his right into my battered jaw. I staggered back and fell again, then struggled up, tearing off my coat so quickly that it hit Coe in the face. Lurching forward, I aimed a haymaker at his face, but at that instant, Coe slipped on some puddled whiskey, dropping clumsily to one knee. My violent punch, finding no target, spun me around in a circle. Coe lunged at me and we fell to the floor together, wrestling, grabbing, and kicking like a pair of berserk animals.

"Hickok's feud with gambler Phil Coe started quietly enough," Nichols later wrote, "a minor disagreement over the favors of a certain young lady who—to protect her reputation—remained nameless during their subdued conversation."

"You'll never touch Susannah Moore again!" Coe screamed.

"Susannah Moore?" I yelled. "Susannah Moore means nothing to me!"

"The trifling disagreement was to fester and become inflamed however, resulting in the legendary gun duel at the Alamo Saloon."

Coe had me pinned down to the floor now, panting in my face.

"I'm going outside now," he told me. "Right outside that door. I'm going to wait for you; and when you come out, come out shooting. Understand?"

He banged my head on the floor for emphasis. "You *understand*?" he repeated loudly.

Letting go, he pushed to his feet and started to adjust his clothes, looking down at me.

"If you don't come out in the next five minutes, I'll come in and kill you." He kicked my leg. *"Understand?"*

He turned and stalked away, and the saloon was deathly still, every patron looking either at him or at me.

The batwing doors squeaked loudly as Coe went outside, and every gaze shifted instantly to me. I was, by then, standing slowly, trying to look unconcerned, but too dizzy and unnerved to manage the deception very well.

I moved on wavering legs to my coat, almost took a header as I leaned forward to pick it up, then straightened and donned the coat with as much aplomb as I could muster and looked around for my hat. One of the customers picked it up and brought it to me. I took it with a regal nod. "Thank you," I said, shocked at the revealing tremor in my voice.

I felt for my pistols. One of them was missing and I looked around for it. Another customer picked it up and carried it across the room to me. Him I only nodded at, pushing the pistol beneath my sash.

Turning to the counter, I poured myself a drink, attempting as best as I could to look unruffled despite the shaking of my hand, which caused whiskey to spill on the counter. I tried to raise the glass to my lips, but my hand was trembling so uncontrollably that I couldn't do it.

I felt myself beginning to crumble. I pressed my lips together hard to prevent their quivering. All the years of pretense had fallen away. Dread contorted my expression—as much for the fact that the dread was on display as fear for my life. I could not bear standing there, allowing them to witness my disintegration, yet neither could I make myself walk to the front door.

With a sense of haunted affliction, I turned and, limping badly—my hip was hurting again—I headed for the side door, feeling every eye in the saloon fixed on me.

I opened the side door and went outside. Shutting it, I leaned back, shivering, breath straining through my clenched teeth. Shakily, I reached beneath my coat and drew both pistols. Holding them extended, I began to limp toward the street. It is difficult for me to say these things, as you may well imagine, but I was in utter torment, every lie I'd lived by now revealed, my mind naked before my terrors and my self-contempt.

I stopped and peered around the building edge. Coe was standing just outside the entrance, waiting for me. I felt terror mounting to a peak and knew that I had to deal with it or break entirely.

Lunging from the alley, I shouted "Coe!" and fired both pistols simultaneously, sending two lead balls into his stomach, the impact of them flinging him backward, a look of shock on his face.

I now was frozen to the spot from which I'd fired, knowing that I'd just committed murder.

Then an even more horrible occurrence happened.

Hearing the sound of running footsteps behind me, I

whirled in mindless terror and fired both guns at the figure rushing toward me.

"And having catapulted Phil Coe to his maker with one clean shot between the eyes, Hickok, hearing the approach of further enemies, whirled with one astonishingly graceful motion, drew both pistols once again, and delivered three more scoundrels to their just reward."

The figure rushing toward me was my deputy, Mike Williams.

My repeated shots not only killed him but, flying astray, wounded two townspeople who had the misfortune to be standing too close.

An official paper was submitted to me shortly after the event.

"Be it resolved by Mayor & Council of City of Abilene," it read, "that J. B. Hickok be discharged from his official position as City Marshal for the reason that the City is no longer in need of his services."

Treading the Boards

In traditional drama, tragedy is not supplanted by farce. In real life, no such sensible condition prevails.

In need of income, I agreed to work for a man named Doc Carver, who had signed a contract to deliver one hundred live buffaloes to Kansas City for shipment to Niagara Falls, where they would appear in an exhibition.

This had never been attempted previously and, when I ventured out with the capturing party, the question uppermost in everyone's mind was: What would a buffalo do when roped? A pair of Sioux Indians with the party were dubious about the prospects.

The day we went after our first buffalo is one I am not likely to forget.

After searching for some time, I caught sight of an old bull and rode after it.

The first rope I threw had too large a loop which, unfortunately, slipped back across the buffalo's hump.

The remainder of this sorry incident is best described by an item in the Lincoln *Daily State Journal*.

"The rope on the buffalo's hump gave the animal all the advantage, and with a surge he turned Wild Bill's horse head over heels. The greatest pistol man the West has ever known described an ungraceful arc in the air and landed headfirst on the prairie.

"Getting to his feet, Bill spat grass and buffalo dung from his mouth and watched his horse, still fast to the buffalo, disappear toward the horizon.

"It did not help his feelings when one of the Oglala braves rode up and commiserated with him: 'You ketchem d———n tonka heap gone.' "

Thus occurred my first experience with show business.

My next one was quite different, albeit worse. A momentary mouthful of buffalo dung beats, hands down, the piles of horse manure I was buried under during the theatrical season of 1872–73.

I present same sketchily.

I held the woman with my left arm whilst, with my right, I fired at some whooping offstage Indians.

"Fear not, fair maiden!" I cried. "By heaven, you are safe at last with Wild Bill, who is ever ready to risk his life and die, if need be, in defense of weak and helpless womanhood!"

The audience erupted with a chorus of cheers and whistles, pounding their hands together.

My career was launched.

Alone in my hotel room, I lay on my bed, drinking whiskey and reading a book on English history to forget the nonsense of the play I was in.

The settlers were trapped in the burning cabin, father, mother, and daughter. The father fired two shots through the window, then flung aside the rifle in despair.

"That's the last of our ammunition, Mandy!" he cried. "Them outlaws are going to get us now for sure!"

"No!" the daughter cried back, clinging to her mother, both females blubbering pitifully.

Now the father lunged to the window, shaking the canvas wall of the cabin.

"Wait!" he cried, "I see a figure in the distance!" (Pause.) "A man on horseback!" (Pause.) "I believe it's *Wild Bill!*"

Audience cheers, whistles, foot stamping, and applause.

A dreadful imitation of galloping hooves offstage, a flurry of fired blanks.

"See how gracefully he moves!" the father cried. (Pause.) "He's getting closer!" (Pause.) "Closer!" (Long pause.) "He's *here*! Wild Bill is here!"

Cheers. Applause. Whistles. Stomping feet. I charged into the doorway, a pistol in each hand. Drunk, I stumbled on the threshold and sprawled into the room.

The audience roared with laughter.

The beginning of the end.

They had me recount a story about a horse named Black Nell that I'd ridden in the war.

According to the tale, this remarkable equine, at a whistled signal, would follow me into a saloon and climb onto a billiard table, where she stood on all four legs, several patrons sitting on her back. After which, I would mount her and have her bound across the front porch and into the middle of the street in one leap, a distance of some thirty to forty feet. Remarkable creature. She should have been on the stage instead of me.

Finally, I had to stop the account because it was too ridiculous.

They tried to get me to tell how I'd killed a giant grizzly bear single-handed but that I refused to do from the outset.

The gypsy woman lived in a shack on the outskirts of town.

"Good evening," I said as she opened the door. "I'm—"

"Tell me nothing," she instructed me. "I will be given information by my sources."

"Yes; of course," I said.

She led me into a small room illuminated by a single burning candle and, at her gesture, I settled on a chair across from her.

She closed her eyes and made some mumbling noises, then began to chant beneath her breath; it sounded like the chanting of an Indian.

How long she did this I have no idea, but finally she opened her eyes and seemed to look at me, although she may have been looking at visions of which I was not aware.

Then she said, "You suffer."

I felt myself begin to tense at these words.

"You suffer because . . ." She drew in a rasping breath between her teeth. ". . . you *killed*."

I should not have come, I thought. *I don't want to hear this.*

She looked around and murmured, "What?" as though someone had just entered the room and spoken to get her attention.

I sat rigidly, staring at her. *I should not have come,* I thought again.

"Yes," she said. "I understand." As though the new party in the room had spoken to her once again. She nodded. "I understand, do not be upset."

She turned back to me.

"A man is with us," she told me. "His name is Mike. He asks, 'Why did you shoot me when I only meant to help?'"

It seemed as though all breath had just been sucked from me. I couldn't speak, couldn't move.

"You understand?" the gypsy woman asked.

I do not recall how I endured that meeting. Not that I

remained with her that long; I left as soon as possible, thanked her, paid her, and departed.

Back in my hotel room, I drank myself unconscious, terrified to fall asleep in the usual way lest the dead come floating to me in a dream and kill me with fear.

I stood in the stage saloon, leaning on the counter, declaiming slurringly to a group of men.

"McCanles jumped into the room, his gun . . . leveled to, uh, shoot," I said. "But he wasn't quick enough. My . . . pistol ball went through his heart."

"Can't hear you, Hickok!" someone shouted in the audience.

From the corners of my eyes, I saw the stage manager watching me, grinding his teeth in frustration at my intoxication and inability to remember lines.

"His death was . . . was—" I faltered, cleared my throat, went on. "His death was followed by a . . . *yell* from his gang." I knew my voice was fading, but I didn't care. "I . . . said to myself. Only, uh . . . six shots left and—" I sighed and finished glumly, "nine men to kill."

"Can't *hear* you, d———n it!" screamed an angry voice.

Three hours later, snow fell steadily as I stumbled from the saloon and started to trudge along the sidewalk, trying to walk upright, but scarcely able to do so. I moved weavingly through the darkness and the snow, Wild Bill Hickok, Hero of the Plains.

It ended on a rainy night in March in Philadelphia.

The set was that of a street, men standing and sitting on barrels and boxes, listening to me as I limped back and forth, in my usual inept fashion, trying to ignore the periodic boos and hisses and insulting taunts from the audience.

"I was . . . in a hotel," I fumbled, "in . . . Leavenworth City and I . . . saw these—loose—loose characters about as I ordered a room. I had . . . uh . . . had considerable money—"

"Can't *hear* you!" someone yelled down from the balcony. I glanced up, wincing at the lights, which hurt my eyes.

"Come *on,* come *on!*" another member of the audience shouted.

"What happened *then,* Bill?" one of the actors on stage prompted. "What happened *after you got the room?*"

I started limping back and forth again, saying, "I had— lain some thirty—"

"Louder!" raged a man.

"I had lain some thirty minutes!" I repeated loudly, mocking whistles and applause greeting my increase in volume.

"—lain for thirty minutes on the bed when . . . as I . . . as I suspected, I heard some men at my door. I . . . I pulled out my revolver and . . . my Bowie knife and, uh—"

"—your whiskey bottle!" someone in the balcony yelled. The audience laughed and I looked up, forced to lower my stinging eyes once more because of the spotlight's glare.

"What happened *then,* Bill?" asked an actor.

"I had . . . lain some thirty minutes on—" I started.

"You already *told* us that!" someone shouted.

I stiffened angrily, looking around, then felt a chill run up my back at what I saw moving to the edge of the stage. I peered at the nearest box.

Agnes was sitting there, tears running down her cheeks. I murmured her name.

"Louder!" cried a number of men.

I stared at Agnes, thinking: *That she should see this . . .*

"What happened after you pulled out your revolver and your Bowie knife, Bill?" one of the actors asked me desperately.

I could only stare at Agnes, wishing that I was far away from this agony.

"Did they open the door, Bill?" the actor asked. His voice broke as he added, *"Wild Bill?"*

I could not go on. Even the audience seemed to realize it, for they gradually grew still.

Then, a wondrous moment, ending the excruciating pain.

Agnes stood and extended her arms to me.

With a sob that I hoped nobody heard, I limped forward, climbing into the box, where I embraced her, pressing my cheek to hers, my tear-filled eyes closed tightly, *"Agnes,"* I whispered. *"Agnes."*

"Bill," she murmured.

And in that vast enclosure crammed with people, we were, nonetheless, alone together.

My Attempt on
the Life of Wild Bill

M y abortive effort to assassinate Wild Bill Hickok—at
least in a limited fashion—occurred the very night
that Agnes came back into my life.

With no attempt at social niceties or courting graces, we
retired immediately to my hotel room where I (and I hope
she) enjoyed the most fruitful sexual union I had ever
known in my life; fruitful because, deeply intermingled
with the pleasure of the physical experience were the added
elements of gratitude, happiness, and, most of all, love. It is
a combination I can recommend most highly or, as Hamlet
expressed it, "A consummation devoutly to be wished"—or
something on that order.

It was when we were lying together, warm and satiated
by our most rewarding act of love, that I essayed to make
Wild Bill take the big jump to, at least, obscurity if not the
actual wooden overcoat.

"You still haven't told me why you didn't come to Kansas City, Bill," she said, by the use of that name perhaps
planting, in my brain, the seed of what transpired.

"Well," I lied (I think I became fully aware of that for
the first time), "I had the offer of this play, you see—"

"That awful play," she interrupted. "You aren't going to

do that anymore; I just won't let you. It's beneath your dignity. You're too important a man to let them use you like that." (Another seed planted by her comment.)

"No," I promised her, "I won't do it anymore."

"Good," she said, looking grimly pleased. "No wonder you drank. To be made a fool of in that way. A famous man like you."

Another seed. I seemed to sense it germinating in my mind.

"Why didn't you write me, Bill?" she asked. Bill again. The germination continuing.

"I was ashamed of what I was doing," I answered quietly.

It was a beginning.

She didn't sense what was about to happen. Can I blame her? Not at all; I can only blame myself.

"You should have come to Kansas City," she said. "You could have joined the circus as a—guest of honor or something. It would have been much better than appearing in that dreadful and humiliating play."

"I suppose," I answered, secretly mulling, contemplating.

"To hear those stupid people . . . *braying* at you," she said angrily. "At *you*. A man whose boots they aren't fit to polish."

She held me tightly and possessively and we almost made love again, but something kept me from it; a need to express, to reveal, in a word, to *confess*.

"Agnes," I said.

"Yes, darling," she replied.

"The reason I . . . didn't come to Kansas City . . . wasn't the—play. It was . . ." My voice drifted into silence. This was a difficult move to make for me, albeit she was the only person in the world I would even have considered making it for.

"What, Bill?" she finally asked when I did not continue.

I swallowed, very dryly, and set myself for the tribulation I sensed it was going to be.

"The newspaper stories," I began.

"Newspaper stories?" she said.

"About what happened in Abilene."

"Bill," she said, appalled, "you don't think I believed them, do you?"

For an instant of leaping hope, I thought that she already understood.

But then she went on. "Nobody believed them. Everybody knows how newspapers lie. Especially the *Abilene Chronicle*. Obviously, they represent people whose toes you stepped on when you were marshal."

Gently, chidingly, she slapped my cheek.

"Bill," she said, "you didn't come to join me in Kansas City because of *that*? Shame on you. Haven't you any more faith in me than that? Don't you think I know you? Know how brave you really are? Do you think a few newspaper stories could change that? *Do* you?"

Good God, I thought. I had hoped to point out to her that the newspaper stories, especially the one in the *Abilene Chronicle,* which more than intimated murder, had not been overstating the case in suggesting that my killing of Coe had been deliberate. But before I had a chance to do so, Agnes had rallied to my defense and cut the ground right out from under me.

"Well . . ." was all I could respond.

I almost gave it up then and there; the effort seemed too onerous to face. But the need to unburden myself was too overpowering; I knew that it was, literally, as the phrase goes, now or never.

"Agnes," I began again.

"What, Bill?" she asked.

I paused again; it seemed, to me, a long time before I asked, "Agnes, do you love me?"

She sounded surprised if not injured in countering, "Why do you ask that, Bill?"

"*Do* you?" I persisted.

She seemed about to respond in pique, then relaxed. Still perplexed if no longer offended by the question, she said, "You know I do, Bill."

I paused again. Then, bracing myself, I replied, "My name is James, Agnes. James—Butler—Hickok."

"I know that, Bill," she said, still not understanding.

"What I mean is that I'm not . . ." I drew in a quick breath and finished, "*Wild Bill* Hickok."

"Bill—" she started.

"*James,*" I corrected, cutting her off.

"All right," she said, "I know your name is really James. It's just that I've become accustomed to calling you Bill. It's the name everyone calls you. You never told me *not* to call you Bill."

"I know, I know," I admitted, "but . . . well, it's just a nickname, Agnes. A nickname some old lady gave me years ago; she wasn't even *thinking* who I really was when she gave it to me. But it doesn't mean a thing."

"It does to me," she said.

I felt myself grow tight inside. Was this attempt going to become a total failure? "You know what I mean," I said, hoping it was true.

It wasn't. "No, I don't," she responded. "I *don't* understand what you're saying, Bill—I mean . . . well— " Her voice trailed off, and I knew that she did not elect to apologize for calling me Bill but, rather, was somewhat edgy about me insisting, at this late date, that she call me by my given name.

I wouldn't back off; I was into it, and I intended that she know and understand, no matter how difficult it was for me to do so.

"What I'm saying, Agnes," I went on, "is . . . there is a

real me and a . . . a *made-up* me. Those stories . . . mostly by Colonel Nichols . . ." I scowled at myself for giving him that undeserved title. "They're *exaggerated*," I finished.

Agnes smiled. "But I know that," she said. "Everybody does. No one takes him seriously."

"They don't?" I murmured; it was news to me.

"Of course not," she said. "It's the way things are done. They call it yellow journalism."

Another leap of hope, clutched and smashed as she continued. "It doesn't detract from what you've really accomplished," she said. "Just because the stories are exaggerated doesn't mean they aren't fundamentally true, does it?

"You *did* kill seven men at Rock Creek. You *were* a hero in the War Between the States. You *did* turn back that mob. You did kill Dave Tutt in Springfield. You *were* a heroic scout for General Custer, a heroic sheriff in Hays, a *magnificent* marshal in Abilene. Stories can't alter facts, Bill— all right, James."

She smiled with amusement. "You may not have killed hundreds of men and Indians, but you've certainly defended yourself with honor any number of times. Isn't that right." She waited. "*Isn't* it?" she insisted.

I didn't know what to say or think, not knowing whether to feel aghast at how versed she was in my legendary past or to be frustrated by the difficulty I was having getting through to her.

"Well . . . yes," I said, retreating. "Yes; of course." I couldn't let it go at that, however. "It's just that," I continued, "well . . . my reputation. Wild Bill, Prince of Pistoleers. Gun Master of the Border. It's . . . *ridiculous*."

I felt a tremor of foreboding to see her expression tighten at my final word.

I could not back down, though; not when I had gone so far.

"I want us to be married but—"

"Oh, Bill," she cried, hugging me so tightly her leg thumped against my hip, making me wince. "I want that as well! With all my heart!"

I drew back, trying not to show my reaction to her hurting my hip, and said, "Well, when I've made a decent raise and can afford to ask you for your hand—"

"But Bill—*Jim*—I have the circus, we'd have more than enough to—"

"No, no," I said, feeling thwarted by the sidetracking of what I really wanted to discuss. "I want to make some money first. But that's not the point. The point is—"

"What, Bill, I mean *Jim*."

"*That's* the point," I pounced on it. "This *Bill* thing; *Wild* Bill, in particular. I can't have you marrying me, thinking I'm a—great *hero* or something."

"You're too modest, Bill," she said.

I almost groaned, repressing it with effort. "No," I said. "*No, Agnes*."

She didn't respond and, once again, uneasiness gripped me. Was I destroying our relationship by doing this?

To my dishonor—at least, my discredit—I went on, conditionally.

"I've killed men, yes," I said. "Dave McCanles and—one other at Rock Creek, *not seven*. Dave Tutt in Springfield. Bill Mulvey in Hays. Phil Coe in Abilene." I swallowed. "Mike Williams in Abilene, that by terrible mistake.

"But *that's it*, Agnes. Not hundreds. Not even dozens. Just the ones I've mentioned. And if you'd seen how—"

My voice would not allow me to go on. The total truth was not only difficult for me to reveal, it seemed d———d near impossible.

"You see . . . Agnes," I said, "I want you to love me."

"I *do*, Bill, I *do*."

I looked at her accusingly. She tried to look repentent,

but I could see that she was more inclined toward exasperation. *"Jim,"* she said, "I do love you."

"Me?" I demanded. "Or some . . . character who doesn't even exist?"

I knew from her expression that she still didn't comprehend what I was trying so hard—albeit unsuccessfully—to convey.

"I mean—" I started.

"I love *you,* Bill." Was that a scowl? *"Jim,* I love you."

I put my arms around her and held her close. Was I asking too much of her? Was I being unjust? After all, she had committed no crime; she was blameless of fault in all this. It was *my* doing, all mine.

"And I love you, Agnes," I told her ardently. "I love you more than anything else in the entire world. That's why I want you to know the truth about me. So you won't think you're married to some—*fiction.* You know what I mean."

"I understand," she said. But did she?

"I know you do," I said, regardless.

I waited. Then, at last, I had to add, "I've been afraid a lot of times."

"That's only normal, Bill," she said, catching her breath in irritation as she realized that, once again, she'd used my nickname.

Was I lulled by the tone of her voice? I'll never know. But I continued, "I didn't leave Hays because I had the offer of a better job in Abilene. I left because—"

Realization of what I'd been about to say brought me up short. *How far could I go?*

"What, Bill?" she asked. She didn't even react to using the name now; I believe she felt that it was all right to do so since it was the name I was so widely known by.

"Well—" I hesitated. Did I dare?

Self-anger made me go on. I would not give way when I'd come this far. I must not, I resolved.

"I'd arrested Custer's brother and put him in jail," I told her, "and he said he was going to—*kill* me, so . . ."

Impossible; I simply couldn't tell her the naked truth; talk about *cowardice*.

"Well, there was . . . there were seven other soldiers with him and I just . . . I didn't think I could handle eight at once so . . ."

I retreated even further toward a stated ignobility.

"It was the only time, though," I continued. "I mean . . . as you said, I *was* the marshal in Abilene, I *did* scout for Custer, I *was* in the war. The stories weren't *all* made up by a long shot." I wanted to end it now. I knew that it had been a failure and wanted to get out of it as quickly as possible.

"I'm glad we had this little talk," I said. "It just wouldn't be right to have you marry me, thinking that your husband was *The Hero of the Plains,* performance nightly, six days a week, matinees on Wednesday and Sunday afternoon."

"No," she said—very quietly, I thought.

I never brought up the subject again and we have never spoken of it since. I know I *tried* to let her know the truth, but how much she was willing to accept the facts I don't know to this day. I needed her too much to make any more of it, and if she was or still is disturbed by the notions I raised in that talk, she has never mentioned it.

I tried to put Wild Bill to rest—at least in our relationship—but I am not sure whether I succeeded, even in part. Did I, in fact, replace him, in her estimation, with that pitiful impostor I have been on too many occasions in the past? I hope not.

Does she understand at all? Or do I expect too much of her? How could she understand my circumstance when I have never truly managed to do so myself?

Miracles in Kansas
and Beyond

I still loved Agnes deeply but feared that I had done some injury to our relationship by what I'd said during that conversation.

Accordingly, I felt a need to separate myself from her in order to give her the time to adjust and recover from my words. I didn't feel that she really perceived what I was trying to convey but believed that enough had been said to create a cloud of uneasy suspicion in her mind.

For that reason, using the perfectly valid excuse that I was going to seek out a means of income other than the theater, which we both agreed was hardly worth the pain and aggravation to me, we parted company after a few days, promising to correspond and keep our love alive with words.

To be honest, I had the apprehension that I had destroyed our relationship by what I'd told her. This produced a double reaction in me: one of sorrow that I might have lost the one person who could make a difference in my life but also, and almost equally disturbing, that if our relationship could not survive the truth, it was too flawed to pursue in any case.

With these conflicting emotions hovering in the air

above my head, I left Agnes and sallied forth. Wrong word
there; to sally forth implies an expedition or excursion.

I merely removed myself physically from her company,
my emotional tail between my legs.

During 1874, a year of miracles for me, I accomplished the
following:

I was in New York City being lionized by one and all.

I was visiting friends in Springfield, Missouri.

I was killing Indians out West.

I had a gunfight with two of Phil Coe's relatives and
killed them both.

I was, myself, killed in Galveston, Texas.

I was also killed in Fort Dodge, my body "riddled with
bullets."

What I really did was somewhat less dramatic.

I took a position leading a party of English hunters
whose sole intent seemed to be the extermination of all
wild game in Colorado. Their carnage grew so demented
that a company of cavalry was dispatched to see to it that
the Britishers did not exterminate all the Indians they saw
as well. I did not last very long on this adventure, so thoroughly disgusted was I by the mindless butchers, who
came close to surpassing the Grand Duke Alexis and his
1872 mass slaughter of the buffaloes.

About that time, I began to experience more and more difficulty with my eyes and began to wear tinted glasses to
protect them from the glare of the sun.

A visit to a doctor in Topeka elicited his diagnosis that
I was suffering with an infection caused by the colored fire
used on stage during my theatrical touring. When I asked
him if the problem would decrease in time, he could give
me no assurance of that; it could, conceivably, get worse
in time, he said.

Which, of course, made life a little more delightful than usual. I took to tucking my hair beneath my hat and that, along with the darkly tinted glasses, served to disguise my appearance well enough; not to mention my enforced use of a cane whenever cold weather brought on rheumatism in my hip. Why I didn't have my hair cut short as I would have liked to, I shall never know. Perhaps a residue of false pride would not allow me to eradicate one of my Wild Bill talismans.

While I was in Topeka, I had a curious experience.

I went one night to an establishment called the Colorado House to play some poker and enjoy some drinking.

I had not chosen to disguise myself and, as I entered, everyone saw me and began to cheer, immediately making me sorry that I hadn't entered incognito. However, the deed was done, and I was either to accept it or depart; I chose to remain.

While I was standing at the counter having a drink, a man came up behind me. Seeing his reflection in the mirror, I turned quickly, tensing.

Seeing that, he flinched and drew back, both hands in the air. "I come in peace," he said, his voice so shaky that I almost laughed, but managed to confine my amused reaction to a smile. "What can I do for you?" I asked.

"Sir, a gentleman is playing poker over there [he pointed] who I thought—*we* thought—you might enjoy meeting."

"And who might that be?" I inquired.

"Clay Halser, Mr. Hickok."

I could not prevent a sudden stricture in my chest and stomach muscles. Halser was, in fact, what I was in legend: a genuinely brave, courageous man whose exploits as a shootist and lawman were well-known in the nation, much less the West. *Meet* him? The idea chilled my blood. What if he was really as aggressive as I'd read? Wouldn't

his immediate inclination be to try me and add yet
another—sizable—notch to his gun?

All this rushed through my head as I stared at the man.

"I wouldn't want to disturb his game," I said as casually as I could.

"Oh, you wouldn't be," the man said eagerly. Before I
could prevent it, he had turned and bustled off. Not wanting to be perceived as anxious in any way, I turned back
to the counter and poured myself a libation of whiskey,
downing half of it in a swallow, grateful for the soothing
warmth of it in my stomach.

In the mirror, I saw the man come bustling back. This
time I didn't turn to meet him, knowing it to be un-
necessary.

"Sir?" he said.

I let him stand a moment, unacknowledged.

"Mr. Hickok?" he asked.

I turned and nodded. "Yes?" I said as though I didn't
know why he was there.

"Mr. Halser said that he'd be honored to meet you."

"Honored?" I asked.

"Oh, yes, sir, his exact word," said the man.

I felt the stricture slowly loosening. I grunted as though
thinking it over, then shrugged and said, "Oh, very well."

I crossed the room behind him, sensing every eye on
me. "Meeting of the Giants!" I saw the blazing headline
in my mind. "Two Gun Masters Face-to-Face!" Inwardly,
I cursed Nichols yet again for making me think in terms
of his overblown journalistic jargon and wondered what
Halser thought of the "colonel" since he, too, had received
the royal treatment in Nichols's magazine and newspaper
articles.

As I neared the table where he sat, a man stood up
and, in an instant, I knew a number of things about Clay
Halser. He was no imposing giant, being, I would estimate,

approximately five foot nine inches in height and built very slenderly. He was not heavily armed, no weapon visible at all, although I assumed that, living under similar circumstances as my own, he had to keep at least one weapon on him for defense.

Mostly, I saw that, if anything, he was in worse physical and mental condition than I was, his hair streaked with gray, his features haggard and ashen, his eyes virtually burned out. I saw in them the same emotional depletion I saw in my own eyes when I looked at myself in the mirror. I had no idea what he had looked like earlier in his life but, to me, it seemed as though he must have lost considerable weight as well, his clothes hanging loose on his frame. As he extended his hand to shake mine, I saw a very visible tremor in it.

"Mr. Hickok," he said.

"My honor, sir," I replied. "I have admired your career."

He seemed genuinely flustered by my words. *"My* career?" he said, incredulous. "Good God, sir. Compared to yours—" He made a scoffing sound as though to relegate his own career to some inferior position.

Two thoughts occurred to me almost simultaneously: one, how prematurely foolish I had been to presume that he would want to challenge me and, two, that I felt a disquieting sense of sympathy, even pity for him. The only thing that might have caused me to react with even more inner distress would have been if I had known his age. I took him, by appearance, to be well in his forties when, actually, he was barely thirty-one.

After our initial handshake, we retired to a corner table where I evoked a smile from him by noting that we both sat with our backs to the wall.

He asked me then if I remembered "hurrahing" him in Morgan City some eternity previously. I told him that I honestly did not, but when he described the incident during which I had treated him with brusque dismissal, I told him I was sorry I had done so. "However," I said, "I imagine that you understand, now, why I acted as I did."

"I do," he said. "Being a cow town marshal is not the most relaxing job in the world."

We enjoyed a mutual chuckle over that. "No, it certainly is not," I agreed with him.

He glanced around the room and smiled at what he saw; a bitter smile, I noted. "You know what they want," he said.

"Of course," I replied. "For us to pull down and blow each other to bloody ribbons."

He chuckled. "I could not have said it better," he responded.

I must say that, all things considered, it was a pleasant evening. Only one thing marred it for me: the fact that I had to maintain, as always, the fiction that my life had been as heroic as his. Not that he presented it as such. Indeed, a more modest man I never met. Still, I knew that all the exaggerated stories about him were—unlike those about me—based on truth. It made a profound difference, although I tried not to show it in any way. I liked him very much and wish, to this day, that our exchange had been as honest on my side as it was on his.

We discussed for a while the interesting parallels in our careers, both born in the Middle West, both on the Union side during the war, both cow town marshals, both known through the bloated hyperbole of Nichols and writers like him.

Both—this we laughed at heartily—appearing in self-exalting plays, required, in essence to play the fool. I suspect our laughter was laced with acid, but we enjoyed it nonetheless.

He told me then—no laughter here, completely solemn—of an incident where he had been convinced he'd seen the ghost of a man he'd killed. I did not respond at first, but felt a prickle of gooseflesh over my body.

When he was finished with his strange and sorrowful story, I told him that I'd read a number of books on Spiritualism and even gone to see a gypsy medium who had told me things she could not have known by normal means.

I told him that there was a woman in Topeka who claimed she could communicate with the dead, but I could see from his reaction that he wished no part of that.

At last, we spoke about the subject that was uppermost in both our minds: our position in the West, the nation, and, for all we knew, the world.

"We are victims of notoriety," I told him. "No longer men but figments of imagination.

"Journalists have endowed us with qualities that no man could possibly possess. Yet men hate us for these very nonexistent qualities.

"Our time is written on the sands, Mr. Halser," I told him. "We are living dead men."

I had never thought about my situation in those terms but, once I had expressed it so, I realized how true it was.

At that moment, it seemed to me that I had nothing to look forward to but death.

My History Concluded

I am nearly finished now with my account. I need not fear that anyone will, ultimately, read it. Even if they came upon it, they would, more than likely, burn it as a somber, boring narrative.

But I will continue, thus wrapping up the ends.

The year 1875 was not a banner one for me. No miracles occurred or were imagined.

Instead, I started down the slope of drink and lechery again, albeit briefly.

I don't know whether it began after my experience with Clay Halser. It may well have, for I never felt more of a fraud than I did from that night on.

In addition, for more than several months I heard no word (of love or otherwise) from Agnes. Because of this, I became convinced that she no longer cared for me; that I had, in fact, turned her away from me with my clumsy attempt at revealing the truth about myself.

In a state of despair, I succumbed to old weaknesses once more. Yet even in this renewed surrender to intemperance, I presented a spurious facade to all I came in contact with, intimating (even overtly stating) that the reason for my dissipation was a melancholy reaction to the closing in of civilization on the free soul that I was. Pure, un-adulterated buffalo chips!

I got into the odious habit of joining crowds of tender-feet at the bar and regaling them with high-blown, windy accounts of adventures with "red fiends" and "white rogues," all the while soaking my inner man with gratis bottles of whiskey.

I reached my lowest point in June of that year when I was charged with vagrancy and a warrant for my arrest was issued. Unable to face this humiliation, I fled the city, returning some months later where, although the charge was still outstanding, I was able to move about once more.

Happily, by that time, I had heard from Agnes once again and was relieved to discover that she still cared for me. As I have indicated, she did not mention our conversation and, gratefully, I did not raise the topic, vowing never to speak of it again.

This made me think, in the fall of 1875, of the concept of preparing these memoirs. I had, through the previous months, accumulated the sum of $1,600 through various means (gambling, involvement in hunting expeditions, etc.), which, while it was certainly not enough to provide a comfortable life for Agnes and me, did provide me with the wherewithal to write these memoirs, the bulk of which I have done. I feel some guilt about not sending part of this money to my aged mother and hope that she has not felt a sense of resentment toward me for my dereliction. As excuse, I can only offer that my main concern was (in addition to preparing this book) amassing enough money so that I could offer Agnes a married life with a decent standard of living. I certainly did not intend to live permanently off her circus earnings.

I did consider accepting one of the many offers tendered to me to write a chronicle of my adventures, but knowing what kind of heroical tommyrot these people would expect, I could not force myself to the task. As I have told you, I actually did keep a journal for a number of years, choosing to incinerate it rather than promulgate its thick-headed absurdities.

So I commenced to prepare my memoirs.

And now we are in 1876, unusual festivities taking place around the country, this being the centennial year of the Declaration of Independence.

On March 5, Agnes and I were married at the Cheyenne residence of S. L. Moyers and family, friends of Agnes.

Agnes, being the honest woman that she is, wrote down her true age on the wedding license: forty-two. Being still a gentleman—if nothing else—I did not write down my true age (thirty-nine) but, instead, put down that I was forty-five.

If ever I felt inclined to kill (and you now know how nonexistent that inclination has always been in me) it was because of an article written about our wedding in the Omaha *Daily Bee*.

"Hickok has always been considered as wild and woolly and hard to curry, but the proprietress of the best circus on the continent wanted a husband of renown and she laid siege to the not oversusceptible heart of the man who had killed his dozens of both whites and Indians. The contest was short, sharp, and decisive, Wild Bill went down in the struggle clasping his opponent in both his brawny arms, and now sweet little cupids hover over their pathway, and sugar, cream, and honey form a delicious paste through which they honeymoon."

Indeed! Whoever wrote that drivel should be staked out naked on an anthill on a summer's afternoon!

Agnes and I had two fine weeks together sullied only by a somewhat heated discussion regarding our means of income, she stating that she could earn five thousand dollars a year plus all expenses in any number of circuses, me retorting—unequivocally—that no wife of mine would ever work.

As fortune would have it, the discovery of gold in the Black Hills of Dakota a few years earlier had created a nationwide furor, and by the middle of 1875, men were beginning to swarm to the Hills like crazed ants. By April of this year (1876), the mining camp that had become most prominent was Deadwood Gulch. It was to there that I determined to travel, hopefully to make a strike and provide for Agnes for the remainder of our lives and find myself a respectable niche in life.

My first attempt to reach Deadwood was to announce that I was raising a company to travel to the Black Hills, not only for safety's sake but to economize on supplies and, reaching the gold region, to comprise an impressive settlement of miners. The fare per person was to be in excess of thirty-three and a half dollars.

Unfortunately, a lack of adequate applicants forced me to cancel this project and, instead, travel to Deadwood in the company of the Utter brothers, Steve and Charley, who own and operate a four-horse shipping company.

I arrived in Deadwood on July 12.

The city (probably too grand a name for such a primitive location) sits at the end of the gulch, which is a dead-end canyon.

It consists of one street filled with tree stumps and potholes, hastily constructed frame buildings on either side. The street is, during daylight hours, jammed with men, horses, mules, oxen, and wagons. Saloons outnumber stores three to one and, in general, the lure of gold and the fleecing of men who might find it has attracted every low-grade denizen capable of reaching the community. *Was I one of them?* I wondered at the time.

My eyes had been bothering me considerably and, upon arrival in Deadwood, I felt it advisable to see a doctor. I had seen a number of them in Cheyenne but none had put forth the same opinion as to the cause of my optical affliction.

With this in mind, I approached a burly man unloading a wagon. "Pardon me, sir," I said.

The man turned quickly to reveal as unprepossessing a countenance as I have ever seen, so dirty and odor-ridden that gnats hovered about him.

"You lookin' for a fat lip?" he said.

"I beg your pardon?" I replied.

"Never mind, never mind," he cut me off. "What do you want?"

"Could you tell me where I might find a doctor?" I inquired.

He pointed. "That way, bucko," he answered. "Dr. Kelly, ten doors down."

"Thank you," I said.

"What's the problem?" asked the ugly man. "Dose of the clap?" He chuckled, revealing a set of rotten, crooked teeth with numerous gaps. I backed away, brushing at a gnat attacking my nose. "Thank you again," I said.

"Say hello to Kelly for me," he said. "You won't be the first dose of clap I sent to him."

Upon which, he cackled madly, gurgled, hawked up an oyster, and let it fly, just missing me. "J———s C———t," he said, turning back to his work.

As I walked away, I saw Charley Utter standing nearby, grinning.

"By all that is holy," I muttered to him, "who is that horrible man?"

Charley laughed and answered, "Calamity Jane."

"That is a *woman?*" I said, incredulous.

"If you can call her that," said Charlie. "Some folks claim she's a hermaphrodite."

"My God," I murmured.

"I think she makes a better man than a woman," Charlie said.

I will say no more about that incident except to comment that, not knowing what dire events may have occurred in this creature's life, I cannot criticize her. At any rate, I do not expect to cross her path again.

For that matter, if I do happen to see her coming, I will most likely cross the street to avoid contact with her.

Why, after all the doctors I have seen elsewhere, with their multiple diagnoses of my problem, it took a hick doctor in a mining camp to tell me what the problem really is, I have no idea. But it was Dr. Kelly who let me know what was really wrong.

"You want it straight, Mr.—?" he said, breaking off when he reached my unknown last name—not really unknown, I suspect; I think he knew exactly who I was.

"Butler," I told him.

"Ah, yes." He nodded. "You want it straight, Mr. Butler?"

"What is it?" I asked.

"Glaucoma," he said. "Advanced. Looks to me like gonorrheal ophthalmia."

His words stunned me, my first horrified thought being: *Oh, dear God, have I infected Agnes with a disease picked up from whores?*

"How advanced?" I heard myself inquire. It seemed like the voice of someone else.

"You want it straight?" asked Kelly.

"Yes, damn it, *yes*," I replied.

"You could be blind in a matter of months," he said.

I left his office in a daze. I had felt that there was something chronic going on in my eyes, but *that*? The realization was staggering. *Blind in a matter of months.* What was I to do?

As I was limping along the plank walk, my cane slipped through a crack in the wood and, staggering, I fell clumsily to one side, sprawling into the street, my spectacles falling off, my hat falling off so that my hair (which I customarily pushed up inside my hat) fell loose.

A man stepped over to help me up. "You all right, mister?" he asked.

"Yes," I muttered, standing up.

He looked more closely at me. "Hey, ain't you—?" he began.

"No," I interrupted him and, quickly, picking up my spectacles, hat, and cane, moved away from him as rapidly as possible. As I did, another man joined him and I heard him say, "Sure looks like Hickok to me."

"Hickok!" exploded the second. *Why not climb up on a rooftop and shout it?* I thought angrily. "I thought he was *dead!*"

Hearing the Magic Name, a third man joined the pair and their voices rang out above the noisy bustle of the street, "Did you say *Hickok?*" "Yeah! That's him! Right there!" *"Wild Bill Hickok* in Deadwood?"

So much for incognito.

I complete these memoirs sitting on a rough cot in a tent. It is nearly the end of July.

I wonder if it is nearly the end of my life, as well.

When it is general knowledge—as I'm sure it will be— that I am on the verge of blindness, some aspirant, more daring because of my failing eyesight, will go up against me and, unless I can hit him by the sound of his revolver being drawn (an unlikely feat), it will all be over.

Even if that doesn't happen, what kind of life can I lead in darkness?

I have been taking mineral drugs prescribed by Dr. Kelly, and from what I can make out in my hand mirror, it has taken its toll on me. My skin is almost gray, my eyes are dull and lifeless. I look dead already.

I read, a while back, of the death of Clay Halser in Silver Gulch; he was shot down by some adolescent boy who had the good luck (or bad luck as it will probably turn out) of having Halser's pistol misfire on the first shot. God rest Halser's soul; I hope he is in peace, and that, when my time comes, I will be disposed of by a man worthy of the name, not by some ambitious fool seeking only notoriety.

Mentioning that makes me wonder, as I have on more than one occasion, if the souls of the men I have killed still linger about me like that of Mike Williams. I pray to God that they do not and, most of all, that I will never have to see them standing before me, white-faced and accusing.

So I draw near the conclusion of this manuscript. I hope that I have made it clear that I am no more wild than a butterfly and that my name isn't Bill. For that matter, my last name has been misrepresented as well, more times than a dog has fleas; I have been, among other family monikers, identified as Hitchcock, Hansock, Hickock, Haycock, Hicock, Hiccocks, and Hiccox.

To wrap things up: I have come to the final judgment that I am not a man any longer. I am a figment, a concoction, an overblown invention born of low-grade whiskey and high-grade journalistic distortion; of street and saloon gossip and dime-novel bombast.

It is not that I have been a total waste as a human being. I have accomplished *something* in my life; just something less than has been cast abroad. The truth lies somewhere in between the two extremes.

I have written to Agnes and, heaven pity me, lied to her once more, unable to tell her the truth; at least, I can try to hold on to her love at a distance, if not in her presence. I have told her that I never was as well in my life and that we will have a home yet and will be happy even though I know that it will never happen. I bade her good-bye, calling her my dear wife and, after signing J. B. Hickok, adding—a final act of cowardice because I fear to lose her?—*Wild Bill.*

To amuse her (I hope it does) I added a second note written in the style of the uneducated boor so many people believe me to bc.

As to the future, God only knows; I do not.

However, as Lincoln put it, "The best thing about the future is that it comcs only one day at a time."

Or, as Benjamin Franklin wrote (words I live by nowadays): "Blessed is he who expects nothing, for he shall never be disappointed."

Addendum

I thought I was finished—in more ways than one—but fate (if that is what it was) has intervened, and my tale goes on, albeit briefly.

I was lying in my tent one gloomy, overcast afternoon, much in need of a bath, a shave, and a change of clothes, when footsteps sounded outside. By instinct, I reached for my new .32 caliber Smith & Wesson—my first cylinder-loading pistol—then changed my mind and lay back down. If it was Death's tread I heard, let it be. That may not have been my exact thought, but certainly that was the gist of it.

If it was Death, it cleared its throat outside the tent flap, then inquired, "Mr. Hickok?"

"Who is it?" I asked, relatively certain at that point that it wasn't Death at all but some more prosaic entity.

"John Stebbins, Mr. Hickok," said the voice.

"Who are you?" I asked.

"Stebbins, Post and Company, sir," he answered. "I am here representing the merchants of Deadwood."

Instantaneous disinterest on my part; I did not respond.

He cleared his throat again. "May I come in?" he asked.

"No," I said. I wanted him to vanish.

"Oh," he responded. "Well . . . of course." Another throat-clearing. "We've been thinking, Mr. Hickok," he went on (I knew what he was going to say before he said it), "Dead-wood needs a marshal bad and we were wondering if you—"

His voice had faded off by then. I stared into a memory, a gauzy, ethereal remembrance of Agnes standing on a horse's back as it cantered around the circus ring; a vision of the first night I had seen her in performance and fallen in love with her.

I soon realized that Stebbins was still talking. When his words ended with an audible question mark, I said, irritably, "What?"

"I said, would that be agreeable?" he repeated.

"Would *what* be agreeable?" I demanded; Lord, but I'd become a surly wretch.

"Why . . . two hundred dollars a month and half the col-lected—"

"I'll *think* about it," I interrupted. Anything to get rid of him.

"That's all we can ask, Mr. Hickok," he said. "All we can ask."

He was silent for a few moments before clearing his throat again. I almost groaned aloud. "Uh . . . Mr. Hickok?" he said.

I closed my eyes; obviously the man was never going to leave. "*What?*" I asked.

"There are six men in Saloon Number Ten. Shootists from Montana. A real bad lot."

"So?" I muttered, wearily.

"They say they're going to kill you."

That was adequate to make me open my eyes.

"I just thought you should know," said Stebbins.

"Thank you," I replied, as far from feeling gratitude as any man could be.

"That's all right," he said. He really thought I was grateful. "They said they'd be there all afternoon and into tonight." He cleared his throat. Dramatic emphasis? "Waiting for you," he concluded.

I heard his footsteps moving off. I stared up at the canvas overhead.

"Sure," I said, "I'll go right down and kill them all."

I tried to sleep but couldn't. I sat up, but that was not enough. I stood and paced a bit. No, not enough by half. Something was rising in me; I could feel it like a dark, acidic liquid being slowly poured into my stomach, then my chest.

I could not remain there. Hastily, I threw on my jacket and, grabbing my cane, vacated the tent. I walked and walked and *walked* until I was alone in the wilderness, limping back and forth like some caged, restless beast.

The more I paced, the more I realized exactly what it was that was rising in me. It was anger and resentment, yes, but mostly it was self-contempt. I picked up a stone and tossed it in my palm as I paced. The rage and hatred I felt toward myself kept mounting and getting hotter until it felt as though the acid in my body had caught fire, its flames a searing pain. My pacing grew more agitated. Back and forth and back and forth.

Suddenly, it all erupted, the fury and disgust flooding upward in me. I stopped and hurled away the stone, screaming at the top of my voice, my tormented howl ringing and echoing off the walls of the canyon.

Across my mind, a rush of scenes appeared; a flash of painful recollections so rapid I could scarcely keep track of them: my boyhood terrors, my panic at Rock Creek, my flight in the war, my unintentional heroics with the mob, my pathetic shooting of Dave Tutt, my dread at Fort Riley and during my scouting days. My ridiculous killing of Bill

Mulvey, my fleeing from Tom Custer's rage, my false displays in Abilene, my fear of Thompson, my almost literal murder of Phil Coe and Mike Williams, my humiliating stage experience, my bloated reputation, the lies, the lies, the *lies*.

From the very center of my being—neither shouting it nor raising my voice—I said, *"Enough."*

Unhurriedly, I walked back to my tent and brushed my best clothes, polished my boots; cleaned my pistols; bathed and shaved and groomed my hair; dressed slowly and meticulously. Done, I looked—albeit ghostly—much like the Wild Bill Hickok of old, that persona created by others and emulated by me: The Hero of the Plains.

I pushed the two revolvers underneath my sash (a .32 would not suffice on this occasion) then left the tent and walked down to the main street, using, as was customary, my cane.

When I reached my goal, I removed my blue-tinted spectacles and put them in an inside pocket, glad that it was not a sunny day. I started toward Saloon Number Ten, then stopped and slung my cane aside; I would not utilize it. Drawing in a deep breath, I walked the remaining steps to the saloon without a limp, clenching my teeth so as not to facially reveal the pain it caused me.

I reached the saloon, took one more chest-inflating breath, then pushed inside, slamming the batwing doors against the wall.

The six men were at the counter, just now turning as I came inside. Seeing me, they tensed, and I braced myself for confrontation.

When none of them immediately went for his weapons, I spoke.

"I understand," I told them, "that you cheap, would-be gunfighters from Montana have been making remarks about me. I want you to understand that, unless they are stopped, there will shortly be a number of cheap funerals in Deadwood."

I had no idea where the words were coming from, but they kept on coming, regardless.

"I have come to this town not to court notoriety but to live in peace," I said, "but I do not propose to stand for your insults. So if you *vermin* have a true desire to extinguish my life, here is your golden opportunity."

The sextet stood immobile, staring at me, and a rush of glorious grit took hold of me; I raised my hands. *"Well?"* I demanded. "Either fill your hands or get your yellow a———es out of here!"

The six were cowed, I saw with triumphant delight. One of them actually tried to smile! "We was only joshing, Mr.—"

"Out!" I roared, jerking my left thumb over my shoulder.

I stepped aside and, for the first and probably only time in my life, truly resembled the Prince of Pistoleers (if a sallow-faced one) as the six cowboys (for they were not really gunmen at all) trudged sheepishly for the door, filing by me, one by one. As the last one passed, I could not resist kicking him soundly on the rump, wincing at the jab of pain it cost me but enjoying it immensely. "And don't come back!" I shouted after them.

The patrons of the saloon applauded, cheering. "Hurray for Wild Bill!" one of them cried.

It was my moment. I had waited for it all my life, but there it was at last. I smiled beneficently at the saloon's customers and enjoyed a drink with them.

So now my memoirs are unquestionably done—and with a happier ending withal. I feel a sense of confidence I did not feel before this incident; assurance that I will, in fact, find gold and make a strike toward wealth's security.

I will continue taking medication and my eyesight will be, if not restored, at least improved enough to allow me to enjoy the remainder of my married life with Agnes, who, I am equally assured, will—in time—come to a better understanding of me. I will not make any further abject confessions to her but will, instead, gradually instill into our life a more realistic atmosphere so that she comes to know me for what I am—at least to a large proportion.

In brief, I feel a sense of positive persuasion about my future. And, on that note, I sign these memoirs,

James Butler Hickok

Afterword

So ends the final entry in these odd, revealing memoirs. Two days later, Hickok was assassinated.

I have spoken to one of the men who was sitting at the card table with Hickok when Jack McCall moved up behind him and shot him in the back of the head. His name is Captain Massie.

As he describes it, Hickok entered the saloon, the same one in which he had triumphed over the six Montana "gunfighters," Nuttall and Mann's Number Ten, a little after noon. He was dressed in full finery: his Prince Albert frock coat with all the appropriate accoutrements.

A card game was in progress, its players Captain Massie, Carl Mann (the saloon's co-owner), and Charles Rich. Mann signaled to Hickok, who moved over to the table where he was invited to join the game.

He accepted, asking Rich if he would move so that Hickok could sit with his back to the wall, as was his custom. Rich demurred, laughing, telling Hickok that no one would dare come at him after what he'd done two days earlier.

To Massie's surprise, Hickok made no issue of the point

whatever but sat down with his back to the room and asked for fifteen dollars' worth of pocket checks, which were brought to him.

As the game progressed, Massie noticed Hickok's peculiar behavior. He told me that Hickok seemed possessed of some strange, inner calm, as though he had come to some resolution within himself. His smile was faint and almost distant, his voice restrained and modulated. In short, Massie seemed to be telling me, Hickok behaved like a happy man—a man at peace with himself.

"That was a magnificent show the other day, Bill," Massie commented.

"Grand, Bill. Absolutely grand," Mann added.

To which Hickok replied quietly, "A gentleman could do no less."

He regarded his cards, nodding to himself, Massie fancied. Then he said, "I am descended, as a matter of fact, from the Hiccock family of Stratford-Upon-Avon, Warwickshire, England. A noble line."

A moment later, Jack McCall cried, "D——— —n you, take that!" and fired a bullet into Hickok's brain.

Having read Hickok's memoirs and interviewed Captain Massie, I am led to the inescapable conclusion that Hickok allowed his death to occur.

How else to explain his casual willingness to sit in a position he had not allowed himself to sit in since his life became constantly in jeopardy?

Captain Massie's description of Hickok's behavior crystallizes my opinion: that he seemed possessed of some strange, inner calm, as though he had come to some resolution within himself.

I believe that he had.

He had proved his courage by confronting the six men—whether they were gunfighters or not is irrelevant. Hickok believed at the time that they were and faced them down, regardless, with a display of mettle he had never demonstrated before—or, if he had, he had certainly never mentioned in his memoirs.

Having displayed this proof of courage not only to the world but, more important, to himself, he had achieved a high plateau of gratification and, more important, self-respect. So much so that his final comments speak of a positive persuasion about his future.

In the several days that had passed since the dramatic incident, I believe that Hickok may have felt a sense of anxiety that he would, in spite of his accomplishment, backslide to his previous state of mind. He knew that he still faced imminent blindness, despite his hopeful words to the contrary. Accordingly, he knew that he could not provide his wife with the company of a full man but would, instead, have to call upon her to take care of him in his sightless condition; a prospect that must have been anathema to his pride. Moreover, he knew that the chances of him making a sizable strike in the Hills were beyond remote.

These things all under consideration, I wonder if he did not deliberately sit in such an unaccustomed position; if he did not—with the near psychic oversense of the professional gunfighter—actually *know* that McCall was moving up behind him to end the conflict of his existence with a single shot.

I believe, in short, that Hickok was ready to die.

Between two pages of his memoirs, I found a scrap of paper on which Hickok had scrawled a brief verse. I do not know if he, himself, had written it or if he had found it in a book of poetry and responded to it because it reflected his thoughts.

Whatever the case, the verse reads as follows:

> *To win a single battle*
> *is not to win a war*
> *And the hero soon discovers*
> *he is still the man he was before*

Frank Leslie

SHADOW ON
THE SUN

I dedicate this book to my dear friend Chad Oliver.

See you later, pal.

WEDNESDAY

I

A mile outside of Picture City, they had set up a tent for the meeting with the Apaches. A troop of cavalry from Fort Apache had been dispatched to the conference, and now two lines of horsemen faced each other on the cloud-darkened meadow—one line the saber-bearing cavalrymen; the other the blanketed Apache braves, impassive-faced, sitting on their ponies like waiting statues.

Everything looked drab and colorless in the gloomy half-light—the grass and bushes drained of their late autumnal richness, the horses dark or dun, the costumes of the soldiers and Apaches composed of solid, cheerless hues. Only here and there did color show—lightly in the weave of a blanket, more boldly in the slashes of yellow stripe along the dark pant legs of the cavalrymen.

Between the lines stood the tent, its canvas fluttering in the cold, October wind. Inside its small interior, six men sat on folding stools: Braided Feather, chief of the Pinal Spring band, 287 men, women, and children; his son, Lean Bear; Captain Arthur Leicester, United States Cavalry; Billjohn Finley, United States Indian agent for the area; David Boutelle, newly arrived from Washington, D.C., as observing representative for the Department of the Interior; and Corporal John Herzenbach, who was there to write down the conditions of the treaty between the government of the United States and Braided Feather's people.

Finley was speaking.

"Braided Feather says that his people must be allowed to sow and gather their own grain and work their own sheep and cattle herds," he translated to the captain.

"This is their prerogative," said Leicester. "No one intends to deprive them of it."

Finley interpreted this for the Apache chief, who was silent a moment, then replied. Finley translated.

"He says it is known to him that many Apaches in the San Carlos Reservation have had their fields destroyed and their livestock taken from them," he said.

The captain blew out breath, impatiently.

"His people are not going to the San Carlos Reservation," he said.

Finley spoke to the Apache chief and, after a pause, Braided Feather replied.

"He wants to know," said Finley, "how his people can be sure they will not be sent to the San Carlos Reservation, as so many—"

"They are being given the word of the government of the United States of America," Leicester broke in pettishly.

Finley told Braided Feather and was answered. He pressed away the makings of a grim, humorless smile and turned to the captain.

"The Apaches," Finley interpreted, "have heard this word before."

The two young men sat among the high rocks, one of them looking out across the meadow with a telescope. From where they were, the tent was only a spot on the land below, the facing horsemen only two uneven lines that almost blended with the grass. Only with the telescope could the one man make out features and detail.

If Jim Corcoran had raised the telescope a jot, he would have seen the buildings of Picture City, dull and faded underneath the cloud-heavy sky. As with the horsemen at the conference, two lines of buildings faced each other across the width of the main and only street.

If Jim had turned and climbed the steep incline behind them to its top, he might have seen the dot of Fort Apache sixteen miles due west and, perhaps, caught sight of the smoke from White River chimneys eighteen miles northwest. He would have seen, too, surrounding him like a dark green island in a sea of desert, vast forest land, and, in the distance, the snow-crowned peaks of Arizona's Blue Mountains.

But Jim was only interested in the conference taking place below. Earlier, he'd talked his older brother Tom into leaving the shop to come out and watch it.

"By God," he said, lowering the telescope, "I never thought we'd see the day ol' Braided Feather'd get to feelin' peaceable."

"We never would've either," said Tom, "if it hadn't been for Finley."

"That's right enough," said Jim. He raised the telescope again and chuckled. "Christ A'mighty," he said, "an honest Injun agent. They're as hard to find these days as honest Injuns."

His brother grunted and glanced up briefly at the leaden sky. Each time he looked at it, it seemed to have descended lower.

"She's gonna start to pourin' soon," he said. "We'd better hightail us back to town."

"Aw, let's wait awhile," said Jim. "The meetin' can't last much longer."

"Jim, they been a hour already," said his brother, checking his watch. A raindrop spatted across the gold case, and he wiped it off on his coat sleeve.

"See, there's a drop already," he said. "We'll get soaked."

"Just a mite longer," said Jim, looking intently through the telescope. "We can ride back fast if she starts up."

Tom put his watch away and looked over at his brother. When was Jim going to grow up? he wondered. He was eighteen already, but he still acted like a kid most times. It made their older brother Al mad. Well, that was nothing much, Tom thought, smiling to himself. What *didn't* make Al mad?

Tom yawned and drew up the collar of his coat.

"Suit yourself," he said. He'd wait a little longer anyway. "Can you see good?" he asked.

"Yeah, real good," said Jim.

Overhead, there was a swishing sound.

"All right, all right," Captain Leicester said irritably. "Any breach of treaty on our part releases his people from the agreement. Good God, what does the man want?"

He aimed a stony gaze at the clerk, then looked back suddenly, interrupting Finley as the Indian agent began translating for Braided Feather.

"That goes both ways, of course," he snapped.

When Finley turned again to the Apache chief and his son, he saw that, although they had not understood the content of Leicester's words, his tone of voice had been apparent enough. There was a tightening twitch at the corners of Lean Bear's mouth, the faintest additional glitter in the dark eyes of Braided Feather.

Finley pretended not to notice. He nodded to the two Apaches, then asked a question. The chief sat in silence awhile; across the table from him, Leicester shifted restlessly, the wooden stool creaking beneath his weight.

Then Braided Feather nodded once, curtly, and his son grunted, lips pressed together. Finley turned to the captain.

"It is agreed then," he asked. "The band will be supervised by an Apache police force?"

"We have already discussed that," said Leicester.

"Further," said the agent, "that the band will be subject only to Apache courts and juries to be formed?"

"Presuming that the members of said courts and juries are acceptable to the United States government," said Leicester.

"They will be formed with that stipulation," answered Finley. "The point is: The Apaches must be allowed to govern themselves and, when necessary, act as their own judges, mete out their own punishment."

"Presuming that this right is not used merely as an excuse for laxity of discipline," said Leicester, "it is acceptable."

"They will govern themselves then," Finley said.

Leicester nodded wearily.

"Yes, yes," he said. He turned to the clerk. "Put it down," he said.

Corporal Herzenbach dipped his pen point into the vial of ink. The sound of it, as he wrote, was a delicate scratching in the tent, just heard above the flapping of the canvas.

Over the distant mountains, thunder came rumbling at them like the chest-deep growl of some approaching beast.

"Come on, let's get out of here," Tom Corcoran said. "It's gettin' set to bust wide open."

"Aw, just another minute," pleaded his brother, the telescope still pressed to his eye. "You talk as if we was a hundred miles from town."

"The way it's fixin' to rain," said Tom, "we could get ourselves soaked in two seconds."

"Y'think maybe the meetin's takin' so long because it

ain't workin' out right?" asked Jim, changing the subject so they wouldn't go right away. He wasn't in the mood for riding back to town just yet. Al would just put him to polishing rifle stocks again.

"Y'think so?" he asked again.

"Who knows?" Tom said distractedly. "Who the hell can figure out an Injun's brain? Braided Feather's been turnin' down treaties more'n ten years now. Wouldn't surprise me none he turned down another."

Jim whistled softly. "That wouldn't be so good," he said. "Braided Feather's a real son of a bitch. I'd hate t'see him on the warpath again."

"Yeah," said Tom. "Come on, let's go."

"Y'think maybe—what're ya lookin' at?"

Tom Corcoran was squinting upward. "I thought I heard somethin'," he said.

"Heard what?"

"I don't know."

"Where, up there?" Jim looked up at the cloud-roiling sky.

"Yeah."

Jim snickered. "I expect it was a bird, Tom," he said.

"Yeah, sure, you're funny as hell." Tom lowered his eyes and shivered once. "Come on, let's beat it."

"Oh . . ." Jim Corcoran stuck out his lower lip. Well, no help for it, he guessed. It was going to be a working afternoon and that was the size of it.

"So," he said, shrugging, "let's go then."

The sound passed overhead again, a faint, rushing sibilance.

"There it is again," said Tom, looking up.

"I didn't hear nothin'," said Jim.

"You wouldn't." Tom lowered his gaze.

Jim chuckled, standing up.

"You scared o' birds?" he asked.

Tom flat-handed him on the arm, and Jim lost his balance, almost dropping the telescope. He laughed aloud as he staggered.

"*Birds*," he said.

Below, their horses nickered restlessly. They strained at their ties.

"It is agreed then," Finley told Braided Feather in the Apache tongue. "No rifles or pistols will be kept by any of your people.

"When one of your men needs to hunt, he will go to the soldiers who rule the reservation. There, he will be given a weapon and a pass which will allow him to hunt for a certain time with the weapon. When the time is ended, the rifle or pistol will be returned to the soldiers.

"I have tried," he added to the chief, "to get permission for these guns to be held by the Apache police, but it cannot, immediately, be done. Later, when the soldiers understand, as I understand, that your word is good, I am sure we can get the weapons put under the control of the Apache police. Is that agreeable?"

Braided Feather nodded.

"It is agreeable," he said.

"Is it also agreeable," asked Finley, "that the making of *tulapai* will be limited so that none of your people can drink so much that they might commit an act which would break the treaty?"

Before the chief could answer, Lean Bear spoke angrily to him. Finley did not interfere in the brief exchange between Braided Feather and his son. He glanced over at Leicester and saw the captain gritting his teeth. He looked at Boutelle, who sat, legs crossed, looking at the two Apaches with hard, critical eyes.

Soon Lean Bear had relapsed into a thin-lipped silence, and Finley's gaze sought that of the chief.

"It is agreed," said Braided Feather, "if it is also agreed that no white man will be allowed to offer whiskey for sale to any of my people."

Finley passed this along to the captain, who nodded, a sour expression on his face. Leicester's stomach was upset. There was a dull pain in the small of his back, his wife had been frostily rejecting the night before, and he was sick and tired of haggling with these damned, arrogant savages.

Quickly, sensing the decline of cooperativeness in the air, Finley went over the remaining conditions of the treaty while the captain squirmed uncomfortably on the squeaking stool. The two Apaches, father and son, sat without expression. David Boutelle sat, lips pursed, appraising Finley's words, and the corporal clerk sat with the pen poised between his ink-spotted fingers, waiting for instructions.

Outside, the chill October wind rustled the browning grasses, ruffled the blankets of the Apaches and the dark coats of the cavalrymen, stirred the horses' manes, picked at the canvas of the tent, and was a cold current on which flying things could ride.

They were almost to their horses, which they had tied up in a space below the rocky shelf on which they'd sat.

"You think Al will be mad because we came here?" asked Jim. Now that they were actually going back to town, the thought of Al's angry impatience was distressing him.

"What's the difference?" asked Tom. "If he don't get mad at that, he'll just get mad at something else."

Jim chuckled nervously. "That's a fact," he said. "I think we got us the touchiest brother in the whole territory."

"Don't I know it," said Tom.

Only the week before, he'd had a fistfight with Al out

behind the shop. His ribs still ached from the drubbing he'd taken.

"Hey, I hear it now," Jim said abruptly, looking up. His gaze moved along the rock face beetling above them, but he saw nothing.

"What is it?" he asked.

"I dunno." Tom looked up, curious again. "If it's a bird, it's a hell of a big one."

"Maybe it ain't a bird," said Jim. "Maybe it's somethin' in the rocks. Y'know? Maybe a—"

It came at them with such speed that they had no chance to move. One second they were scuffling down the slope toward their horses, the next, they were paralyzed in their steps, faces frozen into masks of dumb horror. Jim was quick enough to fling an arm up, but neither of them had the time to scream.

Even if they had, their voices would not have been audible above the terrible, piercing screech that filled the air around them.

2

The storm had broken now. Sheets of angling rain swept across the land. In seconds, dust had become mud, dark and viscous, trees and bushes ran water from every wind-lashed leaf and twig, and the distant mountains faded from view behind a curtain of deluge. Men could not keep their eyes open in such a rain. When it struck their cheeks and brows, it stung like whip ends.

Hastily, the tent was struck and the troop rode off at a gallop for Fort Apache. It would take them at least two hours to reach their destination. By then, their uniforms would cling to them with chilling weight and the insides of their boots would slosh with water.

Captain Leicester, teeth gritted against the driving rain, led the way across the meadow toward White Canyon. Already, in his mind, he could see the day in its hapless entirety: the long ride back to the fort, his reporting the results of the conference to Colonel Bishop. The walk to his house, the slinging of his soggy-brimmed hat to the floor, the peeling off of his drenched clothes, the muttered cluckings of his wife. Then the first sneeze, the first trickle at his nostrils, the first chest cough, and off he'd be on the way to a prime cold with all its attendant miseries.

"Damn!" He let the curse go knifing into the wind-scaled rain and, for the effort, got his teeth wet. Damn it! He set his lips into a thin, trembling line. And why, he thought, *why*? For a pack of lice-infested, mule-eating Apaches! Damn them! The sullen, staring, brooding, leather-faced savages!

Captain Leicester dug his spurs in. "Come on!" he raged. "Come on, damn you!"

When David Boutelle, wet and uncomfortable, tried to guide his horse toward the White River Hotel, a swarm of animated townsmen swept him instead toward the Side-winder Saloon. There, along with a laughing Finley, he was virtually lifted from his saddle by the cheering men and borne aloft toward the smoke-blue, shouting din of the barroom.

As the two of them were carried through the batwing doors, a cheer went up from the assemblage. Steins and glasses were banged on tables and bar, two-fingered whistles needled at the air.

Then Boutelle and Finley were lowered jarringly to the floor and guided by their shoulders to the counter where glasses waited and Appleface Kelly, dripping rain, slammed his hamlike palm on the dark counter and bellowed for whiskey. The barroom sounded deafeningly with boot-scuffling, ragged-cheering men as they pushed happily to the counter.

When every glass and stein was filled, Appleface slammed his palm on the counter again, and, at the pistol shot report of it and Appleface's shout to "Hold it! Hold it!" everyone fell silent. Boutelle tried to get away, but he was held in a trap of smiling, eager men.

"Boys!" said Appleface. "This here's a gala day! Our wives and kids can finally walk the streets of Picture City without bein' scared of every shadow! We can work our jobs without expectin' arrows in our backs from some damn, murderin' Apache! And for that we got t'thank one man here."

Appleface beamed and pointed at the Indian agent.

"*Billjohn Finley!*" he declared.

"Hooray for Billjohn!" shouted someone.

"Right!" said Appleface. "Hip, hip—"

"Hooray!" howled the men.

"Hip, hip—"

"Hoo-*ray!*"

"Hip, hip—"

"Hoo-RAYYY!" Boutelle winced at the ear-piercing noise.

Then there was only the sound of mass, convulsive swallowing, followed in seconds by the sounds of fiery coughs, stamping boots, and thick glasses being set down heavily on the counter.

Eddie Harkness and his uncle skimmed along behind the bar, uptilted bottles in their hands, gurgling amber bourbon into the glasses. Boutelle put down his glass, still three-quarters full, grimacing at the hot bite of the whiskey in his throat. He looked around for a way out. He'd made his gesture, now he wanted to go.

"And here's to Mr. David Boutelle from Washington, D.C.!" yelled Appleface. "Hip, hip—"

"Hoo-*RAY!*"

Boutelle smiled thinly and tried to leave, but glasses were being raised en masse again and he was pressed in by the shoulder-to-shoulder drinkers. He took another sip of his drink and clenched his teeth.

Finley noticed the younger man standing in his wet clothes, and when the cheers had abated and the men had gone back to their separate groups of drinking and gaming, he worked his way over to Boutelle.

"You'd better go get yourself a change of clothes," he said.

Boutelle smiled politely. "I intend to," he said. He looked at Finley's rain-darkened coat. "What about you?"

"Oh, I'm used to it," Finley said pleasantly. "I've slept out many a night in wetter clothes than these."

"You don't talk like a native of these parts," said Boutelle, finally getting enough room to take off his hat and shake the raindrops to the floor.

"I'm not," said Finley. "I'm from New Jersey, but I've lived here over seven years."

"Rutgers graduate?" asked Boutelle.

Finley nodded. "That's how I got this job," he said. Rutgers University was the sponsor for the Apache nation.

"I see." Boutelle slid a clean square of handkerchief from his inside coat pocket and patted at the perspiration that scored his upper lip. The hot room was beginning to reek of steaming wool. This, added to the pungent odor of cigar and cigarette smoke, made Boutelle's stomach edgy.

"Well, I've got to go now," he said, picking up his hat.

"How long will you be staying in town?" asked Finley.

"Not long," replied the younger man. "Just until the Apaches are established on the reservation."

"Uh-huh." Finley nodded. "Well, that should be about a day or two."

"Mmm." Boutelle put his handkerchief away. "We'll see."

Finley knew what the younger man was thinking, but he said nothing. Boutelle, like the majority of newly arrived people from the East, believed, quite firmly and—to them—logically, that the Indian nation was composed of treacherous savages, rarely to be taken at their word, never to be trusted. Indians were, like any wild animals, to be penned in, watched over, and kept from doing evil.

Finley imagined that Boutelle was one of the legion who conceived of Indian reservations as some kind of open-air zoo.

He would say nothing, however. It was not his place to lecture. Besides, Boutelle would be gone in two days at the latest; there was no point in risking friction. Even if he did say something, it would not likely alter Boutelle's trend of thought. Words rarely changed a young man's attitude.

"Perhaps I'll see you later in my office," he said to Boutelle.

"Perhaps, Mr. Finley."

Boutelle made his turn from the bar without noticing the approach of the small Indian. The first he saw of him was as an obstacle in his path, and he twitched back as the Indian ducked aside.

"What do you want, Little Owl?" Finley asked in the Indian tongue.

The old Apache glanced timidly at Boutelle, then looked at Finley once again, his dark eyes abject. At his right side, his hand rubbed slowly on the leg of his grease-stained buckskins as though cleaning itself.

Finley grunted once and reached into his pocket. His hand moved quickly to Little Owl's and met it, palm to palm. The gesture took only a moment, and then the small Indian was padding down the length of the bar away from them.

"Did you give him drinking money?" Boutelle asked in surprise.

"Just a loan," said Finley.

"I thought giving liquor to the Indians was against your principles."

"As a rule, it is," Finley said apologetically, "but—well, I guess I just can't think of Little Owl as an Indian. He isn't really anymore. He's a hang-around-the-town Indian, hasn't even got a tribe to call his own. He lives outside of town with his wife and children."

"At the town's expense, I presume," Boutelle said acidly.

"No, no," said Finley, lying a little. "Little Owl works during spring and fall roundups. He's a pretty good little puncher."

Boutelle glanced down the counter and saw the old, stolid-faced Apache carrying a stein of beer into the back room.

"*He* works with cattle?" Boutelle asked.

"Yes, quite a few Indians do," said Finley, taking a cigar from his pocket. He bit off the end and spit it into the gaboon. "Not that they're very good at it," he went on, smiling. "They're too timid with the stock."

He chuckled at the expression on Boutelle's face.

"You've never thought of Indians as being timid, have you?" he said, blowing out a cloud of smoke. "They are, though. They hate to take a risk, any kind of risk at all. That's why they plan their battles so carefully. That's why a chief like Vittorio has lasted so long. He figures things out to the last detail."

"You sound as though you admire him," said Boutelle. He was terribly uncomfortable in these sodden clothes and in the hot airlessness of the saloon, but it was his duty to learn as much as he could about the sort of man who was, after all, representing the United States of America.

"You have to admire a good general," Finley was answering easily, "even if he is your enemy. Didn't we admire General Lee?"

"General Lee did not foment his war."

"Neither did Vittorio, Mr. Boutelle," the Indian agent said quietly.

The younger man cleared his throat.

"I fear we differ on several essential points," he said.

Finley shrugged and grinned cheerfully. "That's what makes life interesting," he said.

Boutelle nodded curtly. "Yes. Well, I really must be getting back to the hotel. These clothes . . ."

"Yes, yes, by all means," said Finley in honest concern. "Get yourself into a hot tub. Down some whiskey. Drive the wet right out of you."

Boutelle managed a politic smile. He knew that Finley was elated at having brought these savages to bay after more than seven years of trying. He had a right to, of course. Even if he did conceive of them as noble primitives instead of the murderous brutes they were.

"You wish to see my report before I send it off to the Capitol?" he asked.

"No, no, I'm sure it'll be fine," Finley said amiably.

"Very well." Boutelle nodded once and turned away.

Finley watched the younger man pick his way across the crowded saloon floor. Twenty-five years old, he thought, maybe twenty-six. Graduate of Yale most likely, maybe Harvard. Father in the law profession or in some legislature or both. Maybe even in Congress. Mother a society grande dame in New York City, Boston, some such place. His future a well-secured plan: politics, a proper wife and children, respectability, the quiet dignity which true wealth makes easier. The descent, more than likely, into stodgy complacence, into . . .

And, then again, maybe not, thought Finley with a self-deprecating shrug. It was unjust of him to write the young man off so easily. Was he, at thirty-seven, already taking on the dogmatism of old age? No sense in planning the poor boy's future all at once. There were always shadows in a man's personality that hid surprises. Besides, he was too happy today to feel critical of anyone. Appleface Kelly was right. It was, by God, a gala day!

Finley grinned at Kelly as the bulky man sidled up
to him.

"Say that Boutelle is a stiff-neck, ain't he?" said Kelly.

"Oh, he's all right," said Finley. "What's your pleasure,
you great hulk?"

Kelly ordered whiskey and put it away with immacu-
late speed. Flushed from drink, his face was almost to the
color of his name.

Al Corcoran came in at four.

Just before he did, Finley had slipped back to his hotel
room for a change of clothes. Now he was back at the
saloon, chatting with Kelly.

"Somethin' I always wondered," said Appleface. "Who
in Sam Hill named you Billjohn?"

"Simple," Finley answered. "My father wanted to call
me Bill and my mother wanted to call me John."

"So they struck them a bargain!" said Appleface.

"Right!"

The two of them were laughing when the double doors
were pushed open and the tall, heavyset man came in, dark
slicker dripping. Stopping at the foot of the counter, he
looked around the crowded room, his eyes coldly venomous beneath the shadowing brim of his Stetson.

When his gaze reached Finley, he came walking over.

"Hello, Al," Finley greeted him. "How'd it—"

"You seen my brothers?" Corcoran interrupted.

Finley's smile faded. "No, I haven't, Al," he said.

Corcoran's lips flared back briefly from gritted teeth.

"Anything wrong?" asked Finley.

"I just told ya," Corcoran said angrily. "I don't know
where they are."

Finley nodded. "Perhaps they went out to watch the
meeting with Braided Feather. A lot of—"

"Then where are they now?"

"They might have decided to take cover somewhere until the rain lets up."

"They had work t'do," said Corcoran, by the statement indicating his disagreement.

"I see." Finley shook his head. "Well, I don't know what to suggest, Al. I wouldn't worry about it though."

"No, you wouldn't," Al said bluntly. "You like Injuns."

Finley looked surprised. "What?"

"You heard me."

"I heard you, but I don't believe I—"

Finley broke off and stared at Corcoran in rising amazement.

"Al, are you trying to tell me—" he began.

"If those goddamn Apaches have anything to do with this," said Corcoran, "you can kiss your treaty good-bye."

Finley set his glass down heavily.

"Have you any reason at all for saying that?" he demanded.

"I *said* it," snarled Corcoran.

Finley pressed down the tremor of anger rising up inside him. "Listen, Al," he said, trying to take Corcoran's arm.

The brutish man pulled away.

"Al, you're wrong," said Finley. "You have no reason to—"

"They're my brothers, Finley," Corcoran said tightly.

"I know who they are, Al," said Finley. "And I'm telling you that the Apaches had nothing to do with them not showing up."

"They better show up soon," said Corcoran.

Finley's breath shook a little.

"They will, Al," he said quietly.

"They better."

Finley gestured, trying to clear the air. "Look, Al, if I can help you—"

He broke off abruptly and stood there watching Corcoran move for the doorway. He kept staring at the doors even after they had stopped swinging behind Corcoran's quick exit.

"What?" He started to turn to face Kelly.

"You think the Apaches could've—"

"*No*," snapped Finley, "I don't."

But his fingers on the glass, when he picked it up, were white across the knuckles. And after he'd swallowed half the drink, he set it down and paid for it.

"I'll see you later," he said.

"Y'need some help?" asked Appleface.

"No, that's all right," said Finley. "I'm just going to help Al find his brothers. I'm sure they're somewhere in town."

"You worried, Billjohn?" asked Kelly.

"No, no, of course not," said Finley, forcing a smile, "but Al is."

He patted Appleface's shoulder. "I'll see you later," he said.

The smile began to fade as he turned away from Kelly. Before he reached the doors it was completely gone, and all the pleasure of the consummated treaty had turned into a cold, nagging distress.

ittle Owl sat wondering what his brain looked like. In his youth, he'd watched two of his older brothers kill a white man. They had picked up the white man by his feet and smashed his head open against a rock. What had spilled across the dry surface of the rock had been the white man's brains, they'd told him. It had looked grayish, wet and slippery. It was still throbbing when he touched it.

But that was long ago. He could not understand why he should be thinking of it now. He had only been a small boy when it happened. Had it meant so much to him that now, when he was old, he should sit thinking of brains and wondering what his own looked like?

Abruptly, he remembered. Last week—or was it last month?—Doctor Phil had talked to him, right here in this room behind the barroom of the Sidewinder. Doctor Phil had been drunk. He drank a lot because he, too, was often tired and wanted to forget his tiredness. And he had been here, sitting across the table from Little Owl, telling him what his brain would look like if he kept on drinking.

The old Apache could not remember what Doctor Phil had said. Something about a sponge eaten away, he thought. He couldn't recall exactly. Memories were evasive now,

uncertain in time and content. As if, somehow, it had
rained in his head and everything was soaked together into
a common, irresolute mash.

The thought amused Little Owl. Outside it was raining—he could hear it falling in the alley beyond the
window—and in his head it was raining, too. The spaces
between his brain matter were like alleys between the
buildings of Picture City—muddy and dark. He was destroying his brain by a rain of beer and whiskey. Yes, that
was what Doctor Phil had said.

Or was it?

Little Owl opened his eyes slowly and stared at the grain
of the table. He looked at the limpness of his hands lying
on the table with the empty, foam-flecked stein between
them. What time was it? he wondered. Was it nighttime?
Or was it morning? No, it couldn't be morning because,
out in the other room, he could still hear the laughter and
talking of the men, the clinking of glasses, the occasional
scrape of a chair leg on the floor.

Little Owl straightened up with a soft groan. He had
been slouched in the chair and his back hurt. Maybe he
should leave the saloon and return to his wickiup, he
thought. Yes, that was what he'd do. He watched his leath
ery hands slide off the table and felt them settle on the
arms of the chair. Pushing down, he got himself into a
standing position, his legs limp and watery beneath him.
Everything around him was hazy at the edges, as if he
were looking through the parting in a mist. Only those
things he looked at directly had any clarity of line.

Little Owl walked across the room with careful deliberation. Maybe Finley was still there, he thought. Maybe
Finley would give him some money to buy a stein of beer.
Then he could go back to the table again and drink some
more. He liked the feeling it gave him to drink, the numb,
bodiless sensation. When he was deep in it, he could

return to the village in the mountains and be a boy again. He could run and laugh and wrestle in the clean, high air, ride horseback again, shoot his bow and arrow, fish in the cold, rushing streams. In memory, he could fill his stomach with roasted meat and lie, at peace, in the thick, hazy warmth of his father's wickiup.

The old Apache stood waveringly at the back of the barroom, looking for Finley. A sinking of disappointment pressed at his stomach. The Indian agent was gone. Little Owl sighed. He should go back to his wickiup. He should bring some meat to his children. Yes, that was what he'd do.

Appleface Kelly turned at the slight tug on his sleeve.

"You scroungin' again, you mangy old bastard?" he asked, then snickered. "No more," he said in Apache. "Get out of here."

Little Owl grunted and stood there, staring at Kelly with blank, obsidian eyes. Kelly turned his back on him, and after a moment, the Apache shifted his feet and headed slowly for the doors.

Before he reached them, Finley entered.

The Indian agent's slicker glistened from the rain and his hat was soaked through. Little Owl waited while Finley took them off and hung them on a wall hook.

Finley managed a smile as he turned. "Still here?" he said in Apache.

The old Indian still waited. Finley looked at him soberly a moment, then, sighing, reached into his pocket.

"Now listen," he told the Apache. "Take this money and buy food for your children. You understand?"

Little Owl stared at him a moment, then, with a grunt, he nodded once. Taking the money, he walked past Finley and pushed through the swinging doors. Finley watched him go. Poor lost soul, he was thinking. None of the dignity of his race left. Completely off the red road. Just a part-time cowboy who spent the major part of the year

cadging for drinks and sitting in silent drunkenness, looking into a past in which he was a man and not just a "damn
scrounging Injun."

Appleface Kelly looked over as Finley leaned against
the bar beside him and ordered whiskey.

"You find 'em?" asked Kelly.

Finley shook his head. "Not yet," he said.

It was not raining as hard as before. It came down now in
straight, almost soundless curtains. The air was colder
though. It made Little Owl shiver as he padded along the
plank walk toward the south edge of town. He should have
brought his blanket with him, he thought before remembering that, months before, he'd given the blanket in exchange for half a bottle of whiskey. Or had it been years
before?

At first, he didn't notice the man on horseback riding in
the same direction. When he was young, he would have
sensed the man's presence instantly, long before his eyes
had seen him. Now, when the muffled sound of the hoofbeats reached his ears, Little Owl started and glanced over
his shoulder dizzily.

It did not come at first. Little Owl saw only the outline
of a man on horseback. He turned his gaze back to the
front and kept on walking.

It was only after half a minute had passed that he realized the man was following him.

The old Apache squinted back across his shoulder again,
trying to see more clearly. Who was the man? Did he know
him? Little Owl grunted to himself, sensing the first twinge
of nervousness. He walked a little faster, trying not to show
it. He'd been through this sort of thing before. There were
always white men who took pleasure in trying to frighten
any Indian they came across.

Only when the man rode past him and reined his horse

in up ahead did the small Indian stop. He was standing at the head of an alley which ran between the post office and the bank. He stood motionless, watching the man dismount and tie the horse to a hitching post.

Then the man began to walk toward Little Owl.

The old Indian shuddered. He squinted hard, trying to make the man out, but his eyes were not good anymore and all he could see was the tall, broad silhouette coming at him. Only his hearing, still acute, picked out every detail of the man's approach—the sucking of his boots in the thick mud, the creak of the planking as the man raised his weight to it, the slow, thudding fall of the man's footsteps on the walk.

Then it began.

It was not a conscious reaction in the old Apache's mind. It was something deeper, a stirring in some long dormant center of awareness. Little Owl stood woodenly, staring at the man. Unwilled, a sound of disbelief rose suddenly in his throat. He sucked in fitfully at the cold, wet air and felt his heartbeat stagger.

The man kept walking toward him. Little Owl could see his eyes now. They seemed to glitter even though there were no lights around to be reflected. Help me, Little Owl thought; help me. He tried to cry the words aloud, but his tongue was like lead in his mouth. And even as he tried, he knew that there was no one who could help him, no one who could stop the approach of this tall, silent figure.

Little Owl began edging to the side, wordless mumblings in his throat. His lungs kept laboring for breath that would not come. It seemed as though he suffocated in some cold, dark emptiness. And the man kept coming at him with unhurried strides. No, thought Little Owl, it could not be.

It could not be.

Suddenly, the Apache whirled and lunged into the al-

ley, moccasins slapping at the mud. He glanced over his
shoulder with terrified eyes and saw that the man still
came. A sob exploded in his throat. He tried to run faster,
but he couldn't. Something was dragging at his legs. His
feet were stone. Gasping for breath, he ran along the alley
in a daze until he reached the fence that blocked his way.
There he spun around, a dry, convulsive rattling in his
throat.

The man stopped, close. He was very big, broad-
shouldered, a massive statue of a man. Little Owl pressed
against the cold, wet fence, looking at him. He could not
speak or breathe or think. All he could do was stare with
frozen eyes, unable to comprehend the horror that stood
before him.

The man spoke in Apache.

"You will help me," he said.

Little Owl jerked back against the fence, a dull cry pulling at his lips. The man took a step closer. Little Owl tried to
scream, but only a witless bubbling came from his mouth.

"*You will help me,*" said the man.

Abruptly, the eyes rolled back in Little Owl's head and,
with a gagging whine, he crumpled to the ground, landing facedown in the mud.

The man came over slowly and stood beside the body.
He looked down at it with unmoving eyes, eyes without
emotion. Then he turned and walked back out of the alley.

Finley set his glass down. "I'm off again," he said.

"Where to now?" asked Appleface.

"Well, they're not in town," said Finley, "I'm sure of
that. I guess I'll have to help Al look around outside of
town."

"Is that where he is?"

Finley nodded. "He rode out about an hour ago."

The Indian agent laid a coin beside his empty glass.

"See you later," he said, then smiled wryly. "Seems like I already said that," he added.

"What are you knockin' your brains out for?" Appleface asked him. "The Corcoran boys ain't your worry."

"Al thinks the Apaches are involved," said Finley. "That *is* my worry."

He punched Kelly lightly on the arm. "And I don't like to worry," he said.

"Don't get wet now," Appleface told him.

Finley chuckled. "I'll see what I can do," he said.

He walked across the room and put his hat and slicker on, then pushed out through the doors and started north toward the livery stable. Finley didn't see the tall figure coming up the walk from the opposite direction.

Inside the saloon, Kelly picked his drink up and carried it across the room to where the Dailey brothers, Lon and Earl, were playing blackjack.

"Get in the next hand, boys?" he asked.

"Sure," said Lon. "Sit down."

Kelly had barely settled in his chair when the man came in.

"Hey, hey, hey," muttered Appleface.

The Dailey brothers glanced at him, then, as Kelly tipped his head toward the doorway, they looked in that direction.

Lon Dailey whistled under his breath.

The man was big. So big that the clothes he wore, though made for a large frame, clung to him tightly, the sleeve ends high on his thick wrists, the pants cuffs riding far up on his mud-spattered boots.

"Who the hell is he?" Earl Dailey murmured.

"I never seen him before," said Appleface.

By now they were not the only ones in the saloon looking with covert curiosity at the man. He did not seem to notice it, however, or, if he did, he gave it no attention.

As he stood immobile in the doorway, the rain-dripping hat too high on his skull, his gaze moved slowly, searchingly, around the room.

"What in hell's he lookin' for?" Lon Dailey whispered through his teeth.

"*Who* in hell's he lookin' for?" Kelly whispered back, masking the movement of his lips with a squeezing tug at his nose.

"I'm glad it ain't me," whispered Earl Dailey.

Appleface squinted at the man suddenly.

"Is he an *Injun*?" he wondered aloud.

The three of them looked carefully at the man. Strangely enough, they couldn't tell if he was an Indian or not. If swarthiness were the only test, there would have been little doubt. But they had all seen white men burned by the sun to a similar pigmentation. It was the features themselves that weren't right. The arrangement of them did not place a definite stamp of Indian on the man. Nor was he clearly a white man either. The harsh angularities of his face seemed, in fact, to go beyond the limits of either possibility. Somehow, it seemed closer to being an animal than a human face.

As the man started toward the counter, the collar of his coat slipped down.

Only the general noise in the room kept Appleface's voice from being heard as he said, "*Holy jumpin' Christ!*"

Around the entire circumference of the man's neck was a red, uneven scar, thick and crudely stitched.

The three men sat staring at the stranger as he halted before the counter. They saw Eddie come walking over, saw him glance involuntarily at the scar, then with a quick, nervous swallow, force a smile to his lips and ask the man what his pleasure was.

They couldn't hear what the man was saying; only the deep rumble of his voice was audible. They saw Eddie pour a drink hastily, but the man didn't touch it. He spoke again and Eddie answered. Even from where they sat, they could see how the young bartender seemed to shrink back from the man.

Abruptly, the stranger turned and headed for the doorway.

"Say—" Eddie called after him.

The man stopped and looked over his shoulder, his dark eyes boring into the bartender's.

"W-what about your drink?" asked Eddie, trying to look affable.

The three men couldn't see the expression on the man's face, but they noticed how a muscle twitched in Eddie's cheek.

"M-my money, I mean." Eddie seemed to be speaking more from instinct than desire. His voice was not strong, but it had grown so quiet in the saloon now that everyone could hear it.

The man didn't seem to understand.

"Money?" asked Eddie. He swallowed. "For the drink?"

He held up the glass, obviously regretting that he'd spoken at all. Then, putting down the glass, he dug a coin out of his vest pocket and held it up.

The stranger looked down at his clothes. Awkwardly, he slid his big right hand into the pants pocket and drew it out, coins clutched between the thick fingers. Stepping to the counter, he dropped them, and two of the coins rolled toward the back edge of the counter. Eddie lunged for them.

"Hey, that's too much," he said.

But the man was already halfway to the doors. Eddie called after him once again, then said no more. Blank-faced, he watched the big stranger push out through the batwing doors and disappear. One of the men at the table nearest the doorway got up and peeked across the top of the doors. After a moment, he turned back and shrugged exaggeratedly to his friends.

Appleface got up and walked over to the bar, where he talked with Eddie. In a minute, he was back.

"What'd he want?" Lon Dailey asked.

"Eddie said he asked after a small man in a black suit," he said. "A man with a little beard. A man of learning."

"He asked in English?" asked Earl.

Kelly nodded. "Yeah."

"What'd Eddie tell 'im?" asked Lon.

"Eddie said he thought the stranger must've meant Perfessor Dodge," said Appleface.

"Dodge?" Earl grimaced. "What in hell would he want the perfessor for?"

Kelly shook his head. "I dunno," he said.

"Eddie tell him where t'find the perfessor?"

"I guess he did," said Kelly.

The three men looked at each other for a moment. Then Earl Dailey cleared his throat.

"What the hell," he said, reaching for his cards. "Whose play?"

4

Harry Vance sat mumbling behind the desk of the lobby of the White River Hotel. He was mad, good and mad. Ethel had made him come out and sit there. You never knew on a night like this, she'd said. All sorts of people might be coming in for rooms. You never knew.

Well, Harry knew. Good and well, he knew. Ethel didn't think for a damn second that there'd be any extra guests that night. She was just mad about last night and this was her little way of getting even with him. She couldn't get honest mad with him, couldn't—wouldn't—tell him what was really on her mind. Oh, no, never in a million centuries! She was a woman, wasn't she? Did a woman ever tell a man what was really on her mind? Ever in the whole history of mankind?

Hell, no! She waited till the next night and then got even with him by asking him to do something she knew full well there wasn't the least bit of need to do. Like sit here in the cold, empty lobby waiting for a guest who'd never show up. Sure, that was a woman. All tricks and deceits and never an honest-to-God explanation. Never.

Christ Almighty, you'd think they were a hundred years old apiece! The way she got so mad every time he tried

anything with her. A hundred damn darn years old apiece.
Christ!

He was glaring down the black well of his thoughts when
the bell over the door tinkled and a stream of cold air
rushed across the lobby floor.

Focusing his eyes, Harry Vance saw the tall man entering. Then, hastily willed, a smile of calculated hospitality
creased his round face, and he leaned forward as if preparing himself to leap over the waist-high counter and embrace the man in cordial welcome.

"Evenin', sir, evenin'," he said genially. Well, by Christ,
they could sure use an extra guest or two. Things were
darn slow this month. Darn slow.

The tall man moved across the rug slowly, his boots
leaving wet, mud-streaked imprints on the carpeting. Oh,
God, he hadn't wiped his feet off! thought Harry, an agony of prescience straining behind his smile. Ethel would
be furious.

Well, the hell with Ethel! he decided suddenly, eyes
steeling. They could have locked the place up, but no, she
had to send him out to sit in the lobby and wait for a guest.
Well, here was a guest, by Christ, and he was tracking up
the floor. So, the hell with her. Let her clean up the damn
spots!

The man stopped before him.

"Yes, sir," Harry said, swiveling the book around and
plucking the pen from its holder. "Just stayin' for the night,
are ya?"

The man didn't even glance at the pen which Harry held
out for him.

"Dodge," he said, his voice deep, guttural.

"Sir?" Harry Vance's smile faltered a little.

"*Dodge,*" the man repeated.

"Dodge City?" Harry asked. He thought he understood.
The man couldn't write and was too embarrassed to

admit it. He was telling Harry he was from Dodge City. Well, that was all right so long as he had coin. Harry would—

"Pro-fessor Dodge," the man said carefully.

The smile was gone. Harry's expression was removed, impersonal. This was no paying guest.

"He ain't here," he said.

"What—room?" asked the man. He spoke as if speaking was an ability laboriously learned, a skill not altogether mastered.

"Twenny-nine," Harry said automatically. He tightened. "But he ain't here," he said. "I *told* ya. He's on one of them field trips. He's a—"

He broke off as the man turned and headed for the staircase.

"I said he wasn't in," he called impatiently.

The man began walking up the steps, boots thudding measuredly on the worn carpeting.

"Hey!" Harry squinted after the man. "I said he wasn't in!" By Christ, he was getting mad now. He'd—

"*Harry.*"

Vance almost vacated his skin as the voice snapped behind him. He grunted in pain as, lurching spasmodically against the counter edge, he hurt his stomach. He whirled, indignant.

"What're ya creepin' up behind me for?" he asked.

"Who is that man?" asked Ethel Vance, pointing toward the stairs.

Harry swallowed his indignation and added it to the indigestable mass already in his frustration-bound stomach.

"I don't know," he said. "He just come in and asked for Perfessor Dodge."

"He's not in," said Ethel.

"I know he's not in," whined Harry. "I told him so."

"Then what's he going up for?" demanded Ethel.

"He's going up because—"

Harry broke off. "I don't know why he's goin' up!" he said, exasperated. "I didn't tell 'im to. He just went."

"Then you just march up there after him, Harry Vance," she ordered. "I won't have strangers walking around in my hotel."

There it was God Almighty. *Her* hotel! As if he hadn't worked like a damn horse to make it a going proposition. Just because her old man left it to her in his will. Her hotel. Christ.

"Well?" asked Ethel.

"Well?" Harry echoed faintly. "What?"

"Are you going up there?" she challenged. "Or are you just going to stand here and let him break into our rooms?"

"Oh, for—" Harry twisted irritably. "He ain't no robber."

"How do *you* know?"

By Christ—the thought drove an icy needle into his heart—how *did* he know? Suddenly, he saw that man again, standing across the desk from him; tall, swarthy, with those dark, implacable eyes. Good Christ, he might even have been an Indian! And the way he spoke, almost mechanically. Harry shuddered. And he'd yelled after the man like—

"Are you *going*?" demanded Ethel.

"Yes, yes, of course I'm going," he snapped. He stepped away from his stool and lifted the counter board. Then he hesitated.

"Well?" she asked.

Swallowing, Harry lowered the board and moved over to the drawer. Pulling it out, he reached inside and picked up the loaded derringer. Ethel looked at him with nervous speculation.

"What are you doing?" she asked, somewhat less authority in her voice now.

"Well," he said, "you can't tell. How do we know who he is?"

For a moment, he felt a stir of pleasure at the alarmed expression crossing Ethel's face. Then the cold prickle of dread was on his spine again and he found himself raising the board once more, found himself advancing toward the staircase.

"Wait," Ethel said suddenly.

Harry twitched and looked around. "No need for—" he began to say, then shut up. Well, the truth of it was he was more than glad for Ethel's company. There was something reassuring about her presence for all her furies and edicts.

The two of them started up the steps.

"You didn't get his name?" she asked.

"He didn't give it," answered Harry.

For some reason, they both spoke in whispers as if, tacitly, it had been agreed between them that the stranger in the hotel was a menace.

"You—think he has a pistol?" asked Ethel.

Harry swallowed dryly. "Probably," he said. He tried to sound casual but failed.

At the head of the staircase, they turned left and moved cautiously into the hallway. They both stopped.

"*Where is he*?" asked Ethel.

Harry stared down the empty hallway. "I don't know," he murmured.

"You think he's in the perfessor's room?" she asked.

"How could he be?" countered Harry. "The perfessor always locks his door when he goes out. He has valuable specimens in there."

Ethel swallowed.

"Then where is he?" she asked.

"Maybe he thought I said thirty-nine," suggested Harry. "Maybe he's up on the third floor."

"Go look," said Ethel.

Harry tightened angrily. Oh, sure, the thought came. Go look. As if he was a big hero or something. As if . . .

Drawing in a shaky breath, he started up the staircase. That man was awfully big. Awfully big.

At the third-floor landing, he stopped and braced himself, one hand resting on the bannister. All right, mister, his mind rehearsed sternly, what do you want up here? You got business? He swallowed again. By Christ, he thought.

He stepped forward quickly, snapping back the hammer of the derringer so that the curved trigger came clicking down to his finger.

The hall was empty.

Harry blinked. Well, what the hell? he thought. What in the blue blazes?

"Harry!"

He started violently, his heartbeat lurching so violently it felt like a horse's kick against his chest wall. Whirling, he thudded down the steps, derringer extended.

"Come here!" called Ethel. It was not exactly a call of distress, it seemed to Harry, but then you never knew how someone like Ethel might react in a moment of danger. Maybe even sudden peril would fail to alter her habit of demanding.

But she was all right, standing at the end of the hallway by the window. Harry walked toward her quickly, testing the door to Professor's Dodge's room as he passed. It was locked.

"What is it?" he asked.

"You leave this window open?" Ethel asked, and there was something in her voice other than demand, Harry noticed.

He had said no before it struck him what the import was of his saying it. He stared out the window at the precipitous drop to the street below.

"You . . . think he *jumped*?" he asked.

Ethel pressed her lips together. "That's *impossible*," she said angrily.

They both looked out the window. Could a man jump that far? wondered Harry. Wouldn't it break his legs?

Then Ethel said, *"Harry,"* in a faint voice.

"What?"

"Look."

His gaze fell to where she was pointing, and he saw the imprint of boot tracks ending at the window.

Harry gaped. There was a swelling in his chest and stomach as if all his organs were expanding. No, there had to be another explanation, his mind claimed instantly. No man could jump twenty-five feet to the ground nor could he climb along a wall that was devoid of footholds or hand-holds.

"Of course," he said, speaking before his mind was set.

"What?" There was a rare sound of grateful attention in Ethel's voice.

"He's in the perfessor's room," said Harry.

"But you said the door was locked," she objected weakly.

"Sure." He plunged on, unwilling to allow the sight of those boot prints to distract him. "He locked it from the inside after he went in. He must have a skeleton key."

"But—what about the window then?"

"Don't you see?" he argued. "He tried to trick us. He opened it up to make us think that was the way he left."

"I don't—" She stared at him blankly. Then, abruptly, she pointed at the boot prints. "What about them?" she asked.

"That's a trick, too," said Harry, trying to outtalk the speed of fear. "He could walk to the window, open it, then move backwards in the same prints. That's an old Injun trick."

He snapped his fingers, making Ethel twitch.

"He *is* an Injun!" he said. "I thought so when I seen him."

"An *Indian*?"

They both looked at each other intently, and suddenly Harry knew what she was going to say and it made him cold inside.

"We'll have to look," she told him.

A shuddered breath passed Harry's lips. *We'll have to look.* The words echoed in his mind.

"You have the key?" she asked.

Harry tried to swallow.

"Well, have you?"

He murmured, "Yeah."

"Then . . ."

No more to be said. The two of them edged over to the door, and Ethel put her ear against it, face twisted with concentration.

"I don't hear anything," she whispered.

"Maybe he's not there anymore," Harry said hopefully.

"Then where is he?"

"I don't know," Harry whispered pettishly. "Are all the other doors locked?"

"Yes. They—"

They both recoiled against each other as a door down the hall suddenly opened.

David Boutelle did not see them. He walked along the hall briskly and turned right onto the staircase. They heard the sound of his descending boots.

"M-Mister Boutelle," mumbled Harry.

Ethel drew in a deep breath.

"*Open the door,*" she said.

"Yes," he said, although his mind said *no*.

The hand he slid into his pocket was cold and shaking. His fingers twitched when they touched the key. He drew it out and slipped it into the keyhole. It rattled there.

"Shh!" hissed Ethel.

Harry closed his eyes. "Will you—?" he began to request.

"Open it fast," said Ethel.

And be ready to use your gun, Harry's mind completed the instruction. He drew in a ragged breath. Through the open window at the end of the hall, he could hear the rustling fall of rain, the clopping of a horse's hooves as it passed the hotel. All right, mister, his mind began again, put your hands up. You can't go breakin' into this hotel without—

He shoved the door open and jumped in quickly, gun raised to fire.

The room was empty.

It was not until immediate fear had gone that the discomfiture of the earlier dread returned. If the man was not in here or in the hall, if he could not possibly have jumped from the window to the street—*where was he*?

Harry stood in mute perplexity while his wife stepped over to the light bracket on the wall and turned up the flame.

The room seemed truly empty. Harry closed his eyes and shivered. What in the blue blazes of merry hell, he thought, is going on?

"Well, he must have gone out the window then, that's all," he said, trying to push down the fear rising inside him.

"But—"

"Who knows why?" he anticipated her. "Maybe he heard us coming up the stairs and got scared. Who knows? But he sure ain't in here."

"Harry, the . . ." Ethel swallowed with effort. "The . . . closet," she said.

Harry could not repress the groan in his chest. Was there to be no end to the woman's alarms? Well, he was getting tired of this, he told himself casually, as if his heart were not threatening to discharge itself from its place. Striding quickly to the closet door, he flung it open.

It was empty.

"There," he said. "Now let's stop this nonsense." He was so relieved that, for a second, the room swam before his eyes.

"Well . . ." she murmured indecisively.

"Ethel, he ain't *in* here," Harry said, feeling a bolt of dread that she might start telling him to look under the bed, look behind the armchair over by the window, look behind . . .

"I . . . guess not," Ethel said.

"Come on, let's go."

Ethel turned down the flame, and they went out into the hall again.

"Shut the window," she told him as he closed the door and relocked it carefully. She started down the hall, muttering to herself, "I still can't see how anyone could jump from that high."

"Well, he did," said Harry. And, by Christ, he was going to believe it, too.

When the door had closed and dark silence filled the room again, the man lifted the window and stepped inside.

He stood for a moment beside the armchair, looking around. Behind him, down in the street, a horse was trotting by and he twitched his head around. He looked at the street, raindrops inching slowly down his cheeks.

When the horse had gone, he turned back again. He walked across the room and twisted up the oil flame, the burnished glow of it crowding darkness into the corners. Then he moved over to the bureau and drew out the top drawer.

He looked down impassively at the cuffs and collars stuffed in messily, the mound of starched handkerchiefs. He opened another drawer and stared at the shirts and ties, the undergarments, the books. Abruptly, he shoved the drawers shut. These things were of no value to him.

He stood before the bureau mirror looking at his reflection—tall, copper-skinned, dark-eyed, the hair ebony-black and long. Steadily, he looked at the reflection of his carven face.

Then his hand, which rested on the bureau top, stirred and brushed against something. The man looked down. It was a specimen of gneiss rock. He looked at the veiny structure of it, then his fingers closed around it slowly and his gaze lifted again to the mirror.

He had to find Dodge. He had to find him soon. Fury began to stir in him, and he looked at the wavering reflection of his face in the mirror, at the mounting shapelessness about his features. Only the burning eyes remained steady.

As he stared, the gneiss rock, hardened by centuries, crumbled to dust between his straining fingers.

5

The pendulum clock on the wall behind his desk was just striking for the ninth time as Finley unlocked his office door and went inside.

Standing in the darkness, he peeled off his dripping slicker and tossed it on the bench beside the door, dropping his rain-soaked hat on top of it. Slowly, he removed his damp jacket and hung it on the clothes tree.

"There," he murmured.

Walking over to the desk, he lifted off the top of the oil lamp and lit the wick, turning the flame up high. Then, replacing the top, he clumped over to the stove.

There was still a bed of glowing embers near the bottom from that morning's fire. To this he added newspaper scraps and kindling until the flames fingered up brightly. Then he dropped in heavier chunks of wood. He kicked the stove door shut, pulled a chair up in front of it, and settled down with a sigh. Groaning tiredly, he pulled off his boots and dropped them on the floor. That was better.

He was just relaxing, eyes shut, deliberating whether or not it was worth the effort to get up and make a pot of coffee, when there was a single, hard rap on the door. He grunted and opened his eyes. Pushing slowly to his feet, he walked across the cold floorboards in his stocking feet and opened the door.

"There you are," he said, "I've been looking all over for you."

"Have ya?" Al Corcoran looked exhausted, his eyes rimmed with red, his face drawn and colorless.

Finley stepped back quickly and drew the door open wide. "Come in and get warm," he said. "I'll put some coffee on."

Al came in, and Finley shut the door, pulling down the shade that covered its top half of glass.

"Now look, Al," he said, turning, "before you start—"

"They ain't back yet, Finley," said Corcoran. It was almost a warning.

"I know that, Al," said Finley.

"And they ain't holed up in some cave," said Corcoran. "And they ain't out ridin' in the rain."

"Al, there are a hundred places in this area they could be," said Finley. "You can't expect to find them on a night like this. I've been out looking for them, too, and I couldn't see a thing. So—"

"So *nothin',*" Corcoran interrupted. "You gonna do anything or not?"

"Al, I've done all there *is* to do tonight," Finley told him. "In the morning, we'll—"

"In the morning be damned!" flared Corcoran. "For all I know they're lyin' out there somewhere with—!"

He stopped abruptly, breathing hard, as someone knocked on the door. Finley gritted his teeth and stepped over to it.

"Yes?" he said.

"Boutelle," said the voice.

Oh, *great*, thought Finley. This was exactly what he needed right now. Exhaling wearily, he opened the door.

"Come in," he said.

Boutelle's eyebrows raised slightly when he saw the brooding Corcoran standing there. "Good evening," he said, nodding once. Corcoran grunted.

"If you'll excuse us for a second, Mr. Boutelle," Finley said, "I'll be with you directly."

"Of course," Boutelle said crisply. He walked over to the desk, glancing briefly at Finley's unshod feet.

"Now, listen, Al," Finley said quietly, hoping Boutelle wouldn't hear. "So help me God, Braided Feather had nothing to do with this. You'll be making a terrible mistake if you think he did. It's something else. You have to believe that. At least until—"

"Why should I believe an Injun lover?" said Corcoran through his teeth.

It was only the slightest tensing of skin across Finley's cheekbones, the least flinting of his gray-green eyes, but Corcoran went rigid as if preparing for a fight.

Finley forced away the angry tension.

"We'll forget you said that, Al," he said.

"You don't have to—"

"Al." Finley's fingers tightened on the heavy man's arm. "Take my word on this until morning. That's all I'm asking you to do. As soon as it's light, we'll go out and find them."

He paused a moment. "All right?"

Corcoran stared at him for a few seconds. Then, jerking his arm free, he turned on his heel and walked over to the door. It slammed loudly behind him.

Finley closed his eyes and blew out a heavy breath. Then, bracing himself for the inevitable, he turned.

"Braided Feather had nothing to do with what?" asked Boutelle.

Finley felt a heavy sinking in his stomach. Dear God, now he was in for it.

"Just a small misunderstanding," he said.

"Regarding what, Mr. Finley?"

Finley didn't answer.

"I would appreciate your telling me," Boutelle said stiffly. "Anything concerning the Apaches—"

"This does *not* concern the Apaches," said Finley.

"Apparently, the gentleman who just left thinks otherwise," said Boutelle.

"He's wrong."

"Please let me be the judge of that," said Boutelle. "What *does* he believe, Mr. Finley?"

Finley sighed. Well, what was the purpose in trying to keep it a secret from Boutelle? It would only make him more suspicious. Casually, as if relating something of little consequence, Finley told the younger man about Tom and Jim Corcoran's disappearance that afternoon. He did not emphasize Al Corcoran's idea about it.

"And they haven't been found yet," said Boutelle. It was not a question.

"Let's say they haven't shown up yet," said Finley. He forced a smile to his lips. "Now, can I be of service to you, Mr. Boutelle?"

Boutelle ignored this.

"Why are you so positive the Apaches had nothing to do with it?" he asked.

Finley clenched his teeth.

"I'm positive," was all he said.

"You talk, Mr. Finley," said Boutelle, "as if no white man has ever been robbed and murdered by an Apache before."

"No white man ever *has* been by Braided Feather's people," snapped Finley.

"I suppose—"

"That was *war*, Mr. Boutelle," Finley interrupted, anticipating what the younger man was going to say. "I, myself, killed eight men during the war with the Confederate states, but I don't think of myself as a murderer."

"I suggest, Mr. Finley," said Boutelle, "that you are, with some deliberation, blinding yourself to a condition only too prevalent. I realize fully that the idea of your hard-won treaty being already broken is not a—"

"You're *wrong*, Mr. Boutelle." Finley shuddered. How long could he hold his temper? He was close to the edge now.

"It has been well established," said Boutelle, "that any number of Indians— Apaches included—periodically desert their reservations—after first collecting their government-issued supplies, of course—and rob and murder white men!"

Boutelle drew in a quick, angry breath.

"Quite periodically, Mr. Finley," he said.

Finley looked darkly at the younger man. Already, he could see Senator Boutelle standing erect and gesturing in the halls of Congress, booming out his splendidly phrased maledictions against the Western Savage. His checks puffed out momentarily as he blew out jaded breath. It was useless to get furious with such pomposity.

"Let's just wait before we make up our minds, shall we?" he suggested.

Boutelle's smile was the thin, supercilious one of a man who is convinced of his own opinion.

"For your sake, Mr. Finley," he said, "I hope you're right."

Finley nodded. "Now, can I help you?" he asked.

"I had meant to consult you about my report to Washington," said Boutelle. "However, under the revised circumstances—"

The younger man stopped talking as there was a faint tapping on the door. Finley turned his head and looked in that direction. "We are really popular tonight," he muttered to himself as he padded over to the door and opened it.

A short, squat Indian woman was standing there. At the sight of her, Finley's annoyed expression softened a little.

"What is it?" he asked in Apache. "Is something wrong with your husband?"

"He has not come back tonight," she answered. "I thought you would know where he is."

Finley looked unhappily exasperated. "I sent him to you," he said. "Hours ago I sent him to you."

There was a flickering in the woman's eyes. Finley rightly identified it as fear.

"He's still in town then," he reassured her. "Look for him in the Sidewinder or at the Silver Hall."

Already, he thought he knew the answer. The old Apache had taken the money given him and gone to the Silver Hall Saloon instead of going to his wickiup as Finley had told him. It would not be the first time.

"And if I do not find him?" the Indian woman was asking.

Finley smiled. "You will find him," he said.

The Apache woman nodded. "I thank you, Finley," she said.

Finley patted her shoulder as she turned away. Closing the door, the Indian agent turned back to Boutelle.

"Was that to do with those two missing men?" the younger man asked.

"No, no." Finley shook his head. "That was Little Owl's wife. She's looking for him."

"Little Owl? Was that the Indian you gave drink money to before?"

"Yes."

Boutelle smiled scornfully. "He's probably lying somewhere in a drunken stupor," he said.

The Indian agent grunted.

"Probably," he said.

Boutelle looked contemptuous. "Indians," he said.

"No, Mr. Boutelle." Finley shook his head, and his voice had an acid edge to it. "Civilization."

Little Owl's wife shuffled through the misty rain, her dark eyes searching.

Something had happened to her husband, something evil. Of that she was certain. As certain as she was of the blood running in her veins, of the heart pulsing heavily behind her breast. Last night, as she lay awake listening to the bubbly snores of Little Owl and the children, outside, high in the cottonwoods, an owl had hooted. The sound of it had turned her flesh to ice.

This morning she had told Little Owl about it. We must leave, she had said; the hooting of an owl is a bad omen. We must go to another place.

But Little Owl had only shaken his head and refused to speak of it. He had been too long among the white men. The instincts of his fathers had died in him, and he no longer believed in signs and omens. It was at that moment, as he turned away from her in silence, that she knew something would happen. Little Owl's failure to believe would cause it.

She did not enter the alley for a long time. First, at Finley's word, she had gone to the Sidewinder Saloon and peered inside, holding one of the swinging doors ajar. But Little Owl was not in there. Nor was he in the Silver Hall Saloon, sitting, as he usually did, at a corner table with a stein of beer in front of him.

And he was not anywhere along the boardwalks. Often, when he had drunk so much that he could not get back to the wickiup, he would curl up on a bench along the walk. She would find him there and help him onto the back of their pony. The horse she would not let him take from the wickiup because she knew that he would only sell it for drink money.

And what an endless anguish it was in her woman's heart to have her husband, mute and without fire, allow her to forbid him anything. In his younger days, when they had lived among their own people, he would have beaten her if she dared to withhold anything from him. He would have flung her to the ground and shouted at her in a fury, *I am the head of our family and no squaw will tell me what to do or not to do!*

It was the measure of his fall that he no longer offered to beat or strike her, no longer contested her words at any time. He only grunted and shook or nodded his head and shambled toward Picture City for drink. Yes, it was an evilly distorted world they lived in now.

She did not see Little Owl at first when she entered the alley. She did not believe that she would find him there, but she knew that she must look in every place before she dared return to Finley and ask for his help. What if he asked her—Did you look in such a place?—and she had to answer, in truth—No, I did not. No, she must try all the places before she—

Then she saw her husband lying in the mud.

It was two things at once to her; first, an icy constriction in her bowels and stomach, a thumping pressure at her temples. Yet, at the same time, almost a relief because the sight of him there was proof that the omen had been true and that some values in their life, at least, remained as they should.

It was not until she bent over him, however, that she knew his death and the hideousness of it.

A sound of animal pain tore the lips drawn back from her teeth, and with a sharp intake of breath, she scuttled backward. In her haste, she slipped and fell. Scrambling to her feet again, she started running, all the black horrors in her world pursuing her.

By the time she reached Finley's office, she could hardly breathe. Wheezing, she fell against the door, clubbing weakly at the glass.

Finley had to catch her when he opened the door.

"*What?*" he asked her in Apache.

She could not speak. Only sobbing gasps escaped her lips as she pointed down the street.

Hastily, Finley ran over to the stove and pulled his boots on. Then, grabbing his jacket off the clothes tree, he hurried outside, feeling the clutch of the woman's hand on his sleeve as they started along the walk. Behind them, he heard the fall of Boutelle's following boots.

She would not go up the alley again. She stood pressed against the side of the bank, shivering impotently as Finley and Boutelle walked in to where the body lay. Finley squatted down and turned Little Owl onto his back, his hand sliding underneath the Apache's buckskin shirt.

"Dead," he murmured.

"Is it one of those two men?" asked Boutelle.

Finley didn't answer. Reaching into his shirt pocket, he took out his match case. Opening it, he struck a match and lit the wick of the tiny candle inserted in the case. Then, roofing the flame with his palm, he held it close to Little Owl's face.

"*Good God.*" Boutelle's voice was faint.

If ever a look of heart-wrenched terror had been imprinted on a man's face, it was on Little Owl's. The dark features were stiff with it; the mud-caked lips drawn back frozenly in a hideous grin of fright, the dark eyes open wide and staring. It took an effort for Finley to force down the lids of those horror-stricken eyes.

"What in God's name happened to him?" a sickened Boutelle asked.

Again, Finley didn't answer. He ran the candle flame along the length of the Apache's body, looking for a wound. As he did, the tight pain in his eyes began changing.

"There's not a mark on him," he said quietly. The very quietness of his voice seemed to underline the words.

"His heart then," said Boutelle. It sounded less like a statement than an uneasy question.

"I don't know," said Finley.

Letting the rain douse the candle, he shut the cover of the match case and slid it back into his shirt pocket. Then, raising Little Owl to a limp, sitting position, he lifted the dead Indian across his shoulder.

It was remarkable how light he was, Finley could not help thinking. It was as if once the weight of self-respect had gone from Little Owl, his body had complied with the loss, grown fragile and honeycombed with the weightlessness of defeat. Some men, in loss, grow heavy, thought Finley. Some merely wasted away like Little Owl.

He didn't notice where the eyes of Little Owl's wife were looking as he passed her. If he had noticed and thought about it, he would have guessed that her gaze was averted because she was afraid to look upon death until the actual moment of bodily preparation.

He was unaware of the fact that she had seen the tall, broad form standing in the shadows across the street from them. He was unaware that the stricture around her heart was so close to that stricture which had killed her husband that she, herself, almost lost the power to breathe and stand and almost went pitching forward into the mud.

Darkness wavered behind the woman's eyes. Horror sucked at her breath, licked across her brain with a cold, rasping tongue. Only the greatest exertion of will kept her on her feet. With a drawn-in gasp of air, she pushed away from the bank and followed Boutelle closely. She must not look at the tall, dark figure, she knew. He must not realize that she knew of his presence. If she died now, then all was lost.

Back inside the office, Finley lowered the body to the bench beside the door and covered it with his slicker. The expression on Little Owl's face, as it was hidden away, fused itself into Finley's consciousness like a brand seared into flesh.

"I'll take him to your—" he began to say in Apache before he realized that Little Owl's wife was not there.

He looked over at Boutelle. "Where did she go?" he asked.

"I didn't see," the younger man answered. He couldn't take his eyes off the covered figure on the bench.

"Wasn't she with us?"

Boutelle swallowed. "I thought so."

Finley went over to the door and opened it. Stepping out onto the walk, he looked toward the south end of town but saw nothing. Grunting, he went back inside and closed the door. He walked across the office and entered the small hallway that led to the back door. He found the door slightly ajar. She had gone this way then. But why? She should have stayed and gone with the body when Finley took it to her wickiup for burial preparation.

Shaking his head, Finley closed the back door firmly and turned. And this had started out, in the words of Appleface Kelly, as a "gala day." Well, it had, very early, turned into something far different.

"Why did she leave?" asked Boutelle.

"Apache dread of death," said Finley, not wanting Boutelle to know any more than he did.

"What do you suppose happened to him?" Boutelle asked.

"I don't know," said Finley.

He would, most certainly, not answer that question. Boutelle had shown no desire to understand the Indians' point of view. It would do little good for him to tell Boutelle that, as far as he could see, Little Owl had been frightened to death.

She had run, hobbling, all the way to the tethered horse, then walked the horse far out of Picture City. Only there, breathless, a stitch knifing at her side, had she dared to mount and gallop to the wickiup.

She stayed there only long enough to wake her eldest girl and tell her to watch over the other children until her mother returned. She did not tell the girl that Little Owl was dead. There would be time enough for that in the morning.

Right now there was a ride to be made.

Quitting the wickiup hastily, the Apache woman mounted the pony and kicked at its bony sides. The old animal surged forward underneath her, its thin legs driving at the muddy earth. Little Owl's wife set her teeth and braced herself for the ride.

It was a long way to the camp of Braided Feather.

THURSDAY

6

The two of them were in Corcoran's Gunsmith Shop. Al Corcoran was pulling down a rifle from the wall rack. No, Al, pleaded Finley, you're *wrong*. Al Corcoran didn't say a word. He began to load the rifle. Finley knew that he was going to go after Braided Feather and shoot him. Don't be a fool! he said. If you do that, you'll start the whole thing over again! The treaty won't be worth the paper it's written on. Corcoran said nothing. Al! cried Finley. He jerked the rifle out of Corcoran's hands and threw it on the floor.

Corcoran went over to the wall rack and took down another rifle. For God's sake, Al! said Finley. He tore the rifle out of Corcoran's grip and flung it on the floor. Corcoran drew the pistol from his holster. Al, don't, said Finley. Corcoran squeezed the trigger, and Finley felt a bullet club him on the chest. He fell back against the workbench. Corcoran was walking toward the door, the smoking pistol in his hand. The next one is for Braided Feather, he said. No, it isn't, Finley said vengefully. He drew his pistol out and tried to fire it, but the trigger stuck. When he jerked it desperately, it broke off against his finger like brittle glass. Oh, God! moaned Finley. He lunged for one of the rifles on the floor.

Before Corcoran could get out the door, Finley fired three bullets into his back. Al flung forward onto his face, and Finley staggered to his feet. You won't break my treaty now, he said. I won't let you. He fired another bullet into Corcoran's body.

Then, outside, there was a thundering of hooves. Braided Feather and his men came galloping toward the front of the shop. Finley ran out to tell them that the treaty was safe, but as they galloped up, they threw two torn and bleeding bodies at him. Suddenly, Finley knew he had been wrong. No! he cried. No! I can't be wrong!

Finley jolted in his bed. He sat up, gasping.

Outside and down the street there was a rising thunder of hoofbeats. For a second, Finley sat dazed, staring at the window with sleep-drugged eyes. Then, with a brusque motion, he flung aside the covers and dropped his legs to the floor. He stood and raced across the carpet to the window and jerked up its shade.

It was barely light. Main Street stood empty in the gray of morning. But the thunder was coming closer, and Finley turned his head to the left. Instantly, his mouth dropped open in dumb astonishment.

Galloping into town were approximately three dozen Apache braves.

Finley gaped down at the street with eyes that could not believe what they saw. He looked for the leader of the party and saw, with added shock, that it was Braided Feather. He stared down blankly as the Apache chief went rushing by, the hooves of his horse casting up gouts of mud.

Then, whirling abruptly, he raced to the bed and jerked his nightshirt off. He was dressed in twenty seconds, his arms and legs a blur of agitated motion. Jerking on his boots, he jumped up and sprinted to the door, snatching his hat from the bureau as he passed it. The door went crashing against the wall as he flung it open and sped into the hallway.

He met Boutelle as he half-skidded across the second-floor landing, his hand squeaking on the bannister. The younger man, a long coat thrown over his nightshirt, feet thrust bare into his boots, looked at Finley angrily.

"So much for your treaty!" he snapped.

Finley didn't take the time to answer. Darting past Boutelle, he descended the stairs in a series of step-engulfing leaps. Boutelle followed hurriedly.

"What's wrong, Mr. Finley?"

Finley shot a glance to one side as he raced across the dim lobby. He saw Mrs. Vance in her nightgown standing in the doorway to her and Mr. Vance's apartment.

"Don't know, ma'am!" Finley answered breathlessly. He jolted to a halt before the door and jerked it open, the bell tinkling sharply.

"Is it an attack?" cried Mrs. Vance.

"No!" he shouted over his shoulder as he plunged into the chilly morning air. Turning right, he began to run again along the plank walk. Down the street, the Apaches had drawn their ponies up in front of the general store. At first, Finley didn't see what they were looking at.

Then he caught sight of the man sitting there on the general store's porch.

Within earshot now, Finley skidded to a halt in time to hear Braided Feather address the man in Apache. The agent stopped so abruptly that Boutelle, running close behind, almost rammed into him.

Across the street, the man remained seated, his eyes on Braided Feather as the chief spoke.

"What did the Indian say?" Boutelle whispered, not recognizing Braided Feather.

"He asked the man what he wants," Finley translated

hastily, his gaze fixed on the seated man. Who was he? Finley wondered. Why had Braided Feather ridden all the way to Picture City just to see him?

As Finley wondered, the man stood slowly and moved to the edge of the walk. The agent noticed how the Apaches seemed to cringe at his approach, how the ponies nickered in restless alarm and tried to back off.

The man answered Braided Feather.

"What did he say?" whispered Boutelle.

Finley's face had grown suddenly taut. He did not seem to have heard the question.

"What did he *say*?" Boutelle repeated angrily.

"He wants to know where the Night Doctor is."

"Who?"

The Indian agent waved him off and leaned forward, listening intently as Braided Feather spoke again. He heard a sound in the chief's voice he had never heard before— the sound of fear. It made him shudder.

"We do not know," Braided Feather was telling the man, edging his horse back slowly as he spoke. *"We do not know."*

The man smiled coldly.

"It does not matter," he said. "I will find him."

Suddenly, Braided Feather jerked his horse around and drove heels to its flanks. In an instant, the other Apaches followed his lead and the street was shaking with the impact of driving hooves.

"Wait!" Finley shouted to the chief. But if Braided Feather heard, he gave no sign of it. Face a carven mask, eyes held straight ahead, he drove his horse toward the edge of town. In a minute, every Apache was gone.

Finley stood for a few moments, staring in the direction they had gone. Then, slowly, his gaze shifted to the man.

"What in the name of heaven is going on?" demanded an angry, confused Boutelle.

Finley shook his head, looking at the man.

"Are those the Apaches we met with yesterday?"

"Yes."

"Are they trying to—"

"Hey, what in hell's going on around here?"

The two of them turned as Appleface Kelly came stomping up, wearing a long, gray overcoat over his nightshirt. His eyes were puffy with sleep, and there was a growth of dark stubble on his cheeks. In his hands he carried a rifle.

"I thought there was a treaty with them bastards," he said.

"There is," said Finley. "This has nothing to do with the treaty. They rode in to see him." He gestured toward the man across the street.

Appleface squinted at the man. "Him again," he said.

"You've seen him before?" asked Finley.

Appleface told him what had happened at the Sidewinder Saloon the night before.

"He asked for Dodge?" said Finley. This thing was getting beyond him.

"That's what Eddie Harkness figgered he wanted," said Appleface. He glanced across the street. "Wonder who in hell he is anyway," he said.

"Maybe we'd better find out," said Finley.

"I would like to—" Boutelle began, then stopped as the Indian agent stepped away.

"Watch y'self," Kelly muttered after him.

Finley nodded once as he started across the muddy street toward the man, who, apparently oblivious to the agent's approach, had gone back to the chair and was looking toward the hotel again.

Finley stepped up onto the walk.

"Good morning," he said.

He was not prepared for the sudden tightening that took place in his stomach muscles when the man's eyes turned to his. It took an effort of will to keep his voice from faltering.

"My name is Finley," he said, trying to sound casually affable. "I'm the Indian agent for this territory."

The man looked at him without answering.

"You—speak English?" asked Finley. Kelly had said that he did, but there seemed to be no reception in the man's face. He eyed Finley without blinking, his face as still as a rock.

"If I can help you in any way . . ." Finley went on, talking more from instinct than design. "I know the Indians who just spoke to you and—"

There was a sudden glittering in the man's eyes which made him stop.

"You know the Night Doctor?" asked the man.

Finley felt a chill lace through the muscles of his back. The way the man had asked it, almost hungrily.

"I know of him," said Finley.

"*Where is he*?" asked the man.

Finley realized in that instant that he would not have told the man where the Night Doctor was even if he knew. He had no reason for this except a feeling in his gut.

"I don't know that," he said.

The man turned away, no longer interested in Finley. Why does he want to see the Night Doctor? the agent wondered.

He was about to say something about knowing Professor Dodge when the man raised his head a little to see who it was that was riding into town down beyond the hotel. And Finley saw the scar.

He couldn't take his eyes off it. They were still fixed to the discolored line of tissue when the man turned and looked at him.

Finley drew in a quick breath and forced his eyes up.

"I'm sorry," he said.

Looking into the man's eyes was like staring into two black pits.

"That must have been . . . quite a cut," Finley heard himself saying.

The man's brutally appraising look altered. Abruptly, almost terribly, he was smiling, but it was not a smile that bore warmth for Finley or for anyone.

"Someone cut my head off once," he said.

Finley shuddered. "Really?" he said, but the bantering tone he tried to put in his voice failed completely.

He stood looking into the man's black eyes for another moment. Then, without another word, he turned and stepped down off the walk. He knew he had learned nothing, that if anything he had been made a fool of. Yet he also knew that he'd had to get away from the man, that he couldn't have stood there by him for another second.

Reaching Boutelle and Kelly, he turned right and started back for the hotel. The two men fell into step beside him.

"What'd he say?" asked Appleface.

"Nothing," said Finley. He didn't want to talk about it.

"Who is he?" asked Boutelle. "And why did the Apaches ride here to see him?"

"I don't know," Finley said tensely. "He told me nothing."

"You think there's gonna be trouble with the Injuns?" Kelly asked.

"If they'd come in to make trouble," Finley told him, "they could have wiped us out. You know that."

Appleface grunted. "That's so." His step faltered. "Well . . . I better get me some clothes on before I get arrested. I'll see ya later."

"All right." Finley kept walking determinedly toward the hotel, trying to rid himself of the cold and frightened restlessness in his gut. He'd never felt like this in his life, and he neither liked nor understood it.

Kelly fell out of step and turned away from them. As

he walked back to his boardinghouse he kept glancing across the street to where the man sat. Who in the hell is he, Kelly wondered, that Braided Feather should come riding all the way into town just to see him?

"The man told you absolutely nothing?" Boutelle asked after Kelly had left them.

"Only that he wants to see the Night Doctor," Finley said, hoping this would satisfy the younger man.

"Who in God's name is the Night Doctor?" asked Boutelle.

"An Apache shaman," Finley answered. "A medicine man," he added as Boutelle started to say something. "He was a member of Braided Feather's tribe."

"Was?"

Finley grunted, glancing back over his shoulder. The man still sat in the same position, looking up at the hotel. Finley traced the line of his gaze and saw that it ended on the second story—perhaps on the window of Professor Dodge's room, it occurred to him. Although how the man knew where Dodge's room was, was another question added to the rest.

"Is he dead?" asked Boutelle.

Finley started. "What?"

"The Night Doctor," Boutelle said acidly. "Is he dead?"

"I don't know," said Finley.

"Why did he leave his tribe?"

"He didn't leave it; he was driven out," Finley answered. "Braided Feather outlawed him."

"Why?"

Finley pushed open the hotel door and started in.

"For tampering," he said.

"What do you—"

Boutelle stopped. The Vances were in the lobby, turning from one of the windows where they had been watching. Realizing the state of his dress, Boutelle headed directly for the stairs. After he was dressed, he'd confront Finley again and this time, by heaven, the agent had better give straight answers and stop this nonsense about any Night Doctor. If Finley thought for one second that he could condone the Apaches' obvious disinclination to abide by the conditions of the treaty—not the least of which was the clearly stated rule that they were to keep away from Picture City—he had another think coming. And on the day after the meeting, too! Good God, did Finley think him an idiot?

Finley, at that moment, was thinking of anything but Boutelle's mental capacity.

"No, it wasn't a war party," he was assuring Mrs. Vance. "They were here to see a man. Which is what I want to—"

"Yes, we saw," said Mrs. Vance. "He's the same one who came here last night."

Quickly, she told Finley about the previous night. As she described the open window and the footprints ending in front of it, the agent stared at her almost blankly.

"You think he . . . went *out* the window?" he asked.

"I don't see what else he could have done," she said.

"That scar, did you see that scar on his neck?" added Harry Vance.

Finley nodded, feeling as if he were involved in some ridiculous dream and not actually standing in the hotel lobby talking to the Vances.

"Tell me," he said, "did he happen to mention *why* he wanted to see Professor Dodge?"

"No, he didn't," Harry said. "Just went upstairs and . . ." He shrugged weakly.

Finley shook his head and grinned wryly. "Sure makes a lot of sense, doesn't it?"

"It makes no sense at all," said Mrs. Vance, as if he were speaking seriously.

"You say you don't know when Professor Dodge is coming back?" Finley asked Harry.

"No, he didn't say," said Harry. "Never does."

"I see. Well, when he does come in, will you tell him I want to see him right away? Before that . . . other fellow gets to him."

"Yes, sir, I'll do that," Harry said.

"Good."

Except that things were far from good, Finley thought as he went up to his room to shave. He kept trying to put the bizarre details into some kind of pattern, but they wouldn't fit together. How could you connect such shapeless pieces as a stranger who might or might not be an Indian; a stranger who wanted to see an outlawed medicine man and a professor of archaeology; a stranger with a jagged scar around his neck ("*Someone cut my head off once*") whose presence gave one a sense of sickened dread; a story about this man jumping from a second-story window without injury; and Braided Feather, a fearless Apache chief, riding in to see the man, then fleeing as if devils pursued him? These things made no overall sense—or, if they did, the sense was lost to Finley.

He was just relocking his door when it occurred to him that there might be two more details to be added, details which would make the pattern, should it emerge, even darker.

The death of Little Owl. And the disappearance of Tom and Jim Corcoran.

7

At eight o'clock that morning, Al Corcoran rode into Picture City with the corpses of his brothers.

He did not look to either side of the street, did not note the shocked faces of the people who came out from their stores and houses as he passed. He did not notice the man sitting on the porch of the general store. He rode on woodenly, eyes staring and glassy, mouth set into an ugly, lipless gash, gloved hands curled tightly round the rein ends of his mount.

Following behind on a lead walked the horse that had belonged to his brother Tom. The two bodies lay across its back, covered by a frayed blanket. They had been put there, faces down, their arms and legs hanging loosely, the wrists and ankles tied together. One of the men was barefoot, the feet pale white and gnarled with dark blue veins. Across the wrists of the other was a darkened spiderweb of dry blood. The two bodies stirred with the motion of the horse as if they were trying to move.

Corcoran rode directly to the Indian agent's office before reining up. Slowly dismounting, he wrapped the reins of his horse around the hitching post and, ignoring the stares of the people around him, strode to the plank walk, stepped up onto it, and went to the office door. He did not go in. Turning the knob, he shoved the door open as hard as he could.

Inside, Finley and Boutelle looked up in shock as the door crashed against the wall.

"*Al . . .*" Finley's voice was startled.

Corcoran did not reply. He stared in at the agent, gloved hands fisted at his sides. Finley pushed up from his desk and hurried to the door. Corcoran didn't move, blocking his way. Finley stopped in front of him and looked over the heavy man's shoulder. There was a tightening on his cheeks as he saw the bodies.

"Where were they?" he asked.

"Out where the Injuns were," muttered Corcoran.

Finley blinked. Then, as Corcoran stepped back, he moved out onto the walk, eyes stark with pain. This was the moment he had dreaded most since yesterday. Abruptly, a fragment of his dream flared briefly in consciousness: him coming out of some building, seeing the two bleeding bodies. He shuddered and stepped down off the walk into the mud. Corcoran followed him.

Finley stood beside the second horse, his hand closed around a cold, white ankle. He felt sick with premonition. These two, still bodies could plunge everyone in Picture City into a bloody nightmare again.

"Now tell me it wasn't Injuns," Corcoran said between his teeth. "*Tell* me, Finley."

Finley drew in a fast breath of the cold, morning air. "Al—" he started.

With a sob of fury, Corcoran tore the blanket away.

"*Tell me it wasn't Injuns!*" he cried.

Across the street a woman moaned softly and had to be supported. On the walk, Boutelle gagged and caught onto one of the columns that supported the balcony overhead.

"*Oh, my God,*" Finley murmured.

One of them was naked, his blood-drained body raked with deep, blue-edged gullies, half his chest torn away. The other, the one who had been Jim Corcoran, had no face—only a blood-oozing mask of shredded meat. Here an eye was missing, there an ear. Gouges deep enough to lay the hand in sideways had been slashed across backs and bellies. Nerve and artery ends hung like black ribbons. In one thigh, bone showed. From the half-missing chest, rib ends stuck out jaggedly, their ivory darkened by blood.

Finley could not speak or draw his eyes from the butchered remains. He felt his heart thumping slowly and heavily in his chest. Horror swept over him in waves that seemed to blot away the sane world which he had managed to cling to until this moment.

He hardly felt the hand on his arm as Corcoran turned him. He stared blankly at the trembling, wild-eyed man.

"You get them soldiers," Corcoran muttered hoarsely. "You get them right away. You hear me?"

Sucking in breath, Finley disengaged Corcoran's shaking fingers and picked up the blanket lying on the mud. Carefully, he laid it back across the two bodies and closed his eyes for a moment, trying to force back into himself the strength he needed.

Then he turned back and took Corcoran's arm.

"Come inside," he said.

Corcoran jerked his arm away. "I'm takin' them to Packer's," he said.

"Al, we—"

The heavyset man turned away, moving almost drunkenly. He stopped in mid-step and looked back over his shoulder.

"I'm comin' back here in a couple o' minutes," he said. "If you ain't ready t'go for the soldiers by then, I'll go after them murderin' bastards myself."

"I'll be here, Al."

Corcoran untwisted the reins of his horse and started walking it away. Behind, the second horse lurched forward, the two bodies twitching at the abrupt movement. Finley stared at the arms and legs as they began to hitch and sway. He wanted to call after Corcoran, but his voice would not function. He knew he should go with the nerve-shattered man, but he needed a little time to get hold of himself. He stood, wordless, watching Corcoran move away toward Packer's Funeral Parlor.

It wasn't Braided Feather. That was the only thought his mind could manage. Yet what good would it do to say that to Corcoran now? What dissuasion could it possibly be to a man who had found his two brothers in that hideous state and, with his own hands, put them on horseback? By any judgment of sanity, he should ride immediately to Fort Apache and get the soldiers, send them after Braided Feather's tribe.

Finley shuddered. That was the crux of it, he realized. This *wasn't* sanity. It was all a maniac's dream. No Indian had done that to the Corcoran brothers. Only a giant animal could have torn them so. Was that possible? Finley thought suddenly.

No. It was that man. Behind all sensible thoughts, the secret place of his mind knew that somehow that man was responsible. But how? The conscious mind could not imagine an answer. How could one man do what had been done to those two, husky young men?

There was only one course he could think of in the midst of all this, to ride to Braided Feather's camp immediately—or to the reservation if they had already reported there—and find out who the man was and why the Apaches feared him. He'd take Corcoran along. He didn't dare leave the grief-maddened man to himself. He had planned to wait for Professor Dodge's return, but there was no time for waiting now; that was frighteningly clear. Something had to be done immediately.

Boutelle followed him back into the office—a paler, far less steady man than had left it minutes before.

"And you defend them," he said, his voice thickened by the horror he had just witnessed.

"No Indian did that," was all that Finley could think of saying.

"Then what did, Mr. Finley?" demanded Boutelle.

Finley sank down heavily on the bench where Little Owl had lain the night before. He'd taken the body to its wickiup an hour earlier. Yes—what did? his mind repeated. And what had made the old Apache die without a single mark on him?

"I don't know, Mr. Boutelle," he answered. "I only wish I did." He exhaled slowly. "I only know it wasn't Braided Feather's—"

"Finley, you're blind!" cried Boutelle. "Or mad—or worse!"

At any other time, Finley would have lost his temper at such vitriolic, accusing words. Yet now, off balance, he only looked up defenselessly at the younger man's infuriated expression.

"Are you going to the fort?" challenged Boutelle.

Finley rubbed a hand across his dry lips. What answer could he give that would not brand him as brainlessly submissive?

He could only shake his head, not in answer so much as in reflection of his perplexity.

"I see," said Boutelle, and for a second, Finley almost envied the simple clarity with which the younger man saw the situation, devoid of complications, of perilous possibilities.

"Then I'll ride there myself with Mr. Corcoran," said Boutelle. "I shall have dispatched a—"

"*You will not.*" Anger came at least strongly enough to stiffen Finley's words and make him stand abruptly. "Now you listen to—"

He grabbed Boutelle's arms as the younger man started turning and twisted him back. "I said *listen!*" he snapped.

"If you think—"

"There's more involved here—"

"Get your hands off me!"

"—than just a senseless Indian murder!" Finley drowned him out. "Use your brains! What possible good could Braided Feather have gotten out of murdering two of our citizens on the very day he agreed to a peace treaty with us! After ten years of constant battle! No! I say, no! It wasn't Indians!"

"And I say only an Indian could do what was done to those men!" Boutelle lashed back. "I say only an Indian could *conceive* of it!"

"You don't—"

"I'm riding to that fort, Mr. Finley!" the younger man yelled. "With you—or without you!"

"*You are not!*" roared Finley, his hands tightening so hard on the younger man's arms that Boutelle winced. "I'm the authorized agent for this territory and until I'm re-placed, it's my decision to make! And I say there'll be no soldiers yet!"

Boutelle's repression of fury was easily visible. Finley could almost see him swallow it.

"Very well," the younger man said in a tight, quiet voice. "Very well, Mr. Finley. You are quite correct. Your authority supersedes mine."

He paused, looking at the agent with cold contempt.

"At least for now," he said.

Spinning on his heel, he moved for the door. Finley started to say something, then changed his mind. Let him go, he thought. Maybe righteous indignation would keep him occupied for a while, the preparation of damning reports to Washington.

Well, there was no time to waste in concerns about Boutelle. Grabbing his hat and jacket, he stepped outside.

"Oh, Jimmy," he called to a young boy passing by.

"Yes, sir." Jimmy Taylor came over to him.

"Like to earn a short bit?"

"Yes, sir."

"I'm expecting Al Corcoran back here any second," Finley told the boy. "Will you tell him that I'm going to the hotel for a minute, then I'm going to the livery stable for my horse."

"Yes, sir."

Finley pressed the coin into the palm of the boy's hand. "Tell him to wait right here, Jimmy. Tell him I'll be right back. You understand?"

Jimmy nodded. "Yes, sir, I understand."

"Good." Finley patted his shoulder and turned away. What if Dodge came back while he was gone? the thought occurred. He'd better tell Harry Vance to tell the professor to stay in his room until he got back.

Blowing out breath, Finley stepped off hurriedly, wondering how in God's name he was going to talk Al Corcoran into going in peace to the Apache camp.

Al Corcoran came out of Packer's Funeral Parlor and started walking the horses down the street. He was going back to Finley's office now and Finley had better have his mind made up.

Corcoran shivered fitfully, still feeling sick. He was sure that he would never forget the experience of carrying his brothers into Packer's back room. He could still smell that raw-meat odor of them in his nostrils, still see in his tortured mind their torn flesh and protruding bones as he laid them down on the tables in the dim, chemical-reeking room.

He sucked in raspingly at the air. The Apaches would pay for this, by God. One way or another, he'd get out to Braided Feather's camp for revenge—even if he had to go alone with a high-powered, telescopic lens rifle. There would be payment in full, he swore that to himself and to the memory of his brothers.

He was thinking that when he saw the man.

At first it failed to strike him. He walked on past the store, his mind too deeply intent on thoughts of vengeance to notice the evidence before his eyes. Then, abruptly, he stopped and looked back so quickly that it drove sharp twinges of pain up his neck.

The man was wearing Tom's clothes.

For a moment, Corcoran couldn't move. The enormity of it seemed to paralyze his muscles. He stood, immobile, his eyes fixed on the tall stranger who sat on the porch of the general store, looking toward the hotel.

Then the fury came, breaking Corcoran loose from his paralysis, moving through his veins like a current of acid. Slowly, mechanically, he walked across the street and tied his lead horse to the post.

He took a deep, trembling breath and unbuttoned his jacket, pushing the right side of it back with his hand. For a moment, he rested the curve of his hand on his pistol butt.

Then, lowering his hand, he stepped up to the edge of the walk.

"You," he said.

The man's gaze turned and lowered to the murderous eyes of Al Corcoran.

"Where did you get those clothes?" Corcoran asked slowly. He shuddered at the sight of this savage-looking man, but forged ahead.

The man was silent, his dark eyes perusing Corcoran's face.

"You hear me?"

The man's lips curled upward slightly in a scornful smile.

"I do not understand you," he said in Apache.

Corcoran shuddered with animal hatred. "An *Injun*," he whispered through his teeth so softly that only he could hear it.

Abruptly, he reached back and slipped the Colt from its holster. The man's gaze dropped to the barrel end pointed at his chest.

"What are you doing?" he asked in Apache. There was no alarm in his voice.

"Get on that horse," said Corcoran, gesturing with his head. He felt his finger tightening on the trigger and willfully loosened it.

A man came out of the store and stopped in his tracks at the sight of Corcoran's drawn pistol. Corcoran noticed him from the corners of his eyes.

"Get back inside," he said.

"I do not understand you," the stranger said, as if Corcoran had spoken to him.

Corcoran's chest heaved with shaking breath. Jerkily, he moved back a pace and gestured toward the second horse with his pistol barrel. He emphasized the movement by a loud cocking of the Colt's hammer.

The man still did not look disturbed. He glanced over at the hotel, then, without a word, pushed to his feet. Stepping down off the walk, he released the reins of the second horse and mounted it with a single, fluid motion. There he sat waiting while Al pulled his own horse free and mounted it hastily.

"All right," said Al, "now *get*." With the pistol barrel, he pointed toward the north end of town.

The man drew his horse around and started walking it down the street. Behind him, pistol held across his saddle, rode Corcoran. This was one Apache Finley wasn't going to save, he was thinking. Finley wasn't even going to know about it. Maybe the agent was right about it not being Braided Feather, but he was wrong about it not being an Indian—because, right there ahead of him, tall and steady on his horse, rode the Indian who had killed his brothers. The one who was going to die in the same way they had.

"Hurry it up, will you, Sam?" asked Finley.

"Yes, sir, Mr. Finley." The old man dropped the saddle across the mare's twitching back and started working on the straps.

Finley stood impatiently on the straw-littered floor of the stable. His fingers flexed restlessly inside his gloves as he sighed deeply. Yesterday, about this time, he had been in the Bluebell Restaurant with Boutelle, having his steak and eggs. The day had looked promising.

How much could change in twenty-four hours.

He glanced toward the old man and saw that he was almost finished now. Moving to the horse, he rechecked the straps hastily, then nodded. "That's fine, Sam." Raising his boot to the stirrup, he lifted himself to the saddle quickly.

"See you," he muttered and nudged his boot heels against the mare's flanks. Its shoes clattered noisily across the stable floor, then squished into the mud outside. Finley reined it left and rode down the street to his office.

Jimmy was still there, leaning against one of the balcony columns. As Finley drew up, the boy straightened and came over to the edge of the walk.

"Hasn't he come back yet?" Finley frowned.

"No, sir."

"You're positive you couldn't have missed him?"

"Yes, sir, Mr. Finley. I never caught sight of him."

"I see." Finley clenched his teeth. "Well, thank you, Jimmy." Pulling the mare around, he heeled it into a quick canter down the street.

A minute later he was rushing out of Packer's front door, his face a mask of alarm. Was Al already taking things into his own hands? Had he ridden to Fort Apache by himself or with Boutelle? Or worse, armed himself and started off for Braided Feather's camp? The agent looked around indecisively, the fist of one hand hitting at his leg. Good God, was there to be no end to this insanity?

He was riding past the store when he saw that the man was no longer there. Reining up quickly, he dismounted and jogged inside.

"Mr. Casey, did you see where that strange man went?" he asked.

He didn't expect the answer he got.

Corcoran rode behind the man, his .44 leveled at the broad back. Every few seconds he had to consciously restrain himself from squeezing the trigger and sending a bullet into the stranger's body.

He didn't want to do that yet. He wanted to save that for last. First, he wanted to make the man beg for his life, to cry for mercy. Or, failing that (these damned Injuns sometimes died without a sound) he wanted, at least, to kill him slowly, inch by inch. Not with one merciful shot.

Corcoran pressed his teeth together and shivered. He had never wanted to kill so much as he did now. His eyes glittered as he stared at the man ahead. Damned butcher, he thought. The Indian must have sneaked up on his brothers from behind. This had been no face-to-face attack, that was for certain. His brothers had been strong, husky boys.

No one Indian, no matter how strong, could have done what had been done to them unless . . .

Corcoran's breath hissed out between his lips. Damned murdering bastard! he thought. When I'm through with you, they not only won't know who you were, they won't know *what* you were.

Raised in his stirrups, Finley galloped out of Picture City, eyes scanning the meadow for Corcoran and the man. He had to find them now, before . . .

He grimaced painfully. Before what? his mind demanded. There was no answer. Only vivid memories of a dead, staring Indian so terrified that his heart had stopped and of two hideously mutilated bodies. Only premonitions of a horror that went far beyond all fears men came to live with and accept.

Corcoran tightened his reins and pulled the bit back in his horse's mouth.

"Stop," he said.

Ahead, the man, without glancing back, pulled in his horse and halted it. They were in a small, tree-ringed glade that slanted down gradually toward a narrow, rushing stream. It was a place hidden to anyone but those within a range of several yards. Corcoran didn't want anyone to stop this play.

The man sat motionless on his horse as Corcoran dismounted. The heavyset man walked slowly across the ground and raised his pistol.

"Get down," he ordered.

The man raised his leg backward over the horse's body and settled easily to the ground. It drove a fiery bolt of rage through Corcoran to see the pant leg of his brother hitch up across the boot top.

"Raise your hands," he said.

The man raised his arms, his expression one of unconcern. Corcoran stiffened, a tight, venomous smile forming on his lips.

"I thought you didn't savvy me," he said.

Was that a smile? Beneath his glove, the fingers that held the Colt went white across the knuckles.

"I understand," the man said calmly.

With a savage cry, Corcoran jumped forward and slammed the pistol barrel across the man's skull.

Without a sound, the man staggered back a few paces, then caught his balance. As he straightened up, the raised collar of the jacket he wore slid down, revealing the livid scar. The sight of it jolted Corcoran, but not enough to drive away the murderous fury in him.

"You son of a bitch, Injun scum," he said in a soft, tense voice. "I'm gonna cut you into meat."

The man stood erect again, seemingly oblivious to the trickle of blood across his forehead.

"Wipe that filthy smile off your—"

Corcoran broke off suddenly and smiled crazily himself.

"No, go ahead," he said through his teeth. "Smile, you Injun bastard. That's how they'll find your head—*smilin'*." He looked down at the scar. "That's gonna make me a perfect line for cuttin'."

A chuckle sounded deeply in the man's chest.

"Go on, laugh, you bastard!" said Corcoran, his voice breaking.

The man did laugh. Eyes glowing with a savage amusement, his lips flared back, his laughter rocking terribly in the air. Hatred boiled up behind Corcoran's eyes. With a deranged sob, he pulled the trigger and fired a bullet into the man's chest.

Finley jerked the mare around and looked in all directions. Dear Christ, was he too late already?

In the distance, a second shot rang out and echoed off the hills.

Corcoran stood frozenly, staring at the man. His mouth hung open; a line of spittle ran across his jaw.

The man stood smiling at him.

Corcoran fired again, instinctively.

The man twitched back a little but did not fall. A hollow sound of disbelief stirred in Corcoran's throat.

"Who are you?" he asked, but the words came out only as a jumble of brainless sounds.

The man took a step toward him.

"No." Corcoran edged back, his eyes wide with terror.

The man kept coming. With a sobbing gasp, Corcoran fired again, and again. He kept pulling the trigger even when there was only the click of the hammer on empty chambers.

"All gone," said the man.

Corcoran cried out hoarsely as he backed against the tree. He pressed against the gnarled trunk tightly, shaking his head in tiny, fitful jerks, his eyes bright and staring.

"*Who are you?*" he gasped.

The man stopped a few paces away.

"*Look*," he said, and he stretched out his arms.

Corcoran recoiled against the tree, the beginning of a scream strangled in his throat. He stood there for a moment looking at the man with eyes that had lost their sanity. Then his vibrating legs gave way, and he slid down to a half-sitting position on the tree roots, looking up stupidly at the man and what the man was becoming.

When the monstrous shadow fell across him, he tried to scream, but there was no strength in him. Mouth yawning open in a soundless shriek, he went limp against the tree. He barely heard the inhuman screech that filled his ears.

A trembling Finley pulled up his horse.

He didn't want to enter that glade. A moment before, Corcoran's two horses had come bursting out of it and passed him, their eyes mad with terror. He wanted to turn and follow their frenzied gallop across the meadow. The scream still seemed to ring in his ears—a sound the like of which he had never heard in all his life.

Only after a long while could he force the shuddering mare to enter the glade.

It seemed to be deserted. No tall figure stood there waiting for him; there was no sign of Al Corcoran. Finley sat stiffly on the fidgeting horse, his eyes moving over the silence of the glade.

Then he saw the pieces.

8

Thirty minutes before he saw the low line of Picture City's buildings in the distance, Professor Albert Dodge knew in a flash of angry revelation that he was going back to Connecticut.

He'd had enough, more than enough. Odd that it took this last abortive foray into the hills to make him realize it. God knew the disenchantment had been mounting for at least a year. Perhaps this last, frustrating trip was a disguised blessing.

Under the circumstances, he wasn't sure who was more of an idiot—"Appleface" Kelly or himself for believing Kelly. "Oh, yes, sir, Perfessor. There is sure as hell some broken pots out there, some bones, too." Dodge could hear the man's assured voice repeated in his memory. "Moron," he muttered. He'd soon discovered that the pot shards were dry clay formations and the bones leftovers from wild animal kills.

Then it had begun to rain.

Rain? he thought irascibly. More like horseback riding underneath a waterfall. In less than twenty seconds he'd been drenched. No shelter at first. He'd tried to stop beneath the overhang of a piñon tree. That had been a waste of time. After several minutes of that, he'd been forced to move on, the rain alternately coming straight down on top of him or blowing into his face with the violence of buckets of water flung at him by some deranged antagonist.

On top of that, his horse had slipped and fallen.

By the time he'd located the small cave, he was dripping wet and screaming vehement curses at Kelly, the sky, the land, life itself.

The cave helped precious little. He'd crawled into it nonetheless, over still-moist animal droppings and the remains of small, partially devoured creatures he could not identify.

There he had cowered, while the rain poured down, at last falling into a sluggish sleep despite his dread that some wild animal—a coyote, a cougar—might clamber into the cave and attack him. It would have been a fitting conclusion to Kelly's Folly, he thought. To be ripped asunder by some ravenous beast.

All he'd gleaned from this infernal little outing was a fallen horse, a bruised side, a chilled body, and mud-caked clothes where he'd fallen from the horse. He was lucky, he supposed, that he didn't have a broken leg or worse; the damned, skittish animal could have landed square on top of him.

No, he was going back; that was suddenly, definitively settled. Back to Fairfax College if they'd have him. What a fool he'd been to leave there in the first place, and for what? Heat, wind, dust, rain, snow, the company of fools and no archaeological results worth a tinker's damn.

Unless one counted that single, bizarre experience. Dodge shuddered. Would he never be able to shake it from his mind? Well, that was not surprising. He was, as a matter of fact, astounded at himself for not having left the territory immediately after it had taken place.

Except, of course, that it had taken no more than a

month for logic to refute the apparent evidence of his senses. Really, it couldn't have happened as he recalled. Something in the drink the shaman had given him. For protection, the old man had cautioned. Perhaps something in the fire smoke he'd been compelled to inhale throughout the ceremony. Even—it was not inconceivable—that the shaman had placed him into some involuntary state of mental control.

But certainly—*certainly*—he could not have actually seen what he thought he saw.

If only I had a pick, a shovel, Finley had kept thinking.

What he'd been compelled to do was torturous and ghastly. He'd seen victims of Indian raids in the past, seen a village of Apaches slaughtered by the cavalry.

He'd never seen anything remotely like this.

He didn't want to dispose of the pieces but knew he had no choice. If anyone from Picture City—or God forbid from Fort Apache—saw what had happened here, there would be no doubt whatever in their minds that Braided Feather's tribe had violated the treaty with a massacre.

He might not have even known it was Al Corcoran if it hadn't been for the head lying yards distant from the mangled body parts, as though it had been hurled aside in some maniacal rage.

The look on Al Corcoran's blood-streaked face was virtually a duplicate of the one on Little Owl's face—an expression of total, unutterable horror.

Finley had kept his eyes averted as he'd reached down until he felt Al Corcoran's hair. Then gingerly, grimacing, sickened as he did it, he'd picked up the ripped-off head and carried it back to where the dismembered body lay.

He'd hoped, for several minutes, that the rain had been severe enough to soften the earth so that he could dig a

shallow trench with his knife and hands. But scant inches
below the muddy surface, the earth was, as always, brick
hard, making that impossible.

He'd been forced to gather together the shredded, torn
remains and cover them as best he could with large stones
and small boulders. Throughout, he'd tried to look at something else, anything else but the hideously butchered leav-
ings of what an hour earlier had been a man.

It was not always possible. Jarring sights kept stinging
at his eyes and brain. Corcoran's left hand and wrist dangling purplish veins and arteries. His right arm, the hand
clutched into a rigid, white fist. His left leg almost pulled
loose. The trunk of his body, chest and belly, ripped apart
as though by the claws of a raging bear, his internal organs strewn across the blood-soaked ground.

He tried not to think about what might have done this
to Corcoran. He knew only that it wasn't any of Braided
Feather's people.

But what it had been was something he could not address at the moment. It was enough to cover over Al Corcoran's torn and mutilated form.

He could not allow himself to visualize what sort of
being was capable of such horrible savagery.

As Dodge rode into Picture City, a bitterly ironic memory
struck his mind. Him ranting to the Fairfax Board of Gov-
ernors that archaeology was supposed to be a living sci-
ence, not some musty, dry-as-bones collection of facts
dredged up in classrooms.

"Oh, yes," he muttered sourly. Well, he'd be happy to
return to musty fact collections just as soon as stagecoach
and train could get him back to civilization.

He looked down at himself as the horse clopped slowly
toward the hotel. Never had he looked more pitiful. By

God, he'd have these damn clothes burned before he left town. But first a bath, sleep, and then a decent meal with copious whiskey as a side dish.

Then—*hallelujah*—to the stagecoach office to reserve a seat on the morning coach to White River and all parts east. Back to genteel, sensible surroundings.

"Amen," he muttered.

He left the horse at the livery stable. Thank God he'd only rented the use of it. Selling it could take forever.

"Looks like you took a tumble," the man at the stable said with a grin.

Dodge only grunted and turned away, feeling a slight sense of pleasure that he'd never bothered to learn the man's name.

The journey along the plank walk to the hotel made him wince. His stockings were still damp inside his boots, and his mud-stiffened trousers rubbed against the skin on his legs; the long coat, still wet, weighed him down oppressively.

"So *there* you are, Perfessor," Harry Vance said as Dodge entered the lobby. "You been out all night?"

"Obviously," Dodge answered curtly. "My key, please."

Harry slid the key from its slot and handed it over. "Lots of excitement here this morning," he said.

"Oh?" Dodge turned for the staircase.

"Yes, sir. Ol' Braided Feather and a passel of his braves come riding in."

Dodge stopped and looked around. "Why?" he asked.

"Seems they come to see this man," Harry answered.

"They came in to see a *man*?" Dodge sounded dubious.

"*Some man* though," Harry said. "Matter o' fact, he come in here last night lookin' for you."

Dodge felt a slight chill waver through his body. "Me?" he asked.

"Yes, sir. Asked for you by name. Weird-lookin' duck he was."

Dodge swallowed; his throat felt suddenly dry. "Why, what did he look like?" he asked. He felt as though somebody else had asked the question.

"Well, he was powerful tall," Harry said. "I mean *powerful* tall, mayhaps six foot five inches."

"Yes?" Dodge asked, barely audible.

"He looked sort of like an Injun, but I don't think he was," Harry said. "Had a"—he gestured vaguely at his neck—"big . . . thick . . . *scar* around his neck, *all* around it. Awful-lookin' sight."

No, thought Dodge. He thought he heard a faint voice speak the word aloud in his ears. No, it wasn't possible.

"Told him you wasn't here," Harry said, wondering about the blank stare on Professor Dodge's face. "He went upstairs anyway. That was peculiar, too. He had mud on his boots and tracked it on the carpet in the upstairs hall. But the tracks, they stopped by the window at the end of the hall. The window was open and the man was gone. We thought maybe he'd gone in your room so we took a look, 'scuse that. He wasn't there though. So he must have jumped from the window. From the second floor though?"

Dodge felt as if he were about to faint. His head felt very light and there was a buzzing in his ears. No, this is wrong, he thought. It wasn't happening. It couldn't be.

"Where —" He coughed weakly. "Where is he now?" he asked. He was appalled at how weak and strained his voice had become.

"Ain't seen him since this morning when the Apaches rode in to see him," Harry said. "You know who he is?"

His voice trailed off on the last two words of his question because Professor Dodge had turned away and moved abruptly toward the stairs. Doesn't look too steady, Harry thought. He watched the professor start up the steps, holding tightly to the bannister. Was it his imagination or had the blood drained from Dodge's face? He certainly looked disturbed enough. Who *was* that weird duck anyway? He'd have to tell Ethel about this right off.

Dodge heard the thump of his boots on the steps but could barely feel his feet. He seemed to have gone numb all over. He kept shaking his head with tiny, jerking movements. There had to be another explanation for this. It could not possibly be what it seemed.

He twitched in shock as a sob broke in his throat. "No," he whispered.

He half-ran, half-walked down the hallway, unlocked the door to his room and pushed inside. Closing the door quickly, he relocked it, his hand so palsied by fear that he could barely manage it.

Then he stumbled to the bed and dropped down on it heavily. He felt completely drained of strength. He had not felt such a sense of dread since that night in the shaman's wickiup when . . .

"No!" He drove a fist down weakly on the bed. It couldn't be! It was impossible!

Impossible.

When Finley got back to town, he left his horse at the livery stable and started toward the hotel. He wanted more than anything to strip away his clothes and take a hot bath, he felt so befouled by what he'd had to do. He could still smell the sickening odor of Al Corcoran's mutilated flesh.

It was when he was taking his key from Harry that he asked offhandedly if Professor Dodge had come back yet.

"Yes, he has," Harry told him. "Just got back about"—he checked the wall clock—"oh, fifteen, twenty minutes ago."

"And he's in his room?" Finley asked.

"Far as I know," Harry answered. "Leastwise, haven't seen him leave."

"What's the number of his room?" Finley asked.

"Twenny-nine."

"Thanks," Finley said, turning away.

The bath would have to wait, he thought. Dodge was the only one who might be able to shed some light on this unnerving situation. He couldn't imagine why that grisly-looking man would want to see Dodge, but at least it was a start—and all he had to go on at the moment.

Reaching the second floor, he walked to the end of the hall and knocked on the door to Room Twenty-nine. He twitched his head a little to the left, thinking he heard a gasp inside the room. Then there was dead silence. He waited for Dodge to open the door.

When nothing happened, he knocked again, a little more loudly.

There was no response. Could Harry have been wrong? he thought. Had Dodge gone out again?

He knocked once more and said, "Professor Dodge?"

There was no answer. "Are you in there?" he asked loudly.

Silence. He grunted in frustration and started to turn away.

"Who is it?" he heard Dodge ask from inside the room, his voice tight and barely audible.

"Billjohn Finley," he answered.

"Who?" The question sounded faintly.

"Finley." He grimaced with irritation. "The Indian agent."

Silence again. Now what? Finley wondered. Was the man going to let him in or not?

"What do you want?" Dodge asked. There was no mistaking it now; what he heard was the voice of a frightened man.

"I'd like to talk with you," Finley said, trying to keep the aggravation out of his voice.

"What about?" Dodge demanded.

For Christ's sake, Finley thought. What the hell is wrong with the man?

Then he thought of everything that had happened since yesterday. If Dodge was part of it, it was not surprising that he'd sound disturbed.

"I want to talk to you about that man," Finley said, somehow knowing that Dodge would know exactly what he meant.

Silence. What was Dodge doing? he wondered. And was he actually going to open the door?

"Are you alone?" Dodge's thin voice drifted through the door.

"Yes," Finley answered.

Another few seconds passed. Then Finley heard the door being unlocked. It didn't open. "Come in," Dodge said.

Finley opened the door and stopped short.

Dodge was pointing a derringer at his chest.

Finley's hands flew up, palms spread. "For God's sake," he said.

The professor lowered the derringer. "Come in, come in," he said. As Finley did, Dodge shut the door quickly and relocked it. That lock wouldn't do much good if that man chose to break the door open, Finley thought.

Then he was looking at Dodge's face, knowing in an instant that the professor was very much a part of the strange events which had taken place. The small man's expression, while not as exaggerated by shock, very much reminded him of the look on Little Owl's face. The look on Al Corcoran's face.

The look of a man confronted by total, overpowering terror.

9

Finley glanced toward the bed. Dodge had thrown two suitcases across the mattress and begun to pack them—if flinging articles of clothing into them with clumsy haste could be defined as packing. More evidence, he thought. Not that he needed it now. Dodge's appearance and manner made it more than apparent that he was getting ready to flee.

"Leaving?" he asked.

The professor's Adam's apple bobbed convulsively. "What do you want?" he asked.

"I think you know what I want," Finley told him.

"I have no idea—"

"I want to know who that man is," Finley broke in. "I want to know why he wants to see you. Why he asked about the Night Doctor. I want to know why Braided Feather and his braves rode all the way in from Pinal Spring to see him. I want you to tell me what's going on, Professor."

"I have no idea—" Dodge started again.

"I think you do," Finley interrupted angrily. "The man asked for you in the Sidewinder Saloon. Then he came here and asked for you. He—"

"I don't know who he is!" Dodge cried. He turned away abruptly. "Now if you'll please go, I have packing to do."

"I don't think you can run away from him," Finley told him quietly. "Four men are dead already and—"

He broke off at the look of stunned dismay on Dodge's face. "What?" the professor murmured.

"Four men have been killed," Finley said. "One of them was frightened to death. The other three were torn apart by God knows what. Now, I know—"

He broke off a second time as Dodge began to shake, making faint whimpering sounds in his throat as he stared at Finley.

The agent felt a burst of pity for the little man. "For God's sake, Professor," he said. *"What is going on?"*

He couldn't tell at first what Dodge was saying, his voice was so weak and trembling. Then he heard the words, repeated and repeated. "I can't, I can't, I can't."

"Why?" Finley stared at him, feeling as though he were involved in some bewildering nightmare.

He drew back a little involuntarily as Dodge moved toward him. He felt the small man's shaking hand clutch at his arm. "Please," Dodge said. *"Please.* Take me into custody."

"What?"

"Arrest me. Lock me in the jail," Dodge begged.

"Professor, I'm the local Indian agent, I'm not the—"

"Take me to Fort Apache then," Dodge interrupted. His eyes were brimming tears now. "Hand me over to the cavalry."

"Professor, you are going to have to tell me what is going on."

"I *can't!*" Dodge cried in agony. "There isn't time! I have to be protected or—"

He stopped abruptly.

"Or?" Finley said.

"Please take me with you," Dodge said. "When I'm safe, I'll tell you what it is, I promise you."

"It would help if you told me now, Profess—"

"No! It wouldn't! There isn't time!" The little man was weeping now. Finley felt the sense of dark alarm within him growing. Who in God's name was that man that he could cause such blind terror in everyone he encountered?

As he led the professor out through the front door of the hotel, he started in surprise as Dodge jerked back with a hiss, pulling his arm free and shrinking back into the doorway.

"What is it?" Finley asked.

Dodge couldn't speak. He made a faint noise of dread as he stared out at the street. Finley looked in that direction and winced.

Across the street, the man was just dismounting from one of the Corcoran horses. But they had galloped off, Finley thought in confusion. How did the man . . . ?

"What are we going to do?" Dodge whispered, terrified.

Finley drew in a deep, restoring breath. He wasn't going to let this thing completely spook him, he resolved. He simply wasn't.

"We are going to walk to my office, Professor," he said as calmly as he could. "Then we are going to the stable, get two horses, and ride out of town to Fort Apache."

He wondered if Dodge had heard a single word he'd said. The little man could not remove his stricken gaze from the man across the street. Finley looked in that direction. The man was just sitting down in the chair again to watch the hotel.

"Come on," Finley said, taking hold of Dodge's arm.

"*No.*" The little man hitched back in blind alarm.

Finley grimaced with anger. "Professor, I'm going down to my office now. Come with me or stay here alone."

Dodge looked at him in a sudden panic. "Don't leave me," he begged.

"Then come with me," Finley said. "I'm not going to stay."

He stepped off, glancing back. Dodge hadn't budged. He was still gaping at the man across the street. Again, Finley looked in that direction. An icy shiver ran up his back.

The man was looking toward the hotel doorway. Could he see Dodge? Finley wondered.

He looked back at Dodge, who still stood frozen just inside the hotel doorway.

"Professor," he said, "the street is filled with people. The man isn't going to go after you with all these people around."

He glanced around. There weren't that many, he saw. He wasn't going to tell Dodge that, however. "Come on," he said, "I'm going now."

"Wait," Dodge pleaded pathetically.

He came out slowly, pretending that he didn't know the man was across the street. Finley glanced aside, stiffening as he saw the man rise suddenly. Jesus, was he going to approach Dodge anyway?

He grabbed the professor's arm and started leading him toward the office.

"Just walk smoothly," he said. He had to force himself not to glance across the street. Not that he'd know what to do if the man was crossing toward them. Confront him? Run?

"Is he coming for us?" Dodge asked in a faint voice.

Finley almost glanced aside despite his resolution not to do it. He clenched his teeth and looked ahead determinedly. "Just walk," he said.

He could feel the rigid tension in Dodge's arm as they moved down the street, their boots thumping on the plank walk. Finley couldn't help himself from glancing at the window of Chasen's Dry Goods. He saw the man reflected, still across the street, watching them. What did that mean? he wondered. That he'd changed his mind about seeing Dodge? That he wouldn't accost Dodge unless the professor was alone? He couldn't help wondering what the man thought of him for leading Dodge along the street.

He had his answer when they reached the office. As he opened the door and ushered Dodge inside, he could not prevent himself from looking toward the man.

He shivered as he saw that the man had moved along the opposite side of the street. Already, he was standing almost directly across from the office.

The look he directed at Finley chilled the agent's blood. It was a look of murderous hostility.

Swallowing with effort, Finley went inside and shut the door with a cowed sense that there was probably no door that could shut away the man if the man chose to enter.

As he turned toward the office, he was startled to see Boutelle across the floor from him, standing with Barney Gans, who ran a small horse ranch somewhere in the vicinity of Pinal Spring.

From the look of him, Barney had been riding hard, his long coat splattered with mud, streaks and specks of it across his face and hat, on his hands.

"What's going on?" Finley asked.

Boutelle glanced questioningly at Dodge.

"This is Professor Dodge," Finley told him. "I'm taking him to Fort Apache."

"Good." Boutelle's voice was grim. "I'll go with you."

Now what? Finley thought.

"Tell Mr. Finley," Boutelle said to Gans.

"It's the Injuns, Mr. Finley," Barney said. "Braided Feather's band. They left their camp and took off for the mountains."

Oh, Christ, Finley thought. He wasn't prepared for this. "You're sure?" was all he could think to say.

"Yes, sir. I was bringin' in some strays and saw them movin' off."

"Are you satisfied now?" Boutelle demanded. "Is this enough? Can we tell Colonel Bishop that—"

"Listen—" Finley interrupted, then broke off instantly and turned to Dodge. "Can you tell us something to explain this?" he asked. "Mr. Boutelle is convinced that Braided Feather's band is behind all this. I think you know differently. Now will you please tell Mr. Boutelle what's actually going on?"

Dodge gulped. "I can't," he murmured. "I have to leave."

"Professor, *we have got to know*," Finley said irritably. "Mr. Boutelle—"

"Mr. Boutelle is convinced that this is one more dereliction on the part of the Apaches," Boutelle broke in. "One more indication of their utter contempt for the agreement they signed only yesterday!"

Finley grabbed Dodge's arm. "Damn it," he said. "Tell us who that man is and why he wants to talk to you, and to the Night Doctor."

Dodge began to shake, tears rising in his eyes again. "I can't," he said. Boutelle looked at him, wondering how Dodge fitted into any of this. He was convinced it was the Apaches. Still . . .

"Barney, thank you for riding in and telling us this," Finley said to Gans. "I'm going to find Braided Feather and his people and ask them what this is all about."

"You don't think—" Barney began.

"You're going to *talk* to the Apaches?" Boutelle said incredulously. "You're still not going to call in the troops to—"

"Barney, I'll be in touch with you later," Finley said, cutting off Boutelle. "Thank you again."

"That's okay, Mr. Finley," Barney said.

When he'd gone, Finley turned back to Boutelle. The

young man's face was set into a grim expression. I cannot believe how much has gone wrong in the past twenty-four hours, Finley thought. He glanced at the wall clock. Jesus. It hadn't even been twenty-four hours yet.

Bracing himself, he spoke to Boutelle.

"You don't know everything that's going on here," he said. He threw a resentful glance at Dodge. "And it doesn't look as if you're going to right away—any more than I am."

He gestured brusquely toward the bench by the door. "Wait there," he told Dodge. Despite the small man's continuing dread, Finley was losing patience with him. Dodge might conceivably solve this problem with a simple explanation. He couldn't imagine what that explanation might be, but if it was there, Dodge damn well owed it to them.

"I know what you believe, Mr. Boutelle," he said. "I know it makes sense to you. But I'm convinced there's more involved here than a broken treaty."

"*A broken treaty*?" Boutelle said coldly. "Have you already forgotten about those two butchered men?"

"No, I haven't forgotten about them," Finley said, noticing the frightened look Dodge was giving Boutelle. He almost told Boutelle about Al Corcoran, then decided against it; there simply wasn't time.

"I'm going after Braided Feather," he continued. "I have to hear his side of the story before I can decide what to do. I'm sorry, but that's the way it's got to be for now."

Boutelle stared at him in silence. Finley heard the wall clock ticking and saw, from the left side of his vision, the brass pendulum arcing back and forth.

"I see," Boutelle finally replied.

Finley turned away and moved to the cupboard to get his saddlebags and supplies.

"I'll go rent a horse," Boutelle said.

Finley turned in surprise. Boutelle was heading for the door.

"You're going with me?" Finley asked.

Boutelle stopped and looked around.

"Is there any reason that I can't?" he challenged.

Finley thought about it for a moment. "No," he said. "Glad to have your company."

"That I doubt," Boutelle murmured, moving to the door again and opening it. "I'll meet you at the livery stable," he said.

Finley watched Boutelle close the door. He was impressed. It would never have occurred to him that Boutelle would volunteer for such a trip.

He grunted with dark amusement as he turned back to the cupboard. Glad to have his company? he thought. Boutelle was right. He doubted it, too. At least he'd know where Boutelle was, though. That would prevent the younger man from riding to Fort Apache on his own and reporting Braided Feather's flight to Colonel Bishop.

A look of concern tightened his face again. Why *did* Braided Feather take his entire band away from their camp? He'd never known the chief to evidence a moment's cowardice in the past. Now he was taking flight with all his people.

Something was driving them away. Something which obviously terrified them.

He looked at Dodge.

The little man was standing by the window, pressed against the wall, peering around its edge.

"Is he still there?" Finley asked.

His voice made the little man twitch and look toward Finley with a gasp.

"Is he?" Finley said.

Dodge drew in a shaking breath. "Yes," he said, his voice thin. "You *are* going to take me to Fort Apache, aren't you?"

"No," Finley answered.

Dodge looked at him in shock. "You're *not*?" he said.

"Why should I take you anywhere?" Finley demanded. "You're not willing to help me. Why should I help you?"

"Please," Dodge said. "I can't tell you."

"Then go by yourself," Finley snapped.

"Damn you, don't you have the slightest idea of what we're all involved in here!" Dodge cried, startling Finley. "If you knew what that man really is!"

"What is he?" Finley demanded.

"*Something you don't want to know about*," Dodge told him. "If you had the brains you were born with, you'd leave the territory with me and never come back!"

Finley looked intently at the little man. Clearly, Dodge was overwhelmed by dread.

He sighed. No use, he thought. He wasn't going to get anything helpful from the professor. He may as well forego the hope.

"You can go with me," he told the professor. "But I can't take you to Fort Apache."

"But you *have* to," Dodge said in a panicked voice.

"It's in the opposite direction from the way I have to go," Finley told him. "I'm sorry. You know what I have to do."

"You can't just leave me," Dodge said pleadingly.

"I'm sorry," Finley said, gathering supplies together. "I'll stay with you as far as I can. Then I've got to head into the mountains." He looked over at Dodge. "Maybe you want to come with me, see Braided Feather yourself."

Dodge said no more. He stood by the window in silence, peering out at the man.

The next time Finley looked at him, the little man was slumped on the bench, bending over, holding his head in his hands. Finley had never seen a more defeated-looking man. He felt sorry for Dodge again.

But there was nothing more he could do about it.

IO

As they rode down Main Street, headed for the south end of town, they had to ride past the hotel. Across from it, sitting in the chair again, was the man. On seeing him there, it occurred to Finley that ordinarily if short-tempered Elbert Zweig, who owned the grain shop, saw anyone sitting in his chair, he'd charge out and roust him. That there was not a sign of Zweig made it obvious that he had no intention of confronting the man.

He glanced at Dodge. The professor was staring straight ahead, face set into a rigid mask.

Finley glanced at the man in the chair, shuddering as he saw that look again directed at him.

He felt a tightening of reactive anger. Damn the man anyway, he thought. If the Marshal had been around, Finley could have told him that the man had stolen one of the Corcorans' horses; that would be enough to get him thrown in jail.

But could the jail even contain the man, Finley wondered, remembering that glade and the sight of Al Corcoran torn apart like the prey of some wild animal. The last time he'd seen a living thing so mangled was when he'd stumbled onto a hawk devouring a rabbit it had just caught.

His startling of the bird had made it rush up suddenly into the air, scattering the bloody fragments of flesh in all directions.

"You really think that man is involved with what's happening?" Boutelle's voice made him start.

Finley glanced at the man in the chair to see if he'd overheard. If he had, he gave no indication of it.

"Ask the professor," he answered.

Boutelle looked at Dodge. "Professor?" he asked. If the small man knew something about this situation, Boutelle could not fathom why he was so reluctant to reveal it.

"Not yet," was all Dodge said, his lips barely moving as though he didn't want the man in the chair to think he was speaking.

Ten minutes later, they were out of Picture City.

After they were gone from sight, the man stood slowly and moved to Al Corcoran's horse. He swung his giant frame onto the saddle and reined the horse's head around.

He would not lose track of the professor this time.

They saw the grayish-white smoke before they were close enough to see what was burning.

"What could that be?" Boutelle asked.

"Unless I'm wrong, it's Little Owl's wickiup," Finley told him.

In several minutes, they could see the burning structure. Because of the heavy rain the day and night before, its hide walls were still damp, smoldering slowly instead of burning quickly as they would have in drier weather.

Little Owl's widow and children had just finished loading a travois with their few belongings. They looked around apprehensively as they heard the approaching hoofbeats. Seeing Finley, Little Owl's wife said something to her children and they became less restive.

Boutelle looked at them with impolite curiosity as they

rode closer to the burning wickiup. He had not seen Indian women and children before. His only exposure to the Apaches had been the meeting yesterday and the few minutes in town this morning, and that had only been with Braided Feather, his rancorous son, and whatever braves had come along with them.

Frankly, he was appalled by the sight of Little Owl's widow and children. They looked dirty and diseased to him, their clothes in wretched condition. Did they ever wash? he thought. But even as he thought it, he sensed the injustice of that observation. To live like this was scarcely conducive to cleanliness. Not that they care, I'm sure, he thought.

In light of all that, however, why in the name of God were they burning the one shelter they had, meager and mean though it was?

He asked, and Finley told him that it was because of Little Owl, that it was an Indian practice to burn their dwelling places after a death.

"With his body *inside*?" he asked, repelled.

"It's their way," Finley answered.

Boutelle was silent for a few moments before asking, "Can you find out if she knows anything about the Apaches leaving their camp?"

"She wouldn't know anything about that," Finley replied.

"Ask her about her husband then," Boutelle said. "Maybe he knew—"

"Impossible," Finley interrupted. "From the moment she knew her husband was dead, his name never passed her lips, and in no way whatever will she ever refer to him for the rest of her life."

"Really," Boutelle said, not impressed by the information, merely reacting to it.

They stopped by the smoking, slowly burning wickiup,

and Finley, dismounting, spoke to Little Owl's wife. Boutelle could not help but notice the kindness in his voice when he spoke to her. What did the man see in these people anyway? he thought. Their hideous depredations on the settlers of this territory and beyond would certainly seem to disqualify them from the status of acceptable human beings.

He looked over at Dodge. The professor was clearly unhappy about them stopping at all. He kept looking back toward Picture City, his expression deeply anxious. Did he think that man was going to follow them?

Boutelle tried not to allow himself to be misled by what appeared to be complications in what was going on. The facts were clear enough. The Apaches had signed the treaty in bad faith, promptly massacred those two young men, and now were fleeing from the obvious consequences.

The rest was extraneous. That man—as grotesque as he was to look at—could not conceivably be behind all this. Very well, Professor Dodge was terrified of him. Dodge seemed to be an educated man, but that did not prevent him from being credulous as well. Perhaps he'd done something to offend the man and feared reprisal.

As far as the so-called "Night Doctor" . . . Boutelle made a scoffing noise. He had no intention of succumbing to anything which remotely smacked of mysticism. God knew the man with the scar looked powerful enough to commit any conceivable variety of mayhem without being a mystical being. That the Apaches feared him was not all that peculiar. They were a naive, superstitious lot at best and . . .

His train of thought broke off as Dodge said loudly, "Can't we go?"

Finley looked up at him without expression, then turned back to Little Owl's widow and said a few more things to her. Boutelle saw him pat her gently on the back and smile. Then he returned to his horse and mounted. Without a word, he pulled the mare around and nudged his heels against its flanks, causing it to trot away. Boutelle did the same, then Dodge. The three men rode off from what had been Little Owl's home and now was only a smoking framework of poles and burning hides.

"What did you say to her?" Boutelle asked, riding up beside Finley.

"I wished her luck," Finley muttered.

"You didn't suggest she take her family to the San Carlos Reservation?"

"I wouldn't send a *dog* there," Finley responded.

The bitterness in his voice shut Boutelle up. Obviously Finley was in no frame of mind to be rational, he thought. Let it go. Soon enough, the agent would have to accept the facts and have a troop of cavalry sent in pursuit of the fleeing Apaches.

Dodge followed them, relieved when Finley heeled his mare into a slow gallop. The further away from the man he got and the faster, the better he'd feel.

Finley pulled up his horse and twisted around to look at Dodge.

"This is as far as I can take you," he said. "The fort is that way."

Dodge stared at him blankly. "You're really not going to—"

"You can still come with us," Finley cut him off. "Talk to Braided Feather. Tell him—"

"No," Dodge interrupted.

Finley's lips tightened. "Suit yourself," he said. Boutelle saw him struggling with his anger and controlling it. Then Finley spoke again.

"Listen to me, Professor," he said. "This is your last chance to prevent what could well be a catastrophe. You know a lot more than you've told us. Please . . . *please* don't hold back anymore. *Who is that man?* Why are the Apaches running from him? Why are *you* running from him? What does the Night Doctor have to do with it? For God's sake, what's that damn *scar* around his neck?"

It seemed as though Dodge was about to speak. His lips stirred soundlessly, his expression tautly anxious.

Abruptly, then, he looked behind them, hissed as though he saw something, and kicked his boot heels at the horse's flanks, galloping off toward the fort.

"I hope he makes it," Finley said after a few moments.

Boutelle didn't know how to respond. Despite his resolve, his mind kept getting cluttered with these complications, all of them leading to one unanswerable question.

What *did* the tall stranger have to do with what was going on?

He watched Dodge galloping away at high speed.

As though pursued by the demons of Hell.

The Campground was built beside a running stream within a grove of trees, a thick windbreak of pine, spruce, and piñon.

There were eighty-seven tepees covering a clearing of almost four acres. They surrounded an open area of ground in which stood an oversize tepee which Boutelle took to be a meeting lodge of some kind.

Each tepee was constructed of a tripod of poles tightly covered by buffalo skins, their flesh side outward. All of them looked slightly tilted to Boutelle, which he took to be deliberate.

The camp was deserted.

Boutelle's gaze moved across the quiet area. Several fires were still burning low, their wood embers dark red. Pots hung over them as though the Apaches had not even had the time to remove them. Boutelle could smell some kind of food now burning in them.

His gaze shifted to where an ancient-looking steer was standing, motionless, looking off into the distance.

"Why did they leave it?" he asked.

"Too old, too slow," Finley said. "They didn't want to be held back."

"How do you know that?" Boutelle asked.

Finley didn't answer, and Boutelle had the sudden impression that Finley knew a great deal about these people and their land. For a few moments, he felt alien and helpless, then fought it off. No need for that, he told himself.

"Now what?" he asked.

Finley gazed at him, and Boutelle had the impression that the agent wouldn't hesitate to leave him there if it served his purpose.

"Now we find them," Finley answered.

"Where?"

Was that a scornful smile on Finley's lips? The Indian agent pointed. "Thataway," he said. Boutelle was going to question him regarding how he knew, then realized that to someone with Finley's experience finding tracks would present no difficulty. He decided not to speak.

"If nothing else," Finley said, "this should make it clear to you how frightened these people are. Indians can pack and move very fast, including their tepees. That they've left them here—even left cooking utensils—well . . ." He looked at Boutelle grimly. "You'll have to take my word for it," he said. "Let's get out of here."

He swung up onto his mare and started off. Boutelle swallowed, trying to repress a sense of apprehension.

They were heading for the mountains.

Dodge knew he was driving his horse too hard, but he couldn't help it. He cursed himself for not demanding a different horse from the one he'd ridden on his trip into the hills. He should have a fresh mount, one that could move faster.

He looked down at the horse. Its neck was covered with lather. He should let it slow down; it needed a break. He couldn't allow it though. He kept kicking his boot heels against its flanks and uttering demanding cries for more and more speed. The Appaloosa's legs drove down like pistons against the still wet earth, casting up sprays of mud. Dodge glanced down at himself. He was filthy with the stuff.

Forget it, he told himself. *Forget it.* For the seventy-third time since he'd left Picture City, he looked behind. No sign of the man, he saw. Which didn't mean the man was not pursuing him. He had to guess that Dodge was headed for the fort. It wouldn't even require a guess if he'd spotted the place where Dodge had separated from Finley and Boutelle.

He tried to stand a little in the stirrups to relieve the pounding of his body on the hard saddle. He wished to God he were a better rider. It had never seemed a necessity before.

Now it did.

He looked over his shoulder toward the mountains. Already, they were darkening. For God's sake, what had happened to the day? he thought angrily. He had to reach the fort before sunset. The vision of him being forced to gallop in the dark terrified him.

He reached up his left hand and rubbed it across his sweating neck. Despite the chilly air, he felt hot. He should stop and remove his coat, but he didn't dare take the time. He had to keep going. Until he reached the fort, he was in constant danger.

The horse struggled up a rise, and Dodge reined it to a skidding halt, twisting around on the saddle to look again at—

The sound he uttered in his throat was something between a sob and a cry of fear.

In the distance, riding hard, the man was following him.

"*God*," Dodge whimpered.

He drove his heels into the horse's body, and it lurched forward with a frightening groan. *Don't fail me now*, Dodge thought desperately.

The Appaloosa half-ran, half-slid down the slope on the opposite side, reached level ground and broke into a gallop once more. Dodge caught his breath. Was it his imagination or had the horse just lurched as though the strain was too much for it?

He couldn't even let himself consider the possibility. The horse would get him to the fort. *It had to get him there.* He looked over his shoulder again.

And cried out in despairing shock.

The other horse still followed him.

But it was riderless.

"*No!*" Dodge ground his teeth together, kicking wildly at the horse's flanks. He needed a whip, a *whip*! Dear God! *It wasn't possible.*

He looked up at the leaden-colored sky. "No, please," he whimpered. "Please." His heart was pounding violently. His mind kept pleading.

He was looking at the sky again when the Appaloosa's legs collapsed.

Screaming with horror, Dodge was hurled from its back, landing in a twisted heap. Uncontrolled, his frail body tumbled, somersaulting down a rocky slope, the back of his head striking a boulder with violent impact at the bottom.

There was a rushing sound above, a dropping shadow.

Then the man stood at the top of the slope, looking down at Dodge's motionless body.

Ignoring the fleeing Appaloosa, the man moved down the slope, boots crunching on the layers of small rocks.

At the bottom, he stopped and looked down at Professor Dodge's dead body, his dark eyes filled with hatred for the little man.

Abruptly, then, he leaned over and dragged up Dodge's body with one hand, raised it effortlessly above his head and hurled it away with a snarl of feral rage.

The professor's bruised and bleeding corpse landed more than twenty feet away.

II

Finley looked around at Boutelle and saw the younger man kneading at his right leg. Reining back his mare until he was beside Boutelle, he asked him what was wrong.

"Nothing," Boutelle answered. "I just haven't ridden such a distance in a long time."

Finley looked at the sky. "Well, we should stop soon anyway," he said. "We can't go much further today."

Boutelle frowned. He hadn't planned on spending the night out here.

"Shouldn't we be turning back for help?" he asked. "You really intend to confront the Apaches all by yourself?"

"Better than confronting them with Leicester's troops behind me," Finley said. "That would really be a mistake. Braided Feather wouldn't trust me for a moment if I did that."

Boutelle was inclined to disagree but sensed that it would be a waste of time. Grimacing, he removed his glove and dug the fingers of his right hand into his cramping leg muscles.

"Apaches believe that involuntary muscle spasms are signals of evil events to come," Finley observed. Was that the hint of a smile on his lips? Boutelle wondered. He grunted as Finley moved away from him. Naturally, he didn't believe a word of such nonsense, but after everything that had happened, he would have preferred that Finley kept that bit of Apache lore to himself.

Fifteen minutes later, Finley stopped his mare by the side of a small creek in an aspen grove. The chilling October wind was causing the undersides of the aspen leaves to twist around, making the tree appear as though it was dancing with light.

"Don't get down too close to that brush," Finley told him.

But Boutelle was already dismounting.

He gasped at the sudden buzzing noise beneath him. He felt something thick and soft beneath his boot, then cried out at the fiery sensation in his right calf. He looked down to see a thrash of tan-brown movement in the brush and heard another buzzing sound.

He never knew how Finley got to him so fast. All he knew was that the agent had a long knife in his hand and was stabbing down at something. The buzzing and thrashing increased, and Boutelle saw then what he'd stepped on: a brown and tan rattlesnake at least seven feet long.

"My God," he murmured. Now that the initial shock had passed, the pain in his leg was increasing. I'm going to die, he thought incredulously. Out here. Like this.

He saw that Finley had driven his knife blade through the snake's neck, pinning it to the ground. Pulling a folding knife from a trouser pocket, the agent opened it and started slicing a piece of flesh from the still living snake. The rattler kept striking, but the blade through its neck prevented it from reaching them.

"Quickly," Finley said. He grabbed Boutelle by the arm and half-pulled, half-shoved him to a piece of open ground where he threw him down. He pulled up Boutelle's trouser leg and slapped the piece of rattler flesh on the puncture mark.

Boutelle caught his breath. Despite the pain, he felt a drawing sensation, and in less than a minute, to his amazement, the white snake flesh started turning green.

"Hold it against the wound," Finley told him.

Boutelle did as he was told, and Finley quickly returned to the still thrashing snake and cut another chunk of flesh from its body. Bringing it back, he took the greenish piece of flesh away, threw it aside, and replaced it with the new white piece. Boutelle felt the drawing sensation once more and watched in awe while the second piece of flesh began to change in color as the rattler's venom was sapped from his blood.

Boutelle lay immobile on the ground as Finley kept applying chunks of snake meat to the puncture wound until the flesh ceased turning green. It took almost the entire snake before that happened. It was almost dark by then. Finley had to take out his match case and light the wick of the tiny candle so he could be sure the poison had been totally extracted.

"There you go," he said. "You'll be sore, maybe a little dizzy. But nothing more."

Boutelle swallowed dryly. "Thank you," he murmured.

"My pleasure," Finley said, smiling a little.

"That was a big snake," Boutelle said. "I could have died."

"Easily," Finley agreed.

Boutelle shuddered. "I never heard of treating it that way," he said. "Cutting a crosshatch in the skin and sucking it out, yes, but—"

"That doesn't always work," Finley said. "This way is more certain. Hated to kill the snake, but I had no choice. He bit you, he had to cure you."

"Where—" Boutelle swallowed again, the impact of

what he'd just gone through getting to him more and more. He could have died. "Where did you learn to do that?"

Finley chuckled. "From Braided Feather," he answered.

Boutelle had no idea what to reply. Finley grinned at him.

"Bet that leg cramp isn't bothering you now," he said.

While Boutelle rested, Finley unsaddled the horses and tethered them to graze after first letting them drink their fill from the creek.

Then he broke off a pile of aspen twigs and branches for a fire.

"Good wood," he told Boutelle, trying to prevent the younger man from brooding too much about what had happened to him; he knew the danger of that. "Makes a smokeless fire."

Boutelle wondered why it mattered that the fire was smokeless. That man with the scar was interested in Professor Dodge, not them.

"Just as soon no smoke shows," Finley said, as though reading his mind.

When the fire was burning, Finley took supplies from his saddlebags: a slab of bacon, a can of beans, some flour, and a small sack of coffee. "Common doin's," Finley said. "Keep us from starving though."

"You must have known we were out for the night," Boutelle said, trying not to sound accusing.

"I wasn't sure," Finley responded. "I hoped we'd find Braided Feather right away but knew I couldn't count on it." He glanced over at Boutelle. "I'm sorry I can't take you into town to see Doc Reese," he said.

"Do I need to see a doctor?" Boutelle asked uneasily.

"I don't think so," Finley said. "Just thought you might feel better seeing a real sawbones."

"I doubt if he could do any more than you," Boutelle

replied. He was still flabbergasted by the memory of what Finley had done. There was no doubt in his mind that he would have died if Finley hadn't acted so immediately.

It made him feel off balance to owe the agent so much. In a matter of seconds, their relationship seemed to have changed completely.

How could he argue with a man who'd saved his life?

"Coffee's ready," Finley said. He poured some into a metal cup and handed it to Boutelle. "Hope it doesn't curl your hair. It's cowboy coffee."

"What's that?" Boutelle asked.

"If a silver dollar floats on top of it, it's done," Finley answered, grinning.

Boutelle managed a smile. Despite Finley's incredible rescue, he still felt achy and a little hot.

"You all right?" Finley asked.

"Considering the alternative, I'd say yes," Boutelle answered.

Finley smiled and sat down with his cup of coffee. "Drink," he said. "If anything can neutralize rattler venom, it's a good, strong cup of Arbuckle's."

Boutelle took a sip, the taste of it widening his eyes. "God," he murmured.

"Little strong?" Finley asked.

"Just a bit." Boutelle sniffed at the coffee, then took another sip and whistled softly. "I may never sleep again," he said.

Finley smiled, then looked serious.

"Listen . . . Boutelle," he said. "All right if I call you David?" he sidetracked himself.

Boutelle hesitated.

"If it bothers you, I won't," Finley told him.

"No, no," Boutelle said. "That's fine." He paused. "Billjohn, is it?"

Finley explained how he got the name. "Both my folks were satisfied," he said. "At least, they claimed they were. I doubt it, though."

He took a sip of coffee, then removed a cigar case from his inside jacket pocket and held it out. "Want one?" he asked.

"Not right now, thank you," Boutelle answered.

"Understandable." Finley put a cigar between his lips and lit the end of it, drew in deeply, then blew out smoke. "Good," he said.

Boutelle waited. He believed that Finley had been about to say something serious to him a few moments earlier.

"David, do you still think the Apaches are responsible for what's been going on?" Finley asked.

Boutelle felt cornered. Before the rattler bite, he would have responded instantly that of course he did. Now it was a bit more difficult than that.

He elected to do the sort of thing he saw in Washington all the time, the political thing. He reversed the question.

"Do you still think it's that man?" he asked.

Finley's lips stirred in a faint smile, and Boutelle sensed that the agent was aware of what he'd done.

"Look at it this way then," Finley said, confirming the impression. "Does it make sense to you that, on the very day of signing a treaty with the United States—after ten years of war, mind you—Braided Feather would let his braves kill and mutilate the Corcoran brothers—*on their way home from the signing ceremony*?"

Boutelle could not deny that Finley's point was well-taken. Still . . .

"And that, knowing full well that one of the main conditions of the treaty is that they keep their distance from Picture City, he'd ride into town with his braves the very next morning?"

"Well . . ." Boutelle felt his conviction fading.

"They came in to see that man," Finley said. "If they'd come as hostiles, they could have wiped us out at that time of morning. You know that."

"I don't," Boutelle said. "I'll take your word on it, though."

"You do admit they were afraid of that man and left within seconds of seeing him?"

"I . . . suppose," Boutelle had to admit, albeit reluctantly.

"David," Finley said. Boutelle tensed a little at the admonishing tone in Finley's voice; that he did not appreciate. "These aren't dime-novel Indians. These are bone-seasoned Apache warriors. Believe me, there is very little in this world that frightens them. But that man frightens them."

Boutelle nodded slightly. "Well, he certainly seems to frighten Professor Dodge," he said.

"Terrifies him, David," Finley said. "Terrifies him."

He hesitated, then said, "I'll tell you something. He kind o' scares the bejesus out of me as well."

He told Boutelle about his rejected inclination to await the marshal's return and try to put the man in jail for horse stealing. "Not to mention murder," he finished.

Then he told Boutelle about finding Al Corcoran's butchered remains.

"I've seen victims of Apache raids," he said. "They did some pretty god-awful things. But nothing like that."

"Which has been my point—" Boutelle almost said "Billjohn," then couldn't make himself do it. "The Apaches—the Indians—are well-known for their atrocities. You can't deny that."

"I don't deny it," Finley said. "I'm just saying that these atrocities go way beyond what I've seen them do."

"Then how could that man be responsible?" Boutelle challenged. "How could any one man be responsible for these things?"

"I don't know," Finley murmured. He added something in such a low voice that Boutelle couldn't hear it.

"What?" he asked. It made him uneasy to see how obviously Finley swallowed.

"I said, if he *is* a man," the agent said.

Boutelle felt himself shudder involuntarily. "What do you—" He cleared his throat. "What do you mean?"

Finley didn't answer at first. All Boutelle could hear was the crackle of the low fire and sounds in the night, birds and other animals. He stared at the agent's face, firelight reflected on it.

Finley looked away, troubled.

Finally, the agent sighed and tossed his cigar into the fire.

"I'm thinking of the look on Little Owl's face," he said. "You saw it. If ever a man died of fright, it was him."

He hesitated, then continued. "I saw the same look on Al Corcoran's face when I . . . picked up his head," he told Boutelle, who winced at his words.

"You saw the look on Tom Corcoran's face. It was the same look—absolute horror."

He drew in a deep, laboring breath and released it slowly.

"I imagine we'd have seen the same look on Jim Corcoran's face, too," he said, "if his face hadn't been ripped off."

Boutelle winced again. More and more, he was losing confidence in what he'd been convinced of earlier. He tried to believe that it was because of the darkness, the sounds, and the firelight glinting on Finley's harrowed expression. But it wouldn't wash. The Indian agent was right. There were too many abnormal factors in this situation to ignore.

"I'm thinking about the Night Doctor. I'm wondering why that man is so anxious to see a discredited shaman, a medicine man who was banished from his tribe for performing ceremonies he wasn't supposed to perform."

They sat in silence, Finley staring gravely into the fire, Boutelle watching him with a sense of deep disquiet.

"You know," Finley said after a while, "back East, it's civilized and all the mysteries have been dispelled by that civilization. Out here, it's easier to believe that there's still a lot of unexplored ground. A lot of secrets."

He paused again, then added quietly, "I'm thinking of that thick scar around the man's entire neck. When I mentioned it, he smiled at me and said that someone had once cut off his head."

Boutelle wished desperately now that he could speak up and refute the agent's increasingly alarming words. He couldn't, though.

He started as he heard a horrible screeching noise in the distance, looked quickly at Finley. The other man had not responded to the sound.

"What was that?" Boutelle had to ask.

"Owl killing something," Finley said. "Or a hawk." He shrugged. "Maybe an eagle."

FRIDAY

12

While they were riding the next day, heading toward the mountains, Finley following signs Boutelle couldn't see, they began to talk about Indians.

In the daylight––there was even an occasional glow of sunshine to warm the cold air––Boutelle regained some of his confidence in past convictions. The soreness from the rattler bite was almost gone as well, and uncharitable though it was, with little to remind him physically of what Finley had done, it was easier to retrieve beliefs he'd held for so many years.

"About these Plains Indians," he began.

"David, there was no such thing until the Spanish brought in horses."

"And the Indians stole them," Boutelle countered.

"Or traded for them," Finley said. "They were farmers and hunters until they got the horses."

"I was under the impression that the Apache nation—" Boutelle started.

"There *is* no Apache nation," Finley cut him off. "There are only clans and kinship groupings.

"For that matter, isn't it stupid that we call them Indians

at all? What if Columbus had thought he'd landed in Turkey instead of India? Would we call them turkeys?"

"Mr. . . . Billjohn," Boutelle said, grimacing slightly. "What do you want to call them?"

"People," Finley said. "That's what they call themselves. How about the first Americans? They were here before we were."

Boutelle sighed. "I hear your Rutgers background speaking now," he said.

They rode in silence for a while. Then Boutelle spoke again.

"You admitted last night that the Apaches have done some god-awful things," he started.

"And we've done some god-awful things to them," Finley said.

He is really in a bellicose frame of mind today, Boutelle thought.

"As I heard a man in White River say to a companion," he prodded Finley, "*haul in your horns.* By which—"

He broke off as Finley snickered. Clearly, the agent knew exactly what he meant.

"You're right," Finley said. "I'm sorry. I'll try to speak my piece without rattling my tail.

"It's a little difficult for me, though. I was a history major at Rutgers—American history. I wrote my Master's thesis on the Indian situation."

Boutelle was surprised. He'd had no idea the man was that well educated. He felt a twinge of guilt.

"You think the problem started only ten or twenty years ago?" Finley continued. "Indians were living on the East Coast more than forty years ago. Living in peace with their neighbors. In log cabins. Wearing homespun clothing. The Cherokees, the Chickasaws, the Choctaws, Creeks, and Seminoles. They were called the Five Civilized Tribes.

Their leaders could read and write English. Their people intermarried with the whites.

"Then Andrew Jackson decided that they didn't belong there. So he had Congress pass legislation to move the Indians to 'an ample district west of the Mississippi.'" His tone was bitter as he quoted.

"It took nine years to get it done, but by God they got it done," he went on. "Sixty thousand Indians rounded up at gunpoint and marched west under military guard.

"Only fourteen thousand of them survived it."

He smiled and shook his head; it was a smile devoid of humor. "Eventually, the land they'd been given was taken away from them."

He grunted. "That's the way it worked from the start," he said. "We gave them land—that was already theirs, of course. Then when we wanted that land for building or mining or farming or grazing, we took it back and gave them other land further out. Until the land they were given was so bad they decided to fight back. At which point, we began calling them savages."

Boutelle felt as though he should say something to refute what Finley had told him. He couldn't, though. He couldn't think of anything to say.

"I've been an Indian agent for seven years, David," Finley continued. "My job has been to issue supplies and annuities to the Apaches. Annuities that never arrived on time. Supplies that got sold or stolen before they reached me.

"I'm supposed to tell the Indians how nice their lives will be on reservations like the one at San Carlos, which is a malaria-ridden hellhole.

"Of course, no matter what I do, it's hopeless. The Apaches are finished. All the Indians are finished. They got in our way. We wanted their land so we took it. Their days are written on the sand. You and I may not live to see it, but it's going to happen, it's inevitable."

He sighed and smiled bitterly. "Listen, if you think I've got diarrhea of the jawbone, just tell me so. I have a tendency to run on for a day and a half when I talk about the Indians."

They rode in silence for a long while before Boutelle felt compelled to speak.

"Listen . . . Billjohn," he said, "I've lived an isolated life. My family has a lot of money and it made existence very easy for me. I rode, I hunted, I hiked. I traveled the world. Graduated from the best schools.

"My father got me an appointment in the Department of the Interior. I thought I was equipped to handle it. Like so many people back East, I thought I understood the Indian situation perfectly. I read the newspapers, read the dispatches. You're right; I thought of them as savages. I probably still feel that way deep inside. But you've given me a lot to think about I never had before, and I thank you for it."

Finley's smile was broad and genial. He edged his horse close to Boutelle's and extended his hand.

Boutelle tried not to wince at the power of the agent's grip. He managed to return Finley's smile.

Then Finley sighed again.

"Now all we have to do is locate Braided Feather," he said. "Try to find out what the hell is going on."

The dogs were at them first, crashing from the underbrush with angry snarls, lips curled back from yellow fangs, eyes glittering with menace.

Boutelle reined in hard as the running pack began snapping at his horse's legs. His mount began to twist and buck, nickering in alarm, trying to avoid the dogs' teeth. From the corners of his eyes, he saw Finley trying to hold in his mare as well, cursing at the dogs.

Then Apaches were surrounding them, pointing rifles, dark faces impassive. The dogs drew back, still snarling, as Finley spoke to the threatening braves.

At first it seemed it wasn't going to work; the Indians raised their rifles as though to fire.

Then Lean Bear appeared from the woods and, seeing Finley, ordered off his men. Finley thanked him.

"Why are you here?" Lean Bear asked suspiciously.

"I must speak to Braided Feather," Finley answered.

"We are not going back to our camp," Lean Bear told him.

"I understand that," Finley replied. "I, too, am concerned about that man and wish to speak to your father about him."

Lean Bear said something in Apache which, Boutelle thought, was obviously spoken in bitter scorn. Then he gestured to Finley for the mare's reins, and Finley tossed them over his horse's head so Lean Bear could grab them.

He looked at Boutelle. "Give them your reins," he said. "And your weapon," he added, slipping his rifle from its scabbard and giving it to Lean Bear, then handing down his pistol.

Boutelle threw the reins of his horse across its head, and a brave took hold of them. Removing his pistol carefully from its holster, he handed it down, butt first, to the Indian's reaching hand, hoping that he wasn't committing suicide by doing so.

The dogs kept circling, growling and baring their teeth as their horses walked skittishly among the Apaches.

"I gather the dogs don't like us," Boutelle said to break the silence.

"They don't like the way we smell," Finley responded.

Boutelle swallowed, looking around. Through the undergrowth, he could see other braves watching them, some armed with rifles, some with bows and arrows.

"What did . . ." His voice faded, and as Finley looked at him, he nodded toward Lean Bear.

"What?" Finley asked.

"What did he say before? He sounded so . . . *scornful*."

"Try *afraid*," Finley said. "When I told him I was concerned about that man, he said, '*Man*?'"

Boutelle shivered at more than the gathering mountain chill. It was beginning to get dark as well. For some reason, he recalled the ghastly screeching noise he'd heard the night before.

He shook away the memory, irritated with himself for being credulous.

"Well, I think he *is* a man," he said, trying to sound as confident as possible.

"Do you?" was all Finley said.

They were moving now into an open glade, deeply shaded by a thick overhead growth of pines. As they entered it, Boutelle saw, in the center of the glade, stacked preparations for a bonfire. He could use a little fire warmth, he thought.

Finley looked at the fire preparations with a sense of foreboding. He knew what it was. Not a camp fire for heat and cooking. It was too big for that.

They were getting ready to light a ceremonial fire.

Boutelle saw more and more of the Pinal Spring band now. How many members did it have? He tried to recall. In the two hundreds, it seemed. He saw clusters of women and children eyeing him and Finley. Never had he felt so alien to an environment, so out of place. This was their world, and he had no comprehension of it whatsoever.

Now the horses were stopped and he and Finley ordered to the ground. They dismounted, and Boutelle realized abruptly that the older man standing in front of them was Braided Feather. He hadn't recognized the chief because here he was not the sternly dignified figure he had been at the treaty meeting. He looked smaller now, more haggard.

Finley moved to the chief and raised his right hand in a saluting gesture. "I come as your friend," he said in Apache.

"We know you are our friend," Braided Feather answered. "Come with me."

He led them away from the other Apaches to a small shelter that had been erected for him. He sank down on a buffalo robe beneath the overhang and gestured for them to sit. Boutelle glanced around and saw that Lean Bear had followed them. He looked back at the other Apaches and saw that they were tying up the two horses.

"First let me tell you what the Army and the citizens of Picture City think," Finley said to the chief as Lean Bear sat down with them.

"No need," Braided Feather replied. "I know what they think. That we have broken the treaty."

"Yes." Finley nodded.

Boutelle wished that he understood what they were saying but felt awkward about asking Finley to interpret.

"Does Finley think this as well?" Braided Feather asked the agent.

"Of course I don't," Finley answered. "I know you to be a man of your word. I know that this is something else."

"It is." Braided Feather's lips tightened. "Something very different."

"Can you tell me what it is so I can help?" Finley asked.

Braided Feather looked at his son, who looked toward the fire area and the Apaches waiting around it.

"There is no time," Braided Feather said.

"What is the ceremony to be then?" Finley asked, having noticed Lean Bear's look.

Boutelle had no idea what was being said, but when Finley spoke, he was aware that both Braided Feather and Lean Bear grew tense.

"I cannot tell you that," Braided Feather told Finley. "It is big medicine."

"May we watch so we can learn and perhaps assist you in this?" Finley asked.

Lean Bear stiffened visibly and looked at Finley in anger. "This is not possible," he said.

Finley looked at Braided Feather, knowing that despite Lean Bear's position as eventual chief of the Pinal Spring band, all authority was still in the chief's hands.

"I know it is much to ask," he said, "but this is not an ordinary circumstance. I know that something very dark is taking place and want to help if I can. Are you certain you can deal with this alone?"

Boutelle flinched as Lean Bear spoke sharply to his father, then to Finley. Braided Feather was patient with him at first, but as his hotheaded son spoke with more and more vehemence, his father suddenly cut him off and clearly ordered him to move away.

Lean Bear grimaced savagely and lurched to his feet. "This is a bad mistake," he said and strode away quickly.

Finley looked at Braided Feather without speaking. He knew that to say—particularly to ask—any more would be a slight to the chief's position. Accordingly, he waited in respectful silence.

Finally, Braided Feather spoke. There was a sound of sadness in his voice, Boutelle thought.

"You know that my son is right," the chief said. "This is not a ceremony we permit outsiders to witness." Finley felt a chill to hear a waver in Braided Feather's voice. "But this is *not* an ordinary thing, as you have said. It may well be I am forced to ask for your help. This being so . . ."

He stopped and sighed heavily. "We begin when darkness falls," he said.

Boutelle didn't realize that they had been dismissed

until Finley took him by the arm and helped him to his feet.

As they walked away from Braided Feather's shelter, he asked Finley what the conversation had been about.

When Finley told him, Boutelle frowned, not understanding. "All that over a ceremony?"

"White men are never permitted to witness such Apache ceremonies," Finley told him. "They are a very religious people and their ceremonies are sacred to them. The only reason we're being permitted to look at this particular ceremony is that Braided Feather thinks we might help in this situation."

"We?" Boutelle looked dubious.

"All right, me," Finley admitted. He drew in a deep breath. "This is a very special ceremony," he said. "What they call *big medicine*. Extremely important. I still can't believe they're going to let us watch."

"Why did you ask then?" Boutelle asked.

"Frankly, I don't know," Finley told him. "What's happening is so . . . *distant* from anything I've ever seen that I've behaved in a different manner with the chief. A manner I never would have assumed under more normal circumstances."

They walked in silence toward the fire area. Boutelle looked up. The sky, now barely visible through the pine growth overhead, was almost dark.

"Keep in mind," Finley told him, "these are brave men. Brave women. And they're terrified of something. Absolutely terrified. What else would make them flee their camp to perform a nighttime religious ceremony in the high woods?"

Boutelle glanced into the eyes of Apache men, women, and children as he passed them. Was it his imagination that he saw cold dread in every one of them?

13

He had never experienced anything so strange in his life.

In the near pitch-blackness of the glade, the deep, resonant voice of the band's shaman seemed to be coming at him from all directions. The fact that the shaman was speaking in the guttural, rhythmic language of the Apaches which he could not understand in any way made it all the more bizarre to Boutelle as he sat there on the pine needle–covered ground.

He and Finley were located far back from the others so that the Indian agent could interpret for him. In the darkness of the forest, even Finley's whispering voice sounded unnaturally loud to Boutelle. He felt immersed in some grotesque dream, while at the same time knowing that he was totally awake.

"He's telling them that they are all in mortal danger," Finley whispered into Boutelle's ear. "He says that he's going to perform a rite of scourging to prevent this danger from destroying them, man, woman, and child."

Boutelle swallowed. His throat was dry and he felt a strong need for a sip of water, yet knew it was impossible right now. Feeling almost numb, he sat immobile listening, as Finley continued.

"He's telling them that they must give this ceremony undivided attention and never smile or laugh or do a single thing to displease him or he'll be forced to call a halt to the rite, leaving them unprotected."

Smile? Boutelle thought. Laugh? Who could possibly do either under these conditions?

"The ceremony will first inform them how this terror came to be," Finley finished.

Boutelle shivered. In the darkness, fear comes far too easily, he thought. No wonder nighttime was the time when terror flourished.

The shaman had stopped speaking now. In the heavy silence, Boutelle heard only faint rustling sounds as the waiting Apaches shifted slightly on the ground, a few of them coughing softly.

"Who was speaking?" he asked Finley in a whisper, more to hear the sound of his own voice than out of curiosity.

"The band's shaman," Finley replied.

"How did he become that?" Boutelle asked.

"By receiving a power grant from the mountain spirits in a vision experience," Finley answered matter-of-factly.

Boutelle was about to respond, then changed his mind. How could one respond to such a statement? It was too far beyond the world he knew and accepted.

He started as a fire brand seemed to burst forth from nowhere. He saw it moving in the darkness like a flaming insect.

Then the bonfire was ignited and its stacked wood flamed up with a crackling roar.

Now he could see the Apaches gathered in a giant circle around the mounting fire, all of them seated cross-legged, their faces reflecting the flames like burnished oak, their dark eyes glowing as they stared at the fire. Who *were* they? he wondered. What were they thinking? Once again, he felt completely foreign to the moment, trapped in some unearthly vision.

He glanced at Finley. The agent was looking steadily toward the fire. Even he seemed alien to Boutelle now. Clearly, Finley was a part of all this, accepting what was happening without question. An odd image flitted across Boutelle's mind: him dancing at a New York City ball, wearing dress clothes, chatting casually.

The image seemed a million miles and years from this experience.

His legs jerked in reflexively as drums began to thud with a slow, regular beat, one-two-three-four, one-two-three-four.

He looked toward the fire. The shaman was standing beside it. Boutelle could see now how very old the man was, his coarse black hair streaked with gray. He was beginning to speak, his voice rising and falling with a sound reminiscent of the cries of coyotes. He wondered what the shaman was saying.

Finley looked intently at the medicine man as he spoke. The old man was beginning the history of a creature named Vandaih.

First a tall brave emerged from the darkness, moving to the beat of the drums. He danced in erratic circles as though deranged or drunk. When other braves appeared, he withdrew from its sheath a long knife and began to slash symbolically at them. The other braves clutched at their chests and fell to the ground in convulsing death.

Vandaih continued dancing, his expression one of maddened glee. Figures dressed as women danced from the darkness to the one-two-three-four beat of the drums, and Vandaih clutched at them, taking them in symbolic rape.

Finally, two braves grabbed him from each side and forced him into the darkness as the shaman spoke of how Vandaih, for all his sins against his people, had to suffer condemnation.

Boutelle leaned over to ask what was happening, and Finley quickly told him.

He was in the middle of a sentence when they both jumped and Finley's voice broke off as a figure leapt clumsily into the firelight.

The figure was that of a giant bird, its wings made from branches, its head a crude mask which emphasized its curving beak, the figure barefoot, toes curled in to approximate the look of talons.

As the shaman spoke, Boutelle leaned in to whisper in Finley's ear, "What's happening?"

"As condemnation for his grievous sins," Finley told him, "the tribe medicine man turned Vandaih into an eagle."

Boutelle felt a momentary sense of derision relaxing him. An *eagle*? he thought. All this about some ancient Indian transformed into an eagle?

It wasn't over though. The history continued as the eagle form danced crazily in the firelight, twisting in apparent agony and thrashing its giant wings.

"Vandaih, desperate in his blighted loneliness," the shaman continued, "conceived a hideous plan."

Another dancer, dressed as a woman, materialized from the darkness, and after moving with her in a grotesque dance of courting, the eagle suddenly grabbed her and dragged her off into the night.

"He carried off a woman who was not an Indian but whose skin was white," Finley whispered to Boutelle, repeating what the shaman had said.

Boutelle shuddered, angry at himself for doing so. This is ridiculous, he thought. Each new element of the history was more preposterous than the one before.

He leaned close to Finley and told him so.

Was that a smile of amusement on the agent's lips? It seemed too ominous for that.

"If you think everything that's happened up to now is ridiculous," Finley whispered, "you're going to love this new part." The smile, Boutelle now saw, was definitely not one of amusement.

The man dressed as a woman reappeared and from beneath her bulky costume drew forth what Boutelle took to be—

"A *child*?" he whispered incredulously. "He's telling us there was a child?"

The woman moved into the darkness, carrying the child form.

"Thus this child whose father was an eagle and whose mother was a white woman grew to manhood," the medicine man continued. Finley decided not to translate his words to Boutelle. The young man was having trouble enough as it was. He only wished he could be equally disdainful. On the face of it, it was absurdly superstitious. Still, all these things had happened in the past two days. Things there was no way of denying, much less explaining.

And here in the darkness of this forest glade, with the crackling fire and the endless four-beat thudding of the drums and the silent forms of the Apaches as they sat and watched and undoubtedly believed, it was virtually impossible to deny it.

He flinched as another figure jumped out from the darkness.

"So grew to manhood the issue of this unholy union," the shaman went on. "Vandaih, the man now cursed to be for all time an eagle, his father; the abducted and ravished white woman, his mother."

The man now spun abruptly into the darkness to return seconds later, holding wings, a grotesque mask across his face.

"This malevolent child was capable in times of anger or fear of changing himself at will, of sprouting great black wings instead of arms, of creating talons where his hands had been and dreadful, beaked features for a face. In short, to be a hideous creature, part man, part eagle."

Finley felt obliged to pass along this information, even knowing what Boutelle's reaction would most likely be. He whispered into the young man's ear and saw from Boutelle's scowl that his reaction was exactly as expected.

"Do you *believe* all this?" Boutelle demanded of him, his voice loud enough to make Finley shake his head in warning. Boutelle withdrew into angry silence, unable to tell whether it was truly anger that shook him or dread. Was his disbelief becoming more intense the closer he came to losing it?

He started again as an Apache, garbed as a shaman, leapt from the darkness followed by six braves who grabbed the half man–half eagle form and held him by his lashing wings while the shaman drew a knife with a black blade from beneath his robe and appeared to plunge it into the eagle man's chest.

"The people, through the intervention of their medicine man," Finley whispered to Boutelle, "managed to kill the halfling son by stabbing him to death with an obsidian blade, the only substance able to pierce his accursed skin."

He didn't look to see what Boutelle's reaction to that was. He already knew.

The eagle man, now limp, was dragged into the darkness. In a matter of seconds, the braves and their shaman returned, moving, as always, to the one-two-three-four beating of the drums. They carried in their arms what looked like torn pieces of bird and man.

"They also killed Vandaih and the halfling's mother to prevent their further union," the shaman said. "The son, part man, part eagle, they beheaded, burying at separate, distant points the halfling's head and body."

Finley interpreted. Boutelle closed his eyes, trying to resist the rise of cold foreboding in himself. But all he could think of—a chilling memory in his mind's eye—was the thick, jagged scar around the stranger's neck, a scar which could well mark a deep cut that—

No! He bit his teeth together so rabidly that streaks of pain shot through his jaw. He would not allow himself to believe—

He opened his eyes and looked at the fire in dismay.

A small man garbed in black was dancing in the firelight to the one-two-three-four pulsing of the drums. He tried to block his mind from sensing who the figure represented as the shaman spoke. Don't tell me, he thought, silently addressing Finley. But the agent, never pausing, leaned over to translate. "An eon of moons later, a little man with white skin and brightly curious eyes—a man of schooling—came to our Pinal Spring band and requested to see feats of magic performed by the tribal shaman."

The shaman himself approached the little man in black and, clutching him by the arm, forcefully ejected him into the night. As he did, he spoke, "I told this man named Dodge that what he asked was not a thing we could provide. The man was thrust away in anger."

Boutelle felt cold now, almost sick. He tried to resist the mounting disquiet, but it was becoming more and more difficult for him. Too many elements were falling into place. The history of some ancient happening was now a history of today, too close to ignore, much less reject.

The drumbeat—one-two-three-four, one-two-three-four—seemed to alter his heartbeat, taking it over as he watched the small man in black circle the fire and finally come upon an old man seated in the shadows. *Don't tell me*, he thought, but knew it was in vain as Finley translated the grimly voiced words of the shaman.

"The small man with the bright eyes would not be dissuaded, traveling to the far-off dwelling place of the Night Doctor."

For the first time since the ceremony had begun, Boutelle heard a shocking intake of breath from the watching members of the band. The shaman threw them an angry glance but clearly felt that their reaction to this information was justified for he did not rebuke them further, but only went on with his story. Boutelle sat in stricken silence, listening to Finley's whisper, knowing that he was unable now to fight away acceptance of this dreadful history.

"The Night Doctor had been banished from the tribe for tampering with evil powers," the shaman continued, even though he knew his people were aware of this, Finley understood.

The small man in black feigned putting coins into the palm of the Night Doctor, who nodded. Boutelle shook as the drumbeat started to increase in speed though still retaining, endlessly, the one-two-three-four rhythm.

"And, for the gain of Dodge's money, the banished Night Doctor performed an abominable rite," the shaman said. Finley translated the words into Boutelle's ear.

His heartbeat had increased now, driven by the mesmerizing beat of the drums. One-two-three-four—faster, faster. Boutelle sat frozen, staring at the scene taking place at the fire.

The Night Doctor summoning back from the dead the son of Vandaih and joining head to body.

He shuddered as the small man in black leapt off into darkness, bolting from the invocation, causing the Night Doctor's dance to become one of horror as the eagle man escaped.

"The small man, terrified by what he saw—the connecting of the halfling's head to its body—fled the ceremony," the shaman said, "destroying, by that flight, the Night Doctor's control of the ritual and permitting the son of Vandaih to break from his control and move freely in the world again."

Boutelle felt the cold fingers of his hands twitching on his lap as he watched the man portraying the Night Doctor sprinkle some kind of dust over himself and whirl into the darkness.

"The Night Doctor could only cast a spell upon himself and gain protection from the halfling."

The eagle man now leapt into the firelight again, dancing in a fury.

"The son of Vandaih, maddened by frustration, was unable to locate the Night Doctor and destroy him so that he could assure his freedom for all time.

"So the halfling set out instead to find the small man, Dodge. The only person who might take him to the hiding place of the Night Doctor."

Finley stopped repeating the shaman's words into Boutelle's ear, and they sat in motionless silence as the scourging rite commenced.

There was an audible stir from the watching members of the band as ritual dancers appeared from the darkness, four masked figures wearing painted wooden headdresses, short buckskin skirts, and moccasins, their bodies naked from the waist up and painted black, white, green, and yellow. They danced around the circle to the one-two-three-four beat—now slow again—as though searching for something.

Boutelle winced as he looked at the dancers' *gaan*

masks, the laths of which were made of split yucca secured to each other and to supporting framework pieces with buckskin thongs. The U-shaped headpieces slid down on each side of their heads with only slits for eyes and mouth. The colorful headdresses had snakes painted on them.

Boutelle was back in the dream again as he watched the dancers moving in unison to the constant thudding of the drums. They each held matching wands made of sotol laths with three crosspieces with which they gestured as they danced. Boutelle's eyes slipped out of focus and he saw, in front of him, four shapeless forms moving like figures in his dream, the beat of the drums pervading his brain and body.

He started, focusing his eyes again, as another figure suddenly appeared, dancing around the four. He wore a G-string around his middle, the upper part of his body coated with white clay. Like the other dancers, he wore a mask with slits for eyes and mouth. The headdress of his mask was larger, though, with long wing feathers of an eagle as the upright pieces. In his hand he carried the middle tail feathers of an eagle, and the other dancers averted their faces from him.

"Who is he supposed to be?" Boutelle leaned over to whisper.

"The Black One," Finley told him. "A special kind of mountain spirit who protects the Apaches and their territories."

Boutelle nodded, staring at the dancers. Once again, the drumbeats seemed to have taken control of his heart so that he felt a part of the ceremony, as though his consciousness was being absorbed by the sight and sound of it.

He felt himself tensing as the dancers started throwing powder in the air and in the fire where it sparked like short-lived fireflies. He wanted to ask Finley what they were doing but didn't have the strength.

Finley seemed to read his thoughts and leaned in close to whisper, "That's cattail pollen they're throwing. Very important as a ceremonial offering to Usen to help them resist the powers of the halfling."

Usen? Boutelle thought. Again, Finley seemed to read his mind. "The giver of life," he whispered.

Boutelle thought he nodded but didn't. He sat unmoving, barely conscious of his body, attention fixed on the ritual dancers as they circled the dwindling fire, the Black One sometimes leading, other times following. Boutelle noticed that whenever the Black One passed in front of the observing Apaches, they lowered their heads as though afraid to look at him.

He kept sinking deeper and deeper into a thoughtless state, almost stupefied, his eyes held fast to the movement of the fire-lit dancers as they danced in unison to the hypnotic one-two-three-four rhythm of the drums.

He barely stirred as the shaman now appeared, clearly addressing the Black One. He had no idea what the shaman was saying, although he assumed that it was some form of request for protection by the Black One.

Only Finley understood the words as the medicine man first praised the Black One for his strength and omnipotence, then told him what he had to do to the evil and curse-laden son of Vandaih: Tear him into a hundred pieces and bury them at the four corners of the earth, sinking the halfling's head in the deepest waters of the deepest sea.

Boutelle's legs twitched, his glazed eyes blinking suddenly as Finley took him by the arms.

"Come," the agent murmured.

Boutelle almost fell as he stood, his legs without feeling. Then, as Finley supported him, he started walking stiffly with the agent around the outside edges of the still-continuing ceremony.

"What is it?" he asked.

Finley didn't answer, only guided the younger man across the border of the forest floor.

"What is it?" he repeated.

Finley pointed ahead with his free hand. Looking in that direction, Boutelle saw, by the peripheral light of the fire, the figure of Braided Feather moving toward his shelter.

"Why is he leaving the ceremony?" he asked.

"Why indeed?" Finley questioned back.

The old chief looked around as they approached, his expression grave. Boutelle listened as Finley spoke with the chief. Then Finley turned away, leading Boutelle from the shelter.

After they'd walked some yards, Finley sat down and leaned against a pine trunk. Boutelle sat beside him, wondering what was happening. In the distance, he could see the ritual still taking place, the firelight now waning noticeably.

"Finley, what is it?" he asked.

The agent sighed. "It's all a waste of time," he said.

"What?"

"The ceremony."

"I don't understand," Boutelle responded. "Then why are they—"

"To keep their people from total panic," Finley said. "But the shaman and Braided Feather know that the ritual is pointless."

Boutelle stared at him, not knowing what to say.

"The Night Doctor brought this on," Finley told him. "He invoked the demon and only he can put an end to it."

14

Despite his exhaustion, Boutelle had been unable to fall asleep for more than an hour and a half. He had lain awake on the buffalo robe Braided Feather had let them use, beneath the heavy wool blanket Finley was sharing with him. He was warm enough and tired enough to sleep under any circumstance.

Except the one he was living through.

He was amazed—impressed even—that Finley had gone to sleep in what seemed to him to be only a few seconds. He decided that men "out here" were able to do that, blank their minds to imminent peril and find much needed sleep in order to face that peril, rested.

He was not cut from that bolt of cloth. His mind, aroused by dread and apprehension, refused to release him. It kept running like an overwound clock, ticking out endless minutes of thoughts and anxieties.

He kept reliving the ceremony performed by the Apaches. It seemed bizarre to him that Braided Feather and his medicine man—undoubtedly his son Lean Bear as well—could permit the ritual to take place, knowing all the time that it was pointless and in vain.

Beyond that, he could think only of the menace they all seemed convinced they were facing—the son of Vandaih. Could he possibly accept such an incredible notion? A man who in moments of fear or anger could become a creature part man, part eagle?

Over and over, logic sought to dispel the farfetched idea. Even here in the dark forest, deep within Indian country, utterly removed from any aspect of civilization, he found it virtually impossible to believe.

A *demon*?

He tried not to move about in restless distress because Finley lay beside him, heavily asleep. Still, he turned from his left side onto his back, onto his right side, finally onto his back again, eyes staring up at what little sky he could see through the heavy foliage overhead, the thin sprinkling of diamond-white stars.

Invoked a *demon*? he thought.

"For God's sake," he mumbled more than once. He was a graduate of Harvard, for God's sake. This was the nineteenth century, for God's sake. Such things did not take place. Demons belonged in fairy tales, in witches' dungeons, in tales of farfetched horror.

Not in the real world, in real life.

His transition into sleep came unnoticed. He was thinking of the so called creature, then in the next moment, he was speaking about it to Finley as they sat on the edge of a high cliff looking across a massive forest top that stretched immeasurably into the distance.

"Is it safe for us to sit here like this?" he asked. "Aren't we inviting trouble?"

"Of course," Finley replied. "That's exactly what I want. To lure him into our trap."

"What trap?" he asked. "What can *we* do?"

"I have a little something in mind," Finley said.

"Well, that *sounds* good, but what does it *mean*?" he demanded. "How are we supposed to overcome some creature who can—"

"Hold it." Finley grabbed his arm. "I think I hear it coming."

This is madness! Boutelle thought. No matter what Finley said, they had no defense against a creature of such deadly power.

"Finley, I think we'd better—"

It was all he had time to say before a giant, shadowy form came swooping down from above and crashed against them both. Suddenly he could feel the feathery softness of wing feathers against his face and what felt like sharp talons gripping his shoulders.

"Finley!" he screamed.

But the horrendous screech of the eagle man drowned out his voice.

Boutelle jerked awake, sitting up with wide eyes, his heartbeat pounding.

The horrendous screech was real. He heard it again and again. And something else, something infinitely more hideous.

The screams of a dying horse.

He looked around groggily as Finley leapt to his feet.

"What is it?" he asked.

Finley didn't answer, lunging away from him, moving in the direction of the screaming animal.

Boutelle scrambled to his knees and pushed up quickly, staggering a little as he stood. It was still dark in the forest, despite a faint pallor of light in the sky.

He started running after Finley. Tripping on a tree root and almost sprawling, he felt a sting of pain where the snake had bitten him. Then it was gone and he was after Finley again, face a twisted mask of dismay as he heard the horrible screams of the horse—which abruptly ended.

Now he saw that the Apaches were awake as well, some of the braves running the same way as Finley, others milling around in frantic alarm, women and children staring, some of them crying. What in the name of God? he thought.

He gasped in alarm as an Apache pony came lunging at him from the darkness. Flinging himself to the right, he barely escaped being hit, so close to the galloping horse that he felt the breeze of its passing. He stumbled, almost fell, then regained his footing. As he continued after Finley, he saw the shadowy forms of other ponies racing through the Apache camp. Clearly, they had been stampeded by terror.

He found Braided Feather and Lean Bear standing with Finley and some braves around the remains of the horse.

His.

He looked in sickened horror at the torn, bloody carcass. It was as though it had been slashed apart by giant razor blades, bleeding flesh exposed, glistening entrails ripped from place. The horse's eyes were wide and staring; there was foam across its jaws.

Finley was looking upward. There was an opening in the trees above where the horses had been tied. The faintly dawning sky was clearly visible. Plenty of room for some flying thing to descend on the horses, Boutelle thought.

He looked back at the butchered animal, twitching with a faint cry as a final death spasm shook its torn, blood-splattered body. What did this? It was all he could allow himself to think, trying not to admit to himself that he knew exactly what had done it.

He looked over at Finley. It made him all the more

frightened to see the expression on the agent's face. Sickened. Dazed.

Helpless.

"There is only one solution to this," Finley said to Braided
Feather. "Someone has to find the Night Doctor and force
him—"

"*Ask* him," Braided Feather interrupted. "He will not be
forced. It is this very thing about him which brought on
the horror in the beginning."

"I understand." Finley nodded. "What I mean to say is
that we all know the horror will not end until the Night
Doctor ends it."

"No man in my tribe will dare to face this," Braided
Feather told him.

Finley said, "Then I will."

It was silent in the forest. Even though it was well past
dawn, shadowy darkness still prevailed beneath the thick
overhanging of the pine trees. Finley and Boutelle were sitting with the chief. The horses had been gathered back,
the dead horse carried off for disposal, Lean Bear and his
scouts sent out to observe the terrain—and the sky—in all
directions. Boutelle wondered what Finley and the chief
had been saying but didn't dare ask.

Braided Feather finally spoke.

"You would do this?" he asked, almost in disbelief.

Finley's smile was grim. "I don't want to," he said, "but
I *am* the agent for this territory. I am committed to protect the Apaches."

He smiled again, this time adding a rueful sound.

"I never thought my duties would include something
like this," he said. "Still . . ." The smile was gone. "I'm
willing to try. Someone has to try."

Braided Feather leaned toward Finley, reaching out to

grasp his arm. "You are very brave," he said. "I salute your bravery."

"Salute me if it works," Finley told the chief. "Have you any idea at all where the Night Doctor might be?"

"Somewhere in the mountain caves, we believe," Braided Feather told him.

Finley nodded. "Could I take the robe of the buffalo with me then?" he asked. "It is very cold up there."

Braided Feather nodded. "Take it with our blessing," he said.

"Thank you." Finley stood, Boutelle following his lead.

"Wait," Braided Feather said.

The agent and Boutelle stood waiting while the chief looked through his belongings. Finally he unwrapped a wolf-hide covering to reveal a long knife.

Its blade was as dark as night.

He handed it to Finley. "Take this," he said. "It is the only protection I can give you."

"Obsidian?" Finley asked.

The chief nodded.

Finley removed a long knife from its scabbard on his left side. He held it out to Braided Feather. "Hold this, please, until I return with your knife," he said.

Braided Feather nodded. "I will hold it," he said.

As they moved away from Braided Feather's shelter, they saw preparations being made by the Pinal Spring band to leave the camp.

"Where can they go?" Boutelle asked. He added something else which Finley didn't hear.

Finley glanced at the younger man. "What was that last?" he asked.

At first, it seemed as though Boutelle wasn't going to answer. Then he said, very quietly, "If it can fly."

Finley looked at him again. "You *do* believe it then," he said.

"I . . . don't know," Boutelle faltered. "I don't *want* to believe it and yet . . ." He shook himself. "I guess I'll have to ride with you," he said. "My horse—"

"That's impossible," Finley cut him off.

"What?" Boutelle looked at him in surprise.

"I'll be going by myself," Finley said.

"What are you talking about?" Boutelle asked.

Finley told him what he planned to do. The younger man was dumbfounded. "By yourself?" he asked.

"The Apaches are too frightened to go," Finley said. "Someone has to try. It's the only chance."

"That's insane," Boutelle responded, but his voice was so soft and devoid of resolve it undid his words.

They reached their grounded saddles, and Boutelle watched the agent gather together his belongings.

At last he said, "Do you think the chief will let me have one of their horses?"

Finley didn't even look up. "That's impossible, too," he said.

"Why?" Boutelle demanded. "Why is it impossible?"

"Because there's no point in both of us committing suicide," Finley answered.

Boutelle stared at him. "Is that what you think you're doing?" he asked. "Committing suicide? How is that going to help the Apaches?"

Finley sighed. "I was exaggerating to make a point," he said. "I have this." He patted the hilt of the obsidian knife.

"What *is* that?" Boutelle asked. "I wondered when the chief gave it to you."

Finley explained about the knife, Boutelle remembering the ceremony, was not reassured by his words. If anything, he looked more aghast. "That's it?" he asked.

"Against . . . ?" Clearly, he could think of no way to describe the son of Vandaih.

"No, that isn't it," Finley said. "My plan is to find the Night Doctor and have him . . . *revoke* the creature."

Boutelle simply couldn't take in the insanity of it all. He could deal only with one small aspect of it at a time and that he was certain about.

"I'm going with you," he said.

Finley looked up almost angrily, words set to spill from his lips, words of rejecting, discouraging, absolute refusal.

Then he saw the look on Boutelle's face and a panoramic vision of what would surely take place if he continued arguing swept across his mind. He would refute and argue, refuse and deny, and at every turn, Boutelle would counter him with stubborn insistence. He saw all that in the younger man's obdurate look, the expression of a man who, reaching a point-of-no-return decision, cannot be made to change his mind.

There simply wasn't time for that. At any rate, it was no problem anyway.

"All right, you can go," he told Boutelle. "If we can talk Braided Feather into letting you use one of their ponies."

He knew that would never happen. The Apaches were short of horses, many already doubling to ride.

"That won't be necessary," Boutelle answered.

Finley looked at him, frowning. What was Boutelle talking about now?

Then he saw the younger man gazing off to their left, and he turned and looked.

Lean Bear was riding into camp, leading Professor Dodge's Appaloosa.

The professor's limp body was draped across the horse's back behind the saddle.

Finley and Boutelle moved quickly to where several Apache braves and their chief were converging on the pair of horses. Lean Bear stopped his mount, lifted his right leg over the horse's back, and slid to the ground.

"Where did you find him?" Braided Feather asked his son. Finley couldn't understand how the chief knew who it was. It had been years since Dodge made his refused request. Did Braided Feather still remember Dodge's face from that long ago?

"At the foot of the mountains," Lean Bear answered. Finley noted without surprise that neither he nor his father looked directly at Dodge.

He moved to Dodge's body and lifted his head. Boutelle, beside him, hissed with shock.

"That look again," Finley said.

Boutelle swallowed. For several moments, he was sorely tempted to reverse his stance about going with Finley. The agent wouldn't say a thing if he rode back to Picture City on Dodge's horse. It would probably relieve him.

He forced away the impulse. No, he thought.

"I'll be riding the professor's horse," he said to Finley.

The agent didn't respond. He didn't have the strength to argue with Boutelle now. Actually, he was grateful that he wouldn't be alone. He began to untie the professor's body from its place on the horse's back, thinking darkly that in all likelihood he would never see Picture City again.

SATURDAY

15

It was already nearing sunset. Boutelle could not believe how fast the day had gone by. They had never even stopped to eat, chewing on jerky and sipping from canteens as they rode.

He tried not to look to his left. The drop from the narrow ledge was prodigious. He was impressed—as well as overwrought—by the way his horse picked its way along, the hooves of its front and rear left legs scant inches from the brink of the winding ledge. Occasionally, it slipped, making Boutelle freeze with apprehension. Then it caught itself, regaining balance and moving on calmly. He envied its ability to instantly forget near death. Or did it need to forget? Perhaps it was essentially unaware of its ongoing peril. Wish I could say the same, he thought.

He'd stopped looking over his shoulder to see if Finley was still behind. He was afraid that if he did, he'd lose equilibrium and slip. His gaze shifted to Lean Bear riding ahead of him.

They—especially Finley—had been startled when the chief's son had chosen to lead them into the mountains. Obviously he was as terrified of the son of Vandaih as all the others in his band.

When Finley had asked him why he was doing it, Lean Bear had answered (Finley later told Boutelle) that they would never find the Night Doctor without his help.

Knowing his dread, Finley had thanked him, commending him for his courage.

"I am not doing this for you that you need thank me," Lean Bear had responded coldly. "I do it for my people."

"I understand and appreciate," Finley had said without rancor.

Lean Bear had relented slightly then. "You are an honest man, Finley," he'd said. "A brave one."

He'd added then with renewed coldness in his voice, "It is men like *him*"—he'd glanced at Boutelle—"who have brought doom to my people."

Finley hadn't told Boutelle that part when the man had asked what Lean Bear had gone on to say. Finley had told him that the chief's son had said (which he had) that it was bad enough what the white man had done to his people, now a white man (Dodge) had brought down upon their heads the wrath of this demon creature.

Remembering that, Boutelle shivered and pulled the buffalo robe closer around himself. Thank God Braided Feather had given robes to him and Finley. It was getting colder by the moment, the canyon walls scourged by an endless, icy wind that seemed to slash at his face like tiny, frozen razor blades.

He gazed up briefly at the canyon wall. It looked as though it had been hacked into shape by giant, frenzy-driven pick blows. A reddish cast was inching across it, causing shadows to shift and disappear, then reappear in other places.

Was it possible that they would still be on this ledge after darkness had fallen? He could not conceive of anything so terrible. Surely, Lean Bear would find some place for them to stop.

He winced as he saw Lean Bear turn his head to the left and right and slowly scan the sky.

He'd been doing the same thing all day.

Finally, in the middle of the afternoon, Boutelle had twisted around to speak to Finley.

"If he's so concerned about . . . that *creature*"—he'd been compelled to call it—"following us, why is he wearing a *white* buffalo robe?"

"Because that creature, as you call him, *has* to follow us. He must be close by when the revocation is performed."

"And if he decides to kill us *before* that?" Boutelle had demanded.

"He won't," Finley had said. "He wants us to find the Night Doctor for him so he can kill him before the ceremony. That way he'll be free forever."

Boutelle was chilled by the memory of Finley's words. He'd tried to regain some sense of proportion, recalling his family and his life back East, the total reasonableness of his past.

It didn't work. He was in too deep. He knew that despite all efforts he had come to accept the existence of the son of Vandaih—and the madness of their ride into the mountains to seek out a shaman driven from his people for "tampering."

Boutelle shuddered and looked to his left, unable to prevent himself from doing so.

Gigantic rock formations were now visible in the distance, eroded through eons into separate forms that looked to him like massive statuary, strange figures he could almost make out with imagination, strange faces carved by time and wind and water.

Night was beginning to cover the bases of the huge formations, an ocean of black shadows slowly moving upward on them like a rising lap of dark waters.

Soon the reddish light on the cliffs would diminish, the

stone would go gray in the last of twilight, and night would cover them. Then what? Boutelle wondered. Would Lean Bear find a place where they could stop?

And light a fire?

Boutelle shook his head abruptly. No fire, he thought. That would be too easy to spot. They'd be as helpless as that horse had been.

In spite of how it disturbed him, he tilted back his head and looked at the sky.

Had the son of Vandaih been tracking them all day, up so high they couldn't see him, floating on the wind, great wings stretched and motionless, riding the icy currents like a cork on bobbing water, black eyes ever on his prey?

Boutelle glanced over his shoulder, starting slightly as he saw the pale white, shadow-marked circle of the moon. How could it have appeared so quickly? He shivered.

Darkness was almost upon them.

He twitched as Lean Bear abruptly turned and spoke to them.

"The cavern opening is just ahead," Finley told him. "When you see Lean Bear turning into it, follow him fast. We have to hope he doesn't see us disappear."

Boutelle knew exactly who the agent meant by "he" and braced himself to move as he'd been told.

There was no sound but the whistling of the cold wind and the clatter of the horses' hooves on the stone ledge. Moments passed. Lean Bear kept riding forward.

"All right then," Boutelle muttered to himself. Where was the cavern entrance? Why didn't—

The thought broke off, his face tensing in a grimace as Lean Bear suddenly jerked his mount to the right and as though by magic disappeared into the cliff wall.

"Now!" Finley shouted.

Before fear could repress the action, Boutelle drove his knees into the horse's flanks, and, startled, it lurched forward into a trot. Boutelle closed his eyes, convinced that it would slip off the edge, carry him hurtling down into the green valley far below, crushing him on the rocks and . . .

"No," he growled, forcing himself to reopen his eyes.

He had almost missed the cavern entrance. He was forced to jerk the horse around so much that it rose up slightly off its front feet for a horrifying moment. Boutelle was certain that he'd made it lose balance, that it was about to topple backward off the edge.

But at the last moment the horse regained balance and lunged through the opening in the cliff wall. Boutelle hissed as hanging vines whipped across his shoulders and cheeks when he instinctively hunched over and lowered his face.

Inside he pulled in hard on the reins.

The immediate cessation of wind created an illusion of deep silence. Then he heard the sound of hooves—his and Lean Bear's mounts—shifting nervously on the stone floor of the cavern.

He caught his breath, struggling to control his horse as Finley's mount came charging in from outside, bumping against his horse's side, the two animals nickering with alarm.

He and Finley regained control of their mounts, and Boutelle looked around.

There was enough illumination from the sunset—some light seemed to filter in through cracks in the wall—for him to see that the cavern was immense. He had been inside an icehouse in Vermont once, and the air in here was equally as frigid. Even out of the icy wind, Boutelle felt the need to pull the buffalo robe around himself again.

Lean Bear said something, and Finley interpreted.

"He says the Night Doctor will be somewhere in this cavern."

Boutelle only nodded. What was there to say?

"I'd like you to stay here while Lean Bear and I go on," Finley told him.

Boutelle frowned. "Come all this way with you just to stop now?" he replied.

"It could be . . . terrible," Finley said.

Boutelle was about to respond when he realized that his throat had become clogged by fear.

"I'm—" he began. His voice was strangled, and he broke off, wincing. Well, to hell with it, he thought. He cleared his throat with a viscid sound. "I'm not stopping now," he said. His voice was still not normal, but he didn't care. The statement was made.

"David—"

"I am going with you," Boutelle said, determination clearing the sound of his voice.

"We cannot sit and talk," Lean Bear said tensely.

"All right." Finley nodded, sighing. "There isn't time to argue."

"There hasn't been since we left," Boutelle replied.

Finley nodded again and pulled his mount around. "We're ready," he said in Apache.

Lean Bear nodded and reined his pony around, starting into the cavern. Finley followed, Boutelle trailing behind, wondering distractedly what he'd do if he lost track of Finley. You'll die, that's what you'll do, his mind supplied.

Finley was wishing now that he'd talked Boutelle out of coming, forced him to remain behind if necessary. The younger man's goodwill and good intentions would be of little value when—and if—they found the Night Doctor.

For that matter, he wondered what good *his* presence would do when that time came. Since Lean Bear had insisted on leading them, he could also ask the Night Doctor to perform the revocation rite. The Night Doctor had been a part of the Pinal Spring band; Lean Bear was familiar to him. Finley, on the other hand, was a total stranger.

The more he thought about it, the more pointless his presence became in his mind. Which made Boutelle's presence totally senseless. He scowled, then told himself to let it go. What was done was done. He'd made his promise to Braided Feather. That would have to suffice.

He remembered the chief doing something totally unexpected before he'd left. He had embraced Finley, and the feel of the chief's arms and body had made him realize how old and frail Braided Feather really was.

"The future of my people lies with you," the chief had murmured.

Finley had been embarrassed by the chief's show of emotion. Braided Feather had always represented, to him, the epitome of dignity and strength. It had to be the measure of the chief's dread regarding the son of Vandaih that he would display such vulnerable behavior. It had made Finley all the more apprehensive about what he was planning to attempt.

They had gone about a hundred yards through the vast cavern when the light faded into near darkness and Lean Bear stopped to light a torch. The fact that the chief's son had brought the torch along told Finley that he must know the Night Doctor was in here somewhere, or assumed at least that the possibility that he was, was good

The continuing ride through the cavern was an eerie one.

By the random flicker of the torch in Lean Bear's right hand, Finley could see the walls of the cavern, some dripping with water, some dry. High above, stalactites glimmered, pointing down at them like giant blades. Swords of Damocles, he thought. An appropriate fancy under the circumstances.

He looked back to see if Boutelle was all right. The younger man's expression in the wavering torchlight was a grave one. What was he thinking? Finley wondered. Had he finally come to terms with what was taking place? Or was part of his mind still trying to resist the obvious?

As moments passed, Finley felt himself sinking gradually into a half-conscious reverie, the rhythmic clopping of the horses' hooves on the stone floor of the cavern acting on his mind hypnotically. The flame of the torch ahead became the focal point of his vision as it bobbed along with the movement of Lean Bear's pony. After a while, it was all he could see, and he felt himself begin to weave in the saddle, his progression through the chilly darkness slipping from awareness.

When Lean Bear stopped his mount, Finley almost ran his horse into him; only at the last moment did he blink his eyes, refocusing, and yank back on the reins. He saw Lean Bear looking back at him with disapproving curiosity.

Then the chief's son spoke, the sound of his voice making Finley start a little, it sounded so loud to him.

"He is up ahead," Lean Bear told him.

Finley swallowed dryly, nodding. "All right," he said. "Shall we continue on foot?"

The Apache nodded. "Yes."

As Finley dismounted, he glanced back and saw Boutelle getting off his horse.

"I want you to stay here," he said. He cut off the younger man before he could object. "Lean Bear and I must speak to the shaman. You'd only be in the way."

Boutelle still looked as though he were about to contest Finley's words. But then he nodded curtly. "Very well," he agreed.

Finley grounded his reins and walked to Lean Bear. The

chief's son pointed ahead, and Finley, looking in that direction, saw faint light quivering in a corner of the cavern
where the overhead roof declined sharply.

It was the light of a fire.

"I will go first," Lean Bear told him. "Walk behind me
at a proper distance."

"Very well." Finley nodded.

The two men advanced on the flickering light. When
they were ten yards distant from its source, Lean Bear
called out, his voice ringing and echoing off the cavern
walls, making Finley twitch.

"We are here in peace to see the Night Doctor," the
Apache said.

Silence. Lean Bear waited for a short amount of time,
then repeated his words.

There was no response.

Is he here? Finley wondered. My God, he thought suddenly, what if the Night Doctor had died of some affliction? He was an old man, older than Braided Feather. He
might have had a heart attack, died in his sleep. What
would they do if they found only his body?

What *could* they do? he answered himself. It would
mean the final release of the creature into the world.

Did the son of Vandaih have to *know* the old man was
dead before he could be free?

He tensed as Lean Bear started forward again. Finley
drew in a laboring breath and followed him. He looked
over his shoulder to make sure Boutelle had remained
behind.

The younger man was unseen in the darkness. Finley
felt a twinge of concern for him. It had to be unnerving to
be left alone in total blackness, in a cavern he could never
get out of by himself.

Turning back, he continued after Lean Bear, twitching
again as the chief's son spoke loudly.

o see the Night Doctor," he

added, "We will give you pollen and gold

then decided against it. Lean Bear would be

ed by his interference, and he was only guessing that the Night Doctor was acquisitive because he'd taken money from Professor Dodge. That was some time ago. Things had to be different.

They were almost to the fire now. Lean Bear stopped, and Finley moved to his side.

The shaman's living space was scant and primitive. All that was visible was a pair of buffalo robes on the stone floor and an iron pot beside the low fire.

Finley's gaze shifted. Hanging across what clearly was a rift in the outer cave wall was another buffalo robe. But where was the old man? he wondered.

His answer came with the cocking of a rifle hammer to their right. He and Lean Bear looked there quickly.

Standing in a shadowy patch, the Night Doctor had leveled a rifle at them. In the faint glow of the fire reflected on the old man's face, Finley saw the scar-like seams of ninety years marking his skin, his small, dark eyes glittering as he watched them.

"Who *are* you?" he asked, his voice low-pitched and hoarse.

"You know me," Lean Bear told the old man. "I am Lean Bear of the Pinal Spring band. My father—"

"There is no Pinal Spring band," the old man interrupted. "They do not exist."

Finley grimaced. Of course the old man would say that, he thought. He had been driven from the Pinal Spring band. In his mind, they could not possibly exist any longer.

"You know my father, Braided Feather—" Lean Bear started angrily.

"There is no Braided Feather; he does not exist," the Night Doctor cut him off.

Seeing Lean Bear tense and knowing that the old man would not hesitate to shoot him, Finley quickly said, "We have gold and pollen for a boon."

He saw that his words had angered Lean Bear, as he'd expected, but he had to ignore the Apache's reaction. Better he was angry than dead, he thought.

"Who are *you*?" the old man demanded.

"Billjohn Finley," he answered. "Government Indian agent in Picture City."

The Night Doctor gazed at him impassively.

"What boon?" he finally asked.

Lean Bear cut off Finley's voice as he tried to answer the shaman's question.

"You must destroy the son of Vandaih," Lean Bear said.

The old man's reaction was short-lived, albeit unmistakable—momentary shock dispelled by will.

The impassive look returned.

"I do not know any son of Vandaih," he said.

Lean Bear stiffened, leaning toward the old man, only pulling back as the old man raised the rifle to his shoulder.

"You invoked this demon!" Lean Bear lashed out at the shaman. "You must rid the world of him!"

The old man's features twisted suddenly into a mask of savage venom.

"Let the creature live forever!" he cried. "Your people drove me from my wickiup and forced me to this solitary life! I owe you nothing! I delight in your certain destruction, every man, woman, and child!"

16

The shaman raised the rifle to his shoulder once again. "Leave," he said. "Or die."

Finley saw, in an instant, that Lean Bear had moved his right hand to the hilt of his knife. The Apache did not intend that the Night Doctor should continue living, even if it cost him his own life.

"If you fire your rifle, the son of Vandaih will hear it," Finley said quickly.

The old man's narrowed eyes shifted to him.

"What do you mean?" he asked.

"Did you think he wouldn't follow us?" Finley said.

The shaman's face grew visibly taut. "You *led* him here?" he asked incredulously.

"How could we do otherwise?" Finley asked. "You know he must be close by when the revocation ceremony is performed."

Hatred twisted the old man's face. "I'll kill you both," he snarled.

"No matter who you kill, the creature knows we're in here," Finley responded. "And you know what he'll do when he finds us—or you."

The shaman drew in a sudden hissing breath through clenched teeth.

"I do not believe you," he said, but there was little confidence in his voice.

"Believe him," Lean Bear said. "I wore the robe of a white buffalo as we rode into the mountains. I watched the sky as we came. High above, so high that I could barely see him, the son of Vandaih followed. The white man speaks the truth. We knew that the creature had to be nearby during the ceremony."

His pitiless smile made coldness move up Finley's spine.

"He is nearby," Lean Bear finished. Then, without a pause, he turned away from the shaman. "We will go now. You have some minutes left to live, perhaps an hour. Then the son of Vandaih will have found you." Another remorseless smile. "I leave it to the eye of your mind what he will do to you."

Finley remained motionless as Lean Bear walked past him. His gaze stayed fixed on the old man's face. The shaman had to be in a state of horror, he thought. Unless he really didn't believe what they said. But how could he not believe when it was obvious that—

"Wait." The Night Doctor's voice told Finley everything, thickened by dread, quavering as an old man's voice would quaver.

Lean Bear turned to face the shaman. He did not speak. Neither did Finley. No need for our words now, he was thinking.

The old man shuddered, lowering the rifle.

"I will perform the ceremony," he said.

Finley, Boutelle, and Lean Bear sat cross-legged on the cave floor, watching silently.

At first, the Night Doctor had informed them that no

white man could observe the ceremony he was to perform. Lean Bear had not been opposed to that, but Finley had remained adamant. He and Boutelle had already watched the ceremony performed in the Apache camp, he told the shaman. They were part of this entire situation. They *would* observe.

He knew that under any other circumstances the Night Doctor would refuse to yield. But the old man knew that his time was short, that at any moment the son of Vandaih might burst in on them. He could not take time to argue, so he submitted to Finley's demand. While the shaman gathered what he needed for the ceremony, Finley went and got Boutelle, telling him what had happened.

Now the three men sat in motionless silence, watching the Night Doctor bathe.

The sight of it made Finley restive. If the creature had seen them enter the cavern, he could be close by. The time taken for the old man to wash his body could be fatal to them.

Ironic, too, he thought, a humorless smile drawing back his lips. From the smell of the old man and his living space, cleanliness was not an item high on his list of priorities.

Boutelle leaned over to whisper in his ear, "Why is he doing this?"

"He has to purify himself to ask for help from the Great Spirit," Finley whispered back.

He glanced at Lean Bear. The chief's son was scowling at them. Clearly despite their attempt to be quiet, their words had not eluded the Apache's keen hearing.

His gaze moved back to the Night Doctor.

The old man had finished drying himself and was putting on a short, clean buckskin shirt.

Picking up a small pottery jug (he'd gotten all the ceremony elements from a hidden crevice in the cave) he braced himself visibly, then drank, swallowing deeply. He bent over to put down the jug.

Before he'd straightened up, his face was distorted by a spasm of nausea, and making dreadful, gagging sounds, he lurched to the hanging buffalo robe and swept it aside with a brush of his right arm. He lunged outside just in time to void the contents of his stomach.

"What's he doing?" Boutelle asked, sickened.

"He has to purge himself of all impurities," Finley answered. "There must be no food or drink inside him."

"It doesn't sound likely," Boutelle muttered, grimacing as he listened to the violent retching of the old man outside.

Finley noticed Lean Bear shifting restlessly and knew what he was thinking. It was not completely dark yet and as long as the shaman was outside, he could be seen and there was just the chance—

"For Christ's sake, get back in," he muttered.

He relaxed a little—noticing that Lean Bear did the same—as the Night Doctor came back in, wiping at his lips. The buffalo robe fell back heavily across the opening.

They watched as the old man put on a buffalo robe that had been beaten thin with rocks. The ritual robe, Finley thought.

The shaman worked a leather thong across his head. Hanging from it was a round, metallic medallion with figures inscribed on it. Finley saw from the edge of his vision that Boutelle was looking at him for an explanation. He turned his head and shook it slightly. He dared not speak now. The ceremony was too close.

The Night Doctor had picked up a leather bag and hung it at his waist, its strap diagonally across his bare chest. Then he picked up four pottery dishes with handmade candles in them and placed them at four equidistant points of an invisible circle. These were, Finley knew, the four points of the compass—east, west, north, and south.

Removing a tiny piece of kindling from the fire, the shaman lit the candles.

Then he picked up a deep, dishlike pottery container and scooped up wood coals, dropping them into the container.

Immediately, a thick, greasy smoke began to rise from the dish. Before he had set it down in the center of the circle, the smoke was already starting to fill the cave. Some of it rose toward an opening in the cave roof; some appeared to drift through the hide-covered opening. Finley and Lean Bear both tightened as they saw that. Smoke would be visible for miles.

And it was not yet dark outside. . . .

He bent toward Lean Bear, murmuring, "Must there be such a fire?"

"It is part of the ceremony," Lean Bear responded, but clearly he was nervous about the smoke as well.

"What is it?" Boutelle whispered.

Finley gestured toward the fire, and Boutelle seemed to understand.

"Why doesn't he start?" he whispered, then winced as Lean Bear glared at him.

By then, the Night Doctor was removing articles from another leather pouch and holding them one by one in the smoke from the fire. Boutelle assumed that it was to purify the objects: a wand, a knife, dried plants, a small leather bag, feathers from a large bird. Probably an eagle, Boutelle thought.

Finley looked toward the opening in the wall again. The smoke had thinned, but some was still escaping outside. Get started, he thought urgently. If the son of Vandaih saw that smoke . . .

A shudder ran up his back. They'd be helpless.

He drew in a quick breath and looked at the shaman again, eyes smarting from the greasy pall of smoke in the cave.

The old man was holding something above the smoking fire. It looked to Finley like strips of skin or dried flesh. He had no idea what they were.

Only Lean Bear didn't start as the Night Doctor began to dance around the fire slowly and rhythmically, chanting in his frail, hoarse voice. He had the wand in his left hand, the knife in his right, gesturing with them as he danced first toward the east, then the west, the north, and the south, chanting in each direction.

"O, Usen, O, Great Spirit, you are the sun first rising in the east.

"O, Usen, O, Great Spirit, you are the sun descending in the west.

"O, Usen, O, Great Spirit, you are the winter sun in the north.

"O, Usen, O, Great Spirit, you are the rising sun of spring in the south.

"Spirits of fear and death give way to the sun! This is a place of sanctuary! The roof above, a roof of safety! The floor beneath, a floor of protection!

"O, Usen, O, Great Spirit, protect me from evil approaching from the east, the west, the north, the south."

Finley glanced at Lean Bear, seeing a look of wrath on the Apache's face. He could understand now why the Night Doctor had failed as the shaman of the Pinal Spring band, why they had expelled him.

Ignoring all else, the old man was performing a rite exclusively for his own protection.

And they could do nothing about it.

He had no doubt that the shaman was well aware of their helplessness.

You miserable old bastard, he thought.

He started slightly with Boutelle as the Night Doctor took some powder from the small leather bag and flung it onto the fire. It flashed momentarily, then exuded pale smoke which filled the air with a pungent smell that was sweet and sour at the same time.

Boutelle shook himself, blinking hard and swallowing. The smoke from the burning powder seemed to fill his eyes and throat. He could see the Night Doctor only indistinctly. The old man looked to him like some figure from a mad dream. It seemed as though he could hear the thumping of the drum again. The same one-two-three-four rhythm he had heard in the Apache camp. That was impossible, though. There was no drum. It had to be imagination fixing on the rhythmic thud of the Night Doctor's feet on the floor of the cavern—one-two-three-four, one-two-three-four.

He felt himself beginning to sink again into the trance-like state he'd experienced in the mountain clearing. The sound of the Night Doctor's voice rose and fell in volume and in pitch, sometimes mournful and suppressed, other times aggressive, vehement.

Finley sat rigidly, watching the old man perform his rite of self-protection. He noticed sweat running down the old man's body and became aware of the perspiration on his own face, too, and the many drops of it trickling down his chest and back beneath his shirt.

He winced as the shaman suddenly jabbed at his left palm with the knife blade, drawing blood. Dancing on, he held the palm above the fire, letting dark drops of his blood fall into the glowing wood coals where they hissed.

"O, Usen, O, Great Spirit, let this gift of my blood satisfy and please you that you will protect me from whatever evil is around me."

Soon, the old man would mention the son of Vandaih by name. After the sacrifice. But what would the sacrifice be? Finley tensed, his right hand rising to the hilt of the obsidian knife. The Night Doctor was sapped by age. Still . . .

His hand lowered again as the shaman danced to a nearby corner of the cave and pulled a wolf's hide from a bulky object to reveal a cage woven of twigs inside of which a scrawny hen was standing.

The old man's hands moved swiftly. Opening the cage, he seized the chicken by its throat (so it would make no noise, Finley knew) and carried it to the fire, dancing slowly around the smoking dish, extending the struggling hen to the east, the west, the north, and the south.

Boutelle gasped as the shaman, with a blurring movement of his hands, lopped off the hen's head with his knife, then tore the bird in half and dropped its bloody pieces on the fire.

"O, Usen, O, Great Spirit, may the sacrificing of this hen also be accepted by you. May you return this gift by helping me in this time of peril."

What about *us*? Finley thought. Was Lean Bear thinking that as well?

But then the Night Doctor held a folded piece of the animal skin above the fire and chanted, "I have placed the name of Vandaih's son upon this skin, and when I drop this named skin in the fire, you, O, Usen, must, as fire consumes the skin, consume the son of Vandaih, making his body headless and his head bodiless."

Abruptly, he opened the leather bag at his waist and removed something, which he held above the fire. Boutelle felt his stomach twist with nausea.

It was a shrunken, mummified head, and the shaman was swinging it above the fire by its lank, black hair.

"O, Usen, O, Great Spirit, let it be, in this ceremony, that this head is that of the son of Vandaih. O, Usen, please remove this head once more."

Finley felt himself becoming increasingly rigid with anxiety. He'd been wrong. The shaman *did* intend to destroy the son of Vandaih—and the ceremony was approaching its climax. He felt himself leaning forward tensely, eyes fixed on the old man as he danced and chanted in the dim, smoky light, his frail voice more and more agitated.

"O, Usen, who created the night and the day! O, Usen, who created the earth and the skies! O, Usen, who created the darkness and the light! I plead with you to come now and destroy this vile abomination!

"O, Usen, drive away this evil one like dust before the wind! You have the power to crush all things beneath your might! Crush this, my enemy, the son of Vandaih!

"O, Usen, come at once and do what I desire! Let your terrible presence shake the air and destroy the evil that I ask you to destroy! The son of Vandaih, O, Usen! The cursed and murderous son of Vandaih!

"Curse this demon, O, Usen! Hurl him to the bottom of the pit into a lake of fire! First, his foul head, then his foul body, down into the fiery waters of the center of the earth!"

The old man stopped in his tracks and threw up his arms.

"Be gone, son of Vandaih! Be cursed by Usen! Cursed by the earth! Cursed by the sun and the moon and the stars! Cursed—"

He broke off with a gagging sound, face wrenched by sudden mindless terror.

A rush of great wings could be heard outside the cave, a hideous screech, the same screech they had heard while Boutelle's horse was being slaughtered.

"Complete the ceremony!" Lean Bear shouted at the shaman.

But the old man had slumped back onto the cave floor, eyes wide, lips spread, spittle running from his open mouth.

It seemed to Boutelle that everything happened at once. Lean Bear and Finley were on their feet, lunging for the shaman, both crying out at once. The rush of wings became deafening, the ghastly shriek of the creature almost to the opening of the cave. Lean Bear reaching the old man first and clutching at his shoulder, shouting again: Finley repeating the same words.

Lean Bear recoiling in shock and Finley groaning loudly as the old man fell back, dead from fear.

Then the robe across the opening was ripped away, and the huge, winged creature stood before them, face unseen in the shadows. Boutelle had the fleeting impression of a curved beak on its face and talons where its feet should be.

Then all was lost in movement, smoke, and noise as Lean Bear whirled and drew his knife and, with a cry that Boutelle knew was one of hopeless fury, hurled himself at the creature. Abruptly, they were one, a thrashing huge-winged, double-bodied figure, Lean Bear driving his knife into the creature's chest, then screaming out in agony as the creature's head darted forward, its curved beak tearing off the Apache's face.

Twisting around, the creature hurled the dying Indian through the cave opening, and Lean Bear disappeared in darkness, pitched into space and falling to his death without another sound.

Boutelle stiffened, seeing Finley leap toward the creature while its back was turned, the obsidian knife extended in his hand. The agent drove it as hard as he could into the creature's back. But the wings were too thick with heavy feathers and it glanced off a bony rib, barely breaking the creature's skin.

With a cry of pain at the stab of the obsidian blade, the creature twisted back, its left wing smashing across

Finley's outstretched arm, knocking the knife from his grip.

Finley tried to lunge for it, but with a movement so rapid Boutelle could not follow it, one of the creature's taloned feet lashed out and clamped around Finley's right ankle, stopping him abruptly.

The creature started dragging Finley back, its maddened yellow eyes glinting in the firelight.

"*Boutelle!*" Finley cried.

Boutelle moved before his mind could summon the command. Mindlessly, without considering what the pain might be, he grabbed up the fire dish and, jumping toward the son of Vandaih, hurled the glowing, smoking contents into the creature's face, seeing at the last moment its huge beak opening to tear off Finley's face.

The creature shrieked in pain as red-hot wood coals sprayed across its head, burning its eyes and setting fire to the dark gray plumage on its face. It staggered back and bumped against the cave opening, only the spread of its wings preventing it from falling through.

In backing off, the creature had been forced to lose its grip on Finley's ankle. Diving across the cave, the agent snatched up the obsidian knife, and before the creature could recover, he leapt up and flung himself at it, driving the black blade deep into its chest until he felt it pierce the creature's heart.

The cave rang with the deafening screech of the creature's death.

Boutelle stumbled back and fell against the cave wall as he saw what happened. He and Finley stared in open-mouthed astonishment as they watched the giant wings retracting slowly, saw them thin and disappear into the arm flesh closing up. Saw the creature's beak move slowly into the face and vanish with the plumage. Saw the talons withdraw and change back into human feet.

With that, the son of Vandaih was a man again, the man they'd seen in Picture City, lying dead on the floor of the cave, the obsidian knife buried in his stilled heart, dark blood running down his chest.

Finley slumped down clumsily, and he and Boutelle looked at one another. He felt unable to speak. All he could think of was what he had to do.

But that would have to wait. He couldn't move right now.

At last he spoke.

"You saved my life," he said.

"You saved both of ours," Boutelle responded hoarsely. Not to mention the Pinal Spring band and God knew how many others, he thought. He sat down weakly, closing his eyes. My God, he thought. My dear God.

Several minutes later, Finley struggled to his knees and crawled to the Night Doctor's body. Reaching across him, he picked up the dead Apache's knife and turned back to Boutelle.

"Are you up to this?" he said.

"Do I have any choice?" Boutelle asked.

Finley shook his head slowly. "No," he answered, "I need your help."

"All right." Boutelle nodded. "One thing though."

"What's that?"

"I'll deny, to the end of my life, that I ever did this."

"Don't worry," Finley reassured him with a grim smile, "I'll never mention it, believe me."

Boutelle labored to his feet and moved to the spot where the son of Vandaih lay in motionless silence. He sank to his knees beside the agent.

"All right," he muttered. He filled his lungs with a long, deep breath. "I'm ready," he said.

Finley made the first cut.

Forge

Award-winning authors
Compelling stories

. . . .

Please join us at the website
below for more information
about this author and other great
Forge selections, and to sign up for
our monthly newsletter!

. . . . . **FORGE** www.tor-forge.com . . . .